The Best Short Stories 2021

D0088535

The Best
Short Stories
2021

The O. Henry Prize Winners

Guest Editor:
Chimamanda Ngozi Adichie

Series Editor:
Jenny Minton Quigley

Anchor Books
A Division of Penguin Random House LLC
New York

In memory of James Nwoye Adichie. Beloved father.
Gentle man and gentleman.

Contents

Foreword

The O. Henry Prize is the oldest major prize for short fiction in America. Awarded annually since 1919 (with a break in 2020), the prize seeks to provide a prominent platform for short story writers at all points in their careers. The winners' stories are collected and published annually by Anchor Books.

The prize's namesake, William Sydney Porter—better known by his pen name, O. Henry—was an American short story writer whose best-known tale, "The Gift of the Magi," matched selflessness with love in a famously heartbreaking twist ending. In 1906, that story appeared in O. Henry's second collection, which he titled *The Four Million* in response to an op-ed in *The New York Times* claiming that New York City had only four hundred people worth getting to know. O. Henry believed that the stories of all four million people then residing in New York City were worthwhile. After his death in 1910, Porter's friends created the O. Henry Prize in his honor. The annual collection was a community act that put authors at its center from the start. There have been nine series editors shepherding the prize since 1919; I am the tenth, and *The Best Short Stories 2021: The O. Henry Prize Winners* is a relaunch, one that represents my hopes for what these awards can mean for outstanding writers of short fiction around the globe.

We've made some big changes to O. Henry. The two most important are these: we are now, for the first time, considering works in translation, and we have added a guest editor so that each edition can reflect one brilliant artist's unique vision. It is our hope that with a singular guiding vision, the collection becomes an even more enjoyable and cohesive reading experience. We are thrilled that Chimamanda Ngozi Adichie is our very first guest editor.

I used criteria outlined by Adichie (both her critically acclaimed judgment and her subjective personal taste in fiction) to screen about a thousand stories published on literary websites, in glossy magazines, and in literary journals. I read these stories while unexpectedly confined by the pandemic to my home in West Hartford, Connecticut, the same pines in my backyard providing the background for story after story that took my mind traveling far and wide. I passed along a hefty pile of stories to Adichie to judge. During this globally devastating year, Adichie lost her beloved father, and we deeply appreciate the time and attention she devoted to the O. Henry Prize during this difficult time.

In November, Adichie sent her gorgeous introduction from Abba, Nigeria, where she had finally been able to travel for her father's burial. In it, she encapsulates her belief in the stories she has selected and their ability to spark courage, wisdom, and mystery in readers everywhere. *The O. Henry Prize Winners* is a cluster of twenty glimmering stars, each a small consolation, together a small constellation. We hope you are dazzled.

—Jenny Minton Quigley

Introduction

When I first read these stories, my beloved father had just died. It is still difficult to write "died." Grief was a cruel kind of education. It made life become both unbearably pointless and unbearably precious, and I wish I could say that reading these stories brought succor. Nothing did—my grief was raw and raging—but these stories brought a reminder of how the emotions I was feeling had all been felt before. I briefly wondered whether reading through sorrow would scar my choices, cause me to be drawn only to the darkest stories, or, in an emotional revolt, to the lightest. Almost all the shortlisted stories I read were accomplished, and in thinking of which to select, I asked myself: Which story has remained with me?

I am drawn, in general, to stories that feel genuine, that leave me convinced. Gimmicks bore me, as does cleverness for its own sake, for we can get that in other, better-suited forms than fiction. I am drawn to a quality I call heart, a sense that the story matters and has meaning. But matters to whom? To the writer, to the story's own imaginative world.

I think of the best fiction as art that sometimes brings news. The stories here succeed as art, in their ability to be both timeless and also of the moment, in their care with language, and they all also bring news.

When I was first published in the United States, I was wary of readers who told me that my work brought news, because I chafed at the way that fiction by people like me, people from Africa and Asia and Latin America, from the parts of the world on the periphery of economic power, was often read as anthropology rather than literature. The idea of fiction bringing news can still be diminishing, in particular contexts and specific power relationships, but I understand now that all good fiction brings some kind of news, even if it is news we have heard before.

I was particularly charmed by "Things We Worried About When I Was Ten" by David Rabe, which felt so unabashedly true and brought news about childhood and class. I adored "Endangered Species: Case 47401" by Crystal Wilkinson—for being so in touch with its own boldness, its language like music, its superb narrative tension, its humor, and its very specific news about the casual racism that Black American women face.

A friend of mine once said she looked to novels to tell her how to live. I thought of that in reading some of the stories here, like "Freedom from Want," "The Other One," "Brown Girls," and "The Living Sea." I look to stories for consolation, the kind of small consolation that one needs to want to wake up every day; as templates for life; for news of how others live; for reminders that life's mysteries have no keys. Above all else I look to fiction for a kind of wisdom. Wisdom feels old-fashioned, as a word and as an idea, but if there is a unifying theme in these stories, it is that they are all profoundly wise.

I am drawn to a sense of humor but also to a seriousness of purpose, and it is bliss when both manage to exist in one story, as is the case in many here. I am struck too by a tonal similarity; quite a few of the stories, although very different in subject and setting, have a similar gorgeous grave grace—like "Fisherman's

Stew," "Delandria," "Grief's Garden," and "From Far Around They Saw Us Burn."

I admire writers who are able to be very much of the moment and yet timeless, who produce stories that are intensely contemporary but will survive rereading in the next generation, like "White Noise," "Witness," "The Master's Castle," "Becoming the Baby Girl," and "Color and Light."

A successful story, for me, exists in a moral universe, not one where goodness always triumphs, because that would be false, but one with an inherent awareness of goodness. A story might be anti-goodness, but even in being so, it acknowledges itself as not being amoral. Some of the stories here are clearly moral; they have an illuminating purpose, like "Antediluvian," "To the Dogs," and "Scissors," but none are ideological, because while ideology may serve us well in our social and political lives, it makes fiction an exercise in rigid unbelievability.

The idea of believability itself can feel political; it certainly did when I was in a writing program. Someone would pronounce a story "unbelievable" merely because the experience in the story was not personally familiar to her.

The literary world can sometimes feel addicted to comfort, which is why it is valid criticism in America to discredit a piece of literature for not having any redemption. I am resistant to this, what H. L. Mencken wonderfully called the "cult of hope." I love hope, but I believe in stories that deal with hope only when they do not set out specifically to peddle hope.

When I teach writing, I tell my students that it is not so much about "write what you know" as it is about "don't write what you don't know." A subtle difference, but with the latter, one's work is not constrained by the narrowness of personal experience.

These stories are alert to the world, and they have an imaginative humility, which all great art needs—that awareness that we do not have all the answers and perhaps do not need to.

The stories here are written by a wide range of authors on a wide range of subjects, which is a polite way of saying that, despite its being an anthology of stories published in the United States, it isn't a collection by white men with two others thrown in for some flavor.

These stories are set in China, India, the United States, and Nigeria; they are translated from the Danish and Spanish; they have European, Asian, Latin American, American, and African characters.

But this was by default, rather than deliberate. I did not set out to select "diverse stories"—and that expression has an unfortunate taint of charity, as though stories written by anybody other than a white man must be selected by putting on the righteous glasses of diversity. I read for stories that I cared about, and I like to think that because talent is not the sole preserve of any human group, to read with open curiosity and with emotional hunger is invariably to choose a wide range of stories. Still, in stepping back and looking at my final selections, I could not help feeling a slight wariness, a concern that this might be seen as evidence of being fashionable, of a new kind of cultural currency in these times when more attention—and lip service—is being given to the idea of representation in American cultural life. My wariness is itself telling, an indictment of where we still are.

I teach a writing workshop in Lagos every year. A young man, Kelechi, came to the workshop a few years ago. He was a journalist, from a working-class family in the Nigerian southeast, shrewd and intelligent and watchful. One of the workshop participants wrote a story without a plot, a celebration of language, a meditation on growing up in the rural countryside. I found it beautiful. Kelechi was perplexed by it.

"But this is not even a story. Nothing happens in it. And it is not teaching us anything," Kelechi said. Now that I think back on it, I am ashamed of my response to him.

"Well," I said, "I am sorry the story does not teach you how to harvest yams and how to build a house and how to get a job."

My response was shaped by a mainstream idea, a voguish idea among those who make literature and who teach it and who promote it—that to question the usefulness of literature is philistinism of the purest form. And so, my response to Kelechi, in its shameful snobbery, was exactly that. I could tell he was unconvinced. Later, in thinking about it, I remembered stories from my childhood, stories that had obvious moral lessons, stories that we read in class and were then made to answer questions about, the first one invariably being, what is the moral lesson from this story? I have sometimes been asked that question about my own work. What is the moral of the story?

In responding, I would say that it did not have an overt moral, that it was up to the reader. Which I still believe, although I do think that every work of fiction has a worldview, *believes* something and *disbelieves* something. The moral lessons are not of course overt, because that would lead us into the murky grounds of propaganda.

There are schools in different parts of the world that are increasingly downplaying the teaching of arts and literature in favor of sciences and mathematics, the sorts of serious disciplines that lead to reliable employment. And maybe Kelechi's question came from the general idea of usefulness as a concrete thing. What he was asking that day at the workshop was really a much bigger and I think very important question. Does it matter? Does writing matter? Does literature matter?

And so, he was right in questioning the usefulness of that meditative piece. And I was wrong in closing off his question, in adopting the attitude that I did not have to justify what I valued, the attitude that literature is a secret cult and you either get it or you don't.

It is either we talk of literature as a cult that cannot be questioned, or we begin to soften the edges of our definitions. What does it mean to be useful? Does usefulness end in the concrete? We are not a collection of logical bones and flesh. We are emotional beings as much as we are physical beings.

Stories do teach us. Every story teaches us.

We are different in how we dream—this is a lesson.

I read for many reasons, one of which is to be consoled.

Consolation is useful, consolation is necessary.

I'd very much like to learn *concretely* useful things—my knowledge of them, alas, is limited—but I would not want to live if I were not able to have the consolation that stories give me. The stories here consoled me, some more than others, like "Malliga Homes" and "Two Nurses, Smoking," which left me weeping. They brought me news I mostly knew but still needed to hear, that life is what it is, that history can leap gloriously to life, that grief is love and brokenness. They remain with me still, a sensation, a fragment, an emotion, a sense of place, a character. Taken together, they feel to me like a joyous celebration of small consolations. I hope other readers will find in them whatever it is they look for in literature.

—Chimamanda Ngozi Adichie, December 2020

The Best Short Stories 2021

Daphne Palasi Andreades

Brown Girls

Brown Girls

WE LIVE IN THE DREGS OF QUEENS, New York, where airplanes fly so low that we are certain they will crush us. On our block a lonely tree grows. Its branches tangle in power lines. Its roots upend sidewalks where we ride our bikes before they are stolen. Roots that render the concrete slabs uneven, like a row of crooked teeth. In our front yards, grandmothers string laundry lines, hang bedsheets, our brothers' shorts, and our sneakers scrubbed to look brand-new. Take those down! our mothers hiss. This isn't back home. In front yards, not to be confused with actual lawns, grow tomatoes that have fought their way through the hard earth.

Our grandmothers refuse canes. Our brothers dress in wife-beaters. We all sit on stoops made of brick. The Italian boys with their shaved heads zoom by on bikes, staring, their laughter harsh as their shiny gold chains. Our grandparents weed their gardens and our brothers smoke their cigarettes and, in time, stronger substances we cannot recognize. Whose scent makes our heads pulse.

Our brothers, who ride on bikes, lifting their front wheels high into the air.

"Brown"

If you really want to know, we are the color of 7-Eleven root beer. The color of sand at Rockaway Beach when it blisters the bottoms of our feet. Color of soil. Color of the charcoal pencils our sisters use to rim their eyes. Color of grilled hamburger patties. Color of our mother's darkest thread that she loops through the needle. Color of peanut butter. Of the odd gene that makes us *fair and white as snow*, like whatshername, is it Snow White? (But don't get it twisted—we're still brown.) Dark as seven p.m. dusk, when our mothers switch on the light in the empty room. Exclaim, Oh! There you are.

Brown Boys

We stare at brown boys with their obsidian hair, their fingers and cheekbones, and think, He looks like my brother. He looks like the boy from the restaurant where we ordered kabobs, lechón, jerk chicken, plátanos. He looks like the boy at the bodega who rang up our barbecue chips, our ninety-nine-cent cans of iced tea. He's beautiful, we think, but we'd never go *out* with him. We'd never *date* him. Why? Because he doesn't look— You know. Because he looks like— And anyway, he only likes *those* kinds of girls, the Vanessa Kleinberg types, we heard him say so. We stare at brown boys, listen to the way they say *lieberry*. They fascinate us, but we ignore them. Except one day when our class goes down for a visit to the library—*Lie-brair-ree*, we mouth, alone with brown boys behind a bookshelf. Library. Follow my lips. Say it like this.

Territory

It'll be fun, we say, and we take our white boys on a trip to Queens. From the subway we watch high-rises transform to squat buildings and bodegas. We point out city hospitals where we were born, where some of our parents work as janitors, nurses, social workers, paper pushers. This is the playground where we'd chill with our brothers and sisters, we say. Touch the monkey bars dull from children's hands. Around us, a cacophony of Spanish and Mandarin, Urdu and Tagalog and Vietnamese. Our ears are trained to hear them. *Look at this place!* they say. Walking along sidewalks, we hold our white boys' hands. (Or maybe they are the ones clinging on to us?) We pass a little boy dressed in a Spider-Man costume even though it isn't Halloween, as he walks with his abuela.

We hear the *shuh shuh* sound of the brown boys' sneakers playing basketball. Feet blurred, swift as wind. Brown boys say, *Hey— what's good?* and ignore the white boys at our sides. Toss their chins up at us. Fresh, you looking mad fresh, their eyes say. Some of the boys simply stop, ball in hand, as we walk by. *Yo! When you over him, you know where I'm at!* We hear them laughing with their friends and we blush, drag our white boys away. *Coconut!* they call after us. *Bitch!* No matter, we think, as we walk away with our prizes. *What an asshole*, our white boys say, *what was that about?*

But some of the brown boys, when we pass them, call us by our names. Not our American names, but our names spoken in cramped living rooms, those used by our grandmothers to shake us awake. They call us by our names, our names like tiny flowers, and when we hear them, we must do our very best to walk away.

Shadows

Our white boys, our white boys who are now our husbands and claim us at midnight when the moon is half-hidden. Who curl their fingers over our breasts and thighs and say our names. More, we beg. Harder. You are everything. We slide our hands down backs damp with sweat. No one can say we do not love our husbands because we do. We are good wives. Close your eyes, our husbands say. We do. We obey. Feel their lips on our necks, stomachs, hips, between our legs. But when we close our eyes what comes to mind is not our husbands' faces. But his face. Brown boys, the boys we knew and left behind. Faces etched into our minds. Panic—open your eyes, hurry! Good wives, we say. We are good wives.

Walking past a construction site on a gray day in Chelsea, we run into them. Stop, startled. Is that you? brown boy, now grown and dressed in a neon orange vest, asks. We blush at the sight of his mouth, which reminds us of old teenage desire, naked and unabashed, for him. Lower East Side. We meet our friends for happy hour, hand a twenty-dollar bill to the bartender, double-take when he quips, *Still whiskey and Coke after all these years?* We peer at him, recognize the brown boy we wrapped our arms around in a basement in Richmond Hill. While Aaliyah crooned on the radio. *Holy shit*, we say. *How are you?* For the whole night, we do not take our eyes off him. Write our numbers on napkins. Leave, trembling. See brown boy's paintings at an exhibit in the Bowery, catch sight of him walking down Wall Street in a navy suit, ordering dumplings in Chinatown, sushi in Soho. Try not to stare at them, and women, fair-skinned, who link arms with brown boys, whom brown boys hold umbrellas for and kiss on concrete sidewalks.

We travel to New Orleans for a friend's wedding. At a jazz bar named Court of Two Sisters, meet a man playing drums. Drums that sound like a match going out, hissing, building to a crash. Reverberating in the dim room. Louisiana accent like caramel against our New York City mile-a-minute. He slows us down. Reckless, reckless women. Desire, when he turns out the light. We return to our houses, dream of him and that night forever. Or flee our husbands. Leave for that brown boy, now grown. Open your eyes, hurry.

David Means

Two Nurses, Smoking

FROM A WIDE VANTAGE

Two hospital workers, somewhat lonely-looking figures, taking a smoke break, back behind a trailer, leaning toward each other as they talked softly beside a row of neatly trimmed bushes. One had long hair and thin, pale arms that dangled from her scrubs. The other was big, burly, with a tattoo on his arm. Even that day in June—if you paid close attention, driving past— you might've seen desire in the way she pointed her toe and dug it into the dusty concrete while she listened to him, or you might've noticed the way he swayed as he talked, because he liked to riff on the subject at hand, and, lately, the last few times, when she visited with the trailer, he had expounded upon the recent news: a serial-killer nurse who had confessed to murdering, somewhere in Pennsylvania, at least a dozen patients. She, for her part, added a little commentary here and there, because it was a shared story that somehow seemed to make the job a bit easier, the kind of bullshit story that you'd tell to kill time, and she liked his deep, no-nonsense tone, which, she thought, might've come from his stint in the army. He had green eyes that became deeply serious when he was listening.

THE BOND

Began to form in the way they both moved during the breaks—in the solitude they sought between the bushes and the long flank of the trailer, a dirty sliver of parking-lot curb where cigarette butts and litter had blown up. Between them was a secretive energy, a conspiracy formed out of a mutual history. (Or maybe the conspiracy formed a sense of mutual history. Maybe it wasn't so simple.) As a kid she had lived in one of those motels, Holiday Court, that had turned itself over to long-term renters—folks who paid by the week but did so year in and year out when they could, building an easy camaraderie, fighting in the parking lot, spilling blood, bringing the police—the daughter of a fuckup mom with zero parenting skills. A kind, encouraging counselor at her high school named Mrs. Hargrove, who gave her hope, urged her to take a heroic leap to community college, and then nursing school on a scholarship. He'd grown up in Nevada near a town called Ely, on the Shoshone reservation, without a father, spending a lot of his time alone in the countryside, staying out of his mom's way, and then, suddenly, they'd moved east to a trashy apartment in Newburgh, New York, with a new dad who liked to drink as much as his mother did.

THE KIDNEY POUNDER

As she liked to call it, was inside the trailer. Technically, the pounder's called a lithotripsy machine, she said, and it delivers extracorporeal shock waves and breaks up the stones. Around the metropolitan area, and sometimes in upstate New York, she followed the trailer to cut-rate hospitals, assisting whatever doctor had been assigned to it by putting the patients onto the platform, adjusting the Velcro straps, giving her spiel about how this would hurt but not as much as passing a big stone—if it even passed—and then she'd work the device, pushing as gently as possible while the pulsing waves of ultrasonic energy broke the stone apart.

A MALE PATIENT

Would come into the trailer, bitching and moaning, and use the occasion to touch her knee. A woman would come in, gaunt and frail, barely able to walk, resisting all help, clambering onto the platform, brushing away her offered hand.

ALL PAIN

Seemed to be equalized as she worked the machine, pressing the device, hitting the stone hard with ultrasonic energy, until personality and differences seemed to her to be fused into a single point.

THE SCAR

That ran down his neck—just missing his carotid artery, she noticed—and disappeared beneath his scrubs gave, when she asked him about it, an excuse to talk about the war, the time an IED hit his Hummer, blowing a tire off the vehicle, sending shrapnel through the undercarriage and into his buddy's arm. Bleeding bad, his friend screamed that he was dying, that his arm was shredded meat. But the dude's arm was perfectly fine in the end and it was only the fog-of-war shit. I guess I'm gonna live, his buddy said when he finally realized that his arm was still there, I guess I'm OK, Chief.

KIDNEY BOY

Was this kid, barely twenty, a junkie from the looks of it, suffering for a couple of weeks while the trailer was way up north in a place called Watertown, licking a morphine lollipop, with a big stone and a tight ureter, meaning, like, the worst-case scenario: he's not only going to be pounded but it's going to take a couple of sessions and the fragments are going to pass one at a time, and then a ureteral stent will be put in, too. The kid had this crooked jaw from a bad rewire, and when I unstrapped him he kissed me and said I saved his life, said it like he meant it, and I tried not to let him see it in my eyes—you know, the things I was seeing about his future—she told Marlon one day. He leaned forward and listened to her without a word.

DURING

Most of these breaks, the air conditioner in the trailer would pop on, devouring the sounds: the tink of a ball hitting the backstop at the schoolyard across the street, the skittering of litter in the parking lot, sirens and the deep-blue buzz of the hospital itself. When it went off, the summer would reappear, the chirping of birds and the shush of cars on the road beyond the decorative bushes.

KIDNEY BOY

Said I'm not going to make it, and she assured him that he would but heard the truth in his voice and saw it in his eyes. You know how that is, she said. He was seeing what I saw but couldn't tell him.

NOTHING GOOD

Could come from the intimacy of those post-treatment moments, when a patient was disoriented by a joyous sensation of relief, he thought. That was when they did weird shit, reaching out to touch you, saying something about putting you in their will, or even, in some cases, lashing out for no good reason, because you were a bearer of good tidings.

HE RESISTED

Giving her the standard nurse-to-nurse talk about not internalizing the pain of the patients, how they come and go fleetingly. The ones you think are going to live end up dead. The ones you're sure are going to die, who have death in their eyes, end up living, processed out and sent on their merry way. Changing bedpans and lifting armrests and holding shoulders, checking charts, slipping little baggies over the tips of thermometers, inserting IV needles. Then the sensation of going outside for a break and seeing that, although inside a patient has just grunted and gone into cardiac arrest with a no-assist order, the sky, filled with clouds and sunlight and birds, is still throwing itself majestically over the world.

SHE CRIED

About Kidney Boy, and he drew her close, giving her a chance to glance down, through the blue light of his shirt, at a switchyard of ridges where the scar opened up into the crater where the frag had gone in.

THE TRAILER

Arrived every few weeks that summer, and they texted each other and met.

ITINERANT LIFE

Following the trailer from one town to the next, staying in budget hotels, watching television alone in the evenings, didn't bother

her much, because before Holiday Court she and her mother had traveled around a lot, following one asshole after another, and she got used to it, she said one afternoon, brushing her hair away from her forehead and looking out over the bushes to the kids playing on the ball field across the street and then, turning around quickly, gazing over his shoulder at the hill that climbed past the road in the other direction, across the parking lot, where tomb-stones rose up into the trees. It seemed pretty typical, putting a graveyard next to a hospital.

THE DEAD

Had names that stuck in the mind, whereas those of the ones who were cured were released, sent back into the clean, raw rotation of the stars, so to speak, he said. There was always some patient in critical condition, doomed and marked terminal on the charts, who overcame the odds and marched out of the ward surrounded by his family, not even waving goodbye, taking a name off into the future.

MARLON

Liked her white arms, and the way her breasts swayed beneath the fabric of her scrubs, and he thought—when she and the trailer were gone—about the way her ass shifted when she walked, throwing a compaction from one side to the other, revealing to him a complication of form that begged to be touched, giving him, during lonely nights in his shitty apartment, something to imagine: falling to his knees and extending his arms out like one of those mythic figures offering a baby to the sun or to God, gently cradling each side of her beautiful bottom.

GRACIE

Admired the bulk of his body and his dark skin and his muscular heft in combination with the way he shifted from foot to foot when he was standing and the way, when he was on the curb smoking, he looked beyond her to some point on the horizon that nobody could see, pulling his long black hair tighter into the regulation ponytail, holding his head high and working his jaw as he talked, letting his upstate intonations enter his voice, and the way he assumed a weird, regal formality, stopping to bow to her as he emerged from the emergency-room doors, sweeping his arm out to the side, looking grim and lonely until he unleashed his smile in a way that seemed vulnerable and tough all at the same time.

SHOSHONE

Folk loved the wolf, he told her one afternoon when she asked him about life in Ely, Nevada. Wolf could bring people back to life but he didn't do it, because there'd be too many people in the world if he did. I'm not sure how the story goes, but it's something like that, he said, and it was about the only thing my mother ever really told me about our people.

HALF-HOUR

Breaks adding up, one after another, over four months.

THE LONELIEST ROAD

In America is Route 50 in Nevada, and it goes through Ely. Driving it's like losing your soul and getting another one, my mom used to say. My father drove out 50 and disappeared for a year and came back saying that he'd never got off it—the road, I mean—and then she left him, or he left her, or they left each other. I've got fifty versions of that story. Another thing she told me was that folks in San Francisco said they had to drive east to get to the West. She had this hang-up about being from the West, and then there she was, living in Newburgh, New York.

RIFFING

About the serial-killer nurse, expounding on something he'd read online about this male nurse who admitted to killing patients, mostly in Pennsylvania, adjusting morphine drips and rewriting charts, covering his tracks. By that point she had given him the entire Kidney Boy story, how she'd seen in his eyes that he would commit suicide, even the fact that he'd throw himself from a bridge. A few days later, he told one about his buddy who was killed in Iraq. Same old story, IED, blasting up through the undercarriage, tearing a hole and all of that, except this time it wasn't his arm but his head and upper torso, and the light went out of his eyes.

PLAY IT OUT

She was saying. He was hunching his shoulders, his face buried in his hands. The way I see it, that serial-killer nurse isn't a real killer; he can take or leave the death part, because what he really likes is scoping out the possibilities—you know the ones I'm talking about, the pre-op patients who want you to lend an ear so they can decide that you're gonna be a good-luck charm, taking your hand and complimenting your nursing skills, understanding full well the implications of the coming surgery, whatever. You go in and for a minute, even if you try not to, you feel the life *in your hand* and you become aware that one little fuckup on a chart, or a misreading, and the patient could die. Or when you go in to find balloons and cards tacked to a board and see some little kid—always named Sammy or Annie—with a shaved head and pre-surgery marks and you think, against your will, how fucking easy it would be to save the kid from suffering, he said, looking out over the road, streaming his smoke between his teeth, with his eyes on the horizon and his chin jutting.

ON THE STEPS

Of the trailer a few days later, picking up on the subject of the serial-killer nurse, he began to talk again about the impulse to kill, how he'd learned in Fallujah that impulse equals mess, and how there was a guy in the unit who plugged shots whenever he saw fit, and one day some old lady came around the corner with her hand in the air—we hated corners, he said, which was one reason we hated Fallujah—and this guy in our unit just popped her. When we got close to the body, we saw that she had these arthritic hands, fingers curled, so a hand held up like that might've looked like a gun. But it was really just sloppy shit, the truth.

BEAUTIFUL

Inside that moment—his voice quivering, his eyes welling—the wind was rising and the darker clouds were coming in. His eyes were painfully green as the grief twisted his face and the trees near the road gave off a sugary odor and tenderness formed in the quiet. How long was that moment, held in memory between the two of them for the rest of their lives?

FINALLY

He spoke and said, My grandmother had rheumatoid arthritis, and I used to go with her to Ely, to this clinic where she put her hands into a wax bath while I watched, dipping them in and wincing, at first, until she had blue wax gloves. Then he shook a cigarette from his pack and lit up, and they sat and listened to the sounds of summer, looking over the bushes at the baseball diamond and, beyond it, at the top of the school and the white cupola in the sky. When he spoke again, he explained that the dead lady on the street in Fallujah had had hands just like his grandmother's, and then he began to cry, starting with a single, low gasp and a collapse of his shoulders as he buried his face, and she pulled him close.

ONE

Hopes for the great love born of a common pain, for two united souls sharing grief in long, easy banter while they fend off physical attraction and misread each other until everything seems to change one afternoon, smoking behind the trailer on a particularly rough day—a triaged bus accident that included one double amputee, a burn victim (for him), and (for her) a woman who came in with a story to tell about her previous stones and a time when she was so bad, lying on her side in her living room, bucking in agony, that she begged her husband to kick her, and he did just that, walloping her, and her husband was arrested, of course, but it worked, and the stone passed in her piss. The cops wouldn't listen to her side of the story, though, and her husband ended up in jail. Damn right, Marlon said—and then, just after she finished that story, there was the whoop of a siren and an EMS pulled in and they watched while overhead, from a thin stack on the roof of the hospital, a bloom of smoke emerged into the early-autumnal sky, the incinerated aftermath of old bandages and bloodied towels, afterbirths and whatever else could be burned to save the hospital disposal fees.

ONE AFTERNOON IN SEPTEMBER

He said, I love hearing your stories. I love your stories, too, she said, touching his shoulder.

WE SHOULD GET OUT OF HERE

After this shift, take a drive, he said, shrugging his shoulder toward the emergency entrance, where the orderlies were removing a gurney from a truck, lowering it with a count. And she waited to answer, because she wanted him to beg a little, to hear how much his desire had accrued over the weeks—small hand brushes and gestures, one to the next—and because she took care with matters of the heart, the past having taught her that a hit could come as easily as a kiss.

THEY DROVE

Up the old state road through autumn dusk, talking softly and listening to music as the river appeared and disappeared to the right and she fiddled with the old-radio punch buttons, feeling the mechanism moving the pointer as it slid from station to station.

THEY BOTH FELT

The sensation of going north, while he told stories about growing up, the gangs that ruled the neighborhood, the way they used to play along the river, and then, around the switchbacks of Storm King and passing through the desolation of Newburgh, he said, I think this here is probably the loneliest road in America, and they headed out of town, continuing north as the road opened into four lanes and then fell back to two, skirting old estates and monasteries, until they reached a small hotel up on a berm on the left, painted pink, with a quivering neon sign that said River Rest, something from an old movie.

NO

Wait, before they got to the hotel they stopped at a diner, sharing a meal, and then in the parking lot they smoked and leaned back, gazing up at the stars—and if you'd been looking you would have seen them there and speculated on two people lingering in an upstate parking lot, kissing each other gently, and you would've extrapolated a story from that image.

NO

Wait, there were a lot of other conversations, late in the summer and early in the fall, as they stared out at the road and the ball field and the sky, testing each other, teasing, griping about work and life in general, sharing deeper stories that'll never be recorded, not here, and not in memory, so that later, looking back, it would seem that in the fall, on a cold afternoon, they had both decided on a whim to take the leap, to hook up, to go into the future together, to consummate the hesitant, careful nature of their personalities, because they were both damaged, somehow lost, and sensed and felt—you'd have seen if you'd been watching—a suddenly deep need for each other.

NO

Wait, go back to the afternoon she told him the Kidney Boy story, to the way that exchange had worked temporally, the things that were withheld and the things that were expressed, the way she told Marlon how she imagined the kid, whose name was Curt, going up to the bridge, standing on the railing and looking straight ahead—at the bend in the river, the beautiful vista. Go back to the way the exchange transpired—almost wordlessly, but not quite—that afternoon between Marlon and Gracie, and how he said "of course," after she told him Kidney Boy's real name, Curt, and then he laughed and said, All those stoners have short names, like Hank, Curt, Al. How after she'd talked about the broken jaw she abruptly changed the subject to something her dentist had told her about boys (she said boys) coming into the office on Sunday afternoons with bar-fight jaws, broken teeth. Go back to how, after she'd told Marlon about the dentist, an old couple appeared between the sliding doors and began a slow, shuffling walk across the parking lot, holding each other up, and how he paused (holding off on the nursing lecture) and said, How did Curt die? He said it before she could tell him the fact. Not so much guessing as seeming to have a prophetic insight. And she said, Hey, how'd you know? and he shrugged and looked away and listened as she explained that Curt had jumped from a bridge, and then, right then, the wind lifted and litter skittered and an EMS came into the emergency bay and across the street there was the high, metallic, and beautiful sound of kids playing before she began to cry.

NO

Wait, go back to the way he emerged from the sliding glass doors in his army fatigues over his scrubs with his hood pulled up around a face grimly set, his small mouth puckered, as if he were deep in thought, until he got near the trailer and pulled his hood down and shook his head to let his hair out and paused for a moment, extending his arms as if for an embrace, and then said, Heyya, heyya, and gave her a hug while she held the story she wanted to tell him about the crazy old lady up in Poughkeepsie, because she always had one bottled up, at bay, and that was part of the dynamic, the urge to talk to him, and to hear him talk back.

NO

Wait, go back behind the trailer, to that particularly rough day, a triaged bus accident, two DOA and one double amputee, for him, and for her an old man with a stone the size of the Hope Diamond in for the second time, and the lady who argued over her technique with the pounder, giving her grief, and to make up for it decided to tell Gracie her life story, ten stones in five years—was what she said—and a slow passer, taking her time, a regular at the hospital. And then Gracie told Marlon about her mom, about the way her stepfather had beaten them both, and then about Roy, the guy at Holiday Court, this wiry older guy—at least he seemed older to me at the time, she said—who had a motorcycle and took her for rides, and then she stopped speaking and let Marlon see in her face the things she wanted him to see, that she had suffered at the hands of Roy.

NO

Wait, go to the moment when suddenly, out of the blue, a freak snow squall had appeared from a cloudless sky, and he said it was a good omen, and she told him he was full of shit, and they fell into a hysterical laughing fit together as, once again, an EMS came roaring in—siren whooping—as if to counterpoint their joy and delight with the urgency of some other realm, and how that moment, amid the countless others, somehow sealed a fate between them within the shared eternity of those moments.

NO

Wait, go back to that afternoon, when he said, We should get out of this place, or perhaps he said, We should get away from this joint, and shrugged a shoulder back toward the emergency entrance, where—with a clank-and-clattering sound—they were removing a gurney from the truck, lowering it on a count, which was a sign of something horrible, because they only did that for the messed-up cases, the damaged goods, and she waited a few beats to answer Marlon, because she wanted him to say it again, to beg a little bit, to see just how much desire had accrued over the weeks, from one small hand brush to another, from one gesture to the next, because that was all she had in the end: all she had—she sometimes felt—was the small accumulations, one upon the next, because the past had taught her to take care with all of that, to be frugal with matters of the heart. A hit could come as easily as a kiss. The back of a hand could arrive at a moment's notice. This physics was in her bones, in the way she drew herself slightly away, even now, when he reached out to touch her shoulder. She felt herself—with the breeze blowing her hair around her eyes—withdrawing a little bit from the pliant urgency in his voice when he told her that he just felt like getting away. So she waited until he added, I'm not hitting on you, I'm just proposing a drive up the river, and then they both laughed at that. And she waited a few more beats, and then said, Sure, which was, he thought, the most beautiful word in the world.

SO

Now they were in a bed, in the shadowy hotel light, listening to the occasional car passing on the road.

IN THE SAGGING BED

He heaved into her, lifting himself up on his hands, while she held his shoulders, her fingers sliding around to feel the scar coming down from his neck and channeling out in two lines that then met again around his left nipple to form a craterlike hollow, and she drew on her time in nursing school, testing the tissue where the shrapnel went in and stayed in and burned—he'd later say—phosphorous white and hot enough, thank God, to cauterize the wound and seal off the blood vessels. He thrust down and deep and then eased up as she pushed against him—forgetting his scars—until the two motions spun into what seemed to be an airless freedom. He grunted, and she came, too, her finger flicking.

A SOFT WEEPING

Sound—as close to crying as you could get—and when she made that sound he made it, too, and together they were making one sound, and then he rested his weight against her and recalled her hand down there, fluttering, reminding him of the old woman's hand and of his grandmother's, too, because to touch herself she'd had to bend and flex it, and remembering the feeling after the fact he felt sure that he would tell her what had really happened to the old lady in Fallujah, or at least later—much later, years later—he'd see that image and use it to justify having told her about it.

DEEP IN THE NIGHT

He nudged her awake and explained that he was the one who'd gone trigger-happy on the old lady in Fallujah, shooting her as she came around the corner on raw impulse instead of thought, taking her out from twenty yards away.

HE CRIED

Against her shoulder as she said, softly, It's all right, Marlon, you're here now and it's going to work out, you're a damn good nurse, and then it seemed as if all she had ever learned on the job came into play as she spoke soothingly to him, making a gentle patting motion on his back, the kind of gesture you'd use to calm a baby at night—a gentle repeated pat, not too soft and not too hard.

SO THAT

The deepest enigmatic meaning would seem to stay around that image, not just of the two of them crying together but also of the hand itself, as it fluttered alone, which had led to his admission, and for her that image would hold another meaning, because she would remember it, too, vaguely, and replicate the motion countless times over the years, giving herself pleasure, just as she'd often backtrack through her memory of that summer and fall, drawing on the random moments, trying to find the origin point of their love.

Sindya Bhanoo

Malliga Homes

MR. SWAMINATHAN DIED SUDDENLY, as he was walking
back to his flat from the veg dining hall after dinner. He
was ahead of me on the path, and I saw him slow down. His gait
changed from a fast stride to a slower, hunched walk. His left arm
went limp. He lost his footing and crumpled to the ground. If I
had not been swift, I imagine he would have hit his head on the
cement. There would have been blood. But I caught up with him.
Before he fell, I squatted to the ground and put my hands out,
and his head fell directly into my open palms. Carefully, I slipped
my hands out from behind his head, set it gently on the cement
and sat at his side talking to him. His left eye looked lower than
his right. His left cheek sagged, as if it might slide off.

I held his hand until the ambulance arrived. It was the first time
that I had held a man's hand since my husband died. The rectangular diamond on Mr. Swaminathan's gold ring was hard and cold
in contrast to his warm skin. Before they loaded his body onto
the gurney, he opened his eyes, looked at me and said, "Renuka."
Then he squeezed my hand. Whether he was asking me to summon his wife, or whether he thought I was his wife, I cannot say.

He died before he reached the hospital. He was seventy-five years old, the same age my husband would be if he were alive today.

His death was our first. Hard to believe, since this is a place for old people. But Malliga Homes is a new facility, and the first residents, myself included, moved in just two years ago.

The other day, I spoke to my daughter, Kamala, on the phone, and told her how expertly the personnel handled the whole Swaminathan matter. They were prompt in calling for help. The area was cleared immediately, and the ambulance rolled right onto the freshly trimmed landscaping, crushing a row of golden dewdrops that took a year to grow.

"I am so glad to hear that," Kamala said.

Malliga Homes is not a bad place. It is a rather nice place, in fact. Just a bit isolated for city people like me, coming from places like Chennai. The facility sits at the intersection of Thambur Road and NH-181, just outside of Coimbatore. Going to the outskirts of a midsized city gave the developers more space, and allowed them to invest in luxuries that we all appreciate. We have stone tiles in the bathrooms, cabinets made of Thermofoil, those wood laminate floors that are in style now, picturesque landscaping, and Honda inverter generators with eight hours of runtime for when the power goes out, which it does daily.

I am lucky to be here, my Kamala likes to remind me. It is only the second place of its kind in South India, and the units sold out quickly. Still, no amount of expensive stone or carefully worded praise from my daughter can change what Malliga Homes is: a place for those who have nowhere else to go.

We are of the upper middle class, here. We do not come from families who own hospitals or factories, or vast tracts of land. We work for those people—*worked* for those people. Those people belong to a different cut entirely, and will never move here, no matter how beautifully our gardeners maintain the bougainvillea vines and oleander shrubs. Those people will stay in their posh city flats with their many servants and their children nearby. The offspring of the rich are rich, and they do not seek their fortunes elsewhere.

Like me, nearly every resident of Malliga Homes has lost sons and daughters to Foreign. That is the reason why we live in a retirement community–cum–nursing home, rather than with our families. My Kamala left India twenty-five years ago. She is deputy managing director of a company called Synchros Systems, based in a small town outside of Atlanta.

Renuka Swaminathan also has two children living abroad, one in Germany and one in Australia. They must have arrived already, to help with Mr. Swaminathan's *kariyam* preparations.

I am knitting a sweater made of fine green mohair for Renuka. After the *kariyam*, she is going to Adelaide to spend time with her son. I was the one who said, "Better to go. It is depressing to be alone right after." Her son is the manager of a movie theater there. He was not able to finish his graduate degree at the University of Adelaide, but somehow found a way to stay there. "Good for him," I said, when Renuka told me. I meant it.

Those of us at Malliga Homes with children in America rank higher than those with children in Dubai or Qatar. Somewhere in between fall those with children working in Singapore, Australia, England, Germany, and the rest of Western Europe. Africa falls below the Middle East, both because of what people imagine it is like there, and because it is so hard to get to. What our children do, how much money they make, whether our grandchildren are bright or mediocre—all of this matters. It is a tragedy to have a brilliant child and a dunce of a grandchild.

The yarn for Renuka's sweater cost me five rupees per meter, much more than I typically pay, but I decided it was worth it. The sweater will bring out the green in her eyes and it will be good for the Australian winter. I checked the climate in Adelaide on the Net; it can drop down to ten degrees. But also: death turns you cold, and I want Renuka to stay warm. In the months after my husband died, a chilliness plagued my being, even in hot weather.

My husband's death was what brought me to Malliga Homes. After he died, Kamala flew to India and spent two weeks with me in our Chennai flat. She insisted that I leave my red *bottu* on my forehead, and keep all my jewelry on.

"This is not the end of life for you, Amma. I don't believe in such things," she said.

I did insist on taking off my toe rings. I never liked them. Initially, they would not come off; Kamala tried to help, and gave up. They had been on for forty-five years, the silver rings tightening around my toes as I became fatter over the decades, my flesh curling over their edges. Finally, after soaking my feet in soapy water for thirty minutes, I had success.

Kamala collapsed on our cane sofa, the same one she spent years reading on as a teenager, her legs leisurely stretched out while she held Somerset Maugham high above her head. Her eye makeup was smeared from crying. Both of us had done a lot of that.

"Amma, come lie down with me," she said, a cricket ball in one hand and a brochure in the other. My husband loved cricket, and she had been carrying the ball around with her since her arrival.

"Move over," I said.

We lay squished on the sofa, side by side, hip to hip, mother and daughter. That was when she brought up Malliga Homes. She handed me the brochure.

"Open it," she said. "Look how nice the grounds are. Like Brindavan Gardens."

The brochure was from Kamala's friend in America, Padmini Venugopal. Padmini's parents had just moved into Malliga Homes.

"'All the comforts of home, without any worry—and so many friends,'" Kamala read out loud. She looked at me eagerly.

"Consider it," she said.

"What friends?"

"You will make them."

"You cannot force me. What if I had stopped you all those years ago from going to America alone?" I asked.

"This is not the same thing," she said. She sat up and climbed over me to get off the sofa. "It is not the same thing at all."

The following night, I had a small fall in the bathroom. Though I was not seriously injured, Kamala became unstoppable. I could hear the determination in her voice, like when she was a girl and wanted a peach Melba from Jafar's on Mount Road. She would not stop until I relented.

"You are my responsibility now," she said. She was combing my hair, because I sprained my right wrist in the fall and could not do it myself. "I've already made a booking. I paid the deposit today."

After she tied my white hair into a loose bun, she stroked my head as if I were a child. Her own hair, long and braided, was speckled with white.

"It's a two-bedroom," she said. "So we can visit you."

She extended her trip by a week, so that she could move me into Malliga Homes.

Two years have passed and they have not visited. They were all supposed to be here this time next month—Kamala; my son-in-law, Arun; and my granddaughter, Veena. I prepared the bedroom for them as soon as Kamala told me the plan. I bought new sheets and an extra single bed. But just a few weeks ago, Kamala called to say she was coming alone. Arun is busy with work. Veena started a new job.

They would enjoy it here, I think. It is like a resort. There are three swimming pools on the property, and a boy scoops out the leaves with his large net many times each day. The veg and non-veg food is cooked in separate kitchens. We have tennis matches; movies in Tamil, Hindi and English on the big screen in the lounge; yoga; a walking group; a bridge group; and a Hindu prayer group that meets at the small temple we built on the grounds. There are smaller Muslim and Christian prayer groups that meet in residents' homes. Malliga Homes, as Kamala says, is "inclusive."

There is nothing wrong with Alpharetta, Georgia, but for all the space and privacy that America offers, it is a country that longs for life. You go for a drive and the road is endless. One fast-food restaurant after another. Wendy's. McDonald's. Waffle House. The colored lights shine bright in the evenings, beckoning visitors. "Like temples," I used to say. The grocery store is three kilometers from their house. What sort of place is that? One where people are too busy driving to enjoy life. Nobody has time to talk, and yet everyone is seeing a therapist.

"It is only a ten-minute drive to Starbucks," Kamala would say, when we visited. "Should we go?"

Ten minutes. I may as well plant a tree, pluck the beans myself and grind my own coffee, I used to say to my husband. He would gently put his palm over my hand and whisper, "Shush. She may hear you."

He spoiled her. The best school. The best tutors. The clothes she wanted. The books she liked. Let her go to the movies. Let her relax. *No need to make her cook with you*, he would say. *Do not trouble her. Do not upset her. Let her be.*

He was just as bored as I was in Alpharetta, even if he never said so. He, too, hated the burned taste of Starbucks, and how we went the whole day in America—the whole bloody day—without seeing a single person but the mailman, while Kamala and Arun went to work and Veena went to school. I always enjoyed living right in the heart of Chennai, with the noises of the street cluttering my day. Everything I needed was a stone's throw away.

"No point in living in the city in America," Kamala said, back when they bought the house. "Dirty, unsafe, no parking, bad schools." She said "America" but was she also talking about her childhood home? I could not help but wonder.

What do you do with a big, empty house full of rooms that you do not need? She never talks about this, but somewhere inside she must feel it. She is my daughter after all. Her house, with its vaulted ceilings and skylights, it is no better than Malliga Homes.

"At least she is in America." All those years ago, when her Georgia Tech admissions letter arrived, I said this to my husband.

"If she has to go, let it be there."

I dine with the Venugopals, the parents of Kamala's friend Padmini. Over his empty plate, as we wait to be served, Dr. Venugopal cannot stop talking about Mr. Swaminathan's death.

"For me, it is an intellectual curiosity," he says. He is a retired cardiologist. His wife, Lakshmi, fit and elegant, has gray hair but smooth skin, undoubtedly from years of sandalwood paste facials. We are in the non-veg dining hall, and Mr. and Mrs. Sharma are also with us. The Venugopals and the Sharmas always sit together. Only once before have I been invited to join them, when I first moved in. It was a sort of welcome and thank-you. When Kamala signed me up for Malliga Homes, the Venugopals received something called a "referral bonus," by way of a free out-of-station trip to Ooty.

The Sharmas and the Venugopals are sipping gin and tonics. Dr. Venugopal summons the mobile bartender with his fully stocked cart for me. I order a fresh lime soda. Alcoholic drinks cost extra, and I do not like to waste money.

After listening to me describe the way Mr. Swaminathan fell, how his face drooped on one side, how his speech slurred as he said his wife's name, Dr. Venugopal declares that it was most certainly an ischemic stroke, not a hemorrhagic one.

"Absolutely," he says.

He seems thrilled to have determined this. He has a sharp, well-shaped gray beard and a moustache of the same color. His right finger goes toward his moustache and I expect him to pet it thoughtfully but instead, he points directly at me.

"Rare for a stroke to be fatal. I wonder if there were other complications. Head injury perhaps?" he asks, almost accusingly.

I explain the fall, how gentle it was.

Dr. Venugopal grunts, though not in an unpleasant manner. "Humph. Still, that cement. So hard."

"He fell into my hands," I almost say. But I stop myself. It feels like a confession I should not make.

A waiter dressed in white comes around with spicy red dal. The Venugopals and Sharmas allow him to ladle some into the small stainless bowls on their plates. I put my hand over mine to indicate that I do not want any.

"Such a genuinely nice couple they were," Mrs. Sharma says. "Imagine losing your husband like that."

She looks at me, a soloist between two couples, and says, "What I meant to say was, so suddenly."

Such comments don't upset me these days. "It is lonely, but life goes on," I say, smiling.

Mrs. Sharma nods enthusiastically, relieved. The curls in her coiffed bob nod with her. Out of consideration, I change the subject.

"You look nice this evening," I say to Mrs. Venugopal. She is wearing a sleeveless, block-print *salwar kameez*.

"Come shopping with me," she says. "I bought the material at Badshah. And I have a fabulous tailor."

I know she does not mean it. She sees how I dress. I wear ordinary clothes, and rarely buy new things. In any case, I would not spend my money at a place like Badshah.

"Better for the younger generation. Kamala might like to go," I say. "Though I suppose she isn't so young anymore."

The polite thing would be for Mrs. Venugopal to say that her daughter, Padmini, is also not so young, but she keeps silent and I feel like I have betrayed my child.

"Fantastic chicken korma today," Mrs. Sharma says, as she mixes it with her rice. She looks at the Fitbit on my wrist. "New gadget?"

"A present from my daughter," I say. "It counts your steps. Kamala says I must aim for eight thousand a day."

"We golf," Mrs. Sharma says. "We get plenty of exercise from that. No need to track it."

"Yes," I say.

In old age, status is tied to health, what you can do with your body and what you can't. Or sometimes, what you say you can do.

"Padmini bought Fitbits for us also. They want us to live long lives, don't they?" Mrs. Venugopal says.

"For what, I want to ask," Dr. Venugopal says, leaning forward. "For them?"

"Our son only visits every other year from California," Mrs. Sharma says.

"Padmini hardly comes," Dr. Venugopal says. His eyes catch mine and I see something childlike in them, something sorrowful. "I need another drink," he says.

"She is so busy," Mrs. Venugopal says. "This year she was promoted to director."

"But you know," Dr. Venugopal says, his voice a hush. "Renuka is moving." His eyes search my face. "Did you know?"

"No," I say, but immediately, I understand. It happens often to widows and widowers. She is moving abroad to join her children.

"Where to?" I ask. "Germany with her daughter, or Australia with her son?"

The worst would be if she had to split her time, I think to myself. A permanent, temporary resident in two places.

"Neither," he says, his voice still quiet. "She is moving back to

Chennai. Her son and daughter are returning, with their families, purchasing three side-by-side flats."

"But there are grandchildren?"

"Enrolling in our Indian schools."

Dr. Venugopal seems pleased that he has this information, that he is the one who is delivering it to me, Renuka's friend and witness to Mr. Swaminathan's death.

I have finished my food, and do not wish to stay through a second round of drinks. "I am expecting a call from Kamala," I say, excusing myself.

Dr. Venugopal gives me a salute. "Best not to miss their calls. Otherwise, we may never catch them. Give her our regards."

I stand up and walk away. I hear Mrs. Venugopal say that Kamala lives in Alpharetta, and that Padmini lives in Buckhead.

"Thirty-minute drive," she says. "If there is no traffic."

When I get back to my flat, I call Kamala. It's already Saturday morning there, one of the rare windows of time when I can usually reach her.

"I had dinner with the Venugopals today."

"Lovely. I'm so glad you have friends there."

"I found out about a nice clothing store. We will go, you and me."

There is a pause, and then she says, "I may need to delay my trip."

"What for?"

"Work. What else?"

"We have a good Net connection. Come here and work."

"I'm sorry," she says.

"Forget about you," I say, unable to hide my frustration. "Did you ever truly plan to bring Veena here? Or will she always be too busy? She has not been to India in five years."

"Of course she will come to see you. Just not right now."

"Bring her to my funeral."

"Amma!" Kamala says.

I wish to hang up, but I think of my husband, and his palm on mine. I soften my tone. "How is Veena?" I ask.

Kamala sighs.

"Still trying to sort out her life. She has a temporary job at the Georgia Aquarium."

"Doing science work?"

"No," Kamala says. "She cuts up the food for the animals."

Kamala goes on talking, but I stop listening.

I imagine my daughter's daughter as a butcher, chopping dead fish with bulging eyes for living fish with bulging eyes. I nearly comment that I know why Veena is so lost, how she needed her mother, she still needs her mother. But once again, I remember my husband, the way he'd gently warn me to stop. I keep my mouth shut.

After Kamala, I could not have more children. My body tipped into menopause a decade earlier than expected, otherwise we would have given her siblings. But for Kamala, it was a choice. A second child would have been impractical with her career. The one to suffer was Veena, who spent all those hours in childcare, and then came home to that large, silent house, with all the toys and nobody to play with.

Now that I do not visit Alpharetta anymore—I find the journey far too draining—I must recall the house in my memory. The way the front hallway leads to the kitchen with the black and white granite counter, where, every day, I tried to make something tasty for Veena. How the family room is two carpeted steps down from the kitchen. How Kamala was always fearful that I would trip on those steps. Halfway up the staircase to the upper level, there is a small landing, where Veena liked to launch marbles, to watch them roll and putter down the stairs.

When I close my eyes after hanging up the phone, I can hear the sound of Kamala's dishwasher, gushing and moaning late into the night, and her dryer, tossing clothes around and around.

For Mr. Swaminathan's *kariyam*, I wear a light orange Mysore silk sari. Subdued and traditional is best, based on what I know about Renuka. Still, I made sure to go for something colorful. It is a celebration after all. The *kariyam* marks the fourteenth day after Mr. Swaminathan's death, the official end of the mourning period. Though, the mourning never really stops. Not for a spouse. I finished knitting the sweater for Renuka, but I do not take it with me. What use will it be to her in Chennai, a city where the sun is glaring even on the coldest day of the year?

Mr. Swaminathan's *kariyam* is an efficient, in-and-out kind of affair, held not in their flat but in the Malliga Homes common lounge. Their flat is one of the more modest one-bedrooms, and would not have held the crowd. I arrive on time, but the priest has already finished the *puja*.

"Oh, we finished early," Renuka's daughter says breezily. "No need to make everyone sit through it. We wanted everyone to just enjoy food with us." She is a pretty woman in her thirties, with the same light green eyes as her mother. She is wearing an emerald choker around her neck and a peacock-blue silk sari that she keeps adjusting. Children these days don't know how to wear Indian clothes well, I have noticed. Too much time spent in slacks and skirts.

"I heard you are moving back," I say.

"We are," she says.

I do not ask her questions. She has many people to visit with, and no idea who I am. I wash my hands and take a seat in the eating area, in front of an empty banana leaf, right next to Mrs. Sharma.

"Did you hear about the Bhatia scandal?" she asks me. "Didn't your husband work for them?"

"Yes," I say. "But I have not heard."

"Mrs. Bhatia is suing her own son, Brij, for two hundred crores. And her daughter Cherry for one hundred." She shakes her head. "Rich people. They have so much and they fight like this."

"I met her once," I say. "My husband worked for Bhatia Electricals. She seemed like a nice woman."

"Nice to everyone but her own," Mrs. Sharma says.

Men holding stainless steel buckets of food come by to serve us. I mix my sambar and rice together with my hands. Simple food, but such a pleasure to eat something different than what the dining hall cooks prepare.

I speak with Renuka only once, on my way out. She is wearing a plain, cotton sari. She has wiped off her *bottu*, taken off her earrings, bangles and toe rings. She looks naked, and vulnerable. That is what happens. You wear these things for so many years that they become your permanent clothing.

"I am so sorry," I say.

"Thank you for coming," she says, a phrase she must have said many times already.

For the first time, I notice how many wrinkles she has on her face. All over, even across the bridge of her nose. Nevertheless, her eyes are as striking as ever, penetrating and thoughtful.

"He asked for you at the end," I say.

"I am glad you were there," she says softly.

A few days after Mr. Swaminathan's *kariyam*, I go veg for dinner. They are serving dry, salted herring on the non-veg side. I simply cannot tolerate the smell these days, though I once loved it. I sit alone at a table for four in the back of the veg hall. I survey the room, and the sadness of it all hits me. All of us old people, eating in this canteen, abandoned by our children. It is pathetic. Uncivilized, one might even say.

The old should be with the young, the young with the old.

That was how it was for generations: babies sleeping in the arm-pits of their grandmothers, children sitting atop the shoulders of their grandfathers. Everyone in the same crowded home.

Nobody comes to sit with me today and I am glad for it. I might say something morose and develop a bad reputation. I finish my chapati and bean *kottu* as quickly as possible and rinse my hands at the tap.

My Fitbit says I need six thousand more steps before it gets dark. I do not walk my usual route. Instead, I walk to the side of Malliga Homes where the smaller flats are. Where Renuka's flat is. When I get there, I see that her gauzy yellow curtains are open. I look inside.

Empty.

She must have been so anxious to leave. I turn the doorknob and find it unlocked.

I hear someone behind me, and turn around to see Renuka.

"I was just looking for you," I say. I quickly step out of her flat and shut the door, feeling guilty for the intrusion. "You must be leaving soon."

I watch her remove a piece of a green bean lodged between two teeth with her tongue. For a second, I wonder if her children have changed their minds. They would remain abroad, and she would stay with us, alone.

"I made you a sweater for Australia, but it will be of no use to you anymore."

"It all happened so fast," she says.

"My daughter is visiting next month," I say. "She plans to remodel our old flat and live there one day. Perhaps we can walk on Elliot's Beach together."

"Oh!" Renuka says. She hugs me. "Children these days are so willing." I am shocked by her hug, and by my lie. I try to correct what I've said.

"You misunderstood," I say. "She is doing well in America. She just plans to visit often."

"I came to lock up," Renuka says, pleasantly. "We need to sell this place so we can afford the new flats in Chennai."

"I will give you the sweater before you leave," I say. "Maybe you can use it if you walk on the beach in the evenings."

"How I've missed it," she says. "That sea breeze."

I walk all around Malliga Homes until I reach eight thousand steps. I do not know why I lied to Renuka. Renuka, who lived in the smallest flat that Malliga Homes offers. Renuka, whose son is an ordinary movie theater manager. I imagine repeating it. To the Venugopals. To the Sharmas. To the chap who presses our clothes.

For some reason, I am reminded of my own father, who spent his final days in our flat in Chennai when Kamala was just a child. Toothless, he would sip his bland rice porridge and mutter an old Tamil proverb. "This is stranger than that, and that is stranger than this," he would say, as bits of the porridge dribbled down his chin.

It is dusk now at Malliga Homes. In that darkest part of twilight, that ungraspable moment before day turns fully to night, I pause to admire the oleander shrubs. Their white flowers glowing at their dusty, light yellow centers. The thick bougainvillea vines, in brilliant, deep magenta, are creeping over the Malliga Homes compound wall. Some of the flowers are stuck on one side while others, by sheer luck, fall to the other.

Crystal Wilkinson

Endangered Species: Case 47401

ALL BLACK WOMEN got this thrumming thing inside us but don't nobody notice. Which is understandable if you know the history of the world, but that thrum just sits in our bellies and then one day it comes on so strong that we can't stop it even if we want to. And that's when your Statue of Liberty might get climbed. Your abusive husband might get shot. That's when she might quit that stupid-ass job with the manager who says she can't wear dreadlocks. That's when she be in the corner curled up crying her eyes out over somebody black she don't even know that got killed somewhere, again, because that somebody feels like a sister, an auntie, or a cousin. You might see her on the front lines of a protest when she ain't never done no shit like that before—loud and regal and effective. And then when you see her out there yelling and screaming until her voice is hoarse, looking like a goddamn goddess, that's when you'll pay attention but you won't even know why. But what you don't realize is that this thrum been with us always. These are the thoughts that came over me while I was cooking breakfast that morning in my new kitchen, which I'm sure wasn't the first time a black woman had discovered the deep insides of herself, but it was the first time for me.

Big V was moving up in the world, but it had never been my plan to live that far away from my people. Before his promotion, we'd been perfectly settled into this second marriage thang as though there had never been a first marriage for either of us. But since we'd packed up and moved, and Big V was acting a fool, something had climbed into my stomach and was just there, humming.

Big V was his own version of his best self that morning, sprawled out across the new couch, reading the newspaper with one of his work boots planted in the cushion and the other one on the floor. I wanted to say "Vincent Pickens! Get your feet off the goddamn couch!" but I could feel something deep under my skin around my belly shaking, jittering, so I was trying to pay more attention to me, to that feeling, instead of him. Two months in that new house and there was my man with his uniform pressed, his name freshly embossed in blue letters on his white shirt pocket, his face cleanly shaven and his fade shaped up by his own hands, his mouth just a-going, his boots all up on the furniture, all arrogant.

If you didn't look closely you couldn't even see the tiny letters underneath his name that said *supervisor* in rolling cursive, but you could feel *supervisor* every time he moved. He even smelled like *supervisor* with all that cologne on. I sliced potatoes into the skillet for hash, studied my hands, which had started shaking. I wanted to talk to my mama more than I wanted anything else at that moment, but I kept on cooking. Out the window was six stray cats preening and stretching in the backyard. A gray one was perched on the patio chair, fat and round, looking proud of itself. The cats came to the backyard nearly every day to make themselves known. They'd been there since we moved in. Big V didn't pay them no attention, but I did.

"Crazy," Big V said that morning, "these motherfuckers." He was puffing up into somebody's politician right in front of me. You would have thought he was running for president, not leading a production team at the factory. Talking shit, talking about "These are the end of times as we know it. I can tell you that. These motherfuckers are crazy. This man at work, Na-than-iel, remember me telling you about Na-than-iel?" He peered up from the *Herald* and looked at me sideways like he was waiting for me to answer. "Ba'y?!" he said. I wiped my hands down the front of my T-shirt, stirred the potatoes in with the steak, and diced onions into it. He went on, and I responded with the occasional *Hmmp!* and *I know that's right, baby*, but what I was really listening to was the pulse in my own neck thumping.

I looked out the window again and the cats were gone.

By the time Baby Girl moped down the stairs, I had burned the biscuits. Same biscuit recipe I been using all these years, but it was the new stove, I guess. Baby Girl threw her backpack into a chair and flopped down at the kitchen table.

"When we moving back home?" she said, and rolled her beautiful eyes at Big V, who had stopped his proselytizing just long enough to flip on the TV. Big V wasn't her real daddy, but he'd been in her life for the four years we'd been married. They got along but were more like tolerating church members than real family. Or at least that's how it was then.

He looked at her. I threw the biscuits in the trash can. I thought about the long line of women I come from. We some big old country women—big-boned, skinny-legged fine cooks. I pictured my grandmother at her kitchen window in the hills, looking up toward the knobs, the smell of baking bread wafting through the house and all of us waiting to eat. My heart clicked and ticked in my chest, and it seemed like the thrumming thing was just winding and winding like a goldfish in a bowl.

Little V began to cry from his room upstairs, and I dropped the skillet of hash on the floor, shattering the corner of the new tile, which had been white and gleaming like something off of TV just a minute before.

"Damn," Big V said, and looked at me all silly, but he didn't say nothing else. We ate cold cereal for breakfast, which I regret now, and I also regret that me and him didn't even kiss goodbye.

Later that morning, Little V played on the carpet in the living room while I slung cardboard boxes into a corner of the garage and scattered my prized possessions around me in a circle on the kitchen floor. A picture of Mama Sarah and a stack of yellowed recipe cards that belonged to my mama, a box of unopened white linen that somebody bought us as a wedding present, and a whole lot of stuff that had come to mean something to me. I was just standing there looking at all my heirlooms when I saw through the living room window a white woman traipsing up our side- walk, looking like an after-school special with that blond hair curled around her chin. Green sweater with bright red apples and yellow and green 1, 2, 3s, plaid culottes, and white stockings. The doorbell rang just as I was wondering if she had the right address.

"Are you the lady of the house?" the woman said.

"I am," I said, and held the storm door open just a little.

"Can we count on you?" the white woman said, and shoved a clipboard through the crack in the door. A man across the street was sweeping his sidewalk. A woman was ushering a girl into a waiting car. An old woman was sitting on a porch in a rocking chair holding a dog. They were all watching. They were all white people. I held the box of linen across my chest like it was a shield.

The white woman looked past me, to the other unopened boxes scattered across the floor. She rubbed her nose, cleared her throat, and asked if she should come back when things were in order. I didn't say nothing but the thrum was shifting, moving around my belly button in a circle now like a Ferris wheel.

"We've got to have some way to control them," she said, and got to clicking that ink pen against her clipboard. "The peti- tion would . . ." I placed my fist on one hip, which should have been some kind of warning to her because that's how I meant it.

Little V was crawling across the carpet, and I could hear him getting closer and closer to where I was standing. "My word!" the woman squealed when she saw him, like she'd seen one of the kittens from out back. She was still stretching her neck to see inside our house. I could see my new neighbors stopping whatever they were doing midsentence, midcut, midwalk to stare. I took the petition, thanked the woman and shut my door.

"Ain't that some shit?" I said to Little V. I handed him a teething cracker and rubbed my palm across his head and both cheeks. My sweet, sweet boy. I placed the box of linens on the couch and read the paper the woman gave me. "What kind of people write a petition to kill cats?" I said this out loud, but I thought I'd just said it to myself. "Motherfuckin cats!" I said 'cause I just couldn't believe it. Little V stopped his playing and looked up at me just like he knew what I was talking about. "People crazier than hell, Little V," I said.

I took some aspirin.

Out the back window, I watched the stray cats come back out of the woods and stretch themselves in the sun. Little V stayed content as long as I was in sight. He was playing with a toy car, slobbering.

If them cats had been house cats they would have been something else. Magnificent. The black one lounging on the arm of a couch, a man rubbing on its head, or a girl cradling the yellow one like a doll while she watched some cartoons. But they were feral, at least that's what that white woman had called them, but I didn't see too much wild about them. I'd petted one of them when I threw scraps out there. I kept watching, and a few younger ones followed the big ones out, and the kittens began to stretch and yawn.

Beyond the yard was a grove of trees. I was surprised that the trees looked like they had always been there naturally and not like trees planted just to make a subdivision look comfortable. Even from the window, I could spot oaks and sycamores. During the day when it was just me and Little V, that was my favorite thing to do. I loved looking at the trees.

Little V lifted his head. Somewhere a line from Billie Holiday twisted its way through my head. Like the rest of us, my history with trees is complicated, but I'm a black woman who loves me some trees. You not gonna take everything from me and I will tell anybody that. You ain't taking my love for trees away too. Fuck that.

The sky was brilliant, that's my mama's favorite word. I could see the woods straight ahead. To the right and the left, a long row of big white houses which looked just like the one I was standing in disturbed the land. I was sure that where our house stood a farmer tended a field once, or maybe it was part of untended land left wild, at least it seemed that way to me. And even more years back a row of brothers and sisters working a row of corn or tobacco or a young Wyandotte woman picking berries. Now I know some people don't think like this, but this is the for-real kind of stuff I think about. No matter how you think most black women are. I'm trying to tell you about me.

After that, I went out into the garage for more boxes and a quick smoke. That's when I saw a mouse. A different kind of woman would have screamed bloody murder, but I didn't. Its tail was long, curled upward like a thin ribbon. Maybe that's how they grow up here? I was just looking at it when I saw a sparkle in the tiny eye of my first friend from the Midwest. "What's up?" I said. "Howdy do, buddy!" I knew if I could have gotten close, I could have crushed him with one stomp from my shoe. I'd seen Daddy kill copperheads like that on the farm, back home. The amazing power of one focused black man. Whomp! Then suddenly with the heel of a work boot, the crooked world was safe again. But that mouse, just like them cats, just like me, wasn't bothering nobody, so I left him alone.

I called mama and she said, "Yes, I sure do remember. Uh-huh, he sure did," when I asked her if she remembered Daddy stomp-ing them copperheads like that.

We both held the phone and just listened to each other's breaths. "You like it any better?" Mama asked me.

"I don't know. Don't see many black people up here," I said.

"Indiana." She sighed, then harrumphed. "They killed us all out in that part of the country."

"Aww, Mama," I said. "This the twenty-first century."

I thought about the history of the South and I thought about the North too and the things I saw on the news every day and all them black women with a thrumming in their bellies. I wanted to explain to her how maybe they were making a difference. But black people were still dying every day so I couldn't be sure so I didn't say nothing about it. Me and Mama don't talk about stuff like that. But I knew at that moment that the answer sat right in my own gut. I wondered if Mama could hear that epiphany or whatever it was through the phone, or if she ever listened to her own insides, but I didn't come out and ask her. I wanted to tell her about the white woman and the mouse and the cats and even about Big V acting siddity, but I didn't.

"I know what I know," Mama said.

I noticed a spider crawling across the ceiling that I'd have to get to later, but maybe he needed to be free, too. He was minding his own damn business. Ain't that what we all want? Just to mind our own damn business?

Then Mama said, "So, really, baby, how's everything? Really."

What I said was "Fine." But I really wanted to start crying, and that was before anything much had even happened.

"How's my grandbabies?" she said.

"Fine."

"That man of yours?"

"Awesome."

Mama laughed so hard she got choked. "Awesome?" she said. "You know his ass ain't awesome."

"We all good, Mama," I said. And I wasn't lying. I ain't no Miss Cleo. How was I supposed to know about what was to come? Can you read minds? Do you know the future?

After we got off the phone, I held the phone up to my ear a while longer listening to it buzz across two hundred miles, missing my mama like crazy.

It wasn't but a few seconds later that the doorbell rang again.

Here come this white woman with her cat-killing petition at my door a second time. Sometimes I just sit back and try to imagine a whole room of white people sitting around in a meeting talking about killing cats. Is that what y'all doing when so many black people are on cooling boards all over this country? The door was cracked a little, and I heard her open it up all the way.

"Lady of the house?" she yelled, and I came around the corner holding Little V just in time to see her foot about to cross my damn threshold. Did you hear me say MY? What the hell, right? As I rounded the wall from the kitchen, I felt dizzy. I felt a catch run through my stomach that just about doubled me over. I swear before God, I'd liken it to labor pains.

"How you just come up in somebody's house, lady?" I said, and my voice was slow and low because I knew this wasn't going to turn out right. I knew it from that moment right there.

I could feel my face flushing, my ears burning like they were on fire. I juggled Little V on my hip but he was steady trying to get down and play.

"We need fifty more signatures," she said as she stepped backward onto my porch.

"I don't have time for this dumb shit," I said. "I done told you once." And as I was trying to close my door, she stuck her foot right in my front door. Yes. Can you believe it?

"Have you had time to consider our materials?" she said all silly.

I said to her, "Now, I ain't going to tell you not one more damn time." Little V shifted back in my arms away from her. I tried to scoot her foot out with my own foot, but that crazy-ass woman had her heel wedged in good. "How long have you lived here?" she said, and had the nerve to raise her pen up above her clipboard like this, like she was about to write down whatever I said.

"What?" That's what I said. "What?!" Just like that.

Little V was crying because he wanted me to put him down. But I felt like I needed to keep him in my arms through all this. Instinct. Mother's intuition, I guess.

"Do you have a copy of a mortgage or lease that I could see?" the woman said.

I opened the door wider to make sure I heard her right. I leaned my face toward hers, and I'm not lying when I tell you that I wanted the tip of my nose to touch the tip of hers to make sure I heard her right. "What did you say?" I said. "Do I have what?"

She repeated herself, then got a little scared look on her face before she stepped back and removed her foot.

I slammed the door closed but before I could lock it the woman grabbed the doorknob and turned it.

With Little V in my arms I was losing this game of tug-of-war, and by now my head felt like there were marbles rolling around in my skull. That was the worst headache I've ever had in my life. And let me be clear my thrumming was there constantly. I knew how it was going to end up then, and there was nothing I could have done to stop it. She yanked the door open wider and stepped one foot back in. Then come this wooshing feeling just beneath my heart. Woosh, woosh.

Now I'm telling you, it was never my intention to lay hands on that funny-looking white woman, but when she wouldn't remove her foot from my door, I pushed her out as hard as I could. Yes, I did that. I sure did. I pushed her out of my door. She tumbled to the sidewalk. Her pen went one way and her clipboard went another. Her culottes were bunched up around her thighs. All the stuff in her purse flew across the grass and her stocking was torn and it did look like her knee was bleeding, but she wasn't dead.

And you and I know she ain't dead now. I ain't killed nobody. Right? You've sat down and talked to her, right? She's still living.

Some of the neighbors had stopped in their yards, at their mailboxes, in their driveways to watch. I could see a tall white woman wearing a sun hat and glasses peering at me from across the street. She shook her head and adjusted her water hose before going back to watering her flower bed. The mailman started up our sidewalk and then kept on going to the next house when he saw us out there. I threw up my hand at him, and he didn't speak. I closed my door and locked it. Ain't that what people do all over the world? Close their doors, lock it, and think they're safe?

From the couch I peeped through the blinds, and a few neighbors came to her aid and helped gather her things. She banged on the door again and yelled, "We'll see about this!" And then suddenly it was quiet again.

Then later in the afternoon, I was back in the kitchen. Little V was playing with a toy that my mama bought him that bounced back upright every time he would knock it down. The boxes were piled around him, pictures turned on their backs where I wanted them to be hung along the wall. All these pictures with my people's faces on them. Generations and generations of my family. You got a lot of family like that?

Little V was cute all right, most babies are, but when I heard him cooing and blowing bubbles, I could almost feel my heart rising out of my chest that day. He played peek-a-boo with me while I worked in the kitchen, his curly head bobbing back and forth from view. He had gotten to that age where he didn't want me to pick him up as much. I was his mother. Knew he needed me but I wanted something from him too. Comfort? Assurance? I wanted him to live is what I wanted. Thinking about it all made my heart heavy and made me think of the old house, Mission Creek, where I'd played in as a child, clusters of hardworking black people around me like blackberries on a vine, laughing and fussing and loving, all those kind neighbors on Logan Street and those who had passed away too.

I stopped unpacking again and went to the window. I shared the sun coming through the window with them cats, with the mouse in the garage, with the memories of those who had been there before. Given a choice, I would have stayed at that window watching them cats all day and not ever emptied one more box. The stillness, the light streaming through the window slowed the thrum down to something that felt like comfort or pride. I'm not sure how to describe it really. It wasn't safety. I can't say that I felt safe, but I felt like we'd be OK.

It was a long climb up the hill behind Mama and Daddy's house when I was a girl, but I made it at least once a day—bending back tree saplings as I went. Nothing in the world at all wrong with being by yourself. At the top of that hill, I swelled up with happiness. From there I could see Mama's garden, Daddy's fields of corn, our house. I stood with my walking stick hoisted above me like an explorer of the new world, but that's what children do. I thought my children would have that same kind of life, but that's not gonna happen.

Those woods have been bulldozed down to make way for a strip mall. The old farmhouse is gone. No corn. No garden. My mother moved a little closer to town and settled into a smaller house when my father died, but she still raises tomatoes on her patio in a pot. "Lord!" I said to myself, and thought I could hear a rumbling in my back somewhere, but I wasn't quite sure. I stood there shaking the memories out of my head, Little V still crawling around on the carpet by himself. I took some more aspirin for the headache.

A little while after that is when the police showed up. I swung Little V up on my hip and answered the door.

"Ma'am, we've had a report of a situation here," the first officer said, and was standing at my front door with his hand on his gun.

Can you imagine somebody at your front door with a gun when you ain't been in no situation with no police your whole damn life?

"A situation?" I said. Little V kicked his legs, but I was holding on to him tight.

"May I ask what you are doing here in this house, ma'am?" the other officer said. "We've gotten a call."

"What?" My mouth was trying to find words.

"What are your intentions?"

"Intentions?" I said, and looked at him like I'm looking at you right now. I mean, I know you think I'm dumb but I've got three years of college. Sure, I know what intentions are. I just thought it was me who should have been asking about intentions and not them.

When I hesitated the older one said, "We are going to need you to step out here to the sidewalk."

"Why else would I be here? I don't understand. Of course I live here," is what I kept trying to tell them.

"Well some of the folks around, the neighbors here, said that they don't think you live here. Do you have any proof? And they saw you assault a woman here not too long ago. We are looking for the victim."

"The victim?!"

There were still no words. Hell, I ain't got no words now to explain this thing. "I live here," I said again.

"Can you step out of the house, please?"

When I opened the door to try and step outside, I thought I saw a mouse hesitate before it skittered under the couch. It was my peripheral vision so maybe I imagined it, but I would swear to you that I saw that same mouse that was in the garage earlier. He appeared out of nowhere like an omen. All that fancy house and mice running around. If there had been room for laughter, I sure would have laughed, but I stayed quiet. I bounced Little V on my hip and moved him to the other side and my brain was fogged up from all of this, but mostly it was my legs that wouldn't act right or move fast enough.

"Now!" the officer said.

"My baby . . . I need shoes," I said, and then I just stepped out in my bare feet.

"Was there a woman here?" one of them asked. "A white woman?"

"Yes," I said. "Blond. Talking about killing cats."

The older officer wrote something down in a little notebook. The younger one said, "Can you tell us what happened?"

I started at the beginning, but by then my thrum was threatening to leave my body. I tried to think about all them cats dancing among the sycamores in the sun because what was really on my mind was that thing in my gut growing and pulsing. I talked about history, my ancestors, and my mama. I told them about my wedding, about the births of my children. I told them about that boy in the park who had been shot because he was holding a toy gun up in Cleveland. I told them about that famous singer who had raped all them young black girls and nobody had done nothing in Chicago. I told them about the woman who had died in the jail in Texas. "You know good and well that woman didn't kill herself," I said. I said, "What about all them black mothers?" I told them about the three-year-old Minnesota girl who watched her mother's boyfriend get shot to death by police. "This is why black people don't trust white people or the police," I said. When I got to the part of about the humming thing that lived inside the wombs of black women, the officers looked at each other. One looked surprised. The other one had a smirk on his face like that white boy from Covington had when he was talking to that Native American elder. "Covington, Kentucky," I said. I talked about Covington. I talked about Kentucky. I'm from Kentucky, too. Did you know that? I talked and talked, but when I stopped to catch my breath the older officer said, "Ma'am, we're going to have to ask you to put the baby down." He talked to me like I was a dog and not a woman.

"Hand him here," the other one said, "I'll take him."

I know you think I'm crazy but I'm not. I didn't say nothing else but I wasn't about to put Little V down. I'd hold him till his daddy and his sister came home if I had to. I'd hold him until the next time I saw my mama. I'd hold him until black people stopped dying in the streets. And that's when I heard the thrum louder than I'd ever heard it before. I could feel it spreading out from my womb through my entire body, and then it left my body and floated like a summer storm above our heads, above the neighborhood, above the entire country. And one cop had his hand on his gun and the other one kept saying, "Ma'am, I'm going to need you to put that boy down right now."

But I didn't. I wasn't going to ever let go of my baby. Not until all my people were free.

Alice Jolly

From Far Around They Saw Us Burn

WE ARE THE CHILDREN OF CAVAN. Do you know that place? It is a border town, betwixt and between, a place of crossroads—and yet strangely few pass by there. The land around is low and sodden, a place of scrub and straggly pines, lanes and paths leading nowhere. The damp comes up through the soles of your boots and clots in the lungs.

The town of Cavan itself has a wide main street of many fine buildings and yet it seems the sun never shines at an angle to touch the stonework there. Walking the main street, you pass the Central Hotel, the Farnham Arms, Fegans the Draper and Sullivans the General Store. And then, of course, the Convent buildings and the orphanage.

Those buildings are there and yet they are not. For that place is never opened up, the nuns being a closed order, so though the many windows face onto the street, the glass is opaque and obscured by bars. We orphanage girls are never seen except when we go to the cathedral for mass. And should you ever have cause to knock, the nun who unlocks the door will keep to the side so that you may not see her, for that is the way of our world.

. . .

It was the Sullivan family who knew of it first. Sitting up late in the kitchen over a game of penny poker with some of their staff who lived then on the premises, as was the way at that time. And Louis Blessing was there, he who was famous for playing football, for he was gone on Cissie Reilly as worked the grocery counter.

Over the road in Fegans, the drapery store, yet others were still awake. A group of young men returned from a badminton party, lying several to a bed, laughing and joking yet. The streetlights were off, the last Garda foot patrol was back at the station. The only man abroad was James Meehan, the taxi driver, who arrived at the Farnham Arms. Later, he was sure of the exact time. Ten to two.

Then come two o'clock that party at Sullivans broke up. And then it was that Cissie Reilly stood up from the card table and walked over to the window, pulled back the fringed velvet curtain, looked out into the yard to see what weather they might expect the following day. For Sullivans, you see, was next door to the Convent and overlooked the orphanage.

At first, Cissie thought it was a low mist she saw. Others crowded next to her to give their opinions. The night was clear, with no sight of stars but a high, ragged moon with shreds of cloud racing past it. All were agreed. It was smoke, smoke, pumping out of a vent in the orphanage wall.

In the Sacred Heart Dormitory, we orphanage girls felt it first as a settling of boards, the scraping of a hinge, a sound like a yawn, a taste of ash at the back of the throat. But we were feared to get up. Many a night we had lain there needing to relieve ourselves but too frightened to go to the pot. So though we heard Mary Caffey's footsteps go to the cubicle to get Miss O'Reilly, still we lay rigid in our beds.

The building was without light, only the moon slanting silver at the windows. Yet we heard Mary's feet go pat-pat again down the wooden stairs to the first story, along the corridor, up another flight of stairs to the cell of Sister Felix. Then a harsh noise broke on our ears, drilling into the restless night. It was the ringing of the doorbell at the Convent, a sound we did not oft hear.

And this was a long ring, then hardly a moment of silence, then another long ring, followed by many short jabs at the bell. So that then some of the girls who were close to the windows pulled themselves up on their beds so that they might see out. *From the laundry*, they said. *That's where it's coming.*

By then some of us older girls had gone into St. Clare's dormitory across the corridor, or even downstairs to Our Ladies. You would never generally have done such a thing but by then it was not just the bell ringing. Also, from outside the gate came shouting and a blunt thumping. You might have thought it was the sound of a fist slamming, or a foot kicking, and perhaps at first it was. But soon we knew that it must be an axe which was splitting the door.

Suddenly, the lights came on and we all stood blinking in our white nightdresses, standing between the six rows of iron beds. Veronica, Bernadette, and the Cassidy girls. Mary and Susan McKiernan and also Mary Lowry who wore a gold cross around her neck. She had it as a prize from the bishop for she had a calling, was soon to become a nun.

Those up at the window whispered the news back to us. They saw Sister Felix with a key, which she gave to Mary Caffey. Surely, it was the door to the main entrance of the Convent? Then another noise—raucous and jaunty. A car horn—bleeping in short bursts again and again.

Later, it was recorded that it was Cissie Reilly as started the banging. For how else could they wake the sleeping nuns and alert them to the danger? Then the man from Sullivans, John McNally, was kicking with stout boots. Until those young men from Fegans drapery came, them who had returned from the badminton, who brought an axe to smash it in. Some said it was five minutes they were there, others more like ten. But they could not get in.

Louis Blessing, the football player, he had run up the road to the Garda station to raise the alarm there. As he came running back, he found James Meehan, the taxi driver, who had been sleeping with his head on the car wheel. Louis shouted at him *Drive the car down, drive it down.* So Louis got into the passenger seat and they drove down together. Louis said *Blast the horn, blast it loud.* But James, still half asleep, did not take his meaning, so Louis leaned across and pressed on the horn again and again.

When the taxi pulled up outside the Convent gate, Louis said *Quick, man, quick. Drive on now. Get your foot down. To the house of Mr. Monaghan. Surely he will know how we can enter the building.* That he said for Mr. Monaghan was the Convent's farm steward and so was one of the few that came into those buildings.

But then it was that Mary Caffey finally got the lock turned and the door of the Convent was opened. She waved her scattered arms then in the direction of the laundry but John McNally was having none of that. *Get the children out. Do you not see? The fire is spreading.* He spoke then to a nun but she said *No, no, no.* He must go in the laundry first. He said then *Give me the keys.* But she had not any keys.

John McNally looked up at the building, a place he had seen oft before through the windows of Sullivans, so he knew what a maze it was. A knot of staircase and corridors, inside and out, wooden and metal. How might you find your way in or out? Yet he could see the fire escape which was up on a wooden landing outside the upper dormitories.

Some others said to him *We will try the fire escape, you see if the laundry door will give.* But a nun said *No, no. Come down off there, it is the fire in the laundry which must be put out.* So then a group of them ran to the laundry door but it was still locked. The nuns said *No, no, you must wait for the key.* But the men knew better and kicked it in.

Still, the nuns did not want anyone up the fire escape but Louis and Cissie went up anyway. Yet at the second floor they were stopped by a locked door into a classroom. Louis kicked at it, then tried to climb around it, but it would not give. They went back down to find something with which to break it in. All this was said later when the inquiry came.

While all this was passing, we girls were waiting in the Sacred Heart Dormitory, our hands knotted together, the little ones silent and hollow-eyed. Some stood up at the window, or sat on their beds, but some still had their heads under pillows, wanting to sleep. In that harsh and untimely light, it seemed that everything in that room sparkled and perhaps it did. For everything in that Convent shone, the floorboards, the iron beds, the wood of the cupboard doors, even the skirting boards and the ceilings themselves. We were clean girls.

When Miss O'Reilly came into the Sacred Heart Dormitory, she was not at all fussed. When she saw us at the window she said *Stop that now. Get down on your knees and pray. Say an Act of Contrition.* Miss O'Reilly then crossed over into St. Clare's. When she came back, she said *You best go into the other dormitory until the door opens and things get fixed up.*

So we ran then into St. Clare's, pulling the little ones with us. The sound we made woke any there who were not yet out of bed. Yet we noticed even then how the girls got up, called out to ask what the disturbance was but then oft did sink back into bed, their heads being sent funny by the smoke, though you could see but little of it yet.

Some of us then crowded to the window of that dormitory. From there we saw the Garda and a group of others who seemed to be arguing over a mop. Some had gone into the infirmary and were carrying out the babies. Then the bottom door burst open, we heard the sound of it go, and girls started pouring out, their white nightdresses swelling as they ran, their hair long and straggling. They coughed and cried, stumbled, their eyes streaming, their hands gripped at their throats.

They said later that it was James Meehan, the taxi driver, who went to fetch the town's fire brigade. They came then with a hand-cart and some lengths of hose which had been given to them by the waterworks caretaker. Yet at this time they still could not get into the courtyard as the gate was not unlocked, so they had to break the parlor window in the Convent and climb in that way. As they did so, others connected the hose to the standpipe in the street. But soon it was found that the hoses were leaking so badly that, when the water was switched on, it could but dribble out.

My sister, my sister. I must get her down. That shout came from Kathleen, looking for Bernadette. Other voices came up from down the wooden stairs. Then banging and coughing, a sound of choking. But no one came up the stairs, only a wall of smoke. *We need a key for the fire escape. Where is the key?* Everywhere those words were being shouted as people fumbled and searched and questioned.

We need a gas mask. We'll not get through without. These voices we heard from the other side, where the door was, the way out to the fire escape, and a frantic banging as though someone was try-ing to break through a door with a stick. We said to each other *We must pray. We must say an Act of Contrition.* But we could think of no prayers. *We need to have air. We need to have air.*

Then suddenly all was dark—not just our dormitory but the courtyard down below and all the Convent too. We heard then a door breaking somewhere close and a rush of air, which pushed the smoke further upon us. Then another door opening and another rush of smoke. We were blown back into the room by the force of it. Girls tumbled and scrambled, arms and legs locked. *Oh Lord have mercy.*

Later, John McNally and his friend from Fegans, John Paul Kennedy, told how they had got into the laundry and attacked the clothes dryer—for that was the source of the fire, they thought.

When the extinguishers were emptied the men came out gasping for air. One of the nuns begged McNally *Come now, like a good boy, go in and try again.* He asked for a wet cloth and Monaghan tied it around his nose and mouth. Armed again with fire extinguishers brought now from Sullivans store, he went back into the laundry, where the wooden walls were crackling with flames. But McNally soon fell senseless and Kennedy dragged him out.

Come out. Come out this way. The fire escape is open. It was Mary Caffey's voice. But we could not find the way for the smoke was curdling thick. Then Una Smith said to us *What if there are still girls in Sacred Heart? How do we know that all came out?* So some went with her to check. With the tarry smoke and the solid dark, we could see naught. But we ran our hands over the beds, working down all the six rows.

So it was there we found Dolly Duffy, who was deaf. So we pulled her out. Then we were crossing back to St. Clare's but we could not see the way. Then Una said *It is this way. This way out.* But we said *No, no.* For she was running into solid, gusting smoke. We called after her but it was too late and she had gone.

Dolly Duffy also said *It is better this way. Down the wooden* stairs. *Come, come. We must run or we shall burn.* But we said *No, no. There is no way through.* For we now felt sure that all below was alight. But Dolly Duffy picked up an apron and wrapped it over her head. Then she rushed through an Act of Contrition, and though we pleaded and pleaded with her to stay, yet she ran away from us down the wooden stairs.

Later, it was the testimony of John McNally that, when he recovered consciousness, he asked *The children are out, are they not? You have got the children out?* He was shouting it then at those who stood all about but no one wanted to reply. Until he shook Monaghan by the collar. *No, no,* Monaghan said. *The children are up there. Here, take the keys. See what you may do. Blessed Mary have mercy on us.*

So McNally went up the iron staircase, but the smoke was too dense. It was just as he turned to come down that he saw a girl burst out of the other door, and the soles of her feet were burning. She ran screaming across the courtyard, her arms waving, her eyes rolling. Screaming and screaming, her feet blazing fire.

Forty feet up to our dormitory. We knew we were trapped. And yet we said *Get the youngest children out. That's what we must do.* So we pushed them ahead of us toward the closed door. Then we pulled it open, but so strangling and grasping were the fumes which burst in that we could only push it shut again, our eyes stinging and swollen.

We tried then to get to the window, crawling over beds or under them, keeping low to the floor. Until we were looking down into the courtyard. Down below all was chaos and commotion, with many people running to and fro. We heard them shout that the ladders were coming. We opened the windows and bashed on the sections which did not give. Some of us sat on the beds and gathered the smaller children around us. We began to lead them in a decade of the rosary. *Hail Mary, full of Grace, the Lord is with thee. Pray for us sinners now and at the hour of our death.*

Those down below knew that ladders were then the only hope. So they ran through the unlit streets to the market yard, where they knew the town council kept ladders, and tried to raise the care-taker. He had no bell to his quarters but after much yelling and bashing, a window opened. The caretaker was angry to be woken, so he flung the keys down and they were lost in the dark.

Louis Blessing then had found a bicycle and pedaled furiously up to the Central Hotel, where he and several other bachelors in the town had rooms. He burst into the room of Mattie Hands, shouting and roaring. Grabbing hold of Mattie's shoulder, he pulled him from the bed. Mattie saying *Louis, what are you doing, you blessed fool?* For he thought this was some jest.

But soon enough he understood, for Mattie Hands worked with the Electricity Supply Board and had ladders in the back of his van. While Mattie dressed, Louis cycled back to the market yard, where he found people still stumbling around trying to find the key. But it was hopeless in the dark, so they smashed open a door, and finally the ladders were located and the men seized them and ran to Sullivans yard.

On the way, they met a squad of soldiers brought out of the town barracks and now quick-marching in formation up the main street. Coming into the courtyard the men with ladders and the soldiers found a crowd gripped by panic. Sparks, fireballs, and pieces of slate were raining down. Flames and smoke billowed out of every window.

The three top windows were crowded with a sea of childish faces. Screaming, praying, coughing, calling out *Get us out, we are smothering.* Then a girl jumped, rising up first, so it seemed, like some great white bird, then dipping down, falling faster and faster through the air. Even the blankets spread out below could not break her fall.

We were trying to say the rosary again. Dear Lord, we were try-ing. But the little children were all screaming. Once again some of us went to the door and tried to open it but we were suffo-cated by smoke. Mary Lowry, with her gold chain still around her neck, dropped to the floor. Kathleen crawled under the beds to the window.

When we were halfway through the third decade of the rosary, we could go no further. So we joined those others then at the window. I am sorry to say that we were treading on the younger children who were down below and had been knocked senseless by the fumes. We could not do otherwise, as we must have air.

We saw down below poor Maureen who had jumped and Miss Harrington standing near her. But Miss Harrington never went to pick her up. It was Dolly Duffy, though her feet were burnt black, she was the one as went to pick poor broken Maureen up.

Then we saw men putting up a ladder against the wall but it fell short of the window. *Look, look. See, it does not reach. How will we get down?* Back again then to the door to make one last attempt to get out that way but now flames poured in and we could not get the door shut again, such was the force of the blast.

Below we saw the men, and the soldiers also, struggling to extend the ladders. One went up partially but did not reach our window and came off the pulleys. The other had ropes tied around it. The men got them untangled but still it would not extend. So they lashed the two pieces together but, as it went up, it soon swayed and fell apart.

We heard then a rush and crash as the wooden stairs below us collapsed. The men were calling up then, telling us to jump. We said *No, no.* For it was too far down. But still another did jump. A man tried his best to hold her but she too crashed down, smashing her legs. To one side there was a lean-to shed and one girl tried also to jump onto there but she bounced off and hit the ground. After that none of us wanted to jump.

We saw men place a section of the council ladder on the roof of the lean-to shed. One man then came up and stood up close to the window. *Come on, girl. Come on. Jump. Jump.* So one did, then another and another. But when the fourth jumped, the man lost his balance. He and the child fell on the shed roof and the ladder crashed to the ground.

The window then was burning hot. The glass cracking, blowing out, melting down. The floor started to go. Wardrobes and beds disappeared into the furnace. One girl was lying unconscious on her bed, the clothes on her back on fire. Then she disappeared. The two Carrolls were calling for each other and the McKiernans, hollering and spluttering, arms outstretched. Then the floor where they were disappeared. Only those of us on the windowsill now were left.

Praise God a man came with a better ladder, got it extended in seconds. But though we were throat-raw and suffocated, we were afeard to go. He put out his hands and pulled some of us off, placing us on the ladder so that we might get down. But when it came to the turn of Bernadette, who was but seven years old, she tried to go back into the room, such was her terror.

Teresa it was went after her and tried to catch hold of her. But Bernadette still was wriggling away back into the flames, though only a tiny patch of floor was left. So Teresa then got hold of her by the hair, pulled her toward the window, dragged her hand toward the man on the ladder so that he then got her down. Though by then Bernadette's back and hair were all flaming alight.

At the inquiry, it was explained that it was Mattie Hands who finally got the ladders up. Also Dr. John Sullivan, brother of those Sullivans who owned the store. When he got abreast of the window, it was pumping tarry smoke. He had only time to look through for one moment. A heap of children was struggling about the level of the window. Cries were still coming there.

But he could not breathe and came a step or two down the ladder, putting his head under the windowsill where the air was clearer. As he hung there, he heard still the groans and cries from within. Again he pulled his head over the sill but he could see little and the smoke was making him weak. *I would have done anything on this earth to get in but I could not do it.*

As he came down the ladder, flames smashed out through the window above. A roar, a heaving, a smash of timbers. Another as the roof blew right into the night. He called and called then, shouting until his voice was hoarse, but no voice from the window echoed back to him. The time was 2:40 a.m.

The next day, the orphanage was nothing but a burnt-out frame, with damp wisps of smoke curling out through the debris. Only the many iron beds could you see still standing, stuck up in curved shapes, like the rib cages of so many skeleton beasts. And a pile of hoops lying in the yard. All the businesses in the town were closed and a sickening smell spread all about.

Matt McKiernan, the brother of Mary and Susan, who lived twelve miles from Cavan, was told of the fire that morning and pedaled furiously to Butlersbridge, where he went to the post office and called to the Garda, who told him then that his sisters were dead. Although it was Lent at that time, and many were on the tack, yet they did take to the liquor that day.

It was not until darkness was falling that all the bodies were brought out. Then the men shouldered the coffins and took them to the Convent chapel, laid them down near the altar. Over the days that followed, donations flooded in to the bishop and the abbess from all around.

Yet no one thought to get a call through to Matt McKiernan and his brother Hugh, who had lost their two sisters. So when the family came into the town to the funeral, the procession had already gone out to Cullies Graveyard. But Mrs. Carroll, who had lost two daughters, now she was at the funeral, gripping the hand of her surviving daughter, whom she had dressed in a scarlet coat. *I'll never step into a Catholic church again as long as I live.*

Later, we were asked—those of us who still had tongues to speak— about what happened. For an inquiry was established by Judge McCarthy, sent up from Dublin. You must say your age and your work within the orphanage. Cook, portress, maid, needleworker, or laundress. Even though you fainted you must go back the next day. Though at least for the inquiry no one had to walk out in two left boots, as was often the way. Just as we had learned the catechism, so the nuns taught us what we must say.

It was said *Of course, many of those orphan girls are simple.* But we were not simple, we were frightened. Nuns with the rosary on their wrists, the cane hanging next to it. Mother Carmel would strip your clothes from your body, beat you skinless. We were asked again and again *You knew the instructions in case of a fire, so why did you not follow those procedures?* Yet that question was never asked of the nuns.

It was a pitiful business when all was told. That was widely agreed. It was said in the town *The brigade were not fit to wash a bus.* It was also said privately *Course the building burnt so fast due to all that floor polish.* Yet the council were able to reassure the inquiry that faulty equipment had played no part. The ladders and hoses were all in excellent order.

Questions were asked about the fire escape. It was but seven foot away from the dormitory, so why were the children not able to get out? And the lights in the building, why were they switched off? Miss O'Reilly was questioned at some length. *Was there not a full fifteen minutes during which those children could have been brought down?*

Miss O'Reilly could not say, the questioning made her confused. She was also the sister of the mother abbess and so must be treated with respect. *Which nun was it who had tried to prevent the men from going up the fire escape? No, no. That was not what happened.* The question could not be pursued.

Nor was it asked why some of those girls were ever in the orphanage. For many were not orphans. Susan and Mary McKiernan had brothers and a father. But after their mother died they were sent to the orphanage. A neighbor offered to take them but that woman was a Protestant, so she was not allowed.

Yet, in truth, you could not blame the nuns. Sure they took those children in and the state gave them no money for it. They were good women who did their best. Yet still, in the town it was whispered *It was because those girls must not be seen in their nightdresses by the men of the town.*

We are the children of Cavan. Have you heard speak of us? From all around they saw us burn but none could help. Now and in the hour of our death. Sure it was discipline and fear which killed us, not the wire in the laundry clothes dryer. We are still waiting at the window. And Louis Blessing is still bashing at the fire escape with a mop. And Matt McKiernan is still riding his bike to Butlersbridge and to the phone call that will stake his heart.

John McNally, please, please will you bring the ladder up to us? Or must we run to heaven with our feet on fire? They put on our gravestone *Children pray for us*. Thirty-five girls but only eight coffins. It was only Mary Lowry they could identify—her with the gold cross she had from the bishop. All of the nuns safe enough, so God be praised. Many years have passed now. It was long ago. But we are still waiting. Please, will you not put up the ladders and bring us down?

This story is based on documents and personal testimony relating to the fire at St. Joseph's orphanage in Cavan on the night of February 23, 1943.

David Rabe

Things We Worried About When I Was Ten

HIGH ON THE LIST was trying not to have the older boys decide to de-pants you and then run your pants up the flagpole, leaving you in your underwear, and maybe bloodied if you'd struggled—not that it helped, because they were bigger and stronger—and your pants flapping way up against the sky over the schoolyard. They mostly did this to Freddy Bird—nobody knew why, but it happened a lot. It was best to get away from him when they started to get into that mood—their let's–de-pants–somebody mood. *Oh, there's Freddy Bird.* You could see them thinking it. You had to slip sideways, not in an obvious way but as if you were drifting for no real reason, or maybe the wind was shoving you and you weren't really paying attention, and, most important, you did not want to meet eyes with them, not one of them. Because they could change their mind in a flash if they noticed you, as they would if you met their eyes, and then they'd think, *Oh, look, there's Danny Matz, let's de-pants* him, and before you knew it you'd be trying to get your pants down from high up on the flagpole while everybody laughed, especially Freddy Bird.

Meeting eyes was, generally speaking, worrisome. It could lead anywhere. I'd been on the Kidnickers' porch with the big boys when they were tormenting Devin Sleverding—pushing him and, you know, spitting on him and not letting him off the porch when he tried to go. Fencing him in. And I felt kind of sorry for Devin, but I didn't let it show, and I made sure that I stayed on the big boys' side of the invisible line that separated them from Devin, who was crying and snorting and looking like a trapped pig, which he was, in a sense, and waving his hands around in that girly way he had, his wrists all fluttery and floppy, which he should have just stopped doing, because that was how he'd got into trouble with the big boys to begin with. (That was another thing we worried about, a sort of worry inside a worry: along with not wanting to meet anybody's eyes, we had to make sure that we never started waving our hands around like girls, the way Devin Sleverding did.)

So the older boys had formed a circle around him, and if he tried to break out, they'd push him back into the middle of the ring, and if he just stood there, hoping they'd get tired or bored and go play baseball or something, well, then one of them would jump at him and shove him so hard that he staggered over into the boys on the other side of the circle, who would shove him back in the direction he'd come from. That was what was happening when our eyes met. I was trying to be part of the circle and to look like I belonged with the big boys and thought he deserved it, waving his hands like a girl. Just stop it, I thought. His snot-covered, puffy red face looked shocked and terribly disappointed, as if seeing me act that way was the last straw, as if he'd expected something more from me. And I don't know where Devin got the stick—this hunk of wood covered in slivers that had probably been left on the Kidnickers' porch after somebody built something—but he had it and he hit me over the head. I saw stars, staticky, racing stars no bigger than mouse turds. Blood squirted out of my head, and I fell to my knees, and, while everybody was distracted, Devin made his break. I was crying and crawling, and one of the big boys said, "You better go home." "OK," I said, and left a blood trail spattering the sidewalk where I walked and alongside the apartment building where I lived and on just about every one of the steps I climbed to our door, which entered into the kitchen, where my mom, when she saw me, screamed. I had to have stitches.

Another thing I worried about was how to make sure that I never had to box Sharon Weber again. It was my dad's idea. We'd gone down to Red and Ginger Weber's apartment, which was on the ground floor of our two-story, four-apartment building. I was supposed to box Ron Weber, who was a year older than me, but he wasn't home, so Red offered his daughter, Sharon, as a substitute, and my dad said sure. Nobody checked with me, and I didn't know what to say anyway—so there I was, facing off against Sharon, who was a year younger than me, but about as tall. She hit me square in the nose, a surprise blow, and I just stood there.

"C'mon, Dan," my dad said. "Show her what you got." I wanted to. But I was frozen. I didn't know what I could do—where to hit her. She was a girl. I couldn't hit her in the face, because she was pretty and, being a girl, needed to be pretty, and I couldn't hit her in the stomach, because that was where her baby machinery was, and I didn't want to damage that; I couldn't hit her above her stomach, either, because her chest wasn't a boy's chest—she had breasts, and they were important, too, to babies and in other ways that I didn't understand but had heard about. So I stood there, getting pounded, ducking as best I could, but not too much, because I didn't want to appear cowardly, afraid of a girl, and covering up, not too effectively, for the same reason, while Sharon whaled away on me.

"Dan, c'mon, now," my dad said. "What are you doing? Give her a good one."

I couldn't see my dad, because my eyes were all watery and blurry—not with tears, just water.

I guess it had dawned on Sharon that nothing was coming

back at her, so she was windmilling me and side-arming, prancing around and really winding up. My dad said, "Goddammit, Dan! Give her a smack, for God's sake." Red was gloating and chattering to Sharon, as if she needed coaching to finish me off. "Use your left. Set him up." My dad was red-faced, his mouth and eyes squeezed into this painful grimace, the way they'd been when I spilled boiling soup in his lap. He could barely look at me, like it really hurt to look at me.

He grabbed me then, jerked me out the door. Once we were outside, he left me standing at the bottom of the stairs while he stomped up to our apartment. I ran after him and got to our part of the long second-floor porch we shared with the Stoner family just in time to see him bang the door shut. I heard him inside saying, "Goddammit to hell. What is wrong with that kid?"

"What happened?" my mom asked.

"I'm sick of it, you know."

"Sick of what?"

"What do you think?"

"I don't know."

"Never mind," he said. "Goddammit to hell."

"Sick of what? At least tell me that."

"Why bother?"

"Because I'm asking. That ought to be enough."

"Him and you, OK?"

"Me?" she said. "Me?"

I heard another door slam. When I opened the apartment door to peek in, I saw that the door to the bathroom, which was alongside the kitchen, was closed.

My mother was wearing a housedress that I'd seen a million times. It buttoned down the front and never had the bottom button buttoned. She had an apron on and a pot holder around the handle of a pot in her hand. Everything smelled of fish. She looked at me standing in the doorway with the Webers' boxing gloves on. "What happened?" she asked.

"I was supposed to box Ron Weber, because Dad thought I could beat him, even though he's older, but he wasn't home, so Sharon—"

"Wait, wait. Stop, stop. What more do I have to put up with?" She grabbed my arm and pulled me into the kitchen.

"What happened? What happened? What happened?" she said too many times. "Carl," she shouted at the bathroom door. "What happened?"

"I'm on the crapper," he said.

"Oh, my God." She walked like a sad, dizzy person to the table, where she sat down real slow, the way a person does when sliding into freezing or scalding-hot water. She put her chin in her hands, but her head was too heavy and it sank to the tabletop, where she closed her eyes. I stood for a moment, looking down at my hands in the boxing gloves, wondering how I was going to get out of them. What if I had to pee? How could I get my zipper down and my weenie out? I went into the living room, which was only a few steps away, because the apartment was really small. I sat on the couch. I wished I could go up into the attic. It wasn't very big and had a low, slanted roof, but it felt far away from everything, with all these random objects lying there, as if history had left them behind. One of them was Dobbins, my rocking horse, who had big white scary eyes full of warnings and mysteries to solve, if he could ever get through to me. But the only way up to the attic was through the bathroom, which was off limits at the moment because my dad was in there on the crapper. I worked on the laces of the gloves with my teeth, trying to tug them loose enough that I could clamp the gloves between my knees and pull my hands out, and I made some progress, but not enough. So I gave up. I sat for a while and then I lay down on the couch.

Another thing we worried about was that, if it rained and it was night—not late, because then we had to be in bed, but dark already, and wet, the way a good heavy rain left things—and our parents wouldn't let us go out, or wouldn't let us have a flashlight because we'd run the batteries down, then other kids would get all the night crawlers that came up and slithered in the wet grass. We worried that they would all be snatched up by the kids whose parents weren't home, or who had their own flashlights. It was strange to me that night crawlers came up at all, because when they were under the dirt they were hidden and safe. Maybe, though, if they stayed down there after a heavy rain they would drown. I didn't know and couldn't ask them. The main thing was that they weren't regular worms but night crawlers, big and fat, with shiny, see-through skin, and we could catch them and put them in a can with coffee grounds and then use them as bait or sell them to men who were going fishing but hadn't had time to go out and catch some themselves.

When our parents did let us go, we raced out our doors and, in my case, down the stairs, then walked around sneakily, searching the grass with a flashlight, the beam moving slowly, like the searchlight in a prison movie when prisoners are trying to escape. When the light struck a night crawler, we had to be quick, because they were very fast and they tried to squirm back into the holes they'd come out of, or were partway out of, and we had to pinch them against the ground with our fingers and then pull them out slowly, being careful not to break them in half. Because they somehow resisted—they hung on to their holes without any hands. We could feel the fear in them as they tried to fight back, so tiny compared with us, though we were only kids, and, when we got them out, the way they twisted and writhed about seemed like silent screaming. It was odd, though, how much they loved the dirt. We all knew that there were awful things down there. Germs. Maggots. You could even suffocate if dirt fell on you in a mudslide. We almost felt as if we were saving the night crawlers, dragging them out and feeding them to fish. It was impossible to figure it all out.

. . .

Another thing we worried about was having to move. What if we had to move? It happened every now and then to people we knew. Their families moved and they had to go with them. A big truck showed up, and men in uniforms took all the things out of the house and put them into the truck. It had happened to the Ballingers, for example. "We're moving," Ronnie said. "Gotta move," his younger brother, Max, said. And, the next thing we knew, the trucks were there and the men in and out and then the Ballingers were gone. Every one of them. The house was empty. We could sneak into their yard and peek in the windows and see the big, scary emptiness, so empty it hurt. And then other people, complete strangers, showed up and went in and started living there, and it was as if the Ballingers had never been there.

Or Jesus. We all worried about Jesus. I know I did. What did he think of me? Did he, in fact, think of me? At Mass, I took the Host into my mouth, and the priest said that it was Jesus, and the nuns also said that it was Jesus, in this little slip of bread, this wafer that melted on my tongue. You weren't supposed to chew it or swallow it whole, so you waited for it to melt and spread out holiness. Hands folded, head bowed, eyes closed until you had to see where you were going to get back to your pew, and there was Mary Catherine Michener entering her pew right in front of you, her eyes downcast, a handkerchief on top of her head because she'd forgotten her hat, and her breasts, which had come out of nowhere, it seemed, and stuck out as if they were taking her somewhere, were big, as if to balance the curve of her rear end, which was sticking out in the opposite direction. Did Jesus know? He had to, didn't he, melting as he was in my mouth, trying to fill me with piety and goodness while I had this weird feeling about Mary Catherine Michener, who was only a year or two older than me and whom I'd known when she didn't have pointy breasts and a rounded butt, but now she did, and, seeing them, I thought about them, and the next thought was of confession. Or of being an occasion of sin. I did not want to be an occasion of sin for the girls in my class, who could go to hell if they saw me with my shirt off, according to Sister Mary Irma. And so confession again. Father Paul listening on the other side of the wicker window, or Father Thomas, sighing and sad and bored.

Being made an "example of" by Sister Mary Luke, the principal, was another nerve-racking thing that could happen. You could be an example of almost anything, but, whatever it was, you would be a kind of stand-in for everybody who'd committed some serious offense, and so the punishment would be bad enough to make everybody stop doing it, whatever it was.

Or getting sat on by Sister Conrad. That shouldn't have been a worry, but it was. And, though it may sound outlandish, we'd all seen it happen to Jackie Rand. But, then, almost everything happened to Jackie Rand. Which might have offered a degree of insurance against its ever happening to us, since so much that happened to Jackie didn't happen to anyone else, and yet the fact that it had happened to anyone, even Jackie, and we'd all seen it, was worrisome. Sister Conrad, for no reason we could understand, had been facing the big pull-down map and trying to drill into our heads the geographic placement of France, Germany, and the British Isles. This gave Jackie the chance he needed to poke Basil Mellencamp in the back with his pencil, making him squirm and whisper, "Stop it, Jackie." But Jackie didn't stop, and he was having so much fun that he didn't notice Sister Conrad turning to look at him.

"Jackie!" she barked. Startled and maybe even scared, he rocked back in his desk as far as he could to get away from Basil, and aimed his most innocent expression at Sister Conrad. "Stand up," she told him, "and tell us what you think you are doing."

He looked us over, as if wondering if she'd represented our

interest correctly, then he turned his attention to his desk, lifting the lid to peek inside.

"Did you hear me? I told you to stand up, Jackie Rand."

He nodded to acknowledge that he'd heard her, and, shrugging in his special way, which we all knew represented his particular form of stubborn confusion, he scratched his head.

Sister Conrad shot toward him. She was round and short, not unlike Jackie, though he was less round and at least a foot shorter. All of us pivoted to watch, ducking if we were too close to the black-and-white storm that Sister Conrad had become, rosary beads rattling, silver cross flashing and clanking. She grabbed Jackie by the arm and he yelped, pulling free. She snatched at his ear, but he sprang into the aisle on the opposite side of his desk, knocking into Judy Carberger, who cowered one row over. Sister Conrad lunged, and Basil, who was between them, hunched like a soldier fearing death in a movie where bombs fell everywhere. "You're going to the principal's office!" she shrieked.

We all knew what that meant—it was one step worse than being made an example of. Stinging rulers waited to smack upturned palms, or, if we failed to hold steady and flipped our palms over in search of relief, the punishment found our knuckles with a different, even worse kind of pain.

Sister Conrad and Jackie both bolted for the door. Somehow— though we all marveled at the impossibility of it—Sister Conrad got there first. Jackie had been slowed by the terrible burden of defying authority, which could make anyone sluggish.

"I want to go home," he said. "I want to go home."

The irony of this wish, given what we knew of Jackie's home, shocked us as much as everything else that was going on.

Jackie leaned toward the door as if the moment were normal and he hoped for permission but needed to go. Sister Conrad stayed put, blocking the way. He reached around her for the door-knob and she shoved him. I may have been the only person to see a weird hopelessness fill his eyes at that point. I was his friend, perhaps his only friend, so it was fitting that I saw it. And then he lunged at her and grabbed her. We gasped to see them going sideways and smashing against the blackboard. Erasers, chalk sticks, and chalk dust exploded. Almost every boy in the room had battled Jackie at one point or another, so we knew what Sister Conrad was up against. We gaped, watching her hug him crazily. Her glasses flew off. Jackie shouted about going home as he fell over backward. She came with him, crashing down on top of him. They wrestled, and she squirmed into a sitting position right on his stomach, where she bounced several times. The white cardboard thing around her head had sprung loose, the edge sticking out, the whole black hood so crooked that it half covered her face.

Jackie screamed and wailed under her, as she bounced and shouted for help and Basil ran to get Sister Mary Luke.

Getting into a fight with Jackie Rand was another thing we worried about. Though it was less of a worry for me than for most. Jackie and I lived catercornered from each other across Jefferson Avenue, which was a narrow street, not fancy like a real avenue. Jackie lived in a house, while I was in an apartment. He was rough and angry and mean, it was true—a bully. But not to me. I knew how to handle him. I would talk soothingly to him, as if he were a stray dog. I could even pull him off his victims. His body had a sweaty, gooey sensation of unhappy fat. Under him, a boy would beg for mercy, but Jackie, alone in his rage, would be far from the regular world. When I pulled him off, he would continue to flail, at war with ghosts, until, through his hate-filled little eyes, something soft peered out, and, if it was me that he saw, he might sputter some burning explanation and then run home.

As a group, we condemned him, called him names: "Bully! Pig eyes! Fatso!" The beaten boy would screech, "Pick on somebody your own size, you fat slob!" Others would add, "Lard ass! Fatty-Fatty Two-by-Four!"

The fact that Jackie's mother had died when he was four explained his pouty lips and the hurt in his eyes, I thought. Jackie's father seemed to view him as a kind of commodity he'd purchased one night while drunk. The man would whack him at the drop of a hat. This was even before Jackie's father had failed at business and had to sell the corner grocery store, and before he remarried, hoping for happiness but, according to everybody, making everything worse. Jackie's stepmom, May, came with her own set of jabs and prods that Jackie had to learn to dodge, along with his father's anger.

All of us were slapped around. Our dads were laborers who worked with their hands. Some built machines; others tore machines apart. Some dug up the earth; others repaired automobiles or hammered houses into shape. Many slaughtered cows and pigs at the meatpacking company. Living as they did, they relied on their hands, and they used them. Our overworked mothers were also sharp tempered and as quick with a slap as they were with their fits of coddling. And, after our parents and the nuns were done, we spent a lot of time beating one another up.

Still, Jackie's dad was uncommon. He seemed to mistake Jackie for someone he had a grudge against in a bar. But then, as our parents told us, Jackie was "hard to handle." He would "try the patience of a saint," and his dad was "quick-triggered" and hardly happy in his second marriage.

As Jackie and I walked around the block, or sat in a foxhole we'd dug on the hill and covered with sumac, these were among the mysteries that we tried to solve.

"Too bad your dad lost his store," I told him.

"He loved my real mom," Jackie said, looking up at the light falling through the leaves.

"May is nice."

"I know she is. She's real nice."

"He loves you, Jackie."

"Sure."

"He just doesn't know how to show it. You gotta try not to make him mad."

"I make everybody mad."

"But he's quick tempered."

"I'd try the patience of a saint."

More than once, I went home from time spent with Jackie to stare in wonder and gratitude at my living mother and my dad, half asleep in his big chair, listening to a baseball game.

Sometimes in church I would pray for Jackie, so that he could have as good a life as I did.

In daylight, we did our best, but then there was the time spent in bed at night. It was there that I began to suspect that, while there was much that I knew I worried about, there was more that I worried about without actually knowing what it was that worried me—or even that I was worrying—as I slept. The things with Mr. Stink and Georgie Baxter weren't exactly in this category, but they were close.

Mr. Stink was a kind of hobo, who built a shack on the hill behind our apartment building, and he had that name because he stank. We kids were told to stay away from him and we did. He interested me, though, and I looked at him when I could, and sometimes I saw him looking at us. We all saw him walking on the gravel road between the hill and our houses, lugging bags of junk, on the way to his shack.

Then one night I was in our apartment, doing my homework, while Dad was listening to baseball, and my mom was rocking my baby sister in her lap and trying to talk my dad into listening to something else, when this clanking started. It went *clank-clank-clank* and stopped. Then *clank-clank-clank* again. "What the hell now?" my dad griped. It went on and on, and Dad couldn't figure out what it was, and Mom couldn't, either. It started at about nine and went on till ten or later, and Dad was on his way to complain to the landlord, whose house was next door, when he decided instead to talk to Agnes Rath, who lived in the apartment under us. It turned out that Agnes was scared sick. When Dad knocked, she turned on her porch light and peeked out between her curtains, and, seeing that it was him, she opened her door and told him that Mr. Stink had been peeping in her window. She'd seen him and, not knowing what to do, had turned off all her lights and crawled into the kitchen. Lying on the floor, she'd banged on the pipes under her sink as a signal. So that was the clanking. Agnes Rath's signal. Well, a few nights later, a group of men ran through our yard and my dad ran with them, and then, not too long after that, fire leaped up on the hill around the spot where Mr. Stink had his shack, and nobody ever saw him again.

Then Georgie Baxter got married, and moved into an apartment on the ground floor of the building next door to Jackie. Georgie and his new wife, who everybody said was "a real looker," couldn't afford a long honeymoon. They got married on a Saturday, but, because Georgie had to work on Monday, they came back to their apartment Sunday night, and what awaited them was a shivaree. People came from all directions, men, women, and kids, everybody carrying metal buckets or pots and beating on them with spoons to make a huge loud racket. Jackie and I were doing it like everybody else, beating away on pots with big spoons, though we had no idea why, all of us together creating this clamor as we closed in on the apartment building with Georgie and his new bride inside. I stood with my pot and my spoon, beating away, whooping and feeling scared by the crazy noise we were making and the wild look in all the grown-ups' eyes, as if they were stealing or breaking something. I wished more than anything that I knew why we were doing what we were doing.

About a week later, Jackie came and told me to hurry. At his house, he took me upstairs. It was Saturday, and he put his finger to his lips as he pulled me to the window and we looked down at Georgie and his new wife, in their bed without any clothes on, rolling and wrestling, and she looked like pudding or butter. After a while, Jackie fell on the floor kind of moaning, like he had the time we went to the Orpheum Theatre to see the movie *Dracula*. Perched way up high in the third balcony, we'd watched the ghost ship land in the mists with everyone dead, and, when Dracula swirled his cape and lay back in his coffin, Jackie got so scared he hid on the floor. I looked down at him now, and then back at the window, and the pudding woman saw me. She glanced up, and, though I ducked as fast as I could, she caught me looking in her window. If she told, what would happen? Would I get run out of town like Mr. Stink? If she told Georgie, or started banging on water pipes to alert people, would they come swarming and pounding on pots to surround me? My fate was in the hands of Georgie Baxter's wife. What could be worse? Because she knew that I knew that under her clothes she was all pudding and bubbles. It was a horrible worry, but I didn't tell anyone, not even Jackie. That worry was mine alone, and it was maybe the worst worry, the worry to end all worries.

But then Jackie wandered into his kitchen one Saturday to find his stepmother, May, stuffing hunks of beef into the meat grinder. Her head swayed to music from the radio on the shelf above her, and her eyes were busy with something distant. Jackie had gone into the kitchen because he was thirsty, so he stood on a chair to get a glass from the cupboard above the sink. He filled the glass to the brim from the faucet and drank every drop. The chair made a little squeal as he slid it back under the kitchen table. That was when Stepmom May screamed. Seeing the black hole of her mouth strung with saliva, Jackie was certain he had committed some unspeakable crime. She raised a bloody mess toward him, her eyes icy and dead, and he knew that she was about to hurl a half-ground hunk of beef at him. When instead she attacked the radio, yanking out the plug and circling her arm with the cord, he thought that she had gone insane. It was only when she wailed "My thumb!" that he understood. A hand crank powered the meat grinder, moving a gear that worked the teeth inside its cast-iron belly. With her right hand turning the crank, she'd used her left to stuff the meat into the mouthlike opening on top of the apparatus. Her thumb had gone in too deep, and she'd failed to notice, or noticed only when she'd ground her thumb up with the beef. She ran out the door, the radio tied to her arm, rattling along behind her, and left him standing alone, blood dotting the worn-out ducks in the uneven linoleum, and the trickle of hope that had survived the loss of his real mom draining away.

When Jackie told me what had happened, as he did within minutes, it was as if I'd been there to see it, and I felt his deep, deep worry. It played on us like the spooky music in *Dracula*. It was strange and haunting and beyond anything we could explain, with our poor grasp of nouns and verbs. And yet we knew that Jackie needed to try. A downstairs door banged, and Jackie ran from where we stood on my porch, around the corner of the bannister, taking the steps two at a time until he landed in the yard.

Finding Agnes Rath, who nervously peered over her grocery bag at Jackie, he made his report: "STEPMOM MAY CUT HER THUMB OFF IN THE MEAT GRINDER!"

Suppertime was near, so people were coming and going. Suddenly, he heard Red Weber approaching, followed by his wife. Racing up to one and then the other, Jackie backtracked in the direction of their door so he could announce his dreadful news before they trampled him in their haste to get home: "STEPMOM MAY CUT HER THUMB OFF IN THE MEAT GRINDER!"

Henry Stoner, who lived beside us on the second floor, came around the corner, lunch bucket under his arm, and Jackie retreated up the stairs, never missing a step; he took corners, eluded rails. "STUCK IT IN AND TURNED THE CRANK!" he shrieked. "STUCK IT IN AND TURNED THE CRANK!" Mrs. Stoner was home already, her shift at the plant having ended earlier than her husband's. She came out onto the porch and, in a gush of neighborly concern, prodded Jackie for more details.

"How is she?" Mrs. Stoner asked.

"JUST GROUND IT UP!"

"Did you see it?"

But he could not budge from his point. The thing against which he had crashed clutched at him, like the tentacles of that monster squid we had all seen in *Wake of the Red Witch*. Now Jackie was being dragged down through inky confusion to some deep, lightless doom. If he was ever to discover the cause of the terror endangering him and me and everyone he knew, as he believed, and I did, too, the search for an answer had to begin with what he'd seen. "JUST STUCK IT IN! AND TURNED THE CRANK, MRS. STONER! JUST GROUND IT UP!"

"Can we do something for you, Jackie?"

Though he had time to look at her, he had time for nothing more. Mr. Hogan, who lived on the gravel road behind our house and who used our backyard as a shortcut home every night, was crossing. Jackie hurtled down the stairs and jumped in front of Mr. Hogan, who was fleshy and soft and smelled of furniture polish. Startled, Mr. Hogan took a step back.

Before him stood a deranged-looking Jackie Rand. "JUST STUCK IT IN AND GROUND IT UP!" he yelled.

"What?"

"STEPMOM MAY CUT HER THUMB OFF IN THE MEAT GRINDER! STEPMOM MAY CUT HER THUMB OFF IN THE MEAT GRINDER!"

"What?"

"BLOOD!" he shrieked. "STUCK IT IN AND GROUND IT OFF! BLOOD! BLOOD!"

Over the next hour, the four families in our building worked their way toward supper. Last-minute shopping was needed, and errands were run. Butter was borrowed from the second floor by the first floor, an onion traded for a potato. The odor of Spam mixed with beef, sauerkraut, wieners, and hash, while boiling potatoes sent out their steamy scent to mingle with that of corn and string beans, peas, coffee, baked potatoes, and pie. All to the accompaniment of Jackie's "BLOOD!" and "STEPMOM MAY!"

My mother, looking down over the bannister, said to my dad, "He looks so sad."

"Not to me."

"You don't think he looks sad?"

"Looks crazy, if you ask me. Nuttier than a pet coon, not that he doesn't always."

"Don't say that. Why would you say such a thing?"

My father went inside, leaving my mother alone. I felt invisible, perfectly forgotten, standing in the corner of the porch watching my mother witness Jackie's second encounter with Red Weber, who had returned from somewhere. "STEPMOM MAY! STUCK IT IN, MR. WEBER! CUT IT OFF! BLOOD! TURNED THE CRANK! STUCK IT IN!"

Annoyed now, he brushed Jackie aside and snapped, "You told me! Now go home. Go home!"

Without a second's hesitation, my mother called down to invite Jackie up for dinner.

"STEPMOM MAY," he said as he came in our door. "TURNED THE CRANK!" he addressed my dad. "BLOOD!" he delivered as he took a seat. And, glowering at my baby sister in her high chair sucking milk from a bottle, he said, "STEPMOM MAY CUT HER THUMB OFF IN THE MEAT GRINDER!"

"Am I supposed to have my goddamn supper with this fool and his tune?" my dad asked.

"Can't we talk about something else?" my mother said to Jackie.

Outside, a door slammed. Jackie could not rest. He bobbed in what might have been a bow. "Thanks for inviting me to dinner.

It was real good." He was gone, not having taken a bite, the screen door croaking on its hinges.

"Goddammit to hell," my dad said. "What does a person have to do to have his supper in peace around this nut factory!"

From afar, there was the rise and fall of Jackie's voice as he chased whomever he found: "STEPMOM MAY! CUT HER THUMB OFF! STUCK IT IN AND TURNED THE CRANK!"

It was then that I understood. If Jackie understood, then or ever, I can't say. But the answer seemed simple and obvious once I saw it. If Stepmom May could do that to herself, what might she do to him? If she could lose track of the whereabouts of her own thumb, what chance did he have? What was he, after all, but a little boy, a small, mobile piece of meat? Certainly her connection to him was weaker than her connection to her own hand. Would he find himself tomorrow mistaken in her absentmindedness for a chicken, unclothed and basted in the oven? Must he be alert every second for her next blunder? Would he end up jammed into the Mixmaster, among the raisins and nuts?

What might any of our mothers do to any of us, we had to ask, given the strangeness of their love and their stranger neglect, those moments of distraction when they lost track of everything, even themselves, as they stared into worries that were all their own and bigger than anything we could hope to fathom?

I'm not sure how the word spread, but it did. We all heard it and knew to gather in the Haggertys' empty lot. It was a narrow strip that ran down from the gravel road that separated the hill from the houses where we lived. Nobody knew what the Haggertys planned to do with the lot. It wasn't wild, but it wasn't neat and cared for, either, and we all went there as soon as we could get out after supper. We came from different directions and then we were there, nodding and knowing, but without knowing what we knew. For a while, we talked about Korea and the Chinese horde and the dangers that had our fathers leaning in close to their radios and cursing. We got restless and somebody wanted to play pump-pump-pullaway, but other people scoffed. We tried red rover, and then statue, where you got whirled around by somebody, and, when the boy who'd spun you yelled "Freeze!" as you stumbled around, you had to stop and stay that way without moving an inch, and then think of some kind of meaning for how you'd ended up. We did that for a bit, but we all knew where we were headed. Finally, somebody—it might have been me—said, "Let's play the blackout game."

The light had dimmed and the moon was now high, high enough that it was almost above us in the sky, with lots of stars, so we were ghostly and perfect. Our mood had that something in it that made everyone feel as though this was what we had all been waiting for.

To play the blackout game, you'd stand with someone behind you, his arms around your chest, and you'd take deep breaths over and over, and the other boy would squeeze your chest until you passed out in a downpour of spangling lights. The person behind you would then lay you down gently on your back in the grass, where you wandered around without yourself, until you woke up from a sleep whose content you'd never know. We took turns. Jerry went, then Tommy and Butch. I went, and then Jackie was there, and he wanted to go. Freddy Bird got behind Jackie, and Jackie huffed and huffed and sailed away, blacking out. Freddy Bird let go and stepped clear. Jackie toppled over backward. His butt landed and then his body slammed back, like a reverse jackknife, and, finally, his head hit with a loud crack. A hurt look came over him, and a big sigh came out of his mouth: "Oh-h-h-h." More of a gasp, really, and he lay very still. Motionless. Pale, I thought. We all stared. He didn't move. Freddy Bird was no longer pleased with how clever he was.

We waited for Jackie to wake up and he didn't. It seemed longer than usual.

"We didn't kill him, did we?"

"You don't die from that."

"It's because he's out twice. Once from the breathing stuff and once from banging his head."

We waited. Jackie didn't move. I went closer.

Staring down, I had the crazy thought that Jackie Rand was like Jesus. Not that he was Jesus but that he was kind of our Jesus, getting the worst of everything for everybody, getting the worst that anybody could dish out, so that we could feel OK about our lives. No matter how bad or unfair we might feel things were, they were worse for Jackie.

"Should we maybe tell somebody?"

A tiny tear appeared in the corner of each of Jackie's eyes. He was the saddest person on earth, lying there, I thought. The tears dribbled down his cheeks, and then his eyes blinked and opened and he saw where he was. His big pouty lips quivered. He reached to rub the back of his head, and he started to cry really hard, and we knew that he was alive.

Karina Sainz Borgo,
translated by Elizabeth Bryer

Scissors

THEY REACHED CÚCUTA AT MIDDAY. All of them except the
grandmother were hungry. She lay back in the seat, her eyes
fixed on the bus ceiling. When they started making these trips,
old Herminia stopped eating, fearful that her daughter and granddaughter might abandon her on a back road near the border. She'd
turned hunger into a form of self-protection.

At first they'd made the crossing only once a month. Now they
did so every week. They left before first light. They came back
after nightfall, with three small tomatoes sometimes or a packet of
spaghetti that lasted, at most, two days. They boiled the spaghetti
in salted water and ate it for breakfast, lunch and dinner. No matter what goods they managed to get hold of, every trip made her
ache to the bone.

"We told you to stay home, Mamá, but you never listen."

"Uhum," wheezed the old lady, chewing over her fears like she
would some *chimó* tobacco. "You're as stubborn as a mule," Koralia added as she rummaged around in her bag.

She gave in to her daughter's nagging and handed Milagros an
old sweet and a packet of tissues, nothing else. They had eaten the
last mandarins before reaching Capacho Viejo.

"Well, what do you want me to do? Stay home alone?" Herminia muttered. "You'll desert me when I least expect it, never to return."

"Oh, don't talk nonsense, Mamá."

"How could we desert you, Abuela?" piped up Milagros, Herminia's granddaughter, cradling a baby whose explosive screams kept on until the whole family felt shell-shocked.

Herminia endured these expeditions with a deep-seated stoicism. She was a Táchira woman to the marrow. She had the reserved air of the Andean *páramo*, bowed legs and hair pulled into a modest bun. Anyone who had seen her a few years ago wouldn't recognize her now. She'd lost so much weight that her face had collapsed like a popped balloon, the damaged version of the one she'd presented to the world back when she held the reins of her life and the lives of everyone around her.

Now she looked nothing like the rotund woman whom the neighborhood children had called *Arepa Face*. Herminia used to resemble the little corn cakes she had baked and sold from her corner store, which a group of soldiers set alight during a student roundup. Nobody footed the bill for the damages. Ever since, the years had come down on her like a mudslide, until they had buried her entirely.

Herminia was not a sweet woman, and if she had been once, she no longer remembered such a thing. She seldom laughed, and her poplin dresses lent her a rocky, severe look, as if she had donned a curtain rather than clothing. Her husband, Antonio, had died ten years before. One day in the early hours of the morning, his heavily loaded truck lost control around a curve on the Trans-Andean Highway. It plowed off a cliff and into the rocks below. She never dressed in black, though anyone would say she was born with the face of a widow. The old woman's life had not been easy, but she wasn't one to complain. Her mother and grandmother never had, so why should she be the first to do so?

"Abuela, take the baby while Mamá and I go take care of

something," her granddaughter said, brazen as ever. "Don't move from this spot, you hear?"

"Yes, *m'hija*, I heard."

Herminia wheezed and took the child into her arms. She didn't much care for minding her but had learned to see the act as life insurance: having the baby meant that she herself was safe. She was convinced that this was the only reason they would come back for her. She had heard the stories. Before leaving the country for good, families abandoned the elderly. They left them to their luck on the steps of a hospital with nothing but a blanket and a bottle of water. It was the way the elderly died on that side of the border: soaked in fear and asking when their children would come get them.

The old lady looked at the sky, imploring a bolt of lightning to make Santander Park vanish. At that time of day it was full of pigeons and "draggers"—the name everyone on the border gave to the men and women who engaged in barter trade, dragging potential clients by the sleeve. Like the pigeons, the draggers had an unsightly, flea-ridden air. And just as the pigeons pounced on cigarette butts—there was no longer any bread for them to feed on—the draggers fought over the desperate individuals prepared to exchange their back teeth for a few pesos.

Koralia and Milagros disappeared down the street. It took them ten minutes to get to Los Guerreros hair salon. It was a filthy place, bedecked with clippings from eighties fashion mags: teased hairstyles, purple eyelids, vests with bacteria patterns, out-of-date outfits. People were lining up out the door. Not to get their hair styled, but to sell it.

"We'll give you sixty thousand pesos for yours, a little less for your mother's," a woman said when, finally, it was their turn.

"But my hair's long too," said Koralia.

"It's not as shiny, and we only use hair of the finest quality for our wigs."

Koralia lowered her gaze while the hairdresser held a strand between thumb and forefinger.

"It's dry and vitamin deficient. The ends are split," said the woman.

"Well, that's it," said Koralia, "do you want it or not?"

"If we take the full length, it will be twenty thousand pesos."

"Only twenty thousand?"

"And I'm giving you a good price."

"Mamá, quit haggling," Milagros interrupted. "If we add it to my sixty thousand pesos we'll have eighty. That's not bad."

"You're right, *hija*, it's not bad; it's terrible."

"Listen, lady, you can go away and think about it if you want. I can't stand around all day waiting for you to make up your mind."

"Well, I want to, even if she doesn't," said Milagros, not wanting their trip to go to waste.

"Put this on." The woman handed her a black salon cape. "And take a seat over there. I'll go get a hairdresser."

"Are you sure you want your hair cut off, *hija*?" Koralia murmured.

"It's just hair, Mamá. And attached to my head it's not going to buy anything at the market."

Koralia looked at her daughter as if she were waiting for her at the other end of a long tunnel. Then she pulled her hair up in a ponytail and went to find the woman who had made the lowball appraisal. She came back soon after, holding a black cape flecked with dye stains, and took a seat next to her daughter. There were still twelve people ahead of them.

The place seemed more like a barracks than a hair salon: there were no mirrors or basins, only a row of plastic chairs where women waited their turn to get shorn. The hairdressers were hardly worthy of the title. They cut off hair, period. They approached, comb in hand. They detangled sections and then sunk the scissors in. They cropped as close to the scalp as possible so as not to let a single centimeter go to waste.

When finally it was their turn, mother and daughter knew by heart the sound of the blades when they came into contact with the hair. A snip-snap, a removal. Tearing out things to sell to whoever will pay up. They felt like turning and running, or crying. They did neither. Only waited.

Old Herminia was nervous. It was almost six o'clock and the sun was starting to retreat, timid, in the dusk of the border city. The baby was asleep, worn out from all the crying. Hunger was like that: once you got used to it, it numbed any impulse. Where had all the things that once seemed lasting gone, Herminia wondered, surrounded by the filthy pigeons.

Koralia and Milagros appeared. Herminia recognized them by their clothing. From afar they looked skinny and withered, advanced into old age well before their time. She removed her glasses and cleaned them with her dress, wanting to make them out more clearly. Koralia had no hair and Milagros sported only the fuzz of a skinny chicken. They looked as if they were returning from war, not the market. They had two packets of pasta in hand, which they put into the backpack without a word.

Jamel Brinkley

Witness

M Y SISTER THREW OPEN THE DOOR so that it banged
against the little console table she kept by the entrance.
"Silas," she said breathlessly, before even removing her coat, "I
have to tell you something." Which was enough to make me feel
trapped, as though the words out of her mouth were expand-
ing and filling up the space in her tiny apartment. I told her to
calm down and apologized, and then I began making excuses for
myself. I had assumed she would be angry at me because of the
previous night, so I was primed for what she might say when she
got home from work.

"Don't be so defensive," Bernice said. "I'm not talking about
that." She tapped my legs so I would move them and then plopped
down next to me on the love seat. The chill from outside clung to
her body. I saved my reformatted CV, set my laptop on the floor,
and listened.

The man who sang out of tune had been waiting for her again.
He had started standing near the card shop on Amsterdam Avenue during her lunch hour two weeks earlier, and she had quickly
noticed his repeated presence. As she passed him that afternoon,
he faced her directly and gave her a meaningful look, which was

more than he had ever done before. "But all he did after that was keep belting it out in that terrible voice," she told me. "A sentimental song, you know? The sweetness of making love in the morning." Even though he was thin and light skinned and wore those big, clunky headphones—"Not my type at all," she said—Bernice did find him somewhat handsome. But since he didn't say anything, she just went inside the shop. She liked to go in there during her break because her job could be tough. She worked as a guidance counselor for high school kids, soaking up their troubles all day long, and the cards, however hackneyed or sentimental, gave her a daily boost she enjoyed. When she emerged a bit later, feeling affirmed, the man approached her. With the headphones clamped around his temples, his gloved fists tight around the straps of his backpack, he said he was sorry for bothering her, that he hoped she didn't mind but he had seen her walk by the other day and thought, well, she was beautiful. "Meanwhile," she told me, "with the kind of night I had, I'm sure I've never looked worse a day in my life." She didn't shake the hand he offered, but smiled at how flustered he was. His name, which he said was Dove, pleased her, and the way he scrunched his lips together and shifted them from side to side had what she described to me as a clarifying effect.

Bernice laughed now and said, "So, long story short, I said yes."

"What do you mean you said yes?"

"I gave him my *actual* name and my *actual* number," she said. "He's a DJ, and he has a gig this weekend. Maybe I'll go see him do his thing."

I couldn't tell if she was being serious.

"You think I'm crazy."

"I don't," I said reflexively, but only somewhat honestly. I knew that she found our mother's warnings to avoid men on the street excessive. She'd told me once that doing so would be like forbidding the use of a shower because water could get hot and scald. Bernice didn't want to be seen as weak, and she always trusted her own instincts. I didn't have much faith in them, though. In my mind she could be reckless.

The previous night, she had texted and called me in a panic, but I wasn't available for her. I was out with a woman when my phone lit up, so for a long time I ignored Bernice's texts, her calls, and her voice mails, too. The truth was, I found my sister exhausting, the way she could crowd you out of your life with the enormity of her own. The entanglement I was trying to have with that woman, I told myself, was too urgent to be interrupted. I didn't find out what had happened until the morning, when I finally listened to her messages and read her texts. By then she was already on her way to work.

Unable to reach me last night, she requested a car to drive her to the emergency room. She sat in the dingy waiting area for a long time before she was able to meet with a doctor, and she told him what she told me on the first voice mail: "I don't know what it is, but I just feel off. I can't think straight, and my body, it doesn't feel right." She had texted me again afterward, saying that her blood pressure was elevated, but in the doctor's opinion her issues overall seemed minor, most likely stress related. All she needed to do was relax.

"So," I said now, "you're feeling okay?" As the heat hissed steadily into the room, I looked down at the love seat, where I'd been sleeping for weeks while enduring a job search. Perhaps foolishly, I was hell-bent on being in New York, but it seemed like every other Americanist in the country was, too. Bernice had offered to let me stay with her until I got my bearings and found something.

"I already told you. The doctor says I'm fine."

"So you're fine."

"I guess so."

"That's good," I said. "I'm glad. I mean it."

"But they shooed me away, Silas," Bernice said, her voice growing large. "You should have seen it. It all happened so fast, I didn't even get a chance to explain." When she saw the smirk on my face, she glared. "What's so funny?"

"You're doing really well with the whole relaxing thing," I said. "Terrific job. Truly top-notch."

She nudged my shoulder with hers. "Well, I'll be doing plenty of relaxing with my new friend Dove, if he plays his cards right."

"That's awful," I said. "That's just too much. You're always saying too much."

"Doesn't matter how much you talk if people don't listen," she said.

I picked at the edge of my borrowed pillow. The love seat faced the door to the apartment and next to it, above the table, hung a framed photograph taken by our late father, of our mother and us when she was a young woman. In it, Bernice is three, cranky from an ear infection, and I am a frowning infant in her lap. Sitting beside us on a stiff-looking blue sofa, wearing a pale summer dress, our mother smiles with her teeth. "Well, let me ask you this," I said suddenly now, in a brassy imitation of her. "Was that doctor you saw a *white* doctor?"

"Oh god," my sister said, "of course he was." She began shaking her head and we both laughed. "I should have remembered what she always says. What was it again?"

"You remember."

"But when it comes to those white doctors," Bernice cried, now imitating our mother, too, "always, *always*, exaggerate the pain."

Bernie did go to see Dove DJ, and he must have been adept at it, because that weekend sparked a whirlwind romance. Despite the inconvenience of my presence, Dove was a frequent visitor, often after his gigs. Things hadn't worked out with the woman I was interested in, so I was usually there, curled on the love seat, and he would wake me up when he came in, a bit clumsy, unsure in his lankiness as he made his way through the dark apartment. Crates of Dove's records began accumulating around me. When I asked Bernice if she would consider slowing things down, she said, "I'm doing exactly what I want to do, exactly the way I want to do it." Then she smiled and added, "Exactly how I always have." For her, the choice to begin anything significant was a powerful exertion, one the universe couldn't ignore, proof of the force of her will. She felt that if you really wanted to and if you knew how, you could control your life.

Within two months, Bernice and Dove had willed an engagement into existence. The speed of this made our mother furious. When I spoke to her on the phone, she told me Bernice was being a fool, and she refused to come to New York for their marriage at the city clerk's office. I was their only witness. We went through the government's metal detectors and sat together in the crowded waiting room. Finally we were called in for the quick ceremony. Bernice wore a tea-length dress, simple but elegant, the white of it stark against her skin. Dove had on baggy slacks, dark shoes, and a large cream-colored guayabera. With his clothes as loose as they were, he looked ridiculous, and he was as giddy as a child, with all the happiness the occasion called for but none of the solemnity. He seemed possessed of no seriousness, completely unlike the sort of person you should commit your life to. When he extended his arms so he could hold my sister's hands, I waited for him to bungle something. He didn't appear to be reliable at all.

Bernice improvised the presence of our mother by bringing the framed photograph from the apartment. Despite our inclusion in it, the image belongs absolutely to our mother. All three of us are brown, but her skin is particularly dark, full of tiny glints, as though enriched by a day walking in the sun. Her eyes are tired, but happily so, the way people appear sated and spent in the wake of a long, demanding meal. She looks so beautiful and strong that you would be tempted to think her children, in that moment, are beautiful and strong, too. This, our mother's sovereignty, is the source of the photograph's power, and the reason why it's my sister's favorite.

Dove, who had been living with his father, didn't make much money, and the newlyweds' combined income wouldn't have gotten them a better place than the one Bernice already had—rent was still reasonable in that part of Crown Heights. So her apartment soon became their apartment. For two people it was very small. For three it was nearly hopeless. When we ate together, they sat on the love seat and I was relegated to the floor. There were always conflicts about the bathroom. The arrangement began to wear on us more and more. I complained that at night I could hear them, to use Dove's phrase, *making love*. He complained about the photo of us and our mother, so he took it down and replaced it with one of him and Bernice. She complained that he had done this and switched them back, declaring that no one she lived with was grateful for her. After that she kept more company with the books she began bringing home from the library.

The person who lived upstairs was a friendly man who worked as a high school basketball coach. Bernice liked him, though he had a habit of watching games with the volume on his TV turned all the way up. He also walked through his apartment with astonishing frequency, and his steps were very heavy. His stomping constantly threatened the photo of our mother on the wall, shaking it askew. Usually it was Bernice who ran over to straighten it and make sure it didn't slip completely from its nail. But in the three months since the marriage, she'd become more irritated and depressed than I'd ever seen her, and she seemed more interested now in causes than in their effects. So late one night, as the upstairs neighbor stomped and his TV roared, all she did was raise her head from the arm of the love seat, where she had been reading, and sneer at the ceiling.

"This is getting ridiculous," Bernice said. "What time is it now?"

I took the photo down and laid it on the console table, next to a thin, empty vase. I explained that it was exactly six minutes later than the last time she had asked. I pointed at the fully functioning, prominently displayed clock. It was 4:18 a.m.

"Tell that motherfucker I can't stand him anymore," she said. "Tell him next time I see him, he should just gumboot-dance directly on my chest."

Was she talking about the coach or Dove? Neither man had a connection to South Africa, as far as I knew, but my sister's mind had become increasingly global in range. The books surrounding her on the love seat and the floor included library copies of fiction and poetry in translation, various travel writings and studies of cultural practices, histories of colonialism and insurrection throughout the African diaspora. She collected as much information as she could, as furiously as she could, about the lives and trials, real and imagined, of black people everywhere. Willy-nilly, she regurgitated facts and ideas at me. It was an undisciplined affront to my years of graduate training, especially annoying since she refused to explain exactly what she was doing. But it was clear that whatever else it was, this new habit was a way to resist being crushed by the altered circumstances of her life.

When she wasn't absorbed in a book, or overtaken by a depressive sleep—in one way or another conjuring dream routes across the planet—Bernice was forced to deal with local matters. She was running out of sick days at work, and her performance there seemed to be declining fast. She mentioned that parents of the students she counseled had started to complain that she was giving out strange advice. Much of it was about her philosophy of love, which at this point, she told me, was "also a philosophy of hate." At the apartment, she seemed sad and anxious when Dove was out late DJing, but she also fell into despair and rage when he was at home. Not once did I say *I told you so*. It seemed she had come to understand, on her own, that we always overestimate how much we can control our lives.

Dove finally got home that night a little before five. He unlocked the door and shuffled in ass first, bent over two milk crates of LPs. He was one of those DJs who boasted about playing vinyl, but the undignified way he entered the apartment punctured his self-righteousness, as did the sheepishness that came over his features when he turned around and saw the complications on my sister's face.

"Oh, you're still up?" he said now, to both of us. He looked frightened as he pulled his sagging jeans to his waist.

"Silas sleeps *here*," my sister said. "And where am I? Here. Silas can't sleep here if *I'm* here."

"Why do you sound angry?"

"I'm not angry, I'm sick."

Dove rolled his eyes at me, but I gave no sign that I agreed with him. "Well," he said, "why aren't you in bed, then?"

Bernice collapsed onto her side and faced the back of the love seat. Her hair was slicked into a sad curly bun, and her head rested on an open book, a history of compulsory sterilization in Kenya.

Dove began to take a step forward but then retracted it. He often moved this way, as if the floor were booby-trapped. He jerked his head toward the front door and said to me, "Come on, professor, let's go get some grub. I'm paying."

Bernice moaned without turning. "There's food here," she said. "What is it about having a little bit of money in your pocket that immediately makes you want to spend it? Are you a child?"

He glanced at me. "I'm a man," he replied. "The man of *this* house."

"Man. Child. What's the difference?"

Dove didn't argue. He approached my sister with trepidation, moved some of the books aside, and crouched by the love seat, but he seemed unsure of what to say. Except for Bernice's whistling breaths, everything was quiet. Even the coach and his television were idle. Dove cleared his throat and told my sister he would bring her back something good. "Some soup to help you feel better."

"Soup again?" she replied. "You think soup fixes everything. At the farthest reaches of your imagination, out there in the wilderness, explorers would discover a bowl of soup."

"Oh, come on, sweet girl."

"You stink of liquor," she said. "Liquor and sweat and desperation. Please, I'm begging you, just go away."

Ejected from the apartment, Dove sprinted down the stairs. I followed him outside. The sun would be up soon on another warm spring morning. There was a twenty-four-hour diner he remembered. It was pretty far from the apartment, but he insisted that we walk.

"Back in the day," he explained, grinning, "me and my boys would eat at this place after partying all damn night. Man, we were just kids then. I miss those dudes. They're the jokers who gave me the name Dove," he said, and laughed good-naturedly. "Because I'm so light."

"Oh, is that why?" I asked, but he didn't hear the sarcasm.

He shook his head, full of nostalgia. He seemed to find solace in calling forth and repeating the past. "That's when music was good, you know?" Then he began to pontificate on what he called the golden age of hip-hop. He even lectured about producers and the art of sampling. "Old-school is where it's at, man. Why do you think I spin records?"

"I haven't really thought about it," I told him.

"With digital files, the music gets compressed. Details get lost. The depth, the textures: gone. It's actually sad. Nothing's the way it used to be."

I asked what happened to his friends.

"They got married. Had kids. Or they moved. They moved on."

He changed the topic, asking about my job search. I had several new applications out and was now hoping to piece together enough adjunct positions to make a decent living.

"And find a place of your own?" he asked.

"Bernice says I can stay as long as I need to," I told him.

He just hummed in response. Then he asked if the sort of thing I was trying to do wasn't a ridiculous hustle in New York. I said it was. I asked if trying to pay the bills as a DJ in New York wasn't a hustle, too. He nodded. After that we didn't talk. Our interest in each other had been exhausted, and neither of us wanted to talk about Bernice. Dove started singing to himself in his horrible voice.

Maybe he also sensed she was moving on, around and abroad, or further and further back into accounts of the past, escaping with her books to places and times that seemed closed to anyone but herself. From the way she looked as she conducted her arcane scholarship, it seemed easeful to pass the days like that. At least until her husband or brother came home, breaking her loneliness and her peace.

When Dove and I arrived at the diner we were met by construction barriers, a perimeter of chain-link fencing backed with lengths of green screen. The building that had housed the diner was gone, replaced by the gleaming bones of a condominium. A sign showed an image of what it would be eventually, a sky-piercing complex sheathed in glass. Applications for buyers were already being accepted. Dove stared at the sign, headphones snug at his temples, his lips scrunched together. I tried to glimpse what my sister had ever seen in him. Could he have been anyone, any person whose gestures and manner she might have chosen to recognize and accept, or was there something more substantial about him? The way his untucked shirt and jeans hung from his body made him look even more puerile than usual. Maybe it was something related to this, Dove's frivolity, that made her think he would be easy, that she could fit him wherever she pleased. He turned to me, jolted by some notion, and said he knew of another place not too far away, an "old-school" doughnut spot that had great coffee. Was the new plan to bring my sister a doughnut? The idea of it made me angry. I told him I was tired from the walk, that I needed to go home and try to sleep. Dove seemed relieved. "What you *need* to do," he teased, "is hurry up and find your ass a job." Then he bumped my fist hard with his and we went our separate ways.

Everything I saw on the way back to the apartment became the object of my anger. The cracks in the sidewalks, the dust on the parked cars, the slowness of the occasional pedestrian—it all seemed jammed full of stupidity. The city struck me as an impossible place to live. What was I even doing here? I walked on, pausing whenever I passed an open bodega. I told myself I was thinking of what I could buy for my sister, something that would please or help her. But I didn't have much money and, honestly, I was just giving myself excuses to delay. I didn't want to be with Dove, but I didn't want to be in the apartment either. Bernice was just another kind of burden.

When I came into the apartment, Bernice yelled from the bedroom, "Oh Jesus, what kind of soup is it this time?" A month had passed since my walk with Dove, and though it was a sunny afternoon outside, the apartment's main window, which faced an air shaft, made it seem like evening. From the bedroom came sweetly fragrant wisps of musk that added to the gloom. The bedroom was filled with even more smoke. Sticks of incense had been lit, well over a dozen, and scented candles burned. In the middle of this cloying cloud, the bed was strewn with books and other objects, and Bernice's head and torso were elevated on a pile of pillows. She squinted at me in the doorway and I squinted back at her, disturbed by the scene.

"It's just me," I said.

"It's just me," she replied, mocking me, and then stabbed her cloud with a sharp cough of laughter. She watched with a pleased grimace as the wound sealed itself. "Was baby brother out trying to make a lady friend again?" she asked.

"I'm broke and I live on my sister's couch," I said. "Once that becomes obvious, no one wants to be my friend."

"Ghosts," she said. "Ghosting you." Then she studied me again, still just outside the room. "It smells so good in here now, but you can't stand it, can you? I know you can't. That's all right. Don't want you in here anyway. Just stay there and let me look at you. I can see your true nature now . . . I want to see his, too. Where is he?"

"I don't know," I said. "I'm assuming he'll be back later."

"That's good," she said, and then she seemed to shrug. "It's messed up, too."

In addition to her books and the incense, she had recently started collecting a significant number of translucent crystals, which glimmered within the smoke. I asked her now what they were.

"Quartz," she said. "They're healing stones. I ordered them online."

"What do they do?" I asked.

"They're healing stones, Silas. What do you *think*?" Bernice had complained of headaches two weeks ago, and had gone back to the doctor, but was told again that she was fine, and that she needed to work harder to relax. She had taken a leave of absence from work.

"Maybe you really are sick," I said. I wanted her to know I was starting to believe it.

"No shit, detective. Shall I confess to you my pain? Shall I confess my other crimes?" She groaned and rubbed her eyes with the heels of her hands.

I peered in, trying to see her clearly, unsure of what to say. Everything I could think of felt wrong. "Go to the doctor again," I said. "Please. I'll go with you this time."

"No."

"Tell me why you don't want to."

She laughed dryly. "Silas, I've tried. They just keep sending me home. Why would I go where people don't know how to treat me? That's just more helplessness."

"We can try to get you a black doctor," I said. But in truth, I had little sense then that this could make a difference. I hardly went to the doctor myself.

"Okay, sure thing, *Mom*," she said, amusing herself. "Listen, do you know what I read yesterday—no, what am I saying, I just read it—do you know?"

"Bernice—"

"Get this. When slavery was abolished, there were all these little children just walking around, confused, completely separated from their kin. How's that for a picture of freedom. Can you imagine? How scared they were? The danger they were in? Well, do you know what happened next? Other black folks, *strangers*, took them in. Families. Adults who were on their own. Sometimes people who were hardly adults themselves. Saw these wandering children and adopted them, just like that."

"Well, it was more complicated than you're saying," I began, even though African American history wasn't my area of expertise. "If you study any of the oral accounts—"

"Strangers did this, Silas! Not so long ago . . . And it happened here!"

She said *here* as if shocked to find something of use anywhere on the planet. Then she watched for my response, which was to do absolutely nothing. I remained on the edge of her cloud while the coach stomped around above us. Then there was a sound like the spitting of a lit candle. Bernice's body went rigid on the mattress and started jerking. I couldn't move—I didn't know what to do. Her back arched as she continued convulsing, and the spitting sound, I realized, came from her mouth as she labored to breathe. She wouldn't stop her rigid shaking. I approached the bed finally, and saw that her eyes were rolled back into her head. It was the sight of the reddened saliva at her lips and the stain growing in the crotch of her shorts that jolted me into action. I took out my phone, called 911, and was told what to do. I began by removing the books and crystals from the bed, and I stayed with her until the paramedics arrived.

Bernice went through triage, a long wait, an examination, another long wait, and then, after being admitted, a CT scan. By the time Dove showed up at the hospital, hours later, every emotion and reserve of energy seemed to have been boiled out of her. He zipped past her wheezing roommate and stopped short. "It's gonna be okay," he cried out uselessly. "Don't worry, it's gonna be okay!"

Bernice's head rolled slowly on the pillow until she faced him. She gave a wasted smile and tapped her ear. His eyes widened. Up flew his hands to remove his headphones. We could all hear his loud music scratching the air.

"Hey, Mr. DJ," my sister said quietly. She pointed at her monitor and added, "Can you find a song with a pulse that matches mine? Find it for me, play it for me."

I watched Dove from the seat near the foot of the bed. His eyes, full of affection, communicated that he thought she was being sincere. He tiptoed up to her, took hold of one of her hands, and said, "Oh, sweet girl . . ." Then he repeated it with a hint of unruly pleasure. Maybe he was falling in love with her all over again. If so, and if her condition allowed her a choice, she seemed to be indulging him. He held both of her hands in his and, moving his lips wordlessly, looked as though he was renewing his vows.

"The results of the CT scan are negative," I said.

Dove nodded. "Good, that's good."

"When I asked about getting a black doctor they didn't take me seriously," I added.

My sister turned to me. She must have heard the hollowness of my words. I heard it, too, as I had earlier as the hospital staff spoke to me, the same conspicuous tone of lip service. Bernice wouldn't take her eyes off me, and Dove wouldn't take his eyes off her.

"I just read that racist patients have no problems, absolutely none, when they demand white doctors," I said, holding my phone out toward them. "There was this Nazi out in Michigan, he got every black nurse in a ward reassigned so their filthy jigaboo fingers wouldn't touch his newborn alabaster child."

Neither of them paid attention to what I was saying. They were still holding hands, whispering to each other.

"What took you so long?" I asked Dove angrily. "I called you. I texted, too." The irony of my words wasn't lost on me, so they came out with added bitterness.

"I was on the train," he said bluntly, as if that explained everything. Then he let go of Bernice's hands and took off his backpack. "I went and got you something, baby." He reached in and gave her something small and white: a flat, folded paper bag.

My sister rustled the bag. "A card?" she asked.

"Two cards!" Dove said, beaming.

She examined them. One was a get-well greeting with a cartoon dog on it, the other an anniversary greeting with an illustration, the heads of two red roses. "But it's not our anniversary," she murmured.

"I know that," he said defensively. "I picked it for what it says, inside. It's how I feel."

Bernice read it aloud: "'The years may pass and pass, but our love shall never grow old. Knowing you're mine makes me feel so alive. Each day with you shines like gold.'"

After she was done reciting that canned poetry, she smiled weakly. Dove took the paper bag from her linens, smoothed its wrinkles and folds, and then pointed at it. "Check this out, though. Look where I got them from."

Bernice recognized the logo, from the card shop she liked to visit, outside of which they had spoken for the first time.

"So what do you think?" he asked.

She scowled and closed her eyes. "It hurts."

"What?"

"My head," she said. "The medicine they gave me. It's not working. They didn't give me enough."

Dove rushed to press the call button. He was frantic when a nurse didn't come right away. I said I could ask at the nurses' station, but when I stood he blocked my path, insisting he would do it. I really did want to go—to do something for my sister, and to escape that room—but apparently it had to be him. He ran out into the hallway to let someone know my sister needed more for her pain.

After that, Dove would come to her hospital room, hold her hand, and sing. She was quiet around him, but when I was alone with her, she would talk, intent on expressing herself despite the trouble she was starting to have with her speech. I listened. I came to understand that this was the way she remembered our childhood, the way she always wanted it to be between us. I went as far into this fabrication as I could, until it, as well as the notion that she wasn't angry at me for not believing her, started to feel real. When she became too tired to talk, I would read to her from her library books.

Meanwhile our mother arrived in the city to lend Bernice strength. Whenever she was at the hospital, Dove made sure he wasn't there. He knew she didn't approve of their marriage. She would sit in the chair by the foot of the bed, which seemed to calm my sister, but she would rise whenever a doctor or nurse came in, challenging every word they had to say. When the doctor told us one day that Bernice would be able to go home soon, our mother asked how on earth he could think such a thing. When he said the tests were clear, she said, "Well, how many more tests you got?" When he said Bernice's pain was under control, she asked him how he could possibly know.

Despite our mother's protestations, Bernice was discharged. A few days later she suffered a massive stroke. Back at the hospital, she passed away. Our mother and I were there in the room. I had imagined that my sister's last breath would be a tremendous thing, but it wasn't; it was no different than any other. The moment that breath was released, however, her face straightened, settled, went smooth. Our mother felt that Bernice had transformed. "She's my little baby again," she said. "She looks just like she did as a baby."

Her voice was soft when she said this, but afterward it became hard and enormous, like a slab of iron, and she hurled it at every doctor and nurse she saw. She was my sister's guardian, fiercely so, calling them murderers and demanding that they admit they had killed Bernice. She even made it difficult for the body to be attended to.

Dove arrived at the hospital during a respite in our mother's tirade, but the sight of him, ugly with crying, roused her again, and to an even greater degree. She started screaming her accusations at him. He was shocked, stricken; he had probably expected the three of us, in grief, to have a family embrace. I told him to go away, to go downstairs and wait in the cafeteria. He took a moment to compose himself and then complied, but his leaving had no effect on our mother's rage. It got so bad I had to restrain her. I held her in my arms and told her she had to calm down. She turned her head so that our noses almost touched, her eyes suddenly lucid, and wider than I'd ever seen them. "You did this, too," she said, "you're one of them, you're a murderer." She kept saying it, with unblinking composure, until it became a kind of chant. After a long time, her voice shrank into a murmur. Then all she did was breathe in and out, heavily, and allow herself to go limp in my arms.

. . .

Our mother stayed with me in the Crown Heights apartment as we conducted the costly business of settling Bernice's affairs. She slept in the bedroom—Dove had gone back to his father's place in Harlem—and as usual I slept on the love seat.

Dove didn't come to the funeral. Some of Bernice's old coworkers came, as did many of the students she advised. The coach was there, too. I was surprised to see that many people there for her, but their presence, which confirmed she wasn't as isolated as I thought, made me feel worse. When it was my turn to take the lectern and speak about my sister, I couldn't. This wasn't because I hadn't prepared a speech for her. As I sat there in the front pew, words flowed easily into my mind, just as I had expected. It wasn't a problem of being unable to think of what to say. But the words that came were the bloated kind one used to satisfy the unknowable and therefore impossible expectations of others, words that shined a light so dazzling it washed out every distinctive feature. Our mother, sitting to my left, turned to me. Her expression pleaded with me at first, and then demanded I rise, but I was unable to get up from my seat.

When we got home, she put on her eye mask and earplugs and went directly to bed. So she was spared the mess and noise of my sorrow. That night, as the coach lurched around upstairs, I lay awake sobbing. I kept thinking how unbearable the drama of her loss was, and how unbearable my role in it felt, too. An MRI might have saved Bernice's life. I couldn't believe it was so difficult to take care of someone else.

I grabbed my laptop and opened it. As the blue screen glowed in the darkness of the apartment, a memory came to mind, of Bernice and me as children. We were in our parents' bedroom, wearing our mother's clothes, our small feet in her big shoes, our limbs hidden in the sleeves of her blouses, her head scarves draped loosely around our necks. We stood side by side in front of their mirror, looking at ourselves, our mouths reddened and winged from sucking on cherry ice pops. And then she began to narrate tall tales about us, about who we were and what we had done and the business we would conduct brilliantly in the future. I wondered about that. Had it actually happened, or was I just imagining another story she had told me in the hospital? It didn't matter. I hit a key on the laptop to awaken the screen again. I opened a blank document and typed, "My sister Bernice is dead." I wrote it as a simple matter of fact, as a way to begin accepting it, but then I kept typing. The document became something like a eulogy, but a very honest and private one. No flash, no oratory. It was just for me.

Not too long ago, after our mother had left the city and I had finally managed to find work, I reached out to Dove. Almost all of his records were still in the apartment, crates in every room, so he must have stopped working gigs. With Bernice's books returned to the library and her quartz lined neatly on the console table, it was Dove's stuff alone that gave the apartment its oppressive character. He said he would rent a van and come to the apartment to get his records. We decided on the arrangements and it felt like a larger, unspoken agreement had been made between us.

The sound of his singing got louder as he came up the stairs and approached the door. He knocked, and when I opened it he stood there haggard and stooped, and his headphones hung like an anchor from his neck. An unflattering beard grew like patches of moss along his pallid cheeks and jaw. I got two beers from the refrigerator and, for no reason he or I could have articulated, we clinked our bottles together. We sat on the love seat and he glanced at the quartz. Then he looked up at the framed photograph of Bernice, our mother, and me, back on its nail.

"I always hated that damn picture," he said. "Bernice is so ugly in it, just a sad-ass, ugly-ass kid. Me and her took plenty of pictures together, nice ones I framed, but she never put none of them up. Never posted any online. Nothing." He tilted his head back and took a noisy sip from his beer. "Don't tell me you're gonna stay here."

"No," I said, "I couldn't do that. But I have to for now."

He pointed the bottle up at the ceiling. "How's the coach?"

"Gone."

"Gone?"

"Gone," I said. "Why didn't you come to her service?"

Dove turned toward the air shaft. "I just couldn't, okay?" He took a long drink of beer. "Hey, I have to tell you something, professor—no disrespect, all right?" he said. "I'm just telling you in case you run into us on the street or something. I started seeing someone new. I know it's real soon, but it's not like I was looking. I swear to god I wasn't. Truth be told, she came after me. And she's great, she really is. A girl you can't say no to. She's the kind of girl who puts your pictures on the wall." He took his phone from his pocket as if to show me something, but then thought better of it. "She likes who I am, is what I'm saying. She's not ashamed of me, you know."

Any sympathy I felt for him was draining away quickly.

"Man," he said, staring up at the wall again, "I really fucking hate that photo."

"It was her favorite," I said.

"It makes sense, I guess, the way you two turned out. Must have been hard growing up with a mother like that. I mean, look at her. You know, I still have nightmares about that shit she said to me at the hospital." He shook his head. His eyes were wet.

I could have explained to Dove that our mother had been screaming her charges of murder to nearly everyone she saw that day, that in her rage and grief he was just another person she could blame. But I didn't tell him. Nor did I tell him how she had leveled her accusations at me. I didn't want to give him the comfort of thinking he and I were the same.

"*I* killed Bernice? *Me?* I loved her," he was saying now. "All I ever did was love her."

"But how does it feel," I asked, "to know she never loved you back?"

Dove's jaw tightened. "She married me."

I nodded. "But she was already sick then—you understand that, right? What happened to her was already happening. A sick woman married you, but she didn't love you." I was holding my beer so tightly I could have shattered the glass. I set it down on the floor. "She told me she *never* did," I said, which wasn't true, but punishing him was easier than punishing myself. And for the moment, at least, it felt good. "And here you are," I added, "thinking a girl putting your picture in a frame means anything at all."

Dove stood and sniffed, drank the rest of his beer, and set the bottle down on the floor. He stepped away from me and went over to where crates of his records, grimed with dust, were stacked against a wall.

It was clear at once, from how he moved, that my words had broken him, in a way that might never be repaired. He crouched on the balls of his feet and slowly began to flip through his records. I watched as he moved silently around the little apartment. Before he hauled out the crates, his fingers touched every single sleeve of his vinyl, making a methodical inventory. He had to be certain that nothing else he claimed or cared for had been taken away.

Tessa Hadley

The Other One

WHEN HELOISE WAS TWELVE, in 1986, her father was killed in a car crash. But it was a bit more complicated than that. He was supposed to be away in Germany at a sociology conference, only the accident happened in France, and there were two young women in the car with him. One of them was his lover, it turned out in the days and weeks after the crash, and the other one was his lover's friend. He'd never even registered at the conference. Didn't it seem strange, Heloise's mother asked long afterward, in her creaky, surprised, lightly ironic voice, as if it only touched her curiosity, that the two lovebirds had taken a friend along with them for their tryst in Paris? The lover was also killed; her friend was seriously injured. Heloise's mother, Angie, had found out some of these things when she rushed to be at her husband's bedside in a hospital in France: he lived on for a few days after the accident, though he never recovered consciousness.

That time was blurred in Heloise's memory now, more than thirty years later. She'd been convinced for a while that she'd accompanied her mother to France; vividly she could picture her father, motionless in his hospital bed, his skin yellow-brown against the pillow, his closed eyelids bulging and naked without their rimless round glasses, his glossy black beard spread out over the white sheet. But Angie assured her that she was never there. Anyway, Clifford had shaved off his beard by then. "I should have known he was shaving it off for someone," Angie said. "And why would I have taken you with me, darling? You were a little girl, and I didn't know what I was going to find when I got there. I've mostly blocked out my memory of that journey—it was the worst day of my life. I've no idea how I got across London or onto the ferry, though, strangely, I remember seeing the gray water in the dock, choppy and frightening. I was frightened. I felt surrounded by monstrosities—I suppose I was worried that his injuries might be monstrous. Once I was actually there and I saw him, I was able to grasp everything. I had time to think. It's a bizarre thing to say, but that hospital was a very peaceful place. It was connected to some kind of religious order—there were cold stone floors and a high vaulted ceiling, nuns. Or at least that's how I remember it. I've forgotten the name of the hospital, so I can't Google it to check. Probably it doesn't exist now."

"Did you see her?"

"Who?"

"Delia, the lover."

"Delia wasn't the lover. She was the other one. The lover was killed instantly, in the accident, when they hit the tree. They took her body away."

Heloise and Angie were sitting drinking wine at Angie's kitchen table, in the same skinny four-story Georgian house in Bristol where they'd all lived long ago with Clifford, in the time before the accident: Heloise and her older brother, Toby, and their younger sister, Mair. Angie hadn't even changed the big pine kitchen table since then, although she'd done things to the rest of the kitchen—it was smarter and sleeker now than it used to be, when the fashion was for everything to look homemade and authentic. She and Clifford had bought the table from a dealer in the early days of their marriage; she had stripped off its thick pink paint with Nitromors. And then she'd worked with that dealer for a while, going through country houses with him and keeping his best pieces in her home to show to customers. She couldn't part with the old table, she said; so many friends and family had sat around it over the years. And now she was seventy-two.

Heloise didn't have her mother's gift of lightness. Angie was tall and thin, stooped, with flossy gray silk mingling in her messy, faded hair. Vague and charming, she had escaped from a posh county family whose only passionate feelings, she said, were for dogs and property. Heloise was stocky, top-heavy with bosom, and serious, with thick, kinked tobacco-brown hair and concentrating eyes; she looked more like her father, whose Jewish family had come to the East End of London from Lithuania in the early twentieth century.

She didn't think her personality was much like his, though; she wasn't audacious. She had kept the obituary that appeared in an academic journal—Angie said she didn't want it—which expressed shock and sadness at the loss of "an audacious original thinker," whose book, *Rites of Passage in Contemporary Capitalist Societies*, was required reading for radicals. The obituary didn't mention the problem of the lover. And there were no obituaries in any of the big newspapers; Clifford would have felt slighted by that, if he'd been able to know it—he'd have believed that it was part of the conspiracy against him. Probably no one read his book these days.

Sometimes, when Heloise spoke to her therapist, she imagined her father's death slicing through her life like a sword, changing her completely with one blow; at other times, she thought that, in truth, she'd always been like this, reserved and sulky, wary. She knew other children of those brilliant, risky marriages of the 1970s who were taciturn and full of doubt like her. Her parents had been such an attractive, dynamic couple, so outward-turning;

the crowd of friends dropping in to talk and eat and drink and smoke pot was always on the brink of becoming a party. From the landing on the top floor, where their bedrooms were, or venturing farther down the deep stairwell, Toby and Heloise and Mair, along with strangers' children put to sleep on the spare mattresses, had spied over the bannisters on the adults, who were careless of what the children witnessed: shouted political arguments; weeping; snogging; someone flushing her husband's pills down the lavatory; the husband swinging his fist at her jaw; Angie dancing to Joni Mitchell with her eyes closed, T-shirt off, her pink nipples bare and arms reaching up over her head, long hands washing over each other; Clifford trying to burn five-pound notes in the gas fire and yelling to tell everyone that Angie was frigid, that Englishwomen of her class were born with an icebox between their legs. Angic called him "a dirty little Jew," and then lay back on her beanbag chair, laughing at how absurd they both were.

But that was all ancient history, and now Heloise was in her midforties, divorced, with two young children, running her own small business from home—finding and styling locations for photo shoots—and making just about enough money to live on and pay her half of the mortgage. When she met a woman called Delia at a dinner party, the name didn't strike her at first; it was just a name. It was a late summer's evening, and dinner began with white wine outdoors in a small, brick-walled garden, its smallness disproportionate to the dauntingly tall back of the terraced house, built on a steep hill in Totterdown; there were espaliered apple trees trained around the garden walls. The guests' intimacy thickened as the light faded; birds bustled in the dusk amongst the leaves, and a robin spilled over with his song. Venus pierced the clear evening sky. They all said that they wouldn't talk politics but did anyway, as if their opinions had been dragged out of them, their outrage too stale to be enjoyable. Was it right or wrong to use the word "fascism" to describe what was happening in the world? Was the future of socialism in localism? Their host, Antony, put out cushions on the stone seats and on the grass, because of the cold coming up from the earth; he poured more wine. Heloise had her hair pinned up; she was wearing her vintage navy crêpe dress.

She liked Delia right away.

Delia was older than the rest of them, with a lined, tanned, big-boned face and an alert, frank, open gaze; her dark hair was streaked with gray and cut in a gamine style, fringe falling into her eyes, which made her look Italian, Heloise thought, like an Italian intellectual. Around her neck on a cord hung a striking, heavy piece of twisted silver, and as the air grew cooler she wrapped herself in an orange stole, loose-woven in thick wool, throwing one end over her shoulder. Everything Delia did seemed graceful and natural.

Heloise was full of admiration, at this point in her own life, for older women who managed to live alone and possess themselves with aplomb; she was learning how to be single again, and she didn't want to end up like her mother, volatile and carelessly greedy. Delia was a violinist, it turned out, and taught violin to children, Suzuki-style; this was how she'd got to know Antony, because his younger son came to her classes. She hadn't been to his home before, and said that she liked the neat creative order in his garden; it made her think of a medieval garden in a story. And she was right, Heloise thought. There was something Chaucerian about Antony, in a good way, with his pink cheeks and plump hands; soft, shapeless waist; baggy corduroy trousers; tortoiseshell-framed glasses; tousled caramel-colored hair.

"Delia's like the Pied Piper!" he enthused. "At the end of the morning, she leads the kids around the community center in a sort of conga line, playing away on these violins as tiny as toys, past the Keep Fit and French Conversation and the Alzheimer's Coffee Morning, all of them bowing away like crazy at Schumann and Haydn. Some of these kids have never heard classical music in their lives before. And yet it all sounds great: it's in tune! Or almost in tune, almost!"

Antony and Heloise had been close friends since university. He worked for the city planning department, which was innovative and chronically short-staffed and underfunded. Like her, he was bringing up his children as a single parent; his wife had left him and gone back to Brazil. Heloise had secret hopes of Antony. He wasn't the kind of man she'd ever have chosen when they were young together—too kind, not dangerous enough—but recently she'd come to see him differently. It was as if she'd turned a key in the door of her perception, opening it onto a place that had existed all along. How whole Antony was! How nourishing his company, how sound his judgments! She kept her hopes mostly hidden, though, even from herself. She was afraid of spoiling their friendship through a misunderstanding, or a move made too soon.

Delia said that intonation always came first, in the Suzuki method. No matter how simple a piece you're playing, it should sound right from the very beginning. The conversation became animated, because the other guests were parents of young children, too, and intensely concerned about the creativity of their offspring. Heloise thought that Delia looked amused, as if she was used to parents' thinking their children were prodigies, because they liked banging away on a piano. Antony wished that his older boy would take lessons, but he had been diagnosed on the autistic spectrum, and wasn't good at following directions; Heloise thought that this boy was sometimes just plain naughty, though she didn't say so to Antony. When she suggested that she'd like to bring her own five-year-old daughter, Jemima, to the class, Delia told her the time and the venue. There were still a couple of places free. Teaching was a great pleasure, she added. She liked the company of children, and had never had any of her own. Heloise marveled at how calmly Delia talked about herself, not trailing ragged ends of need or display.

"And what about your own playing?" somebody asked her. "Do you still play?"

She belonged to a quartet that met twice a week, she said, and played sometimes with another friend, who was a pianist; they put on concerts from time to time. "I had hopes of playing as a professional when I was young," she added. "I won some competitions and dreamed of being a soloist—it was probably only a dream. But then I was involved in a car accident in France—I damaged my neck and my hands—I was ill for a long time. And that was the end of that."

The light was almost gone from the garden. Antony had slipped inside to serve up the food. He was a good cook; appetizing smells were coming from the kitchen. Through the open glass doors, Heloise could see yellow lamplight spilling over his books piled up on the coffee table, a folded plaid blanket on a sofa, the children's toys put away in a toy box; beyond that, a table set with glasses and colored napkins, a jug filled with fresh flowers and greenery.

"It was such a long time ago," Delia said, laughing to console the others when they exclaimed over her awful loss. "Like I said, I was very young. It was really all very tragic, but don't worry. It happened to me in another life."

It was possible that Delia's accident had nothing to do with Heloise's father. There might have been two accidents in France, two Delias. If it was the same accident, then why hadn't she identified Heloise when they met or guessed whose daughter she was? Heloise was a pretty unusual name. But then, why would Clifford have mentioned his children's names to a girl who was only his lover's friend? Perhaps he had met Delia for the first time on that fateful day: it was likely that she'd come along only for the drive, a lift to Paris.

Anyway, he wouldn't have been talking about his children to either of those young women. He'd have been pretending, at least to himself, that he wasn't really the father of a family, that he could do anything he dared to do, that he was as young and free as the girls were, his life his own to dispose of. And, after the accident, when Delia had endured months and perhaps years of suffering and rehabilitation, and lost her hope of a career as a performer, why would she have wanted to find out anything about the family whose happiness had been ruined along with hers? She'd have wanted everything connected with Clifford to fall behind her into oblivion. Into the lead-gray sea.

Heloise talked all these possibilities through with her therapist; she didn't want to talk to anyone else, not yet. The therapist was wary of her excitement. She asked why it was important for Heloise right now to find a new connection with her father, and suggested a link between the breakdown of her marriage and her feelings of abandonment at the time of her father's death. "What did you do, when this woman told the story of her accident? How did you react?"

"Somehow I was all right. I'd drunk a couple of glasses of wine, I was feeling surprisingly mellow—for me, anyway. And then, when I suddenly understood who she was—or might be—I felt as if something clicked into place, and I belonged to her. Or she belonged to me. Everything belonged together. It was probably the wine."

Antony had called them in to eat, just as Delia was finishing her story, and Heloise had stood up from her cushion on the stone bench, elated. She'd almost spoken out then and there—but she'd had more sense, knew that this wasn't the right time to open up anything so momentous, not in company. However well balanced Delia appeared, it would be painful to have her buried history brought back to life. So Heloise had gone inside instead, ahead of the others, and put her arms around Antony, who was standing at the sink lifting a tray of vegetables from the bamboo steamer. Because of the kind of man he was, he wasn't annoyed at her getting in between him and the tricky moment of his serving up the food, but put down the vegetables and hugged her back, enthusiastically. "Hey, what's this in honor of?"

"Oh, I don't know. Just. Such a nice dinner party."

He said that she looked lovely in her vintage dress with the art deco brooch, like a learned Jewess from Minsk or Vilnius in the old days, and Heloise realized that this was exactly the look she'd been trying for. She put her outfits together, always, with the same effort she might use in dressing a room for a shoot, working toward some idea at the back of her mind, like an old photograph or a painting.

For the rest of the evening, she'd been more lively and talkative than usual, conscious of the extraordinary story of the accident that she was hoarding inside her, charged with emotion and as dramatic as an opera. Watching Delia, she'd enjoyed the way she held her fork, the poised, elegant angle of her wrist and her rather big brown hand; how she sat up very straight and listened to the others with intelligent interest, reserving her own judgment. She did have Mediterranean heritage, as Heloise had guessed, though it was not Italian but Spanish. Her politics were quite far left but not doctrinaire; she was well informed and thoughtful. As she grew older, Heloise decided, she'd like to wear clothes in Delia's easy style, made of homespun wool or linen, dyed in natural colors.

Jemima wasn't a musical prodigy, it turned out. But she enjoyed the Suzuki classes and for a while, in the first flush of enthusiasm, even carried her tiny violin around with her at home, tucked under her chin, and bowed out her answers to Heloise's questions in snatches of "Twinkle, Twinkle" or "The Happy Farmer" instead of words. And Delia in the different context of the classes was a revelation: not kindly and encouraging, as Heloise had imagined her, but crisp and unsmiling, even stern. Making music was not a game, she conveyed, but an initiation into a realm of great significance. The children responded well to this, as if it was a relief that something for once wasn't all about them. Unconsciously, they imitated Delia's straight back, the flourish of her bowing, the dip of her head on the first beat of the bar; they were carried outside themselves in the music's flow. Their parents, too, were intimidated and gratified by Delia's severity. She liked them to stay to watch the class, so that they could encourage good practice at home during the week, and mostly they obediently did stay.

Usually, Heloise sat through these sessions with Antony, and toward the end of the class one or the other of them would go off to pick up the two older boys—Heloise's Solly and Antony's Max—from their football club. Through the crowded busyness of the rest of her week, Heloise anticipated with pleasure this hour of enforced mute stillness, squeezed up against Antony on the community-center benches, in the big, characterless white room, with its missing ceiling tiles and broken Venetian blinds, feeling his companionable warmth along her flank, buoyed up by the children's music. The room smelled of hot plastic from the lights, and of sweat from the Zumba class that came before Suzuki. Sometimes, she and Antony bought lunch together afterward at the café in the center, depending on how wound up Max was from football. None of this would have been so straightforward if Antony's ex-wife, Carlota, the boys' mother, hadn't gone back to Brazil. Heloise couldn't help feeling a surge of selfish relief when she thought of it; she'd found Carlota abrasive and difficult. When she'd told Antony once that her ex-husband, Richard, had complained that she wasn't spontaneous, Antony confessed in exchange that Carlota had called him an old woman.

"Which was kind of surprising, coming from her," he added, with the modest amount of owlish irony he permitted himself, "as she was supposed to be such a feminist."

Heloise had told Antony years ago, when they first knew each other, about her father's accident, although not about the lover, because that had still felt shaming then, private. Angie had always wanted to tell everyone everything, as a twisted, crazy joke: wasn't life just bound to turn out like that! Now Heloise came close, on several occasions, to explaining to Antony her occult connection, through the accident, with Delia: a connection that might or might not exist. Each time, however, the moment passed; Max threw one of his tantrums, or Jemima spilled her water. And she hadn't said anything, yet, to Delia herself—with every week that she delayed, it grew more difficult to imagine bringing up the subject. The whole story seemed so improbably far-fetched, and, even if it had really ever happened, it was a million years ago, in another age. At the Suzuki classes, anyway, Delia was too remote, impersonal: she belonged to everyone; it would have been inappropriate to take her aside and make that special claim on her.

Apparently, Antony was having viola lessons with her, one evening a week. Heloise hadn't known that he used to play when he was younger. She wished she had some such privileged way into intimacy with Delia; she was shy in the face of the older woman's authority, her self-sufficiency. Delia was always perfectly friendly, but she would never join them for lunch; she rehearsed with her string quartet, she said, on Saturday afternoons. Heloise suspected that she took in, too, with some distaste, the mess at their shared table in the café: the chips afloat in spilled water, the older boys high with adrenaline from their game, obnoxiously shouty, eyes glittering and faces hot, hair pasted down with sweat.

Heloise's brother, Toby, was over from LA, where he worked in the music business; he came to spend a few days in Bristol with their mother. Richard had the children on Saturday night, so Heloise went to have supper with Toby and Angie at the old kitchen table. Toby was like their mother, rangy and tall and thin, with silky graying reddish curls; he had the same rawboned sex appeal that Angie used to have—indolent, indifferent to what anyone thought about him, scratching carelessly at the hollow white belly exposed under his too-short T-shirt, leaning back in his chair and stretching his long legs under the table, so that his big feet in scruffy Converse trainers intruded into Heloise's space. He and Angie were mesmerizing when they exerted their allure, auburn like angels; and then sometimes they were unabashedly ugly, ill-tempered, with their pale-lard coloring, blue eyes small with exhaustion, the sex-light withdrawn like a favor they were bored with proffering.

Angie was happy because Toby was there; she was girlish and gauche, clowning. In honor of the occasion she'd made something ambitious for supper—enchiladas that had to be assembled and fried at the last minute—and then Toby mixed LA-style martinis, which she said made her too drunk to cook safely. He had to fry the enchiladas, with a lot of flame and noise, under her laughing supervision, as she hung on to his shoulder. Heloise thought that her mother, despite her fierce feminism, actually preferred the company of men, powerful men. Women's winding approaches to one another, all the encouraging and propitiating, made her impatient; she'd rather be up against men's bullishness, their frank antagonism—she had even enjoyed sparring with Richard. And Angie liked the way Toby made fun of her radicalism, as if she were some kind of Trotskyite firebrand extremist, while she accused him of selling out; they had this teasing, challenging rapport. Still, it was notable that he'd chosen to live thousands of miles away from her.

Heloise had thought that she might speak to them about Delia. Perhaps her mother could tell her something that would make it clear, at least, whether this was the right Delia. But she was surprised, once she was inside her old home, at her reluctance to mention her discovery. She could imagine Angie taking Delia up, inviting her round to talk, celebrating her, the pair of them growing close, bound together by their long-ago disaster. Or Angie might be scathing, and recoil from making any new connection with those days. So, when Heloise told them about Jemima's

Suzuki class, she didn't mention the teacher's name. Angie loved the idea of Jemima's communicating through her violin. She was an inspired, enthusiastic grandmother, throwing herself into her grandchildren's world, siding with them and seeing everything at their eye level; also fretting to Heloise and Mair, when Toby wasn't there, about the teenage son he had in the U.S. and never saw, from a marriage that hadn't lasted a year. Mair complained that Angie had reinvented herself over the decades. "You'd think now that she was some kind of hippie earth mother, dedicated to her offspring. Which isn't exactly the childhood I remember."

Inevitably, they talked about politics in America; Toby knew a lot, in his laconic, disparaging way. Watching out for totalitarianism, they said, everyone had been oblivious to the advent of the illiberal democracies. And what did it mean for the world, if America's compass was no longer set to liberal? But it had never really been set there in the first place, Angie protested. Toby played them his latest music, then went hunting upstairs in a cupboard for a box of cassette tapes from his youth, and came down with a quiz game and a cricket bat. He tried to make them play the game, but too many questions referred to TV stars and football contests they'd forgotten—in fact, to a whole vanished world of perception. Heloise told awful stories about Richard; there was such relief in not having to defend him to her family any longer. By eleven o'clock, Angie was drained, done for. This was something she had to get used to, she said, now that she was an old woman. Weariness came rattling down all at once in her mind, like a metal shutter across a window, peremptory and imperative, so that she had to go to bed. "But I wish that you'd really begin to be an old woman!" Heloise joked, placating her. "It's about time. Shouldn't you be knitting? You're meant to be tedious and repetitive by now. With a nice perm."

"Toby thinks I'm tedious and repetitive already."

Angie couldn't help flirting with her son, wanting his reassurance. Cruelly, Toby smiled back at her, implacable. And she did look old at that moment, under the bright kitchen light, despite her lovely, careless dress with its zigzag print: the loose skin on her face was papery, her shoulders were bowed, her skull shone through her thinning hair. Heloise couldn't help wanting, whatever Mair said, to deflect her mother's attention from certain hard truths. She asked if there was a copy anywhere of Clifford's book; Angie stood blinking and absent from herself, as if she had no idea what Heloise meant. "Whose book?"

"Dad's book. 'The Whatsit of Contemporary Capitalism.'"

"Oh, *that* book. Good God. I've no idea. Why? You can't seriously be entertaining the idea of reading it?"

"I just thought suddenly that I never have."

Toby said that there was a whole box of them, under the bed in his old room. "They're a bit mummified, sort of shrunken and yellow."

"You can have all of them if you want, darling," Angie said. "Get rid of them for me."

"I don't want all of them. I only want one copy."

When Angie had gone to bed, Toby asked why Heloise wanted the book anyway, and she said that she'd been thinking about their father. He rumpled her hair affectionately; in childhood games, she'd been her brother's faithful squire, in awe of his glamour as he advanced ahead of her into life, knowing all the things she didn't know. "I thought I went with Mum to France," she said, "after Dad's accident. But she told me no."

"Why would you have gone?" Toby said. "None of us went. We had to stay with that ghastly family, the Philipses, and they were sanctimonious and sorry for us. I got drunk for the first time on their bottle of gin, really sick drunk, threw up all over their stair carpet, and they couldn't even be mad with me, under the circumstances. I can remember thinking at the time—this is awful, really, considering that Dad was dying—that from now on, under the circumstances, I could get away with just about anything."

Heloise said she'd been convinced, though, that she'd seen their dad in the hospital. "He looked so peacefully asleep, without his glasses: you know, how he was never peaceful in his life." It was awful to think, she added, that their mother had traveled all alone to France.

"She wasn't alone. She had her boyfriend with her."

"What boyfriend?"

"Terry? Jerry? That guy who kept his furniture here to sell it. I couldn't stand him."

"I'd forgotten about him. But that was just a business relationship—he wasn't her boyfriend."

"Oh, yes, he was."

Toby said that he'd once come across Angie "doing it," as he put it, in his mocking, slangy drawl, with the stripped-pine dealer; this was in Clifford and Angie's bed, before the accident. Heloise was shocked and didn't want to believe it; but probably that sex scene was the kind of thing you couldn't make up, unlike a picture of your dead father at peace. And she did remember vaguely that Toby had fought with the furniture dealer, at some point in that awful time after Clifford's death—a real physical fight, fisticuffs, here in this very kitchen. Toby said that effectively he'd won the fight, although Terry had knocked him down. Because it didn't look good, did it? Big beefy macho bloke beating up a skinny weak kid, his girlfriend's kid, making his nose bleed. Angie hadn't liked it. They hadn't seen much of Terry after that.

Heloise began reading *Rites of Passage in Contemporary Capitalist Societies* as soon as she got home that night. She seemed to hear her father's own voice—which she hadn't even realized she'd forgotten—right in her ear, urgent and confiding. This sense of Clifford's closeness made her happy, just as it used to when she was small and he read to her at bedtime, or told her stories about his family or from history—she understood only years later that he'd never really been to Kiev or Berlin or Moscow. He hadn't censored these stories or tamed them to make them suitable for a child; he'd called her his little scholar. His good moods couldn't be trusted, though; he would come storming out of his study, ranting at the children, if they made any noise when he was trying to write. Didn't they care about his work, or believe it was important? Now Heloise was reading the actual words he'd written, describing the barrenness of life under consumer capitalism, the loss of the meaning that was once created through shared belief and ritual. And she seemed to see through the words, with miraculous ease, to the flow of her father's thought.

When she picked up the book again, however, over her coffee the next morning, while she waited for Richard to bring back the children, she got bogged down in its technical language: "the significance of changing notions of value for the development of a capitalist economy," or "the process of differentiation makes sense if we see it as a continuous process of negotiation." It would take a huge mental effort on her part to even begin to master Clifford's ideas, and she wasn't convinced, in her daylight self, that it was worth it. She was afraid that, as the years had passed, the relevance of his formulations might have slipped away, as relevance had slipped from Toby's quiz. The book's pages had an unread, depressing smell. In the end, she lent it to Antony: he was better with that kind of writing than she was. If he felt like dipping into it, she said, she'd be interested to hear whether he thought it was any good. She liked to think of Antony's having her book in his safekeeping.

Then, one stormy Thursday morning in half term, Heloise turned up unannounced at Antony's house with Solly and Jemima. She had rung to ask him if they could come round, but his phone was switched off; in desperation, she'd decided to take a chance, drive over anyway. It had rained every day of the holiday so far, Richard was away, and Heloise had given up inventing things to do; often the children were still in pajamas at teatime. Rain came sluicing across the big windows of their flat, the conifers thrashed at the end of the garden, wheelie bins blew over. The rooms were like caves inside the noise of water, either greenish and spectral or bleak with the lights on in the middle of the day; the children crouched over their screens, whose colors flickered on their faces. Jemima accompanied back-to-back episodes of *Pet Rescue* on her violin; Solly played his Nintendo until he was glazed and drugged, shrugging Heloise off impatiently if she tried to touch him. The idea of Antony's ordered home was a haven in her imagination. He would be struggling to keep up with his work while at home with his children, just as she was; only he was better at it, better at everything. His boys at this very moment, she thought, would be making art, or laughing at an old film. When Antony saw her, he'd know that she'd been trying her best, that the dreary shirt-dress she'd put on was meant to be domestic and sensible. She thought that it was time to make some offer of herself, to find a way to express how she wanted him.

His front door was down some stone steps, in a narrow base-ment area crowded with bikes, and tubs planted with herbs and shrubs; the muscular gray trunk of a wisteria wound up from here, branching across the whole front of the house. Heloise was worried—once they'd rung the bell and were waiting in the rain, which splashed loudly in the enclosed stone space—at not hearing the children inside. She didn't know what to do if Antony wasn't in. She was counting on him. Then the door opened and Delia stood there, in a gray wool dressing gown and nice red Moroccan leather slippers. She had those weathered, easy looks that are just as good in the morning, without makeup; she seemed taken aback when she saw Heloise, and, for one confused, outraged moment, Heloise thought that Delia's dismay was because she'd been caught out—Antony and Delia had been caught out together—in some-thing forbidden and unforgivable. She knew perfectly well, in the next moment, that there was nothing forbidden about it. Antony could do what he liked. He didn't belong to her.

"Delia, it's you! Is Antony home?"

"He just popped out to buy bread for our breakfast. I thought you were him, coming back."

"Breakfast! Gosh, we've been up for hours."

Heloise knew how absurd she sounded, accusing them. "Where are the boys?"

The boys were with Antony's mother, not due back till after lunch. Heloise had blundered into what should have been a lazy lovers' breakfast: fresh rolls, butter, honey, scrolling through the news with sticky fingers, sharing stories. Imagining it, she was stricken with longing. Her children had been counting on their visit, too: Jemima, whining, pressed her snotty face into Heloise's thigh; Solly kicked at the wall and swore. "I knew there was no point in driving over."

"You'd better come in," Delia said. "I'll make coffee."

"You don't want visitors. We're the last thing you want."

"But you'd better come in. We ought to talk."

Heloise still thought that Delia meant they should talk about whatever was happening between her and Antony. The children were squeezing past her already, shedding wet coats, dropping to the floor in the hall to tug off their Wellingtons, making a show of their eager compliance with house rules. Solly would be relishing the prospect of playing Max's games without Max; Jemima was in a phase of exploring other people's houses—she could spend hours staring into their cupboards and drawers, touching everything inside carefully, one item at a time. When Heloise followed Delia into the kitchen, she saw Clifford's book on the table. Delia stood facing her, with her hand on the book, in a gesture that was almost ceremonial.

"If this is your father," Delia said, "it makes a strange connection between us."

At some point later, Heloise told her mother the whole story, though not about Delia's moving in with Antony, not yet, in case her mother guessed that she'd had hopes herself. "There was no tree," she said. "Apparently they spun across two lanes and smashed into a lorry coming the other way. Delia doesn't remember this, but it's what they told her. You made up the tree. And it was Delia, after all, who was the lover; it wasn't the other one. The other one died."

Angie sat listening stiffly, cautiously, as if there were something bruising and dangerous in this news for her, even after all this time. "So what's she like, then, the lover-girl?"

Heloise said that she was hardly a girl. She wanted to say that Delia was cold and shallow and selfish, but she couldn't. "She's pretty tough. She's made a life for herself. I like her—she's a survivor."

"What does she look like? Is she scarred? I hope so."

She wasn't scarred, Heloise said, as far as she could see.

Delia has never been able to remember anything from the time she and Clifford and Barbie set out for France until she woke up in the hospital. Or just about woke up—into a long dream of pain, in which she was the prisoner of enemies speaking some alien language that was neither English nor French. Slowly, slowly, she'd come back from the dead. And now, after all these years, she can scarcely remember Clifford, either, or why he once seemed essential to her happiness. A few things: That he was overexuberant when making love, as if he was anxious to impress. That he was moved to tears when she played Brahms, though he argued that it was all up for nineteenth-century music. And the soft cleft shape of his chin, revealed when he shaved off his beard, disconcerting, as if a third person, younger and more tentative, were in the bed alongside them. They had met at a concert: he was a friend of the father of someone she knew from the Guildhall.

But she can remember getting ready, in the flat she shared with Barbie, that morning they left for France. Clifford was expected any moment, and Barbie was still packing, holding up one after another of the big-shouldered satiny dresses she wore, splashed with bright flower patterns, deciding which looked right for Paris, where she'd never been. Delia was anxious at the prospect of being without her violin for three whole days. She hardly thought about Clifford's wife and children; she discounted them—she was unformed and ignorant and very young, used to discounting whatever got in the way of her music. Was Delia sure, Barbie worried, that it was all right for her to travel with them? Didn't Delia and Clifford want to be alone together? Barbie promised to make herself scarce as soon as they got to Paris.

Delia wanted Barbie to come. Perhaps she was beginning to be tired of Clifford. Or perhaps she wanted to show off her grown-up lover to Barbie, who hadn't met him, or to show off Barbie to Clifford, have him see what lively, attractive friends she had. Barbie wasn't a musician; she was a primary-school teacher. She was a voluptuous blonde, effervescent and untidy, with thick calves and ankles, always in trouble because of her no-good boyfriends, or because she drank too much, or fell out over school policy with her head teacher. Climbing up onto the bed now, she was holding one of her dresses in front of her, singing and pretending to dance the cancan. In Delia's memory, the window is open that morning in her bedroom, it's early spring, she's happy. The slanting low sunlight is dazzling in her dressing-table mirror.

Adachioma Ezeano

Becoming the Baby Girl

1. Me and Muscled Man

IT's EXAM. Tall thin girls don't show up. I wonder if they are all all right. I ask the course rep where they are. He's busy rereading his worn-out, photocopied version of Iweka's *Introduction to Drama*. He doesn't even look at me. I sigh. Prof. Okafor comes in with muscled men. They come with guns and anger. They come with swear words. They stand us up. They search us. The taller one searches me. He touches my breasts and my eyes bulge. My mouth forms a *whaat*? He says, "Why is it hard?" He asks, "Do you have expo there?" "No, I don't bring prohibited reading materials into the exam hall," I say. "You can," he says. "I don't see why you should not," he keeps on saying. "Everybody does it. Only, they have protectors. I will be your protector. Give me your phone number and yourself." I hiss. I call him idiot. I call him useless. I call him stupid. I call him a very, very useless man. My voice ascends with each word. He screams at me to shut up. He turns to Prof. Okafor, tells Prof. Okafor, "This girl carry expo oo."

"That's a lie! That's a lie!"

"Fill out the examination malpractice form, first of all," Prof. Okafor says to me.

"Why would I do that? This guy is just lyi—"

"No, no, you will not call this honorable man a liar. Fill this form out, young lady. Fill it!"

I take the malpractice form from where he piled them on the table, write my name, and wonder, Can they do this to tall thin girls? Tall thin girls wearing power as perfume and flipping long, dangling braids or costly wigs, brandishing beauty and snobbery like they are the only humans in this universe. This muscled man and this professor. Can they do this to tall thin girls?

2. Me on My First Days Here

I sway my hips past people with my lips slightly parted. I walk past people with grins on their faces, past people with inquisitive looks and no shame as they say, "Hey, fine girl." I say to them with determination that I'm not here to be fine girl and agree with myself: I am not here to be fine girl. I braid my hair in a Ghana weave with black Darling attachments, wear the long skirt Dad bought with the oversize shirt Mum bought. Both of them wiped tears with white handkerchiefs when I pulled out my traveling box. I left them behind with our thin yellow dog, Jack. Jack, with his pendant ears. I wear my mother's cat's-eyes and my pointed nose that everyone believes my father made possible. Dad fills me up with *don't forget* advice as he drives me to Lagos Park: "Don't forget where you come from." "Don't forget where you're going to." "Don't forget to choose the right company." When my bus pulls away from Enugu, I try everything I can think of to connect where I'm going with where I come from. When I dab my face with the white handkerchief Dad gave me before he swerved off in his car to go home, it is tears I wipe from my eyes. I hope never to forget.

3. I Can't Be Tall Thin Girls

Three tall thin girls who are colored like sun, who burn through the class, who let out loud clangs of laughter, who put on airs like they are Beyoncé, who say, "Yeah, you guys, what the fuck, yeah, yeah," who wear English like it is a song, who come to class in too few clothes, clothes that look like they'd fit a two-year-old, who wear long hair extensions worth as much as my father's bungalow, who wave their hands and their perfumes waft around and take over the class. These tall thin girls, who are liked by all the boys and all the men in this school, who bad-mouth Prof. Chris and boo Prof. Okafor, who make girls wish to be them. Those tall thin girls who call to me on the Monday of the first week I walk into this new school and say, "That forehead, oh my god, you look like you are Rihanna right now." Those tall thin girls who call to me on the Tuesday of the second week I walk into this new school and say, "Your shirt, girl, your shirt. Mehn, it looks damn so good, really, giirrl." I wear the loose-fitting white shirt Mum bought from her neighbor who sells imported secondhand wears. Those tall thin girls who call to me on the Thursday of the third week I walk into this school. They say, "Your hair, is that natural? The way it falls straight like a river, really, is it natural?" My hair has drunk uncountable cups of cheap relaxer. My hair doesn't fall straight like a river. My hair is not natural.

Now, those compliments have consequences: The urge to constantly google Rihanna. Place her picture side by side with mine. Compare and contrast. The urge to reshape my loose shirts, make them tighter. Starch them. Buy new ones. The urge to cut my hair. Patiently regrow it till it falls like a river. The urge to become tall thin girls, beautiful, effortlessly confident, eager to dole out compliments.

Who wouldn't want to be tall thin girls? Tall thin girls who drive around the school in Venzas and Lexuses; tall thin girls who are gold; tall thin girls who are bold. But I like to think I am not cut out to become tall thin girls. I am the girl who remembers where she is from and where she is going, who chooses who she goes there with. That is what my father has always said to me, and I am the girl who is her father's daughter, so I ignore tall thin girls on the Friday of the fourth week when they say, "We like you. Be us."

Well, I do not completely ignore them. The tallest of them, the one with the face shaped like an egg, skin the color of Angelina Jolie's, looks at me and says, "Heyy, my name is Ella. Can I have your phone number, please?" And my mouth goes to work telling it to her.

4. Me and the Miracles Tall Thin Girls Make

Now it is tears I wipe from my face again. It is holiday, though I am not going home. I am waiting for the school's disciplinary committee on exam misconduct to sit. No one knows when they will, or if they will, and only when they sit will I know if I will be rusticated from here. For now, I do not know. The letter I received many days ago orders me not to travel yet, orders me to stay till my fate is stated. I don't live off campus—only the rich students do that—and the school hostel is closed by management, to be reopened when school resumes in a month's time. So for now, I put up at my friend's house, and don't know where I will go from here. She says she is going to the village to help her mother with farming and trading so they can save for her school fees next session. They will harvest crops and sell vegetables and yams in the open market. She hasn't gone yet. I beg her not to, not to go yet, not until I find somewhere to stay. I like to think she will give me her key when she leaves. She hasn't said so yet. I only hope, keep saying, "Shebi, you'll leave your key for me when leaving, right?" But a daughter not yet free from her mother's loins will wear her mother's pants. So I wasn't surprised when, two days later, the earliest sun not yet blinding the moon, she sprang from her side of the bed and hit my bare shoulders over and over till I stretched and said, "Ah-ah!" Her mother had called, had said, "It's either I see you here now or you see me there now." So, a girl goes home. She shrugs. I ask for her key. She says nothing. I ask for her key. She says nothing. I ask for her key. She breaks into a story of a young girl like us who made millions last month, just like that. So I pack my stuff as she packs her stuff. I stand by the back door, watch her apply her makeup, rub red lipstick, pencil her brows, wipe off the red lipstick, apply a pink stick, use contour on her face and look extra good. I want to tell her she looks extra good, but I'm not sure I want to talk to her yet. I stand there, watch her drag her Echolac out with lips tightly shut, beads of sweat forming on her forehead, wrinkled lines appearing on her face to form a plea, begging me to help with the heavy box. I press my phone instead because I am not here to help if you are not here to help. Still I stand there, hoping she will say, *Here, take my key. Always lock my door o.*

"Come out, I need to lock the door o." I grab my handbag and drag my box out by Papa Okey's shop, where she and I stood last night, talking about the things I don't care to remember now. She drags her Echolac to the street, flags a bike, tells the rider, a man in a black jean jacket, that she is going to wherever. They bid whatever whatever price, and the man in the black jean jacket climbs down, helps her pull the Echolac up onto the bike, and they zoom off, leaving me in what I want to assume is an intentionally collected swirl of dust. A mild way of telling me to fuck off.

I stand there for hours, watching everything: hurrying men and women, girls and boys, strangers zapping off in my dream cars— Venza, RX 350, Porsche, Range Rover, honking cars and buses and motorcycles, bus drivers cursing one another while struggling for passengers; everything, indications of people busy and life fleeting. I stand there, by the side, doing nothing. My mum calls. I ignore it. I ignore it because ignoring is what you do when you know why a particular call is coming in and you know you have no answers yet to those variegated *wh-* questions you are destined to listen to while pressing that phone to your ear. Mum wants to know when I will be home. Who knows? I lean my box against the peeling wall and walk into Papa Okey's shop, buy airtime, load the fifteen-digit pin into my phone, subscribe for a month's data, and open my WhatsApp. Maybe I can find someone I know who is still around, someone who could save me from sleeping on the street. Maybe. There are tons of new messages, from friends at home, course mates asking for this textbook or that, men who want, people who claim they care, then these messages from this I-don't-know-whose number. I check the profile picture. My eyes swell! It is Ella! Ella of the tall thin girls. Like, who in the class gets messaged by Ella?

Mon., 2 Mar.

Hey Bby Gal 11:41 am

Yeah.. . . . Ella,, here 11:41 am

Chat me up asaq. 11:50 am

Asap** 11:51 am

Thu., 5 Mar.

Heyyy, 10:15 pm

Your ignoring my chats now or they are just not delivering? That's fucked up tbh 10:15 pm

This is Ella tho. Don't be a bitch, yeah? 10:15 pm

Friday

Hey!!!!! 10:17 pm

You don't remember me or what? Gal. It's Ella. Ella! 10:27 pm

Audrey's friend. Queen's friend. Ella! Ella!!! 10:28 pm

Are you really ignoring my text 10:28 pm

Yesterday

Babes, 10:01 am

I called you. You didn't pick. 10:01 am

Today

Someone just told me the issue you had with Prof Okafor.
12:05 am

Call me ASAP. We can help you deal. 12:05 am

This sender is not in your contacts

Block   **Report**   **Add to Contacts**

Ella! 10:20 am

I just saw your profile picture now! 10:20 am

Ella! Queen + Audrey's friend? 11:07 am

Jesus Jesus! I am so oo sorry! Like how can I ignore you? 11:07 am

I am so so sorry, ppleaad 11:07 am

Please*** Biko 11:07 am

I didn't have data,, haven't been here for ages now. 11:08 am

Hello Ella, are you there? 11:08 am

Heyy 6:06 pm

Sup with you and Prof Okafor? 6:06 pm

Eh! You heard? 6:06 pm

Lol Ofcoz I heard. Been meaning to reach U. 6:06 pm

Please, I beg you, help me with that man's issue o. Please. I don't know any anyhow in this school. I cannot afford to be rusticated or anything. biko 6:06 pm

Anyone** 6:06 pm

Where are you ATM? 6:07 pm

Papa Oks 6:07 pm

Papa Okey's** shop 6:07 pm

Kk 6:14 pm

You traveled? My battery is low. It shut down soon sef.
6:14 pm

Go and charge biko. 6:46 pm

Charge? No light here oo 6:46 pm

I don't even have a place to sleep 6:46 pm

Wot do u mean u dont hv place to sleep? 7:10 pm

I'll explain when we see 7:10 pm

Stay at that Papa Okey's shop. I'm driving down. 7:17 pm

Will call as soon as I am there 7:17 pm

OMG! OMG! ELLA!!! 7:17 pm

May God bless you eh. Thank youuu 7:17 pm

Ella? Are you here yet? 8:00 pm

Ella?? 8:17 pm

Ella??? 8:25 pm

I am at Papa Okey's shop 8:30 pm

I am parked where he sells kero. Where you dey? 8:30 pm

Are you there??? your phone off already??? 8:31 pm

Missed voice call at 8:32 pm

TAKE YOUR CALLS!! 8:33 pm

I see you. I see you. In brown Venza 8:33 pm

Yea. get in here. I didn't park well. 8:33 pm

I squint as I look into the night, partially blinded by the sparkly streetlights. I pull up my box and drag it to where she has parked. I am a little scared of these tall thin girls. She opens the passenger door for me to get in once I've pushed my box into the back seat. I resist asking for the name of her perfume that makes the inside of this Venza smell like it is a room in heaven. "Thank you very much, Ella. I don't know what I did right to deserve stressing you like this." She says nothing, nods and keeps bending toward her steering wheel, pressing her phone. It is an iPhone, those long, fine ones that are new and make you drool. We sit in silence. Well, more truthfully, I sit in silence. She is on her phone, pressing, exhaling now and then, smiling mild smiles. I stay quiet, don't know how to be next, yet.

Ella coughs before she says, "So where . . . do . . . we go from here, yeah?" This is our very first real conversation and right now I feel her accent. It sounds like she learned from someone who learned from someone who learned from an Americanah, a complete been-to who thinks staying in America is all we have to do to become Jesus.

"I dunno. I had . . ."

"Fuck it! My house. Where are your stuffs?"

"Oh, in the back here."

"By the way, your name is Akunne, right?"

My name is not Akunne. I don't say this. I don't tell her my name is Ofunne either. I only wait for her to buckle her seat belt before I begin to tell the story nobody asked of me. I tell of my temporary roommate, a.k.a. friend, who left me on the street. I tell of Prof. I tell of standing a whole day and watching the world pass.

"Wow," she says. I talk for close to thirty minutes. She says, "Wow." I say how honored I am to be helped by her, how grateful, how I deeply admire her and everything she stands for. She says, "Wow." I tell more because I do not want to sit and say nothing. I talk on: Whatever, whatever, yada, yada, Buhari Buhari. Prof. Okafor is worse than a corrupt president. You know, you know. EFCC should not only drag around politicians that misappropriate funds. Blah, blah. They should also handle humans who are mean to other humans. Or better still, there be a body for this. Yada, yada.

Ella just drives. No more *wows*. No nod. No *yeah*. No *fuck it*. But her silence sways me as much as she sways her head, which she does a lot, using her green-painted, long nails to brush her long, straight extensions from her face. But before she starts playing Davido's "Nwa Baby," she says, "Baby girl, you don't mind staying in my house, yeah? And yeah, the number I chatted you up with, yeah? Save it, yeah? And yeah, I hope you got sexy pictures on your profile, yeah? Because I want to see all them sexiness you got, yeah?" She swiftly sways her head, uses her green nails to push back her hair again before she winks at me. It looks like she's saying: *Welcome to being a god.* I am still wondering if I am ready for this.

5. Me and Tall Thin Girls Are We Now

We wear black dresses. We strut. We go to Prof. Okafor's office. Ella, Audrey, and Queen say I should stay in the hallway. It is nearly empty now, everyone still on break. A few weeks ago, students studded this place, strutting and carrying their files with pride because it is not easy to beat out a million candidates to secure a spot here. It doesn't matter whether that aunt or uncle of yours who knows a someone who knows a someone that collected something small, maybe money or kindness, worked it out for you, and now here you are, an undergraduate. No, it doesn't matter. We are here now, that's all. The future leaders of Nigeria. Tall thin girls open the door to Prof.'s office. Audrey drags me into the room by my right hand, saying, "Come here, baby girl, come here." My eyes meet Prof.'s. He looks away immediately, says to Ella, "See to it that she writes fast, extraordinarily fast." He stands up from his chair, opens his cabinet, brings out the question papers, selects one, and gives it to me. He leaves his office. Ella takes out a textbook, throws it to me. "Use it. Don't waste my time, please."

"You know we will graduate top of our class, yeah?" Audrey says, smiles, pouts her mouth, winks at me.

"Leave her alone! She needs to concentrate," Queen says to Audrey.

"Is she writing with her ears?" Audrey says.

"You guys, don't be like that now!" Ella says, and then turns to me. "Be fast." I sigh, write and write and write. Or maybe, copy and copy and copy. Once I finish, we pile into Queen's ash-colored Lexus RX 330. I ask, "So do you know when the disciplinary committee will sit?"

They look at me, those three tall thin girls. They laugh. They say, "What the fuck, whaa? What the fuck . . ."

6. Becoming the Tallest Thinnest

I wear new tongues now as well as say "yeah," "you guys," "what the fuck," "yeah, yeah," as well as sing English as well as slap the driver who brings me home as well as become Rihanna and Beyoncé and Cardi B as well as wear too few clothes and hair extensions costing the price of ten plots of land as well as empty bottles of skin-toning creams onto my skin till I shine shine like I am sun as well as drain expensive perfumes till people stop to ask how I got such a fine smell as well as became more beautiful than tall thin girls. Even their men say so. They choose me over them. It makes them happy, though, so long as I get picked and they get paid. They say, "This is why we selected you, because you blaze so bright and your brain burns like fire. We know. We always know the right ones."

7. Bad Girl Gone Good Gone Bad

I lose it and stab my shadows when I hear my father's baritone blare over the phone. He calls more now, and when he is done asking how is school, how is class, how are you coping, my university daughter, he says, "Ofunne, be good. Be godly, okay? You will be home for the holiday this time around, right?"

When he calls, I hear him; when he ends the call, I hear him. I remember the last time I saw him, his hands on the steering wheel, his mouth telling me not to forget where I am from. Right now, I am wondering how a girl from where I am from did forget. I am thinking of all the men I have come to know over the past three months. Chief with the stomach like he swallows the continent for breakfast. He was my first. He was my very first because Ella says it brings good luck; having a wealthy man rip your hymen means you will never meet a poor man. Ever! I didn't tell her of Joshua, the boy living behind my new two-bedroom apartment who sneaks in after these chiefs have gone. He begs for tea and t-fare. I give him tea and t-fare and kiss and me. We moan together and I know that even if he had money, I wouldn't want him for that. Then there is Prof. Okafor. And the man with a white beard. And the man who pays for the two-bedroom apartment. And this other guy, Igwe Obiora, who Ella made sure I'd never see again. All he gave me were multiple orgasms and cowries. He said the cowries were original, the original cowries my ancestors harvested human heads for. There are other men, too, people I work hard to forget. The only person I am working hard not to forget is me. I fear that in trying to be me, I missed, became tall thin girls instead.

I stand from my bed, go to church. I kneel. I say, "Heavenly father, forgive me, forget the things I did, accept me back." I skip classes. And when I don't, I sit far, far from tall thin girls. But they come. They knock and knock and knock and knock till I know I can't really dodge tall thin girls.

"Don't call me baby girl. My name is Ofunne." But tall thin girls don't care. They say, "Ofunne is bush, something the governor would not like to call you."

"Which governor?"

They tell me how the minister of education celebrated his birthday when I was idling out. They didn't call me, because I was idling out. They tell me the governor looked through Queen's phone while they gisted, chewed gum, and sipped rum. They tell me that among many pictures, it was my picture he saw and liked. They tell me he said, "Get this one for me na. Ha! See big ikebe! What, what will she cost me?" They tell me they are here to break my idling. When Ella says, "You are going to South Africa with him," I nod, forget my father in heaven, forget the one in Enugu, and say, "Please, call me baby girl once again."

8. It's Johannesburg, Baby

So the governor calls my phone, calls me baby girl. So he says it this way: "beibei girl," like he lacks something in his mouth, teeth or tongue. When he first calls, I wonder which governor this is. I listen as he tells me, "Keep our relationship to yourself, just you should know it." I put everything he tells me in my mouth and swallow it with water. I prepare for the South Africa trip. I ride to the newest boutique in Lekki with tall thin girls. Once we've burned the money he sends for my prepping, we return so I can pack, and for the first time, tall thin girls don't look so glamorous, not more than me. I know they are jealous, not just because they say it and laugh but because I see it in their eyes. I sleep in Lagos today and know that tomorrow I will be sleeping in Johannesburg.

The governor calls. He says to me, "Beibei, we will not go to Johannesburg right now, but we will go very soon." He sends enough money to buy ten Venza cars. Tall thin girls say maybe he saw a thicker girl with a bigger ikebe, oh yeah. They laugh with their mouths wide enough to swallow a river. I want to tell them to get out of my flat, but my voice is too tiny to start a war. I say I want to go see my mum this weekend since the Johannesburg trip is off. Tall thin girls say, "For what?" We sit in my living room, quiet, wearing too few clothes, pressing our phones till Audrey reads out from a popular blog that there is a strike now. We google it and learn that the Academic Staff Union of Universities is negotiating higher salaries for lecturers, and they're meeting with governors. I smile. I say this is really why he postponed Johannesburg. Tall thin girls press their iPhones. I stand to turn on my AC; there is too much going on right now.

9. Johannesburg, for Real

10. Puking Out the Party

The governor buys me a white Crosstour and says, "Keep this car. But keep us to yourself." And so I'm keeping the month we spent in Johannesburg after the strike ended to myself. I mean, I did not even tell tall thin girls what went down there, or else they would be minding me like I was a baby: "Have you taken pills, eh? How much did he give you, eh? Will you see him again, eh?" Well, now I am bigger, from all the dinners, I think, and I am back and yay, I have my own car, and the strike is off, and I am here at a very depressing party at Nkem's house. Nkem is the friend of Aboy, the senior special adviser to the minister of foreign duties. Aboy understands the real meaning of foreign duties. Apart from linking us up with the minister himself, Aboy has connections and gets me and tall thin girls influential men who reek of power and hard currencies and hardness. His ride-or-die babe, Nkem, is drama, and her house is for showing off, with her plasma TV and her washing machine and her Indian hair and her fake smile and her Aboy. I drink vodka and rum and run to the toilet because I retch, and then puke. I don't know why I puke, but I puke again. Nkem comes into her toilet. I am facing the bowl and puking, and the bitch looks at me and says, "What the hell? You've got AIDS now? You slutting tall thin girls! What the hell. What the hell."

11. A Drug and a Drink to Drink

It is exam. I am the only tall thin girl in the exam hall because I tell tall thin girls I want to write all my exams in the hall and not in the office so no lecturer will have the chance to grab my ass. Ella shrugs, says, "Your choice." Now I think I shouldn't have had such guts. It is a difficult exam. My hands shake and seem to be afraid of holding things. My pen won't stay put, keeps slipping through my fingers. In my head, there sit a million humans with hammers and they hit the hammers, and each hitting leaves my head thinner. I want to die, and that is the only feeling that comes close to describing it. That and the hollowness that hugs you only when you lose someone who you once breathed like the air. I lost myself, but I am not sure this is why I feel like I am holding hands with the butchered parts of my body. One of the invigilators taps me from behind, asks me, "Are you okay, dear?" Her voice is soft and patronizing. I am not a charity case and I do not know the best way to say *get lost* if not by handing in my blank papers to this thin woman. She collects them, walks to the end of the hall, and hands them over to the new professor, who doesn't know me and who doesn't know tall thin girls. I stand from my chair, hold the other students' gazes. I am used to holding the other students' gazes. I have become for many girls the star now. If they only knew what it's like. Like being a perfumed dead rat. I go to the table where an invigilator earlier ordered we drop our bags and phones, grab mine, leave. It is an original Louis Vuitton Saintonge. The other tall thin girls would never keep a Louis Vuitton Saintonge, with its smooth calfskin and its soft tassels and its expensive price, on the same table where cheap secondhand bags cluster. Ella would have found handing over her bag a very valid reason to leave the exam. But not me, and this is one of the many things that worries Ella about me. I pull out my phone, an iPhone XS, dial my mother's number, walk to my car. When she says, "Hello, Ofunne m," I pause, exhale, say, "Hello, Mummy."

"Omalicha m, kedu? How was your exam? When are you coming home sef? Ha! It's going to a century since I saw you last o."

"Mummy, my exam, it was bad."

"How? What is the problem? Ogini?"

"I—I don't know. I don't know what I'm doing."

"What's the problem, nne'm?"

"Mummy, I don't know."

"Are you sick? Are you eating well?"

"I am tired, Mummy, very very."

I hear her exhale. She keeps quiet for some time. Then she asks again when I am coming home. I don't know if I am going home. I don't have plans of going home, but I say, "In two weeks' time, Mummy." And nod repeatedly when she asks, "I hope you are still prayerful eh?"

"I will be praying for you here, too, i nula? I will pray. Just have faith. Your exam will be okay."

"Okay, Ma."

"You will pass. Ah! Our king of kings. He's all-knowing, a miracle worker! Have faith, i nula?"

And I have faith. I have faith that the all-knowing king of kings will not make known to my mother the reason I am so tired, the reason I wasn't able to finish the test. He won't make known to her that I haven't stopped puking since Nkem's party; that when we hang up, I will drive straight to Ella's house for some drink she promised will stop my stomach from growing. Because the only thing I need to grow as a baby girl is my bank account, and maybe my breasts and, yeah, my ass. I don't actually think I'm pregnant. I took all measures. But I go to Ella's house because nobody tells Ella no.

Tall thin girls are splayed out on Ella's couch when I open her door that afternoon: Ella reading my worn-out copy of *Purple Hibiscus*, Audrey lying on the floor pressing her phone, Queen holding up a miniature mirror to her face. They want to know how my exam went. I am too tired to recount. Ella repeats, do I know my constant tiredness and headaches and constipations and swollen breasts and vomits and every other whatever can only be attributed to pregnancy? I roll my eyes. Earlier, when Ella said this, I ignored her, as I want to now. But she has a pregnancy test and as soon as I urinate into the brown cup she hands me and return it to her, she immerses the colored end of the strip into the cup. She pulls out the strip and we wait, her singing Ada's "I Testify" and laughing, me sweating and telling her, "Stop, stop, stop that song right now." And then she cackles, holding up the strip and pointing at the two colored lines.

"Oh, yes! Now drink this," she says, handing me a mug. "I will not have a pregnant baby girl."

I have faith that the all-knowing God will not show my mother this, either: me grabbing the mug, drinking the damn thing, wanting to vomit, the taste like rotten fish; me ignoring Ella as she says, "Don't even think about it," when I run past her to the toilet.

When I come out a minute later, Ella doesn't believe me that I didn't puke it up.

"Take this drug." I eye her. Look at Queen and Audrey to say something. Audrey speedily turns to her phone. Queen speedily turns to her phone. I sigh. I throw the drug into my mouth and drink my water. And I say to Ella, "Anything else?"

"No, my madam. Meanwhile, you left your small phone here yesterday o. See it on top of that table."

"I did? Are you serious? I didn't even know to look for it. Ha!"

"Na so the exam do you? So, this is how bad this exam got to you eh?" Audrey says.

"Or is it the pregnancy?" Queen says, then throws her head back and laughs.

Audrey says, "A number you saved as 'Gov' kept calling and calling, like he owns you for real. Is that the governor?"

"I thought you said you were no longer seeing the governor," Ella said.

"I am not seeing any governor. Give me my phone."

Audrey runs to the glassy center table, collects the phone, and puts it into her pocket. I sigh, walk to where she stands. She makes to walk farther, to make me chase her. But then suddenly she stops, pulls the phone out of her pocket, and begins pressing it.

"Give me my phone, Audrey. Ella, please talk to Audrey."

"Audrey, give the phone to her now now."

Audrey throws the phone at me. I dodge it and it hits the floor. The battery and the phone's back fall out. I pick them up, panting as I do so.

"I hope you're not hiding anything from us like this. Ella, see your babe o," Audrey says.

Ella looks at me and looks back at her book, which she is now pretending to read. I enter Ella's room, lock the door, sit there for a while. My mind runs around. I need to sleep, but I don't want to. I unlock the door, go to the living room, where tall thin girls are still lying around, grab my original Louis Vuitton Saintonge, pick up my car key, put on my slippers, open the door, and leave the house.

When I get into my car and lock my door, I dial the governor's number and listen to his campaign song till the governor says, "Hello." I do not let him start up with his usual boring "How thou art, my sugar, you know I love you, my sugar, blah blah, sugar, yada yada, sugar."

"I am pregnant," I say to him immediately, though I don't know why.

He keeps quiet for some time before he says, "You are supposed to be a secret. You are supposed to be secret, sugar."

I want to say I guess this sugar is too sweet to stay secret.

"Is he a boy?" he asks.

"I don't know yet na."

Nothing comes from him for a moment, and I wonder if the network is bad. But it's not. He sighs loudly.

"You are good, all right?" he says. I want to tell him about the drug and drink from Ella, but I worry that will worry him too much and he will worry Ella too much and Ella will worry me too much.

"Don't panic, sugar, tomorrow eh I will come. We will go and see the doctor together. I want a boy. You will remove the baby if the baby is not a boy, you hear?" I don't say anything. He repeats the question, asking, "You hear?" This time I say, "Till tomorrow, please."

He sighs, says he will talk to me later. I want to call my mother, tell her, but I know she will cry that her daughter has lost her faith, has brought dishonor to the family. I want to call my father, tell him, but I know he will sigh severely, say his daughter forgot where she comes from, brought dishonor to the family. I start my car, drive away from Ella's house. I want to go home, but I am not sure home is the two-bedroom apartment I can afford because my body houses an abundance of men. So I keep driving, and keep driving. And keep driving. And keep driving.

Anthony Doerr

The Master's Castle

Basil bebbington from bakersfield isn't good at basketball, wood shop, or talking to girls, but he's fair at physics, and guts his way through technical college, and lands a job grinding lenses for Bakersfield Optometry, and his parents move to Tampa, and Hurricane Andrew floods their basement, and by age twenty-two Basil begins to worry that he's missing out on things—women, joy, et cetera—so on a whim he applies for a job as an optics technician at an observatory on the summit of Mauna Kea on the island of Hawaii.

The interviews take place at sea level, with a rotating slew of astronomers in flip-flops who warn him that the job involves heavy-duty solitude, weeklong shifts alone atop the volcano, "like being a lighthouse keeper on Mars," one says, but Basil is eager to adjust the trajectory of his life, so he signs the papers, completes the training, leases a Jeep, and on the day of his first shift, drives from sea level to fourteen thousand feet in two hours. By the time he gets out of the truck, the wind is throwing snow across the summit, and his skull feels as if a hatchet has been dropped through it.

A tiny flame-haired woman opens the observatory door, seizes him by the collar, and hauls him inside.

"Ow, what wa—" Basil stops midsentence.

"Get in here, Mr. Basil Bebbington from Bakersfield." She force-feeds him four aspirin and twelve ounces of Fresca, and shows him the composting toilet and the telescope—which is not the big Copernicus-type cylinder-with-eyepiece you might expect, but a three-hundred-ton compound mirror thirty-three feet across that adjusts its position twice per second—and she apologizes for the absence of the microwave, which, she explains, made spooky noises at night, so she dragged it to the edge of the road and pitched it off. Her name is Muriel MacDonald, and she's his age, and looks like a woodland elf but moves like a caffeinated jaguar. Before she leaves, she pours him a bowl of Raisin Bran, hands him a Stevie Wonder CD, and says, "When you get lonesome, put 'Higher Ground' on repeat."

By the time Muriel drags her duffel to her Dodge, orange hair blowing everywhere, yelling, "See you in a week!" Basil is 96 percent in love. All that first night he listens to the wind crash against the walls. Fourteen thousand feet below, waves explode onto reefs and tourists gobble deep-fried prawns, but up here it feels to Basil as though life is finally beginning.

He measures wind speeds, radios reports to the astronomers in Waimea, analyzes Muriel's handwriting in the log. At night he puts on "Higher Ground"—

People keep on learnin'
Soldiers keep on warrin'
World keep on turnin'

—and dances idiotically in the mirror barn beneath the burly arm of the Milky Way, and when Sunday finally arrives, and Muriel churns back up the summit road to relieve him, his heart kicks against his sternum like a frog. He makes her coffee, tells her he saw fifty-six meteorites; her green eyes turn like whirlpools; she tells him she believes most stars in the universe support solar systems. "What if," she says, "every star has planets circling around it? What if there are hundreds of billions of Earths? Earths where you can high-jump eighty feet! Earths where little turtle-people build little turtle-people cities!"

All week in Hilo, flush with oxygen, Basil dreams of her, brushing her copper hair, flinging appliances off the summit. Cumulonimbi gather along the flanks of the volcano like battleships, and Basil watches them flicker with lightning: blue ignitions, as if Muriel were a god, incinerating things up there.

One hour each Sunday: that's all the time he ever sees her, sixty minutes on the boundaries of their respective shifts. Yet on the calendar of his life, what hours have shone more brightly? Muriel never touches him, or asks about his week, or notices his haircuts, but neither does she mention a boyfriend, and she always meets him at the door looking woozy and grateful, and ensures the cot in the control room has clean sheets, and one wondrous Sunday, after they have traded shifts for five months, she pokes him on the shoulder and says, "I always say, Basil, if you want something, you need to just go for it."

How many times during the next week, alone on the volcano, does Basil parse the possible implications of that sentence? Did she mean "you" as in the impersonal *you*, or did she mean "you" as in Basil, and "something" as in *her*? And could she have meant "it" as in *doodle-bopping*, as in *jingle-jangling*, as in sexual relations, and has she been waiting all these weeks for him to "just go for it"?

The next Sunday, after seven straight nights at fourteen thousand feet, Basil cuts fifty paper hearts from the pages of a protocol manual, writes a different simile on each—*I love you like a fish loves water; I love you like we're eggs and bacon*—and stashes the hearts all over the observatory: behind doors, rolled up inside the toilet paper, taped to the back of her Raisin Bran. Muriel comes up and Basil heads down, and all that week he imagines her discovering his valentines. She'll be euphoric, flattered, at least amused, but the following weekend, as he is packing for his next shift, the supervisor calls from Waimea to say that Basil has been reported for making inappropriate advances, that a lawyer is involved, that they are going to have to let him go.

He finds a job at an ophthalmologist's in Eugene, then a Lens-Crafters in Pocatello, the ninth-happiest city in Idaho, hoping that an increase in distance will correspond with a decrease in heartbreak, but every few nights he dreams of volcanoes and flame-haired goddesses and humiliation. *I love you like the sky loves blue. I love you like putting up the Christmas tree.* What happens to all the one-sided desire in the world? Does it dissipate into the air, or does it flit around from soul to soul, anxious, haunted, looking for a place to land?

The nineties turn into the 2000s. One Thursday at a foosball tournament, eleven years after leaving Hawaii, Basil is handcuffed by a drunken English department secretary named Mags Futrell who makes fun of his name for half an hour, then kisses him right on the mouth.

Mags drives a Ford Ranger, has eyes like holes burned through a blanket, prefers Def Leppard to silence, and wears a T-shirt to sleep that says, *Lips that touch liquor touch other lips quicker.* She and Basil have a backyard wedding, and mortgage a two-bedroom rancher on Clark Street across from Al's Comix Warehouse, and Mags stays mostly sober through a pregnancy, and produces a bug-eyed infant named Otis, and during Otis's first year on Earth, Basil pushes his stroller up every hill in Pocatello, shedding pounds like he's shedding insecurities, and on his best nights he stops brooding over what life could have been and starts appreciating it for what it is.

But when Otis turns five, Basil catches Mags mixing Jack Daniel's into her morning Pepsi, and discovers a fifth in her glove compartment and a pint in her snow boots, and when he confronts her, she says, "Sure, Basil, I'll cut down on my drinking, how about I only drink on days that end with *Y*." Then she books a room at the Ramada and does not come home for four nights.

Around this time Otis starts wearing an off-brand black superhero cape day and night, every hour of every day—to kindergarten, to dinner, to sleep. Dr. O'Keefe says the boy is responding to "an atmosphere of stress" in his home environment, that he'll outgrow it, but soon Otis is six, then eight, and Mags is regularly heading to the guest room at bedtime with a Solo cup full of enough Wild Turkey to tranquilize a zebra, and Otis won't take off his cape even to shower, and for Basil, driving home from Lens-Crafters every evening has started to feel like a prison sentence.

In October Al's Comix Warehouse goes out of business, and a portly, white-bearded contractor named Nicholas starts putting crews to work on the building, erecting drum towers on the facade, and hanging a portcullis above the entrance, and in March a sign goes up that says, THE MASTER'S CASTLE COMING SOON, flanked by two aluminum skulls on posts with spotlights shooting out of their heads.

Nicholas assures Basil that it's all family-friendly, zoned for "entertainment"—"just keeping it secret to generate interest," he says, and winks over his bifocals, and tries to high-five Otis, who wants nothing to do with high fives from strangers—and although Nicholas has a kind face and even resembles a sawdust-covered, dentally challenged Saint Nick, it's hard not to worry that the Master's Castle is going to be some kind of S & M dungeon, that soon Clark Street will be clogged with perverts in hot pants, that Basil's already battered home value will sink to zero, that his wife needs the kind of help he can't give, that his son might be damaged in some fundamental way, and that his life has descended to a nadir only a few, very particularly sorry lives reach.

Today though, the first of April, Mags wakes before Basil and scrambles a dozen eggs, and announces she's going to clamber back on top of the heap, vacuum the truck, get an oil change, and promises Basil she'll drive Otis to his appointment with Dr. O'Keefe after school, and Basil leaves LensCrafters at four p.m. feeling buoyant, and he empties the house of alcohol—pouring out the cooking sherry, the mouthwash, even the vanilla extract—and prepares a mushroom casserole, and preheats the broiler, and watches an Internet video of a cat doing yoga, and another about a dolphin who turns pink when he's sad, then clicks a link to a story about a new bestselling book called *Memoirs of a Planet Hunter* and Basil's heart catapults into his mouth because the face that blooms across his iPad belongs to Muriel MacDonald.

Same green eyes, same narrow nose, slim, dignified, posed against a pillar in a lab coat, an orange-haired Joan Didion for the telescope set. Even now, after twenty years, to see the pale knobs of her clavicles floods Basil with a longing that threatens to capsize the kitchen.

The article describes how Muriel leads a NASA astronomical team that has discovered 540 extrasolar planets, including a sister Earth sixty light-years away, a rocky world only slightly smaller than ours, with life-friendly temperatures, and now she is slated to win a National Academy of Sciences medal, appear on the *Today* show, and eat lamb shanks with Queen Elizabeth. He downloads *Memoirs of a Planet Hunter*. Chapter 1 opens with seven-year-old Muriel building cardboard rockets. Chapter 2 covers high school. By page 40 she's in Hawaii, interviewing with the observatory.

"Okay," Basil says to the empty kitchen. "Okay, okay, okay."

Out the window Nicholas exits the Master's Castle carrying plywood. The sky is purple. Somehow it has become six fifteen p.m., and shouldn't Mags have had Otis home by five o'clock? Basil slides his casserole onto the center rack, and sits at the table beneath a waterfall of memory.

The way the observatory loomed in the dusk, its dome pale against the sky. The way he'd have to rest his hands on his knees when he'd get out of the Jeep just to catch his breath, heart thudding, dust blowing across the summit. He brought Muriel his grandmother's macaroni and cheese; he bought her a Michael Bolton CD because the guy at the record shop in Hilo said Bolton was the white Stevie Wonder.

> *I love you like Saturday mornings when you wake up and realize*
> *you don't have school.*
> *I love you like the wind loves kites.*

Maybe he came on a little strong, maybe he was a little naive, but at least what he offered was pure, wasn't it?

On page 48, he reads:

> *Every seven days the other optics technician, a man—they were*
> *always men—would roll back up, blinking and slow from the*
> *altitude, and I'd be blinking and slow from seven days of thin*
> *air and sleep deprivation.*
> *I was learning things in the cold nights, in the silence, in*
> *the spray of stars that would show when the big door rolled*
> *back and they poured their ancient light onto the mirror. I was*
> *learning how to see.*
> *When the other optics tech came up, I didn't ever want to go.*

Then it's chapter 3, and Muriel is off to Caltech, the Kepler program, a photo shoot with Annie Leibovitz, et cetera, and is it possible that in the 460-page story of Muriel's life, Basil didn't warrant a single sentence?

He scrolls ahead, scans for his name, uses the search tool—*no results found.* The clock reads seven fifteen p.m., Clark Street is dark, everything smells like a forest fire—the kitchen, his life—and the smoke detector screeches, and Basil opens the oven door to a rolling wave of smoke and hurries his smoldering casserole out the door and flings the pan into the front yard. At 7:20 he's standing on a kitchen chair, yanking the smoke detector off the ceiling, when Mags's Ford Ranger rolls over the curb and skids past the casserole and comes to a stop with its front bumper inside the hedges.

Otis sprints through the front door sobbing, making for his bedroom—no cape flying behind him—and Mags leaves the truck lights on and the driver's door open and comes seesawing through the door with her giant handbag.

"Reeks like fuck-all in here."

"What happened to Otis?"

Mags paws through cabinets.

"Where were you? Where is Otis's cape?"

A half-dozen bottles roll across the floor. "I took it."

"Dr. O'Keefe said to confiscate his cape?"

"Not Dr. O'-flipping-Keefe, me, me, me. I took him to O'Keefe's and then we stopped at the Ramada and everyone agreed that third grade is too old to wear a cape, that all the kids who don't think he's a freak already will think so soon, so I took it."

"You brought our son to a bar?"

"I took him to see people. *Sane* people!" And she slides to the floor, and Basil drops the smoke detector in the sink and puts a frozen pizza in the oven and goes out the front door and backs the still-running, still un-vacuumed Ranger off the lawn and parks in the driveway and sits a moment behind the wheel wondering about distance and the other world Muriel found sixty light-years away.

When he goes back inside, Mags is slumped against the dishwasher. "April," she says, "the month to throw yourself off things." Basil can just see the hem of Otis's cape sticking out of her handbag, so he balls it up in his back pocket and slides the half-cooked pizza from the oven and hacks it into slices and carries two plates and a glass of milk into Otis's room and shuts the door and the two of them sit on the carpet, and Otis sips his milk, and Basil ties the cape around his son's neck, over his parka the way he likes it, and Otis brings its hem to his face and wipes his eyes. They eat their pizza, and the house is quiet, and after a while Otis runs Lego cars over the carpet. Basil imagines driving Otis straight to the Pocatello airport and flying all night and queuing up outside *The Today Show* just as Muriel begins her appearance. She'll see him pressed against the studio window and cock her head in amazement; she'll tell Al Roker—right in the middle of "Today's Take"—that she is realizing only now that she made a mistake, that you never lose by loving, you only lose by holding back, and at her insistence security will escort Basil and Otis onto the set, and Al Roker's producer will whisper into Al's flesh-colored earpiece, *Twitter is going bananas, keep this rolling*, and Muriel will throw her arms wide and say, "Get in here, Mr. Basil Bebbington from Bakersfield," and Basil will look thin on TV, and Al Roker will don a cape in honor of Otis, and by nightfall half of America will be wearing capes, everyone superhero-ing everything, and Al will invite them to spend the weekend in his brownstone, and Basil will cook his mushroom casserole, and Basil and Otis will monitor storms on Al's rooftop X-band Doppler radar, and Al will poke his head through the hatch onto his roof deck and say, "Basil, that was the best goddamn casserole I've tasted in my life," and Basil will say, "Thank you, Al, but please don't swear in front of my son."

Lego men colonize Basil's ankles. He retrieves the carbonized casserole from the yard and scrapes the remains into the garbage can in the garage. Across the street, the twin spotlights of the Master's Castle rise into the sky. He says, "We could go to Florida. Stay with my parents."

Back inside, Mags snores against the dishwasher. He places a pillow under her head, and hand-washes the dishes, and the boiler in the basement exhales its ancient, burnt-hair smell, and when Basil next looks out the window, he sees Nicholas the contractor set something on the front step. The old man gives a wave, and his truck drives off, and Basil is still a moment, then opens the door and there on the front step are two headlamps and an envelope that says, *Seems like you and the kid could use a night out.*

Inside: a skull key chain bearing a single key.

Basil looks at the iPad still on the table, the shape of Mags on the floor, the key in his hand. Then he walks into Otis's room and stretches the band of a headlamp around his son's head.

He leads Otis out the back door so he doesn't see his mother, and they switch on their headlamps and cross Clark Street and stand in front of the Master's Castle. In the strange, purple light it looks large and frightening, a temple risen from some Mephistophelean underworld.

"We're going *in* there?" asks Otis. Basil turns the key, imagining ball gags and pommel horses, middle-aged men in latex trussed up in clotheslines, but in the beam of his headlamp, maybe twenty feet away, he sees what looks like a ten-foot-tall toy castle complete with battlements and turrets and pennants. Spiraling around it are pastures and villages, populated with waist-high windmills and stables, and what appears to be an actual flowing river, and everywhere five-foot-tall miniature oaks hold up thousands of real-looking leaves, and three-inch woodcutters stand beside wagons, the whole thing meticulous and miraculous in the strange light, and Basil blinks on the threshold, confused, overwhelmed, until Otis says, "Dad, it's Putt-Putt!"

To their left, down a cobbled path, stands a sign saying, *Hole #1*, with two putters and two golf balls and a little scorecard waiting on an apron of real-looking grass. Otis, in his big blue coat with his cape trailing off the back and the little cyclopic light of the headlamp glowing in the center of his head, looks up at his father and says, "Ready?"

They pick up the putters, one long-handled, one short, and set their balls in the little dots, and begin.

They play over ramps, through tunnels, under staircases, little wooden ponies drowsing in little wooden stables, mini blacksmiths frozen beside mini anvils, tiny swallows nesting under the eaves of the tiny cottages, everything detailed down to the tongs in the blacksmiths' hands. With each hole they wind closer to the great castle at the center, and Otis keeps score, and they roll their balls over moats, and Basil watches his sweet, mysterious son bend over each stroke, concentrating hard. And so what if he's not a shadow in Muriel's memory? She dreamed her dream after all, found her other Earth, just like Nicholas found his, and sometimes people just love who they love and what can you do about that? There are advantages in not getting what you want. Basil starts computing the realities of moving to Florida—plane tickets, separation from Mags, custody, schools, the size of his parents' condo in Tampa—but rather than feel overwhelmed, he feels light, even dizzy, as if he has rapidly ascended from sea level to fourteen thousand feet and can see the vast glimmering platter of the Pacific stretched out below.

They reach the eighteenth hole, Otis up by twenty, and the castle walls loom in the beams of their headlamps, little wooden guards in guardhouses peering down at them and little archers in archer loops and little golden chains holding up the drawbridge. Otis places his ball on the tee and looks at his father and says, "I'm not ready to give up my cape."

"I know, kid."

"I just need it a little longer."

"You take your time."

Otis sets his feet and whacks his ball straight up a ramp, and it flies right into a hole in the center of the drawbridge, a one-in-a-thousand shot, and some kind of machinery inside the castle comes to life. The three-inch guards lower their four-inch halberds, and the archers on the battlements lower their bows, and lights glow in the windows of the keep and in the towers and in the miniature oaks, and what looks like real smoke rises from chimneys, and the drawbridge comes down like the maw of a terrible beast, and a royal guard of bannermen marches out from the castle and stands to each side, and between them a harpist slides out, moving on some kind of indiscernible track, and begins to pluck her tiny instrument, and though it might be his imagination, Basil hears the tune of Stevie Wonder's "Higher Ground" . . .

No one's gonna bring me down
Oh no
'Til I reach my highest ground

. . . and the harpist plays and the castle glows, and when the song ends she turns, and slides back into the castle, and the royal guard retreats, and the drawbridge rises, and the lights in the windows wink out one by one, and the warehouse goes dark again.

Otis waves the scorecard and says, "I wrecked you, Dad." They lock the door behind them and stop on the edge of Clark Street and switch off their headlamps. Above them a few stars burn above clouds. A jet glides past, flashing its wing lights.

Tiphanie Yanique

The Living Sea

A ROAD OF SAND SEPARATED THE SEAS. Just a thin band of sand, which was the real bitch of it. The beach of death on the right was calm, encircled as it was by a wall of rocks. The living beach, to the left, opened wild to the ocean. We went every Sunday after Mass. Those who could swim proper went to life. But I couldn't fucking swim, so I always soaked in death.

Vega Baja was my home for only a few years. Enough time to learn to swim, to curse when needed, and to meet a boy. Though not at all in that order, I must say. The boy, of course, was Martin. Spelled without the accent, but still pronounced Mar-teen. There were many of us there at the home in Vega Baja. The boundaries of the region were not as they are now. The Caribbean waters were highways, not fucking national borders. So we children went and came. Children from Tortola, from Antigua, even from far away as Trinidad. I came from St. Thomas. Lost children, we was. Orphaned. Martin was from San Juan—a native. Still, he was an abandoned motherscunt, just like the rest of us.

Martin was not a mystery. No one was. The island was American, but Spanish was the language of public school instruction. As far as us picky heads could say, we would all be Puerto Ricans from here on, so before each child's arrival the women would offer the new one's personal history in Spanish. The woman with the private school education and gentle manners would translate the basics into English. This way all of us could be ready with our empathy—no bullying or nastiness. In truth, I cannot believe they did that shit to us. The women. They did not understand a child's need for secrets, the child's desire to tell her own story and make herself new. When Martin finally came it seemed he was a man, not a lost child at all. But there he was. Sleeping on the boys' side of the house with the rest of them.

"My mother is not dead, como dijeron las mujeres," he clarified to anyone who asked anything at all. "Ella esta en San Juan." But what was worse—a dead mother or a living mother who didn't want you? "Es verdad, I do not know my father. Pero él quería conocerme. It is just that my mother wanted to keep me as hers, solo."

It made no fucking sense, of course, but I believed him. He did seem like someone who had been loved most of his life, loved recently. In that way, he was different from the rest of us. We was all in awe of him, jealous to be truth.

We went to Mass every Sunday without fail. The Vega Baja beach after, always. Like church and beach were both holy. But none of us were allowed to climb the rocks on the beach. A local boy had died jumping. Had dived safely, feet first, but still hadn't come back up until he was fucking floating facedown. And then before anyone could save his body, it had been swept through life and out into the ocean. Besides our chores around the farm, this was the only rule at the home. No climbing the maricones rocks. Easy for me. I was scared to fucking death of the water.

The women slept in the same room, together, despite the large farmhouse. Us children slept in the house, too, separated into

the female side of the house and the male. The kitchen and parlor connecting us easily. The women had never had children of
their own, and so did not remember their own childhoods, as
parenthood may cause one to do. We were all at least five when
we came; we could cook simple meals, wash our own clothes, iron
them even. We could communicate in complete sentences, most
of us in Spanish and English. And so the women didn't expect our
innocence, our wildness, our curiosity, our fears. And of course we
didn't speak up to explain. We were grateful, all of us, that they
had taken us in. Even Martin was grateful, I know.

I was the middle girl. Thirteen years old. The elder girl, Darleen, kept a bag of what she said were her own baby teeth around
her neck. She was too odd for regular school, so did her high
school classes via correspondence. The baby girl was six—besides
the burns, she was normal, not even coonoo with water like me.
Her parents had died in a fire and she didn't yet go to school at
all. I alone went to the municipal middle school along with the
stupid small boys. On school mornings one of the women would
braid my hair.

Martin was the eldest boy—fifteen. When he came he was the
only one of us who walked the hour to the high school in the
morning. He began to walk me and the small boys to the small
school, then continue on. He held my hand from the very first
day, like my elder brother would have done if he hadn't drowned
along with my everyone else. Besides braiding my hair, no one
had taken this kind of care with me; no one had even held my
fucking hand in years.

It was on these walks that Martin told his version of how he
came to us.

He had been leaving his school in Río Piedras and seen his
mother at the gate. He was fourteen then and she had stopped
picking him up from school years before. Now here she was holding a board with words on it. In English: *They have stolen my son*

from me. I will kill myself. Please help! Martin was a good student, well-known by the teachers and staff for his diligence in all subjects, evidenced most by his neat penmanship.

Now everyone watched as he walked up to his mother. But his mother didn't seem to see him. He stood in front of her. "Mamá. I'm right here. Look, I'm right here." And he shook his face in front of hers until she met his eyes. "Ay, Dios mío. Estás aquí. They gave you back. Now I can live." For fucking real.

He took the sign from her, ignoring the teachers and students who looked on; they unsure of whether to help this boy or hamper his mother. His mother had been looking for him, so she said, for weeks, even though he'd just left her that morning for school. "Mamá, everything is fine. Estoy aquí. I was at school."

The next morning she was herself again. But now he noticed that herself was freaking strange. Something he had never considered before. She had always been a woman who talked to herself, but he had never before asked about it.

"Estoy practicando," she said now. Practicing? He didn't want to know for what. She had been practicing for this his whole life.

When he left for school that next morning, she kissed him on the mouth. Again, this was something she had always done. But he knew this was not normal. Had known for a while, hadn't he? She took his chin in her fingers and kissed his mouth gently. And for the first time ever he felt the tremor in his crotch and pulled back from her. Outside of the door, he pressed the flat of his hand against the front of his pants until it calmed.

But after school there she frigging was again. At the gate, only this time she was shouting. "They have taken my son! I'm going to kill myself! Kill my whole self!" He rushed to her and grabbed her face until she stared in his eyes and knew him. The students and teachers tittered around.

On the third day, she was crying and she had another sign with more crazy-ass words. The headmaster came out now, but talked to Martin and not his mother. *"She cannot do this again.*

We will call the police. Maybe you need to take some time off from school." Like Martin was a man. They spoke in English to make it all official.

It turned out that one of the women at our home in Vega Baja was Martin's aunt. The Spanish-speaking bitchy one with the mustache who wore pants and boots. The one who rode the horses and never milked the cows. The women had taken him in as family, so he wasn't even a proper orphan. "Martin's mother is dead," both women had told us—a fucking falsehood, we now assumed. We began to wonder if they had told us other lies. If the baby girl was not from Trinidad but from India, as she looked. If Joseph was the five years old he appeared to be and not the ten the women claimed.

"Mi madre está viva," Martin said. "Very alive."

On Sundays after Mass the women walked us to the seas; sometimes we would skip the whole way. Sometimes we would sing. All the children swam in the living, except me. Even baby girl, who was the youngest. I stayed in the death. There, I could walk out to the mountain of rocks and still the water only came to my hips. My brother had known how to swim, but it hadn't saved him.

But on Martin's first Sunday with us he came up behind me in the shallow water. He placed his arm on my back and bent to cradle my legs. I didn't squeal as I knew strange Darleen would have—she was almost seventeen and had novios who were always leaving genips under our windowsill. I let Martin lift me and then gently lower me until I floated in the still water, his hands holding me up. I lay out stiff as a corpse and felt the sun above me.

I knew what my body looked like. I was straight and flat as a board in all directions and now in the water I imagined myself to be a board. Floating, floating in the dead sea. What waves there were, were gentle, and more gentle. Martin's hands below loosened. And then loosened more. I felt the coolness of the water between his hands and my body. I kept my eyes closed up tight. A board, I told myself. A board. I steadied my breathing. The water beneath me warmed. I moved my arm to feel for Martin. But he wasn't fucking there, and I opened my eyes in a panic and flailed, though my feet hit sand quickly.

I looked around and saw him, across the sand dune in the living water, standing against the heavy waves and speaking with little Joseph, who was squatting in the water. Only Joseph's head came above the sea line; it bobbed like it was the only part of him. I looked away, scared as shit and stupid.

How long had Martin left me? How long had I floated on my own? At my feet little sparkling fish swam in circles. I laid my head back, stretched myself out, and then I just floated. I didn't think about my actual older brother. I thought and thought only of Martin.

The next Sunday Martin taught me how to kick. He crouched down and put my palms on his shoulders so that our faces were close, close. And I kicked and kicked. After a month of Sundays I could actually fucking swim.

The boys' side of the house was not forbidden to the girls, nor was ours to the boys. It was an arrangement but not a rule. Often children would fall asleep in the living room, laid out on the rug. On our side the girls all shared a room and the women had the other one. On the boys' side, Martin had his own room, like he alone was equal to the women.

On the Sunday night after the day I finally swam, I left my bed as soon as the other girls slept. I walked through the kitchen and parlor, which were dark. The women always turned in early. Martin's door was locked when I jostled the knob. I stood in front of it, staring at the door, until it opened. His room was moist and black, his windows closed and curtained. When I found his bed, he was in it. He took my chin with his fingers and kissed me on the mouth, his tongue stiff. I thought then that I was the sea, and he was a board and he would float in me.

"Náyade," he said into my mouth. I wanted to say something back to him, but "shark" was all I could think of. And I didn't know how to say it yet in Spanish. His body was hot as he turned onto his back and took me with him. Me in my nightie and his whole naked body beneath mine. "If you love me," he said, "we will get married. But only if you really love."

I tried to look into his face, but it was so dark. "Okay," I said.

"When I am awarded my high school diploma," he said. "When I secure a job. When you have la edad suficiente."

"How old will I have to be?" I asked.

"¿Dieciséis?" he said like a question. Girls regularly left school at sixteen, started work. Sometimes married. There wasn't a girl over seventeen still at the orphanage. Darleen was almost like one of the women herself, though she didn't have their command. I never quite knew what would become of that Darleen. "Sister," she used to call us girls; "brother," she called the boys. Though she never called Martin that. And in truth, I didn't feel like Darleen was my sister then. I had not had a sister, and I didn't know what it should feel like.

"Can it be when I am fifteen?" I asked Martin. Two years was too fucking long to wait to make him my family. I knew well how quickly things could change.

"We can try," he said. And then he lifted my nightie. And it began. His wet fingers, then his wet mouth, then the tip of him already slick. There was a tightness and then a sudden relinquishing and then warmth.

"Mi madre," he said afterward, "loves me very much." I understood.

My mother had loved me, too, until the water took her.

When I left his room, the women were already up and out tending the horses and cows. The other children feeding the chickens and gathering eggs. "¿Dormiste bien, hermanita?" Darleen asked when I rushed to the feed pail. "No, puta," I said. "I haven't slept as yet." I didn't want to tell anyone, but I didn't think it was necessary to lie either.

The TV was on to the news, "Sandra Dayo Conner" the anchor kept shouting in Spanish, like the woman in the black robes was a superhero. The woman without the mustache sat me down in front of the TV, between her legs, to do my hair. Every morning she tackled my head and she complained about its toughness. I always held my face stiff against crying, her tight fist at my roots, the comb raking through the ends. But today she was too focused on the news. "There is a woman in the Supreme Court," she said, "and it is time, negrita, that you did your own hair." Was it the woman judge on the TV, her hand on the actual Bible, that made it clear? Or was it that the woman without the mustache could see that I was more grown, more of a damn woman, than I had been the morning before?

"Puedo trenzar su cabello," Martin said. "I always did my mother's hair." He sat beside the woman. I didn't see, but I felt her get up and then Martin straddled me between his legs and I felt the brush in my hair gently and the comb sliding. On TV, the woman judge was confirmed. She was pretty, with curled hair. Everyone on the TV and there in the home seemed proud of her, and I felt jealous. But Martin focused on me, took so long with my hair that the younger boys left for school without us. Martin twisted instead of braiding—so that my hair looked like gentle puffs on both sides of my head, and not the fierce plaits the woman had always forced.

And that was how it was. Me in his bed every night. Him doing my hair every morning. Us walking to school together and alone now, him holding my hand. And then on Sundays, just us in the death. He never touched me in the water, but any fucking idiota could see I was being touched somehow, sometime. There were my breasts suddenly. There were my hips. But in the water, underneath the sun, I would touch him, too. The water was perfectly clear and I liked to see my hands on him. "Náyade. Sirena," he called me as I moved my wrist. Mermaid, mermaid. Right there for everyone to see. For me to see, gazing into the clear water, watching him, watching my hands. Except no one saw but us. Only we were on the dead side.

Weeks after I had turned fourteen, a thing I knew but that no one took note or notice of, Martin sat me down to twist my hair. He leaned in and whispered into my neck. "You are a woman now." It was true that blood had been on his sheets that morning. I had noticed, but that was how it was sometimes with us. Sometimes it was milk, sometimes it was blood. "No," he said into my ear. "This is your real blood." Did this mean we would marry now? That he could be my family?

On the walk to school he explained. "We cannot continue. You will become pregnant. I will be seventeen soon, but you are still not fully grown yet." I didn't remind him that we were getting married. It was the first time I felt he could abandon me. I let my hand go limp in his, but he squeezed hard.

That night I did not go to him. I lay in bed and wondered what I would do if he left me. I would stay here at the home. I would be like the women, sleeping with other women and working the farm. Perhaps raising other people's children because I didn't have any who belonged to me. The other two girls slept as they usually did. In her sleep Darleen always gripped the pouch of her teeth, like it was precious. But after not a minute Darleen sat up. She looked at me as though she was quite awake. "¿No vas?" she asked. And I realized that everyone must have known. "She got her period," baby girl said, even though that little burnt bitch too had seemed well asleep. "Muy malo para ti," Darleen said, lying back down, clutching the pouch again. "Sister, now all the fun in your life is over."

So my life was over. Again, it was over. But then the knob

rustled and Martin opened the door. Our room was more lit than his, the girls' windows always open with the large moon shining in. "Sirena," Martin called in a whisper. And I got off the bed and went to him.

Instead of going to his room, we walked to the beach with the tide-pulling moon above. It was a school night, so Mass and the beach were still days away. It was the wrong day and it was also too late at night, but still we walked into the water. We went to the living side, which we never did. Which I had never done before. And we did what we'd always done in the death—only now when I touched him he had to hold me with both his hands, so our bodies would not be taken by the waves. Afterward we sat in the sand and watched the big moon and he said, "We can still marry, Mermaid." I leaned my head on his shoulder and he put his arm around me. But he had more. "My mother is getting out of the hospital." He said this with his gaze on the two lobes of life and death.

"Volveré a San Juan. I will go back to being a boy with a mother," he said. "I am not a man. Realmente no."

"You're seventeen," I managed to say, though I was scared as shit.

"Not yet," he said. "And she is still my mother. And now that she is better, yo soy de ella."

I began to cry. And he held me until I wrenched from him. I walked through the familiar dead water, stepped onto the road of sand, and then began to climb the rocks. I had never climbed the rocks before, but if you know anything about how stories work, you know I was heading to those fucking rocks all along.

I did it like I'd gone to Martin's room that first night; I did it without thinking. One finger of blood was crawling down my thighs because I'd left the cloth the women had given me. The rocks were sharp and hurt my feet and I couldn't always see. I stepped on something slimy—I slipped. I felt blood come to my leg, a different blood. But still, I climbed until I saw the other side. Really, I could hear it more than see it. I could hear the spitting spray and I could hear the wind wheezing. And all I could see was the white frothing of the waves, gleaming like teeth in the moonshine. It meant something, to have climbed that rock. It meant something that there, just there, was the true swallowing ocean. But I didn't have the words for the meaning. I was a woman now, but I was still, mostly, a girl. A baby mermaid.

I stood there for a long time. Then I turned back to the shore, to sight Martin. But he wasn't there. I looked into the waters of life and death, and he wasn't there either. And I looked down the rocks and didn't see him climbing after me.

Don't fucking forget that it was the middle of the night. I was a half-hour walk, at best, from the women and the other children. My mother and father and brother had all died by drowning four years before. And now I was high up on the rocks at the beach. I mean, I was only fourteen fucking years old.

I opened my eyes wide and tried to see. Was that another person on the rocks now? A bad person coming to steal me? A wild dog coming to bite me? No, it was just a casha bush shivering in the wind. What was that in the water below? A hungry chupacabra swimming? A shark surfacing? I knew the word for shark by now—tiburón. Like someone's last name.

Maybe that would be me, Sirena Tiburón. Mermaid Shark. But though maybe I was a mermaid, I would never be a shark. My disposition was too warm, despite my hot mouth. I sat on the summit of the rocks and I cursed louder than the sea. I wanted anything living or dead to know that I could scream. I thought of all the bad words I knew: fuck, shit, ass, bitch, mothcrscunt, maricón, puta, cabrón, pendejo. I shouted but the tears also came. I did all that until I was tired. Then I waited. Not for Martin. I waited for the sun. It would come up and then I would be able to see and climb down and then I would wade through death. And then I would go back to the home and go be a little orphan girl again. A girl who didn't belong to anyone.

I waited for hours. My throat was burning from the tears I swallowed. I saw him, my tiburón, when the sun started to rise. He was walking along the beach, calm and cool and his body sloping. It was then that I really noticed that something was not normal about him. That he was not a normal boy. He had, maybe, what his mother had. He didn't resemble a grown-up at all. The woman with the mustache was more man than he.

We hadn't known then that I would be taller than him by the time I stopped growing. We hadn't known then that I would call him Papito, for his small size. But Martin was sick, that would become certain, and I would love him because he was all I had until I had you. A mermaid love for my shark man. Even when he frothed, even when the sickness shook him to a frenzy. But that day, simply by returning for me, Martin had done everything I would ever need. Made you possible. Made this fucking future possible.

He stood at the shore until I climbed down and waded out. He had packed his things. He had packed my things. They were in the same one bag he carried.

"Can you be in San Juan?" he asked, as if he wasn't sure I could exist anywhere else but there between life and death. I nodded. I could be wherever he was.

And that is what we did. We went to San Juan and retrieved his mother. But we weren't like before. We were brother and sister now, neither of us an orphan. He slept on the couch and I in his old room. Sometimes at night he and his small mother, smaller even than he was, would sleep on the couch together. Sometimes I would walk out and see them. I would stand over them. Embraced, maybe like a mother cradled her baby, only this baby could carry her. Hateful bitch, I would think of her but never say. We never spoke of her sickness. We never spoke of my odd arrival—a sudden sister, a sudden daughter. It was like I had always been there, but that I had always been the less loved child. Like any daughter when there is a son. I combed my own hair now. We went to Mass, as always, but there was no more beach.

Martin would do his mathematics and literature into the night. And sometimes in the morning he would still be there at the table, erasing and redoing—that perfect penmanship. On those days, I would sit him between my legs and comb his hair. Wavy boricua hair, like our old ocean. I would tell him how sharp and strong his letters were, how architecturally fine his algebraic fucking equations. I was learning how to really love him, I suppose. The way I would always love. With care. Carefully.

But his mama, she was still sick. If we were ever alone, she would often ask me what I had said, even when I had said nothing. And my Martin was also strange. Sometimes I would reach for him, as I used to. But he would turn an empty look on me and gently step away. He never called me anything but Mermaid. And so that was what Mama called me, too. They said it in English, though my Spanish was good by then. The island was still, always, seesawing Spanish to English—national language versus official. But in our home it was clear. Martin and Mama were nationalist with each other—official with me.

Some nights I lay in bed and touched myself. In the morning I would raise my fingers to Martin's nose and he would wrinkle it as though he didn't know the scent. "You stink," he would say. Like any older brother.

I was no longer a board in the sea. I was no longer the sea with him in me. There must have been an ocean somewhere near, but nestled in our neighborhood, we never went to it. Boys at the school noticed me. I was more developed than the other girls my age. And now when we walked to school I lurched my hand out of Martin's. I stepped away from him. I had been touched too early. Abandoned too early. There was a difficult future ahead of me.

But it motherfucking happened, again, just like Martin had told. Mama came to our school with the placard. Only this time it read: *They have stolen my son and my daughter! I will slash my wrists! I will hang myself from the highest tree!* This time the headmaster didn't wait for us to even step out of the school doors.

"Mermaid," Martin said to me as we watched the ambulance swim away. "I am graduating from high school in just a few weeks. What do you want to do now? We can go back to the dead sea. Or we can go to where you are from."

So I took that boy back to St. Thomas, where my mother and father and brother each had a stone in the Western Cemetery, though their bodies had never been found. A month after we left, Martin's mother hung herself in the Ramón Marina crazy-people place. She'd braided the rope from palm leaves—an art project, the nurses had thought. What I thought was: crazy bitch, but brilliant.

Martin and I married a week after Princess Diana did. We watched the whole long drawn-out thing on TV like it was a fucking tutorial. We'd never seen a wedding before. On our day, other girls and boys were lined up at the cathedral like getting married was style. No one had a dress like Diana's; mine seemed simplest of all. A white dress I'd made myself of cloth I'd stolen from a woman whose house I cleaned. That was my life then. Not like the life Dad and I have made for you and your brothers. But regardless of my plain dress and thieving ways, my Martin looked only at me, like I was a princess. I was fifteen years old. Every Sunday of our marriage we went to Mass and then to the beach. Our ritual.

Together we shark and mermaid had you. Took us some time to get to that. Something about him, his man parts, made it hard. But it was good we managed that, you, because I knew I wouldn't have Martin for long. He had a Jonah death wish. Always trying to find a reason to get himself killed. "Throw me over," he would joke when we took the ferry to St. John for a day trip. Given both our histories, I would take that shit seriously, hold his body close to mine. I would have carried him inside of me if I could. He even tried to join the army, but they said he was slow. Good, I was glad of it.

You were born a decade into our marriage. By then I really was a fucking woman, and I was desperate for you. The doctor, a woman too, had warned that I might feel sad a bit, in the postpartum time. The happy hormones leaving me all at once, when your body left. But it wasn't me who was overcome with the wave of sadness. "Save yourself and throw me in," Martin would say. Until he climbed a mountain, of course, jumped in the water and swam away. Or drowned. Or hit a rock on the way down. Either way.

Who is ever to fucking know if I did the right thing, marrying so young to my shark boy? We were together a decade. Was he keeping himself alive just so you could come? Would he have stayed alive if you hadn't come? Well, I suppose there are entire histories that came before he and I even met, pushing us like currents.

But I decided to live. College, I thought, and it wasn't so hard then as it is now. Didn't cost so much, and if you were smart it could cost less. So I left the island for the States. Did well in college, finished so fast you don't even have any memories of Atlanta—though that is where you made your first steps, learned your first words. I fast found another love to love, another man to bring back to St. Thomas. A good man, the one who raised you. I had the boys, your brothers. Yes, I was vexed to not have Martin with me. Vexed that he'd finally left me and for good. That is how death fucking works. When we moved back to St. Thomas I put up a stone for Martin beside my parents and brother.

And now I am fucking glad to have given you my story. Of how I was afraid, but how love made me brave. And let me tell you, that has been a good enough way to live.

Joan Silber
Freedom from Want

M Y BROTHER'S LONGTIME BOYFRIEND decided to leave him, once and for all. Enough, he said, was enough. If you can't stop arguing after twenty years, when will you ever? Time for a new start for both of them. They would always be friends, of course. He would always care about Saul, but he really did not think that waking up every day in the same apartment was good for either of them.

This speech might have made sense except that my brother had just been diagnosed with some stage or other of liver cancer. (It was hard to get a full story out of Saul.) And the apartment, in the upper reaches of Manhattan, belonged to Kirk, the boyfriend. My brother, a fifty-seven-year-old librarian with no personal savings, was going to have to find a new place to live. For however long he planned to do that.

I was stunned and outraged by the news, maybe more than my brother was. Why had I ever liked Kirk? I had, I always had. With his deep voice, his good haircuts, his quiet merciless jokes. He called me Sister Susie (my name is Rachel, the name was his kidding). Sister Susie was a perky lass, always getting into the gin on the sly. We had a whole set of stories about her and her unusual relations with her dog Spot. Some of his friends thought I was really called Susie.

How could you decide to break up with someone who had a mortal illness? Who could do such a thing? Kirk could.

"The man is a fuck-head," I said to Saul. "And he has no honor."

"We never got along that well," Saul said. "Remember when he picked a fight with me in front of the entire Brooklyn library staff? He was always a pain. And you know how full of himself he's been. He thinks being a digital art director is like being Michelangelo—I always laughed at the way he used the word *creative*. Don't make a big deal out of this. It's not the end of the world."

Kirk had not given him any particular deadline for moving out, and everyone in New York knew couples who stayed together for years after breaking up, while prices rose and good deals slipped away. Meanwhile Kirk and my brother were sharing the same bed every night and were—I gleaned from my brother's remarks—still having what could be called sexual contact. I didn't blame Saul for mentioning it either, showing off a last bit of swagger. And maybe the breakup was just an idea, a flash-in-the pan theory.

Maybe Kirk didn't mean it.

"He says I'm lazy about being sick," Saul said. "I should do more, be proactive. Has anyone used that word since 1997?"

"What is it with him?" I said. "I don't get it."

"He's seeing someone new," Saul said.

"He's *what*?" I said. I had to stop wailing in protest, because it was useless and only increased my brother's suffering. He had his ties to Kirk; he didn't want to hear what I had to say. *No big deal* was his mantra, and there was probably a way to say it in Sanskrit or Pali. Even so, I hated to hear it.

I was his big sister, two years older, but we were both old now. I was the one with the more chaotic sexual history—I'd been with a long list of men and lived with some very poor choices—but time had passed since those days. The daughter of one of my boy-friends (I was never into marriage) still lived with me, after losing patience with both her parents, and she was already twenty-six. I loved Nadia, I was glad to have her with me, but my apartment wasn't really one that could fit her and me and my brother too. An old bargain of a place in Hell's Kitchen. Not that Saul had expressed any interest in moving in.

Was he looking at apartments? Not at the moment. At the moment he was busy going to a clinic where they inserted a needle into his tumors and a high-frequency current heated them to death. I went with him for this—it was not an adorable procedure—and it took a while. Nadia went to pick him up once. And Kirk went the rest of the time. He did.

Saul would go home to sleep after the procedures—who wouldn't?—and he'd lie around with headphones on watching Net-flix for hours when sleep evaded him. The library was giving him time off with no trouble, and maybe he was never going back. He was still losing weight; his nose looked bigger, outgrowing his face. It hurt my heart to look at him. "He could try to eat," Kirk said. "He doesn't even try. I buy things he likes, that he always liked. You know he likes those pecan crunch things. It doesn't matter."

I had my own life, of course, my own work, my own loyalties. I had a decent enough job in human resources (who dreamed up that name?) for a hotel chain, overseeing stingy policies and crazy rate changes. I was the old girl who'd been there forever and knew the ropes. Nadia liked to ask if I could game the system—get bil-lions paid out in insurance for someone who was healthy—but I had to tell her that was beyond me. Nadia had a youthful attitude about the possibilities of cheating. Anyway, one night I was buy-ing us supper at a Mexican place in the West Village that was a big favorite of hers, when I heard someone at a nearby table say, "Okay, be patient. Okay?"

I knew the voice; it was Kirk's. He was talking to a nice-looking dude in his forties, arguing in that weary, reasonable way of his. I knew that tone. It must be his new lover, this not-so-happy guy in a dark suit.

"I've been waiting a while," the guy said.

Oh, were they waiting for my brother to die? Or just to disappear, to crawl offstage? I was choking with fury. Did I want to rush over and make a scene, did I want to stay where I was to hear more?

"Hey!" Nadia said, solving the problem for me. "There's Kirk! Hey, Kirk!"

He took in the sight of us, waved. What a fuck-head. "Look at you," he called out to Nadia, across two tables in between. "You're looking great. Hi, Rachel. This is my friend Ethan." We all nodded at each other.

Even Nadia was taking things in. "Why does everybody all of a sudden know about this restaurant?" she said. "I hate the way it is now, all these people."

"Everybody knows everything nowadays," Kirk said.

"Not for the better either," I said.

"We had a very nice meal," Kirk said. "Didn't you think so, Ethan? We're almost done. Don't mind us. Enjoy your drinks."

And then he turned away from us and murmured something to the Ethan person. He could go ahead and pretend they were in another room, he could do what he wanted.

"They'll leave soon," I said to Nadia. Not that softly either.

Around us a speaker was playing, "Bésame, bésame mucho." The singer was pleading in long notes. We stood our ground, we chewed and drank. Nadia said, "I can't believe he had to bring him here." I didn't know they had left until, halfway through my second bottle of Dos Equis, I looked across and spotted other diners at that table.

"He thinks he's so slick," she said. "Mr. Not-Embarrassed."

"He's like Woody Allen—*the heart wants what it wants.*

Remember when he said that when he ran off with his step-daughter?" Nadia had probably not even been born then, but she'd heard about it. "People think if they're honest about their big cravings, it makes anything okay," I said. "That's a big fallacy of modern life."

I found out Nadia was doing what sounded like praying for my brother. She hadn't been raised in any religion (not with those parents), but she was a great reader online, she taught herself things. In the middle of the night I was in the hallway on my way to pee, when I heard her voice in the living room. "May Saul be better," I heard. "May he be well and happy. May he live with ease. May he live longer."

And who did she think was processing this request? I didn't ask. I didn't want to smudge the purity of whatever she was doing. I listened for her again as I walked down that hallway the night after, but no words vibrated in the air. The next morning, when I got up early, I saw that she slept (as always) flat on her back on the folded-out sofa, and the statue of the Buddha had been moved to a shelf in her line of sight. It was Saul's Buddha—that is, he had brought it to me after a trip somewhere. Thailand? Cambodia? It was a gray stone figure, the size of a gallon of milk, sitting with one hand raised with a flat palm. Fear not, that hand gesture meant. Saul had been a fan of Buddhism—he read books, he went to meditation classes, he explained very well how ego craving was the source of all suffering—but his interest had faded in the last few years. He hadn't said anything about leaning on it now. But Nadia was?

"You don't have to follow all the rules," she said, when I sort of asked. "People get so caught up in that. As if somebody twenty-five hundred years ago was the last one to know anything about spiritual matters. How could that be right?" What I'd heard as prayer were phrases from a Buddhist practice, but she had added flourishes, like setting out a green ribbon (I hadn't noticed) because Saul's favorite color was green.

At least she wasn't kneeling. When I was a child, my mother caught me kneeling by my bed, intoning, "Now I lay me down to sleep, I pray the Lord my soul to keep." (How did I even know that prayer?)

"Jews don't kneel," my mother said.

I got up right away. I sort of loved the urgency in my mother's voice. She spoke rarely about religious matters and sometimes made fun of what I learned in Hebrew school. This was serious. I wanted serious, that was why I was praying.

Like Nadia. All over the world (I traveled much in my wayward youth), people go in for petitionary prayer; they ask for concrete and specific things, even when they're not supposed to, according to their systems of belief. They set out flowers, fruit, candles, money. Tiny models of body parts they want fixed. Votive wishes on papers they pin on trees.

I looked at the green ribbon, a strip of satin left over from a Christmas package. Did she think a Higher Power could bring about what she wanted? "You never know," she said.

"Can't argue with that," I said, though I could have.

Nadia was nine when I first met her. I was dating Nick, her dad, and he had her on weekends. She kept calling me by the wrong name on purpose—Rochelle, Raybelle, Michelle—and looking at me with fiendish eyes. But she got over all that, eventually, and then she was nuzzling and cuddling like a much younger kid and saying she liked my house. She pocketed a spoon when she left (I saw, who cared?). I admired her resourcefulness, her range of attempts to be on top of the situation. She was working hard to watch out for herself. When her father later referred to her as a total pill—he liked that phrase—I said, "What kind of crap is that?"

. . .

Now it was Saul's turn to be a total pill. He talked too much about his ablation treatments, he talked too much about his liver. Once he had been happy to argue about how detective novels were good for the brains of middle-school kids and why online reading was a triumph against capitalism. Now he was like any patient, caught up in the drama of his own ordeals, his schedule of medications, the textures of his own shrinking world. I wanted him to be better than that.

"Sister Susie says you should have a joint," I said. "Your treatments are over. You can do what you want." I lit up while I was spreading this doctrine.

"What *do* I fucking want?" he said. But he took a hit. "There's nothing I want."

"Isn't that an ideal state in Buddhism?" I said.

"That's a gross simplification," Saul said. But he looked at least a little pleased. It was better news than he'd heard for a while.

"Did you know Nadia's been chanting on your behalf?"

"She told me," he said. "What a good girl she turned into."

He really wanted nothing? He had to want to live, if he was going to last a little longer. Indifference would drag him under. But maybe I wasn't paying attention properly.

Before my brother's diagnosis, my life had been in what felt like a good phase. Two crucial areas had shown improvement. An ex-boyfriend—everyone called him Bud—who'd left New York seven years before had started sending me e-mails. He'd gone off to Cambodia to work for an NGO, defending workers' rights, which clearly needed defending, there and here. We'd parted badly but we always remembered each other's birthdays, which was mature of us. On my last birthday, he'd written, "Hands across the water, hands across the sky," lines to a song I used to like. Once he started writing, I was always humming it in my head. And finally, at long last, Nadia seemed to be out of the woods—she'd left behind her habits of moping and quitting and having fits of fury and bouts of despair and going a little nuts. She was back in school, taking computer design classes at FIT that she liked to talk about; she was sane. I walked around feeling secretly smug, as if I'd been right about everything all along.

Which at least made it easier to be nice to Saul when he uttered the same complaints over and over. "I'm nauseated all the time," he said. "I hate it. I can't even barf. I can't do anything."

"You can't read?" I said. He was a librarian, for Christ's sake. The original escapist reader. Thrilled by discoveries, an enthusiast of hidden corners of information. "You want some audiobooks? You could be nauseated and listen at the same time."

"Never mind," he said. "You don't get it."

We were having this conversation in the bedroom of his and Kirk's apartment. He was sitting up in bed, wrapped in a blanket. The night table was a mess of pill bottles, old socks. Did he maybe want to smoke something? "It doesn't help," he said. "Why do people say it helps?"

Kirk was in the living room, tapping on his cell phone. He called out to Saul, "You know there's some of that mango smoothie in the fridge. Easy to swallow. Don't you think you would like that?"

"Why do you think I would like anything?" Saul said.

"Silly me," Kirk said.

Meanwhile, in the midst of this, Bud the old boyfriend had decided it was time for us to Skype each other—Phnom Penh to NYC. Hands across the water. "Rachel!" he said, when we were on each other's screens. I always loved his voice. It was Bud! His hair was shorter, grayer (so was mine but dyed). Had he always had that slight web under his chin? "Isn't this weird, this teledating?"

he said. Oh, we were dating? I could see the room behind him, a beaded curtain over a closet, an open window with green fronds outside.

"Is it hot there now?" I said. "It's snowing here."

"It's in the eighties. You'd like it. You like summer."

I'd been to parts of Southeast Asia when I was a restless young thing—Thailand and Malaysia—but people weren't going to Cambodia then, a postwar mess even to backpackers. "It's still a mess," he said.

"It's a mess here too," I said. I had already told him my worst Trump jokes. "The rich get richer. You know."

"What amazes me in my line of work," he said, "is the strength of people to go on." He had these moments of grandstanding but his points were good. "You see them come out of these factories where they work ten hours a day in suffocating heat, wages so low they can barely eat, and sometimes a girl is laughing at what her friend said. Too tired to move but something is still funny."

I was wondering if Bud could kid around with them in whatever they spoke. "Khmer," he said. "Khmer is Cambodian. It can take them a while to see I'm being funny on purpose."

He probably wasn't as hilarious as he imagined. "You should come visit," he said. "Come to Phnom Penh."

"Sure," I said, as if he really meant it, which I didn't think he did. As if I could go anytime, just like that.

I was at my desk at work when my brother called with a piece of startling news. "Guess what I did?" he said. "I ate a huge bowl of mint chip ice cream. Two and a half scoops. I'm feeling better."

"Icy cold? Is that okay?"

"Went down fine. I might have more."

I laughed. "You were hungry."

"Maybe those needle jabs are working. Maybe I'm getting better. I feel better."

"You do?"

"I don't get that tired when I walk around either. I just wanted to tell you."

"I'm so glad."

"Two and a half scoops. I might have more."

I couldn't believe it—I was too happy to stay still, I was strolling around the room with the phone. Maybe he had more time than we thought. The percentage of people who lived five years after they'd been diagnosed wasn't very high, but a person could be on the good side of statistics. Somebody was.

Later that night, Nadia said, "Well, it was *supposed* to work. That's why he did it."

"Supposed to doesn't usually mean shit," I said, and then I was sorry I had spoken like that to a young person.

"If he's better," my friend Amy at work said, "then you can run off to Cambodia. Have sex with your ex, see Angkor Wat."

"It's too far. You know how far away it is? Twenty hours by plane. At the very least."

"I guess you looked online," she said.

And the airfare wasn't nothing either. Or did Bud think he was paying? We hadn't gotten anywhere near that question.

"Everyone's leaving my brother," I said. "I don't have to join them."

"So I found this nice little apartment," my brother said. "Small but small isn't bad. Decent light."

"You were looking?" I said. "I didn't know you were looking." This made me worry what else I had missed.

"Well, it fell into my lap," he said.

"It's affordable? Really?" Was it over a sewage plant? In nearby Nevada?

"It's in our building," Saul said. "Our neighbor has this studio he wants to sublet."

It was just three floors down.

"This guy wants a big deposit," Saul said. "People do now. Two months' security, one month in advance. I don't know where he thinks I'd be skipping away to. Kirk is lending me the money."

Lend, my ass. My brother's lover was paying him to leave. And they'd be greeting each other in the elevator forever. And everybody was acting cheerful about it.

"I'm looking forward to having my own place," Saul said. "It's been years since I had that."

"Did you want to be alone?"

"No," he said. "But it's fine."

Nadia thought her meditating had caused this improvement for Saul, her focusing on the words with all her strength. Something had gotten him better, against all odds. "I did more than you know. Most of it not out loud," she said. "Don't laugh."

"I'm not laughing."

"What's the other reason? There isn't any."

I wasn't offering any details of science. She looked so happy. She was still an awkward girl, and happiness made her face rounder and bolder.

"Saul thanked me," she said. "He said I was amazing."

My brother's character was improving, now that he was on an upward swing. Sick people had crappy dispositions. "He wants me to design something for the windows of his new place," Nadia said. "I can do that."

Was he going back to work? He'd always had a ridiculously long commute, from Inwood at the top of Manhattan all the way south to Brooklyn, an hour and fifteen minutes, but he used to say he liked reading on the subway. He had an unimpressive salary, decent insurance (I had checked it over), and not that bad a pension. Did he want to be in the library again?

He wasn't saying. He didn't even like it when we asked. When he was little, he loved to announce, "That's for me to know and you to find out," and he seemed to want to say that now. "Later for that," he muttered. To *me*, he said this.

My mother always claimed everyone thought Saul was less stubborn than he really was. I got along better with my mother than he did, and I had trouble too. We'd lost both our parents, within months of each other, a decade ago. Kirk had actually been very good through all that. That was when I still liked Kirk.

All of us helped with Saul's move. Nadia got someone at school to sew the curtains for her—pale greeny cream gathered at the sides, very nice, with misty gray panels in the centers. I scrubbed the place down and bought him a microwave. He was taking a sofa bed and a bookcase out of the apartment, which Kirk and the new boyfriend loaded into the elevator, along with the cartons of Saul's clothes. Ethan, the boyfriend, said, "Good light!" when he entered the room, bowed under the weight of the sofa. He looked different in jeans and a T-shirt, a little stockier.

"I love the light," my brother said. "A new day is dawning here."

He was sitting in a corner while we all worked, and he said, "You know, I really don't need any place bigger."

The new boyfriend looked properly embarrassed. Kirk said, "The couch looks totally great here."

I worried about all this compliance from Saul, this no-problems adaptation to his new situation. Was it sincere? Was it admirable? In my own life, I prided myself on being on good terms with my exes, but I had fought some bitter fights along the way. Nick,

Nadia's father, had been so infuriated by what I once said about his personality that he threatened to kidnap Nadia back. Arrive in the night and spirit her away. He didn't mean it for a second— Nadia didn't think so either—but he was hot with anger; he was, as they say, seeing red. What was Saul seeing now? All that talk of light. I wondered if he was seeing a muted glare, if he had a vision of his long days bathed in peaceful beams, streams of brightness in the air all around him. Blessing and bleaching his months in that room, however many months. He knew more than we did.

And sometimes he slipped into being his former disgruntled self. New York was having a very cold and rainy spring, and when I tried to get him out for a meal of any kind—brunch or dinner or anything—he said, "Who wants to go out in that?" Even when the weather had nothing wrong with it, he was annoyed at the prospect of going outside. The bother of it, the inconvenience. And the food. Did I know how greasy the food was in all brunch places? Did I know anything about what he couldn't eat?

Kirk's new boyfriend had not moved in upstairs—he apparently had his own very good apartment on a tree-lined street in the far West Village. I happened to see Kirk in the elevator, and he did not look pleased about anything, but who knew what that meant? "Hey there," I said to him, and he mumbled, "Oh, hello." Not that he could be expected to be overjoyed to see me.

So what did Saul do all day? He looked things up on his computer, he binge-watched good TV, he reread some Dickens, he did a little meditating. He kept the place neat and relatively clean, a sign of his fondness for it. And did anyone visit but me?

"Friends come. And people from work. And you know who comes a lot?" he said. "Kirk."

I chuckled bitterly. "Does he help?"

"He brings food. We had strawberries the other day. He says he misses me."

I was fucking tired of the caprices of fucking Kirk. "What do you say?"

"I tell him he has to get used to being alone."

How calm my brother was choosing to be. I hoped it bothered Kirk.

And Saul wasn't rushing to go back to work, was he? He wasn't going back. How had I thought that he would?

"Were you ever in Cambodia?" I asked Saul. "Or was it just Thailand?" I was making tea in his kitchen, the one thing he'd let me do. It was a nice kitchen, blue tiles on the wall.

"Just Thailand. Before I knew Kirk. We went up to the northeast, not very visited then. Ever go to that part?"

"Not me."

"Great people," Saul said. "Dirt-poor. I felt like a jerk as a tourist, with my jangling change. They deserved better."

"Freedom from want," I said. "That was one of the four freedoms in FDR's speech. Nobody thinks of that now as a human right."

"So you want to go to Cambodia?" Saul said. "This is new."

"Remember that guy Bud I used to go with? He lives there."

"I think he treated you not very well," Saul said. "As I remember."

"That was then, this is now," I said.

"Famous last words," Saul said.

Nadia said, "So how did people decide who to marry in the old days when they didn't even sleep together? How did people understand what kind of deal they were getting?"

"Don't ask me," I said. "I didn't come in under that system. But you can't go just by sex, you know. Do I have to tell you that?"

"You so do not," Nadia said, rolling her eyes. "But how do people make these colossal bargains about what they decide to put up with?"

I knew this wasn't about her own dating life (which was quiet at the moment) but about her friend Kit, set to marry a person whose merits were entirely invisible to Nadia. How to support her friend but not lie too much: that was the problem.

"Lie," I said. I wasn't her parent, I could talk that way to her.

"She thinks he's smart, and he's really stupid. It depresses me what people do."

"You don't know how it will turn out. No one can tell."

"She thinks she's won the lottery," Nadia said. "She feels sorry for the rest of us."

"People are like that," I said. "I used to be like that."

Saul told me he was thinking more about finances lately. He had made a list of how much he spent on rent, how much on food and utilities, what income he had coming in, how much wiggle room he had. He had a little. "I get benefits," he said. "I'm not destitute. I hope you know that."

And, by the way, he'd made a will, and it was in the bookcase by the big book of Audubon drawings, if I wanted to know.

I thought he'd always had a will.

"Well, no. And this one is good. I had someone, a lawyer, make sure everything was all right."

"You found a lawyer without ever leaving the apartment?"

Ethan was a lawyer.

"Estate law isn't his specialty," Saul said, "but I knew he could get the forms for something simple. He made it easy. I just told him what I wanted. Easy as pie."

"How nice."

"Don't forget. By the Audubon book."

I was tearful when Nadia came home. "Saul decided to have a little conversation about his *will*," I said. "What kind of nineteenth-century novel are we in?"

"I hope he doesn't leave all his money to Kirk or anything," she said, after I'd calmed down and she'd poured us a little wine.

I secretly hoped he was leaving whatever he had to Nadia, a person not legally related to either of us.

"He's not rich anyway," she said.

"It doesn't matter," I said.

That was the question about money, wasn't it? How much it mattered. I used to argue with Bud about that, in the old days, when we liked to talk about which friends were happy. I was always claiming that high incomes soured people and made them anxious and stingy.

"I don't think you should go to Cambodia," Nadia said.

"Who said I was going?"

"I saw on the news they're arresting journalists. It's very unfair."

"I'm not going anywhere anytime soon," I said. I wanted to hop into bed with Bud—that was true, however old we were—but it had nothing to do with the heart of the matter at the moment, which was my brother.

Nadia said, "You mention Bud more than you did."

"Saul knows him. He's not a big fan."

"Excuse me, but Saul is not a proven expert. I wouldn't listen to his opinions about any boyfriends if I had any."

"Who would you listen to instead?"

"Not you either," she said.

What I liked in this was her hopefulness. She was twenty-six, and she was never going to make the mistakes we'd made.

Ethan went with Saul for one of his doctor's visits, on the theory that it was always good to have another person paying attention and writing things down. What kind of world was it, where you needed a lawyer to listen to your doctor? "He asked good questions," my brother said. "We all had a nice chat. But I don't think I'm going again."

How good could those questions have been? In my opinion, Ethan had been no help at all.

"How can you just not go?" I said.

"A question that answers itself," he said.

I believed in freedom—it was my brother's right not to go anywhere—and it would've done no good at all if I'd bossed or begged or reasoned. It seemed that the doctor was no longer offering anything he wanted. Saul had more than one doctor, and they were united in their lack of appealing offers.

"It'll be very relaxing," my brother said. "To stay home."

What home? But the new place had a good kitchen (better than the old place, really) and I believed that if we could keep him eating, he'd have more time. I got this from our mother, always indignant if we didn't finish what was on our plates—"People in other parts of the world would be very happy to eat what you're leaving behind." We were born too late to hear about starving Armenians, but she brought up the people in China (was this about famines under Mao?), and adults were always letting us know that ingratitude about food was dangerous. Did parents in places like Cambodia say this to their children now? Or did the children always eat?

Saul would eat a few things—I could make a very nice corn chowder that he didn't mind and also a Middle Eastern version of fried eggs with mint, oregano, and scallions. Sometimes he ate pad thai from a place nearby. On good days he could be tempted by ice cream in certain flavors. He was a slow eater, like a fidgety five-year-old.

On weekends Nadia came with me to deal with the house-cleaning. We brought the vacuum cleaner down from Kirk's; in the elevator Nadia wore the hose around her shoulders like a boa. Even with all the dust bunnies collecting under the furniture, the place was so small the work didn't take long, and Saul got to make a joke. "How come," he said, "the Buddhist didn't vacuum in the corners of the room?"

"I know this one," Nadia said.

I didn't. "Because," my brother said, "he had no attachments."

"Oh, my God, she's laughing," Nadia said.

"The woman's been inhaling the floor polish," Saul said.

What did that mean, no attachments? Saul used to tell me it meant *don't worry, it won't last, nothing does.* And he said all that was more uplifting than it sounded.

"Don't go to Cambodia," Nadia said, when we were eating dinner that night. I was sure I had made it clear to her I wasn't getting on any planes. "How can I deal with stuff that happens with Saul when you're not here? I'm young, you know."

Bud had stopped issuing invitations to Phnom Penh, perhaps for lack of an enthusiastic response on my part. Maybe he had found someone else. NGOs were full of intelligent single women. We still had our conversations on Skype. I combed my hair, I put on lipstick; I got excited before he called. We flickered on the screen at each other. That was the way it was.

"I asked Saul," Nadia said, "where he'd want to go if he could get his wish, like they do with kids, that wish foundation. I told him he should go to Jamaica. It's where my ridiculous friend Kit is going on her ridiculous honeymoon. I'd take him. It's not that far."

"What did he say?"

"He said he liked it fine where he was."

I snorted.

Adults usually didn't act out their wildest wishes before they died, despite all the movies that used that plot. They had other ideas by then. They left the old ones behind.

.   .   .

Nadia started wearing a green ribbon as a choker, in honor of Saul (it looked good on her, she looked good in everything). As a charm, it didn't work. He had a really bad week; he said an eagle was coming every night to eat his liver. The whites of his eyes looked stained yellow. By phone I pestered the doctor until he prescribed more painkillers. Maybe not enough—scrips were stingy because of the opioid crisis—but welcome for now. "I'm turning on, tuning in, and dropping out," Saul said. "There's a lot to be said for it."

When we were growing up, there was still some rhetoric left about drugs as a source of enlightenment. When I was in Thailand in my twenties, we could buy anything (or my then-boyfriend could) and we sat around stoned on who knows what. Waiting for moments of strange clarity, which sometimes came. Opiated hash, did people still smoke that? Who came up with that combo?

"Do you remember anything?" Saul said.

"I remember my boyfriend," I said. "Except I've forgotten his name."

Saul laughed. He could still laugh. "Sister Susie," he said.

What did I long for? "Are you discouraged," Bud asked on the screen from Phnom Penh, "because of Trump?"

Yes, but I hadn't remembered to think about it lately. We all had different levels of grief, didn't we, a whole hierarchy.

"In NGOs," Bud said, "the aid workers who see the worst are always going out on the town to get stupidly cheered up. Like those Oxfam Brits who hired prostitutes."

He was my cheering up, a very hygienic form.

"What do you do in Phnom Penh?" I said.

He smirked a little. "Well, there's not much to do. Actually, there is, but I don't do it. There's a bar I like. The girls know me, they don't bother me."

I was glad he wasn't bothered.

"You'd love the river, we have three rivers. And the temples."

"What do Cambodians do for luck?" I was thinking of Nadia and her ribbon.

"Some people get protective tattoos. Angelina Jolie got a Cambodian tattoo."

How far away he was. What did it mean to have a romance that was never going to be acted out? It didn't seem so bad to me anymore. In fact it had certain superiorities over contact in person. And it was as real as the outlines of Angelina Jolie's tattoo (which I'd seen online), with its guardian blessings inked out in Pali. Bud had become a wish of mine with no trouble in it.

Kirk was upset. I could tell by the sight of him, rumpled and frowning, when I ran into him by the recycling bins in the basement of the building. I was throwing out a whole bag of empty cans of ginger ale. It was the one thing Saul liked now that he was back to not liking again. The cans were clanging as I dumped them.

"He's not doing well, is he?" Kirk said. "I didn't know how it would be."

"I guess you didn't," I said.

"Don't be against me," Kirk said.

He wanted me to like him too? I might've pushed him into the recyclables, if I'd been a different sort of person. "What's the matter with you?" I said. We seemed to be connected forever, but so what?

"Did he tell you?" Kirk said. "I asked him to move back."

I gasped out loud, a wheeze of amazement. I had just been thinking of getting someone to come in a few hours a day to help, as much as his insurance would cover. Someone good. Not needed now? No longer my business?

"He said no," Kirk said.

"Fuck," I said.

Of course, I was proud of my brother (we don't kneel) and quite surprised. Kirk had been even more surprised.

"He insists that he's happier without me."

Kirk sounded devastated by this bit of news. Which was probably not even true, though maybe it was. Who knew what my brother really wanted? He acted now as if he were in a kingdom whose language was too much work to translate for us.

Kirk was gazing at me, waiting for something he was hoping I could give. "Everybody thinks he's so mild, but he's the stubbornest person on the planet," I said. "No is no."

Kirk said, "Maybe he'll change his mind."

I loved my brother's stubbornness. He didn't have to run around anymore, did he, rushing to get what he thought he should have. Fine where he was. Of course, I envied his freedom, who wouldn't? Only a few days ago I'd gone into a little fit because I'd lost my favorite earrings; they had been a gift from Nadia's father, whom I didn't even like, but I'd had them for years and they looked good on me. "What are you hanging on to?" Saul said. "You had them and they're gone."

This bit of philosophy did stop my wailing. Saul could do that—he could utter a tautology in a way that made it sound beautifully plain and right. "Goodbye to all that," I said to my earrings. Saul was speaking from a spot further on, a better view, speaking with expertise.

Not that he always abided by this. He had spells of being very irritated at me for spending his dollars on overpriced takeout meals or organic detergent—"I'm not made of money." Little pissy amounts of cash. He was afraid of his resources running out. A metaphor there.

Kirk said, "Who knew you would turn into a skinflint?"

How poorly Kirk understood him, what a mess Kirk had made of everything. Yearning and grabbing. Kirk the now-repentant lummox who dreamed my clearheaded brother would change his mind.

Which he did. Five weeks later, Kirk called to give me the news. "We've got him all settled in." Saul was already in his old bedroom watching TV in a newly rented hospital bed by the time they told me. "I'm very comfortable," Saul said. "I have this new kind of pillow under my neck. Ethan got it for me."

"Did they bring up all your stuff? Tell me what you need."

"I think I have everything pretty much."

The one who sounded really, really happy was Kirk. "He looks better already. He does. You can tell by looking at him this is the right move. I never thought he'd say yes. I gave up, I had no clue this would happen. And we got everything done so fast! We did." His voice had gotten giddy and young, he was burbling away.

When I dropped over to see Saul in his new-old lodgings that evening, Kirk was glowing in the doorway. "Ethan made this great little supper that was some kind of mussel stew. And Saul gobbled it up. Well, not all of it, but he ate it. He liked it."

"I ate it in Iceland," Ethan said. "I went there with my mother last year." Ethan had a mother? I never thought about him outside these rooms. "It's gorgeous," Ethan said about Iceland. "Expensive but worth it." What did a lawyer with a fat paycheck care about expensive?

Kirk said, "Ethan can cook, I can cook. We'll keep trying different food."

"We have a whole bucket of empty mussel shells now," my brother said.

My brother with his pinched face, his elbows knobs of bone.

"Ethan's good in the kitchen," Kirk said.

"Now and then I can do something," Ethan said. "But you know how late I work."

"I can't eat late," Saul said. "Don't expect me to stay up. I get tired."

"He ate ice cream too," Kirk had to tell me.

Whatever the report of his chef's skills, Ethan slipped out soon after I arrived. There was murmuring with Kirk by the door, and he was gone.

"Hey," my brother said, when Kirk walked back in, "I don't have to do the dishes now, do I?"

Kirk acted as if that was the funniest thing he'd ever heard. "We just throw them out when they're dirty," he said. Did I actually laugh too?

Soon after, the two of us walked my brother to his old room. Saul showed me the way a person could crank the bed down to make it easy to climb into. "A miracle of science," he said. "It's costing a fortune, I think."

"Good night, sweet prince," Kirk said.

On the way back, I saw from the hallway that Kirk's usually pristine computer studio was a mess, with piles of clothes littering it. It had become the room where he slept. (Alone, it seemed. Not with Ethan at the moment.)

"He's crazy about that bed," Kirk said. "Did you see that? He is."

When the sunlight, which my brother used to love, bothered his eyes, even in this dimmer apartment, Ethan set up curtains around the bed. He had someone construct posts at the bed's four corners, and then he hung the elegant drapes that Nadia had designed—they became bed curtains, like the ones Scrooge had around his bed when the ghosts frightened him.

Even Nadia thought the curtains looked good, the pale green and gray. She was still not a fan of Kirk ("Why do I have to like him?"), but she made an effort when I took her to visit. We were all sitting around the living room, and Ethan brought in tea and a plate of pastel meringue kisses from a bakery, a low-fat delicacy for Saul. "How pretty they are," Nadia said.

Kirk said, "You made the tea too strong. Saul needs it weaker. Can you bring in the hot water?"

I would've said, Get your own fucking water, but Ethan was back with the kettle in a jiffy. "Taste it," he said to my brother.

"Just right," Saul said.

"You're sure?"

Saul was chomping and sipping. Between bites he said, "We watched this thing on Netflix that was really hilarious."

"We were totally into it," Ethan said.

"I couldn't stop laughing in one part," Kirk said.

Nadia got all the details (a Tasmanian lesbian comedian she already knew about) and my brother imitated the woman's accent. Kirk cracked up watching him. "You missed your calling in stand-up," he said.

"He went for the big bucks in library science," Ethan said.

Saul couldn't resist telling how he'd once spilled an entire cart-load of books on a library trustee, a story I'd heard many times before. As had Kirk. My brother told it well this time. Nadia laughed at the oafish amazement of the fallen trustee, Saul's version of his own loony apologies, but the one who loved the tale the most was Kirk. He gazed and nodded at my brother, he clapped and hooted. I'd rarely seen him so happy.

Saul, for his part, had the sly look people get when they've told a joke that's gone over. How pleased my brother was, on that pinched face of his. When we left, Nadia muttered to me in the elevator, "So I guess he's okay there." Her face was still tinted pink from laughing, but now her voice was flat. The whole thing had confused her about the nature of love. I wasn't saying a word either. What did I know? I was thinking that this would become an elemental part of what she'd remember, for who knew how long, that she'd have what she'd just seen. The way they were, just like that—I wanted her to have that.

Jowhor Ile

Fisherman's Stew

N IMI LOCKED THE FRONT DOOR and secured the slide bolt. She turned off the kitchen and hallway lights leading to the room in which now she'd slept for a year. A lumpy shadow of the old Singer foot-pedal sewing machine, heaped with fabric, fell across the narrow bed. Drawing the curtains and sliding open the lower window louver failed to stir a breeze. The wrought-iron window protector still gave off heat.

The lights were going off in her neighbor's house, and the low rumbling from their generators diminished. It was past midnight—no car creaked up the road, no gate slammed shut, no dog, not one voice raised from the stalls outside—everything was as still as it must be on the moon. After Nimi settled into bed she felt a supple movement that lifted the curtain and scattered the fading aroma of supper. That was when she heard the shuffling of feet outside, by the kitchen door, and the sound of someone breathing, waiting patiently. She knew at once that Benji, her husband, had finally returned. The lock clicked. Benji still had his keys. He didn't turn on the light when he entered. Belt buckle clanking, zipper running, and the rustle of clothes falling to the ground: when you are sixty-seven years of age and have shared nearly fifty of those with the same person, you can tell his intentions by the sounds he makes. The carved cupboard of Sapele mahogany and the wall beside it caught Benji's shadow shifting in the lantern's low-trimmed light. It seemed to her that he stood in the gap of the screen curtain, his eyelids heavy with fatigue, as if he'd paddled through miles of smoky streams to get here. She'd always known he'd return, she'd waited for him to come home, as he always did—straight from the workshop, pausing before join- ing her to check on little Alice; or, perhaps, after a brief stop at Uduak's drinking table, where, with his friends, he would knock back shots of schnapps imbued with medicinal roots and bark of trees known to restore vitality and provoke desire in men young and old. With his clothes hooked on the back of a chair in the hallway, he would walk into the bedroom naked as day, the old scar on his arm gleaming.

She shifted on the bed and made room, and Benji met her— loose, sprawled, arched, with parted lips—and then pressed his body against hers. She caught the whiff of dry wood, sweat, and handsaw grease. His callused hands slid round her neck, then cupped her face. His lips shook as his eyes hovered over hers. She took his lower lip into her mouth, calmed it. He was caressing her face with one hand, and with the other he undid the wrapper tied around her waist and flung it into the dark, where a clatter followed the tumbling items on the nightstand, then lowered his head over her belly and navel, making his way down the soft trail of hair.

He stayed there until she retrieved herself with a sharp moan, turning sideways, like a bitch shrugging off her young. She turned and, pressing his shoulders until he was on his back, descended on him. With his balls secure in her mouth, she held Benji until she heard him plead, his voice drifting out the window. She relented, and then raised herself until they were facing each other, breath- ing the same air. He turned sharply as she slid beneath him. With her arm hooked over his neck, she drew her knees up, and held her thighs open like a funnel. In countless heated strokes that ran along the channels of her body, he came in a roar. Afterward, in the deep dark, they lay silent.

He was gone by the morning. When she rose, the pale green walls of the room seemed unfamiliar. She glanced at the old sewing machine, piled with plain cotton and linen, rolls of muslin and gingham, yards of blue-black adire. The handbags on the wardrobe were still untouched in their nylon wrappings. It all came back to her. Alice bringing gifts every time she visited, gifts Nimi hardly touched. Hollow days. She had moved from the bedroom and slept instead on the narrow bed in the sewing room. Last week, when Alice visited with her husband, Asari, and their two boys, Nimi prodded them to leave some clothing behind so they could travel light on their subsequent visits. Alice and Asari had asked again if they could find her a new place, somewhere closer to where they lived at Wimpey, but Nimi had said no, she did not want to move. Now she sat up in bed with her back resting on the wall. Her neighbor Ibifuro was singing in the courtyard, a melodious and militant church chorus. Ibifuro lived in the flat across, with her three children and husband, Enefa—a safety technician on an oil platform in Bonny. Nimi parted the curtain and peered at the tall woman. She was bent over a basin, hands vigorously washing clothes, and her swirling voice trembled: *I will sing unto the Lord, for he has triumphed gloriously, the horse and rider thrown into the sea*. Nimi let the curtain drop. She got out of bed and slipped her feet into the plastic sandals she reserved for the outside. The door whistled on its hinges when she pulled it, and the day swung open before her. The yard was already swept. Normally she rose early to do this and some other chores before her neighbors got up.

You are sleeping well these days, Ibifuro called out.

You are washing, she replied warmly but in no mood for playful banter. How was your night?

We thank God. Ibifuro sighed.

Nimi waited as Ibifuro dunked the striped shirt in her hands back into the basin's foaming water and began to hum the same church chorus, gravely.

You know that woman Dauta, Ibifuro said, that one who calls herself a caterer. You know I introduced her to my friend whose son was getting married.

Nimi could not recall hearing about this Dauta, but from Ibifuro's tone she could tell the introduction had now produced undesirable outcomes.

So imagine how I felt, Ibifuro continued, when I woke up this morning to see messages from my friend and voice messages from people I don't know, that the caterer I brought spoiled their occasion, that food did not go round.

I hate when I'm at a wedding and that happens, Nimi said.

So I called Dauta to ask what happened, and you won't believe it, the woman told me it's not her fault that they paid her to cook for only one hundred people but expected the food to cover nearly three hundred guests present at the reception.

Is that the bad tongue she used to answer you? Nimi asked in disgust.

Ibifuro clucked, as if still shocked at the woman's rudeness. She was not the type of person to stand by and watch her integrity and good name get sullied.

No need to make trouble, Nimi cautioned.

Ibifuro waved it off with a carefree hand. She said, I am going to the pharmacy later, on my way I will stop by her house so I can hear all she has to say to me, and then I'll know what to do. I don't have time to make trouble.

Nimi imagined the wedding reception, held outdoors on a field with colorful canopies or a large tent, a highlife gospel band in full swing, guests in their best clothes, while the bride and groom sat smiling on their special seats, passing a flute of champagne to each other and unaware of the shortage of food and the quiet departures, the cars turning out of the parking lot, taxis flagged down in haste, the small groups walking toward the nearest bus stop. Very unpleasant, Nimi thought. Even at funerals, eating and drinking carried on through the day and into night.

Benji returned to me last night, she said.

Ibifuro's head was down facing the basin. She did not turn around or ask any worried questions. Instead she retrieved a submerged shirt, squeezed and dropped it into another basin filled with clean water.

Nimi, undecided, weighed if she should repeat what she'd just said.

Ibifuro had been there the day the news came about Benji. The two women were shelling egusi in the yard when Chima and Chidi, two men who ran their metalwork stores next to Benji's, arrived to say Benji had been hit by a motorbike crossing Ikwerre Road and was in the hospital. They were remarkably short and stout and good-natured, these men. Nimi and Benji often spoke about them, how they possessed good names in the wrought-iron business, how they plied their trade to complement each other's skills, did not quarrel over customers, how their grit and ambition never excluded warmth. Together the three of them sped along in a taxi toward Braithwaite Memorial Hospital. They did not explain to Nimi why they avoided the main entrance to the hospital and led her instead toward a bungalow at the back. The pathway was lined with hedges of ixora, bloodred and radiant. Her nostrils flinched at the strong smell of formaldehyde. The two men stopped walking as they came in full view of the building, and Chidi placed a hand on her shoulder.

What is happening? Nimi asked. She got no response.

The flower hedges slipped fast before her eyes, the ground was giving way beneath her, her hand slammed against Chidi's chest and grasped his shirt collar tight. His eyes were bloodshot. Madam, madam, he kept saying to her. Chima tried to restrain and console her, but she broke free from them and ran to see where Benji, wearing the shirt Nimi had made from adire cloth with circular patterns running in blue and dead-leaf green, lay lifeless on the stretcher.

As she watched Ibifuro peg her washing on the line, she could taste again Benji's sour morning breath on her tongue. She could still feel on her waist the firm grip of his hands, from where he'd lifted her while on his knees last night, gently, easily, and she reckoned with the words of her people that when we return we do so in the vigor of youth.

Benji came to see me last night, Nimi repeated.

Ibifuro swung round toward Nimi—the bulk of the woman, breasts swaying under her nightdress. A white plastic peg slid out of her hand, but she kept her eyes fixed on Nimi.

Mama, Ibifuro pleaded.

Nimi looked away. She knew what would follow. Ibifuro would immediately call or text Alice, and she would come over. Pastor Osagie would casually drop in the next day to spend time with Nimi. The church's women's group would pick an afternoon to lavish her, cleaning and sweeping, preparing meals for her that would go to waste, while dishing out admonitions. By the weekend, the youth group would gather, singing lustily in her sitting room and offering prayers for blessings on her behalf. All of these she would receive with gratitude, but they would be beside the point.

I saw him only in my dream, Nimi said with a light voice. It gave me comfort.

She took out a napkin and dusted the Formica sideboards and the obeche cabinet in her front room, folded her wrappers and hung her gowns up in the wardrobe in an arrangement she liked. And then she swept the floor of the whole house. There was to be a meeting in church that evening so she sent word she would not make it, claiming an emergency had occurred. Nimi remembered that look she saw on Ibifuro's face when she told her of Benji's return. She thought of her own sleepy-eyed astonishment when she awoke that morning to a bed in disarray. A current ran down her spine. If it was a crack in her mind that had let Benji back into the world, she thought, then her intention was to keep the crack open, widen it. Her plan was to visit the evening market, and then make stew. She knew that if you love a person and they love you back, you can cook for them something that ensures they find their way to you, should they be lost.

It was a little before five when she stepped out of the house and into the street. The sky over Eliozu was alive with an orange light. The slanted, rusty roofs of the houses downhill glinted like gold. With her shopping bag in hand, she closed the gate quietly behind her. Alagbo's sky-blue Nissan Sunny was shimmering at his gate and blocking the entrance, finally back from the mechanic after three solid months of delayed salary. Alagbo had complained about the dire state of things, the cost of a new engine block, and the craftiness of motor mechanics. Nimi made a mental note to call in later to salute him, to greet his family, and to thank God with them that things turned out fine. Chituru sat on a high stool in front of his DVD store, watching two other men play draughts, the pieces sliding and spilling noisily on the wooden board.

Out on the main road Nimi turned toward the market. It was that time just before nightfall when people were on their way home from work, when the air darkened and the figures milling in the markets and the streets may not be people at all. Her eye caught an ice-cream man pedaling home on his bicycle; he was done for the day, no bell ringing, no driving the children mad with want. She felt awake to her own footfalls, to the bright green and yellow head scarf on the woman walking ahead, to the rising murmur of the market as she approached, and to the cars tooting their horns, beetling along in the rush-hour traffic.

She weaved her way through the crowd, sidestepped puddles,

steered clear of the man pushing a wheelbarrow loaded with sacks of onions and grunting, *Chance, chance.* The stalls at the very end of the market were the ones she wanted.

Crabs in woven baskets were clacking away and waving their claws, the giant snails gliding in open buckets, and rows and rows of tables were laid out with tilapia, brown snapper, frozen mackerel wrenched out of misty cartons, silversides and bonga, mudskippers fresh from the river, bulgy-eyed, thrashing on the table and gasping for breath. Nimi stopped to admire a heaped bowl of peppers—blemish-free, slender, and green.

Take two bowls for the price of one, said the young woman in the shed. A nod went from seller to buyer.

Thank you, my daughter, Nimi said. Even the night market was in alliance with her.

When Nimi and Benji were young, before Alice was born, they lived in a little house far outside of town on East-West Road. Benji's workshop was right at the front veranda. People were reluctant to commit to a young, newly arrived carpenter, and there was no denying it, to get those jobs, Benji often exaggerated his experience, inflated the number of years of practice under his belt: I can do it, Ma. I have built that type of armchair before, sir. And he delivered the jobs, not one complaint followed. Still, it was her petty trading that had kept them from starving or returning to the village until he started getting the sort of customers who drove in cars and dropped by the workshop with their children dressed in school uniforms. Then she sold the first set of throw pillows and tablecloths that she ever made. She made headrests and armrests, tablecloths with placemats to match. Nimi sat and sewed, recalling needlework techniques from primary school, adding a flourish to the patterns here and there, with the sound of Benji's hammering and sawing going in the background, until evening, when they packed up and turned in to nest. They stayed up late in those days, talking about she couldn't remember what, long after they had relished the crumbly purity of boiled yam dipped in fire-warmed palm oil and sprinkled with salt. When they stayed up late enough to crave a snack before sleep, Benji would, in no time at all, put together fresh corn, roasted golden, which they ate with ube, buttery and delicate. On one of those nights, while they lay in bed—this was the moment Nimi held in her mind as she scanned rows of fresh tomatoes in the market—Benji pressed his knee into the hollow of her own, slid his foot's instep into the arch of her sole, and said: me and you.

Nimi rolled over and faced him.

When I come back, he said, in our next life, I will find you.

What surprised her was that he had said the words out loud: she had found him to be a man who promised little but did much more.

I will look for you too, she said. That way it will take us half the time.

Lights began to appear in the neighbors' houses as Nimi approached the gate. It had begun to drizzle, quickly hardening into storm. Once she stepped inside her house, she set her shopping bags down, and then she found a towel to wipe her face and arms.

Ignoring the words of the landlord, she made a fire with real firewood, opening the windows to let out the smoke. It would have hastened things to have two pots going, but she was in no rush. She took down a tray and laid out the smoked catfish, the fresh prawns, the periwinkles, the water snails, and the clams. She chopped a fat onion and dropped it into the hot oil. It spat like loud applause. She pulled a log from the fire to reduce the heat. She turned the contents of the tray into a large pot and set it aside. With the onions still sizzling, she poured in a bowl of fresh peppers and tomatoes already blended together for a fee at the market. She let it cook for a while. The aroma filled the room and tickled her nostrils. Last night while they caught their breaths, Benji had put his nose against her hair and inhaled. He had always been stirred by the scent of utazi. From the shelf, she lowered a plastic container where she stored condiments—dried mint, ukashi, uda, utazi, uziza—and crushed some dry utazi leaves into the stew. The fire crackled, and the pot boiled. She unknotted her head scarf and flung it aside. Tonight, after they had eaten the stew with slices of boiled yam, there would be time left to talk.

Emma Cline

White Noise

THE DREAMS HAD MOSTLY STOPPED. Still, he found himself awake, blinking in the dark room. Four a.m. He lay unmoving for a moment under the duvet. His T-shirt was stuck to his back—night sweats, the pillow swampy, the sheets damp. Roll to the other side. Spread out on the chilly sheets. Keep the eyes closed. As soon as both eyes opened, it would be straight to dull business, an organizer already laid out with his morning meds, a bottle of room-temperature Fiji water alongside.

This time tomorrow, he would know everything. Well, not exactly this time, more like ten a.m., but, in any case, all would be decided. He believed, truly, that he would be exonerated. How could he not be? This was America. Maybe there was a moment, a day or two right when this all began, when he believed that this might be it, the end of the road. He understood Epstein's hanging himself in his cell—because what would life look like, afterward? No more dinner parties, no more respect, no buffer of fear and admiration that kept you in a kind of pleasant trance, the world shaping itself around you.

And, yes, there was a moment when people no longer returned his calls, looked away from him on the street, no room at the inn, etc. But, almost as quickly, other people showed up, rushed to fill the void. Came to his Super Bowl party, let him use country houses, consult with family lawyers. He was staying at Vogel's Connecticut house now, for example. A man wouldn't let another man stay in his home if he was truly a leper.

He was fully awake now, adrenaline lighting up his brain, the itch to make plans, get to work. He turned on the bedside light and sat against the pillows. He guzzled the last of the stale water, groped for his legal pad. It was better, he'd learned, after the punishing rounds of discovery, to keep lists on paper. Papers got misplaced, papers disappeared.

He called Joan. "This is off the record," he said, instantly.

Her voice was sleepy. "Hello?"

"Do you agree?" he said. "I need a verbal."

"Harvey?" she said.

"A verbal," he said. "Off the record."

"Sure, Harvey."

He heard someone in the background. "Who is that?"

"It's Jerry. We're in bed."

"Well, get out of bed, OK? This is for your ears only. I'll call back in five."

Joan liked him. Legitimately liked him. She was tough, no-nonsense, but happy to soft-pedal an actor's DUI in return for a lengthy profile, gladly accepted screening invitations and was a reliable fixture at after-parties. They'd had fun times. The junket for the film that he'd triaged out of near-disaster: Harvey had hunkered down in Sag and basically rewritten the script, while the director was hauled out of rehab and barely propped up by a team of ADs. An Academy campaign. The liaison in Japan who took them to Gold Bar—the only white people in the place. Uni on filet mignon, a skinny press assistant hanging around who wouldn't touch it. Who cringed when he put his arm around her, cowering on the banquette. They'd left her at the place, as a joke. As he remembered it. Let her try to find her way back to the hotel at three a.m. in Tokyo. This was before phones, when people got legitimately lost.

And, as he remembered, Joan hadn't exactly gone out of her way to help the girl, or insist they take her home. She had thought it was funny, too.

He dialed again.

Joan answered on the first ring.

"I want to give you the first interview after I'm exonerated," he said. "I do. But I want to make sure you have all the facts, all the facts. 'Cause there is a lot," he said, "a lot that has been suppressed in this case. You would be shocked to find out even a fraction of what the other side buried—"

"OK, Harvey. I'm just walking downstairs, OK? Just hold your horses."

"And this is off the record, Joan."

"Yes, Harvey."

"This time tomorrow"—he corrected himself—"or, you know, tomorrow, not sure when, specifically, this whole case will be revealed for what it is: an elaborate fraud, an attempt to litigate regret and make me a scapegoat. A fraud, it bears saying, that you and your cohorts at the so-called paper of record were willing participants in. A lot of very bad actors there, your colleagues. Some might say there's a civil RICO case to be made against you—"

She didn't respond.

"Joan?"

"Sorry, my kid has an ear infection, I think she's awake. Can you hold on a second?"

He hung up the phone.

Time to get dressed, start the whole mess again. The Loro Piana half-zip, navy, good American blue jeans. The ankle bracelet was slim enough that it actually did seem more like a bracelet. Even as light as it was, it messed with his stride, this little annoyance, ever present, never quite fading into the background. Enough clearance underneath to pull up his thin red socks. Socks from the place the Pope gets his. Tomato red, cotton lisle, made in this tiny shop by the Vatican.

He splashed his face with water. Tightened his belt. He was losing weight. Funny that this was what it took, in the end. Not the hugely expensive doctors, the sachets of vitamins meant to replace meals, the overnight sleep study at Weill Cornell and daily Pilates instruction. All it took, it turned out, was total annihilation. Attempted annihilation, he corrected himself, the threat of annihilation.

"There's been an assassination attempt," he heard in his head, as if from a news announcer, "an attempt on the president's life." This had been a recurring thought lately: an assassination attempt, an assassination attempt. He had survived an assassination attempt. Because how else could you describe what they were trying to do to him? The shocking, incredible resources they had marshaled against one man? He was just a man, just one man in red socks and a too-thin T-shirt, an ache in his left molar, a bad back that was basically on the verge of collapse, all his cartilage scraped away so his spine was a teetering Jenga stack of discs.

A little frightening, the carpeted stairs, his ankles feeling hollow and frail. He gripped the bannister. Better to just take the elevator from now on, one of the reasons Vogel had offered the house up, that cheesy elevator.

Downstairs was quiet, the rooms dark, though a few lights were on in the kitchen. He'd assumed no one was awake, but then Gabe stepped out from the pantry. He was fully dressed, face bright and avid.

"Good morning," Gabe said, smoothly, as if this were a normal hour, as if it weren't only five a.m. Harvey supposed that was what Gabe's job entailed, being perpetually unsurprised. "Can I get you a little breakfast? Coffee?"

"Coffee, yes." Harvey patted his stomach, absently. "Breakfast, no, not yet. My juice, the regular."

"Certainly. The breakfast room is all set up. Let me know if you need anything else."

Gabe brought in the coffee, the glass of juice. Grapefruit juice interfered with Harvey's Lipitor. So lately he was allowed only a splash with seltzer. He missed the full glass, the scathing mouthful that used to start every day. Four newspapers were lined up in tidy order alongside the place mat—he'd gotten used to blurring his vision a little, preemptively, just to lessen the shock upon encountering his own face suddenly on the front page, his name swimming above the fold.

Seeing the photos had been rough, worse than he'd imagined. You let go of a lot of things, had to get used to shame, but it was hard to totally abandon vanity. Harvey hobbling with the walker, the suit that the lawyers had insisted be slightly ill fitting, slightly cheap. They wanted to make everyone feel sorry for him. A strange pose to take, at least in public. It was, he supposed, what he used to do easily enough in private—my mother died today, he said, watching the girl's face change. I'm so lonely, just sit with me a minute, just lie here with me. Patting the hotel bed, over and over. Gripping a wrist with his face in a moue of sorrow—come on, he said, come on. Be a nice girl, not a sour one. I gave you a massage. Now you can give me one. It's only fair.

He aimed the remote at the big television. It took up almost the whole wall, a very Master of the Universe, situation-room setup, a little rich for Vogel, who was, essentially, a money manager. He clicked the remote once, clicked twice. The screen remained blank.

"Gabe," he called out. Nothing. "Gabe," he said, louder, aware of how aggro his voice sounded, a bark, really, exactly what people expected from him. He should watch himself, just get into the habit of corralling certain impulses, though who was here to make a note of any bad behavior except Gabe?

"Of course," Gabe said, taking the remote. He was so anodyne, so mild—hard to imagine him having sex, eating food, meeting any human need. He asked what channel Harvey would like.

News, naturally. On mute.

The sun was not visible yet, but the light had changed. A new day, time to get to work. He dialed the lawyer's number. It went straight to voice mail. He dialed again. The same. And again.

The coffee was cold. Gabe brought a new carafe before Harvey could shout for him.

As Gabe poured a fresh cup, the possibility of God's considering Harvey's fate floated across his mind: a frowning white-bearded daddy gazing down, making a list of his good deeds, his failings. Like maybe this would be taken into account tomorrow. Affect the verdict.

Harvey forced himself to catch Gabe's gaze, forced himself to smile. "Thanks," he said, smiling hard so his eyes crinkled, and Gabe smiled back, pleasantly, though his brow furrowed a little and he seemed to be in a hurry to leave the room.

OK, the day had barely started and already he was being kind, making moves. On the giant screen a blonde in a red fitted dress was leaning on the news desk, staring feverishly into the camera, and Harvey stared back, downing the cup of coffee. She was gesturing at numbers on a green screen, numbers that he didn't understand yet, numbers that meant nothing to him, but soon enough the blond woman would reward his attentions: the context would be explained, the meaning revealed.

He went outside to make a few calls, putting on a waxed barn jacket from the front closet. Sure, all the staff had signed NDAs, but better to be careful. He strode far enough away that Vogel's house—a boxy brick Colonial with flickering gas lamps, likely repro, at the gravel entry circle—was barely in sight, though now the neighbor's driveway was visible. Vogel should landscape this out, so you didn't have to gaze on the neighbors, or, more important, so the neighbors didn't gaze on you.

The sun was up now, a thin disk that offered no warmth, even as dew started to drip from the hedges. Nature was revving itself up. He was chatting to Nancy, the most loyal of the assistants. Nancy, with her MS boyfriend and schizo mother, her sad Minnesota childhood—she would never leave him.

"Harvey?" Nancy was saying. "Kristin wants to come up around three, she wants to leave the city before traffic. Is that OK?"

A turning, a shift—something drew his eye across the vast lawn, above the hedges. A man, opening the front door of the house next door, padding outside in old-fashioned pajamas, a puffy coat. He paused for a moment, tilting his gray face to the chilly sun. Then he walked down the steps and made his way along the driveway to the front gate. Did he see Harvey standing there? He didn't appear to. He stooped to pick up the blue plastic bundle of the newspaper, then walked back to the terrace. He sat on a wooden bench, wriggling the paper from its sleeve.

What was it about the man's face?

"Harvey?" Nancy was saying.

"Sure, sure," he said. "Kristin. Three."

"She's bringing Ruby."

"Mmm."

The man shook the paper open, though now he stopped reading to sweep some debris from the seat of the bench. He was near enough that Harvey could see the two sad clouds of eyebrows, wispy, fading. Why did he know this face?

"And Dr. Farrokhzad is coming at eleven. They'll set up in the guest bedroom. They wanted me to remind you, no liquids for at least two hours beforehand. OK? And definitely no food."

"Got it," he said. Loud enough that the man looked over.

Nancy was droning on—a bankruptcy lien, some claimant who'd worked in the Holmby Hills house coming out of the woodwork. And then all at once he placed the man next door. A shock, but then, when Harvey thought about it, why should it be a surprise? He was a private man, famously so—why wouldn't he be in Connecticut, making a life among these people? Like a secret agent, embedded in plain sight. Harvey hung up on Nancy. His whole body was aimed at the man, his brain vibrating. How could he indicate, in the tone of his voice, his expression, that, yes, he knew exactly who the man was, and, no, he wouldn't make a fuss?

"Morning," Harvey called across the fence, a cheery, neighborly greeting, and Don DeLillo lifted his hand in a wave.

"Nice day," Don DeLillo said. He got to his feet, ambling closer to Harvey.

"Beautiful day," Harvey said, his heart pounding with glee, and it felt like they were speaking in code, a mutually agreed-upon code. A thrill just to make contact. A meeting of equals.

"Field sparrow," Don DeLillo said.

"Hmm?"

"There's a field sparrow," Don DeLillo said. He pointed—Harvey followed the line of his finger until he spotted it: a small brown bird, like a mouse, hopping in the icy gravel. It was dull, the color of dishwater.

"Very rare bird," Don DeLillo mused. "This time of year. Never had one before."

"Interesting," Harvey said.

"I've heard of them showing up after storms, you know. Adverse conditions."

"Right."

They were communicating something, a hidden message coursing underneath this conversation—Do you know who I am? Don DeLillo was asking. Can I trust you? Are you on the level?

Yes, Harvey was trying to send back, straining to be absolutely clear, straining to communicate the entirety of his soul in a pressurized beam of light straight to Don DeLillo's being: yes, you can trust me, yes, I'm on the level.

"Well," Don DeLillo said, squinting at the sun, squinting at the mousy bird. "I'll see you."

"Yes," Harvey said, his eyes unblinking, his voice freighted. "Yes, I'll *see you soon*."

Harvey could visualize the plan, see each step of the process, the whole thing unfolding cleanly in his mind's eye without any hiccups or stutters. *White Noise*, the unfilmable book. Harvey's comeback. Why would he find himself here, on this earth, in the year 2020, if not for this exact purpose?

The rights were available—Nancy found out in two minutes. Of course they were, because everything would go smoothly this time. His head was spinning. He'd seen attempts, back in the day. Recalled a script for that weirdo hockey novel Don DeLillo wrote under a pseudonym, another script kicking around for the football book. Hadn't Rudin had the rights, for a hot minute?

What was that first line? He tried to remember. A screaming comes across the sky! A screaming. Beautiful. Vicious. A great first line. Maybe float a presentation card with the text, not strain to be too literal, try to squeeze an arty image out of it. Just let it land in the original form. *A screaming comes across the sky.* That was confidence. Already he was overwhelmed—calls to make, people to recruit. Draw up some preliminary numbers. But this felt right, exactly right. The perfect thing to jump into the moment, the very second that this circus ended and he was declared innocent. Thank you, he beamed out to the world, thank you. One of the couples therapists had suggested the keeping of a gratitude journal—even his ex-wife had snorted at that idea—but here he was, appreciating his blessings.

The buzz of his phone. The law firm. Finally.

"Hello, team," Rory said. When Rory had signed on to Harvey's defense, the papers had taken great glee in publishing a photo, gleaned from Rory's daughter's Facebook, of Rory in a pink pussy hat and aviator sunglasses, accompanying his daughter to the Women's March.

There were at least five people on the call. Harvey could not quite tell what they were saying. People kept cutting each other off—"If I can just jump in for a second"; "piggybacking off Rory's point about an immediate motion"—and now they were talking about what the next steps would be if there was another delay, what protections they could put in place for the walk out of the courthouse. None of them seemed to address the real question.

"But," Harvey interrupted, "what's going to happen? They're going to say I'm innocent, right? Not guilty. Isn't that what you promised?"

"Now, Harvey," Rory said, his twenty-three-hundred-an-hour voice oozing through the phone. "We are just going through what will happen, hypothetically. Just to cover all the bases. We've mounted a tremendous defense, and I think there's not one thing we could have done better. But. You know. We can't promise anything."

"Then why," Harvey said, wiping his damp brow, "the *fuck* would you say anything?"

The mood shifted.

"Sorry." He was still aware that God was tracking these moments of politeness, these moments of catching himself. Or not catching himself. "You guys read *White Noise?*" he said.

Silence on the line.

"Come on, how many people are on this call, five? Aren't you all Ivy League boys? None of you fuckers read *White Noise?*"

The silence was uneasy.

"Don DeLillo. American master. 'A screaming comes across the sky,' " Harvey said. He said it again, his voice dropped an octave. "A screaming," he said. "Comes across. *The sky.*"

"Isn't that *Gravity's Rainbow?*"

He didn't recognize the voice. "Who said that?"

Rory edged in. "Harvey, excuse me—"

"Who. The fuck. Said that? I don't know you. Why the fuck are you on this call if I don't know you? Isn't that illegal?"

Rory again. "Harvey, that's Ted, he's been in court with us every day."

"I don't fucking know a Ted."

"Harvey—"

"Never mind," Harvey said. "I'll check in later."

"Try to relax," Rory said, "and just remember—" Harvey ended the call.

A quick Google, and, yes, it was fucking *Gravity's Rainbow*. Well. So what. He'd been close, and the gist was the same, wasn't it? A rending of the known world. That was the whole fucking point.

Enough time, before the eleven a.m. doctor visit, to watch some things down in the screening room. They still had him on the list for new releases, though they seemed to arrive a week or two late now, and the union projectionist was hard to coax out of the city. One of the subtle ways he was punished, these days. In their absence, he found himself watching television—up until recently, he had somehow been unaware of just how many television shows there were, the astonishing glut of content that had been barfed out and was just waiting patiently to be consumed.

The screening room was on the lowest level. Easiest to just take the elevator. Squat leather couches, each with a blanket folded neatly on its arm. In the back, there was a refrigerator, well-stocked baskets of food: chips, candy in a drawer. He shouldn't. But he did—a jumbo box of Junior Mints. Who was here to stop him?

He'd been watching a show set in Chernobyl—probably eight or ten mil an episode, if he had to guess. The whole *Saving Private Ryan* chopper thing going on, sooty-faced character actors who looked like guys from his childhood neighborhood in Queens, a passel of dogs roaming through an impeccable set. Incredible, the things they were doing these days. The amount of money, almost perverse! And this got him jazzed all over again, this DeLillo project, because how could anyone argue with this level of production value, this impact? They were the culture-makers, he'd always believed—everything trickled down from people like him, choices made in a certain room in a certain office in Manhattan, choices that shaped the discourse. And even Don DeLillo would respect that. Though how much better to approach him only after the public vindication—hands clean, blank slate.

A handful of Junior Mints mashed against the roof of his mouth. The sugar made his bad molar zing. He stopped, considered a single waxy Junior Mint balanced on the end of his finger. Study the dimpled chocolate, observe the pleasing chestnut sheen. A form of meditation, he congratulated himself.

Like his mantra from that trip to Kashmir—the producers had gone way over budget, Harvey swooping in to whip things into shape. That weekend, George had insisted they all charter a plane to go visit this famous guru. The Beatles got their mantra from this guy, George told them.

It had been a miserable trip, monsoon season or some such, his armpits rashy. All Harvey drank was Coca-Cola and bottles of warm water; he took blown-out shits on the hour. The whole gang of them arrived at this guru's place, the breezy arcades and Dentyne white of the walls. They were supposed to go in, one by one, sit at the feet of this emaciated guru in his caftan. Receive their life-changing mantras, each one specific to each person, your mantra somehow the exact mantra that would correct all your life's ills.

The guru stared out at Harvey from his little skull. Harvey had made himself hold the guy's gaze. As the guru leaned forward, placed a dry hand on Harvey's head, he whispered Harvey's mantra. But Harvey sniffled just at that moment, the Coca-Cola he'd pounded on the way over bubbling up behind his sinuses, and he couldn't make out the mantra.

And here's the rub—the guru would never, it turned out, repeat the mantra.

"Are you kidding?"

But the guru wasn't kidding. Harvey got angry. "Please," he said. "Come on. I'll pay you. Whatever you want. Just repeat it. Write it down if you don't wanna say it. Whatever, OK?"

The man just looked at him placidly.

On the flight back, queasy from the diarrhea meds, his head-phones blocking out the world, Harvey slept fitfully. When he woke up, there was his assistant, across the aisle, alert to whatever his next request would be. She'd gotten a mantra, too. He took the empty seat next to her.

"So." He tented his fingers, leaned on the armrest. "Crazy trip, right? Funny?"

"Yeah," she said, cautiously. "If you're wondering about Helen, she knows we want the full breakdown by Monday, and I'm just waiting to hear back from B team—"

"I don't need to talk about work right now," Harvey said. "I'm just chatting. Can't we just chat?"

Her smile flickered.

"You have a good time?" Harvey asked.

"Um. Yeah. It's been interesting."

"You've never been to India, right?" He was just guessing.

She blinked behind her glasses. "No, never. A really beautiful country," she said. "Really inspiring."

"Right."

The silence made the girl squirm.

"So, you know," Harvey said. "Tell me what your mantra is."

She shifted, uncomfortable. "Come on," she said. Trying to giggle. "You're never supposed to tell what your mantra is."

"Oh, please," he said. "You don't believe that stuff. I think you should just tell me."

"I really shouldn't," she said.

But here was the thing. They both knew, as soon as he asked the question, that she would tell him her mantra. It was just a matter of how long it would take, what the moments between his demand and her capitulation would look like. In the end, it would be the same to him as any other moment of triumph. Only the in-between was different, made up of a different sequence of concessions, the particulars of each person. Some people resisted, some people did not. Some people went still, unmoving; some people started laughing, out of discomfort. He enjoyed it all, even these milder victories—it was like different flavors of ice cream. And, ultimately, he was always sated, the other person breathing hard, squinting, shifting, some new shame in her face.

Now he woke in Vogel's screening room to the looping menu screen, the season over, his hands smeared with Junior Mints. A glance at his phone—twenty minutes before the doctor arrived. An infusion for his back pain, something he'd never tried before.

Enough time to splash his face upstairs, swish around a little toothpaste, change his shirt. His eyes were bloodshot, his throat sore.

Harvey lay on his bed with his shoes on. Or not his bed. Vogel's bed. He missed his own bed. No way to keep the bed, was the gist. His ex-wife wanted the bed, among other things. She got the bed, and most everything else. Now she was sleeping on the horsehair and cashmere. She'd been interviewed by *Vogue*, her portrait taken by that photographer who shot everyone like they were in a Cadillac commercial or a police procedural. Very network. His ex-wife's gaze was downcast; she was a waif dressed in a thick knit sweater and a long skirt, perched on a boulder by the rocky shoreline. She looked brave, sorrowful, as if she'd persevered through a great difficulty. Probably she could not have designed a better exit for herself, as clean and frictionless as slipping away from a party.

Harvey refreshed his e-mail. Refreshed the news sites. He searched his name, scanning the comments sections, a recent habit. Or more of a compulsion, forcing himself to wade through the vitriol until he came across at least one nice comment. He took it as an omen, and as soon as he read that single nice comment he was released. It took a while, this time, but he found one:

Maverick1972: *It's verrry INTERESTING how the girls are suddenly crying when they were asking for jobs and cars at the time! Harvey isn't a monster its not his fault hes got what they wanted and took what he could who would blame him!!!!*

Not the most eloquent defender, Maverick1972, but it gave him heart, a little rush of victory. And why shouldn't he feel confident? One of the younger lawyers had e-mailed him PDFs of all the exhibits, shown him how to scroll through the evidence they'd amassed over the past two years. A simple glance and it was all there: photos of every single one of them, hugging him. Kissing his cheek! Pushing themselves into him, pressing their faces to his face, practically humping him there on the step-and-repeat.

Uncle Harvey, they called him, afterward.

Gabe knocked on the door. Time for the infusion. A new way they were treating chronic pain, a new attempt to mitigate the constant shock from his spine, his body a bombed-out war zone: the only thing that helped lately was the horse pills, swimmy Vicodin afternoons light-headed in the sauna, scratching his chest and arms, slapping his limp dick without any response. He'd forgotten he wasn't supposed to drink water before the infusion, much less house a box of Junior Mints, but probably, like most suggestions, it didn't really matter.

Harvey got to his feet, with some effort. Groped for his phone. An e-mail he'd started to Nancy—cc Lewis, Honor Keating, a few of the sharper guys from the old days, people who'd been waiting to hear what he was kicking around. He was like Bob Evans, he thought, his heart stirring, marshaling Towne and Nicholson to make *Chinatown*. And here it was— the perfect property, his very own *Chinatown*, only better, because it didn't need that little creep Polanski to rewrite the whole thing. Though, it was worth pointing out, look what had happened to Polanski—sex with a thirteen-year-old—anal!—and he'd basically been sentenced to parole, no jail time. Everything ruined by a few unfortunate press photos leaking when he was supposed to be in preproduction.

Despite all that, Polanski was still making movies, still skiing the Swiss Alps with pals and winning awards. Harvey was small potatoes, compared. These were grown women.

How could anyone think Harvey belonged in jail? It was so unlikely. He'd only half listened to the jail consultant, a meeting set up in Rory's conference room. The man had tried to scare Harvey, slamming the table hard when he saw Harvey was on his phone.

"Do you think this is a joke?" the man had screamed, neck ropy above his polo shirt, spittle flying from his mouth and landing, to Harvey's disgust, on his own lips. He wiped it away, deliberately. Went back to his e-mails.

White Noise—they could make a real art-house push, emphasize that this was an old-fashioned movie, a classic. What Bob Evans would call a people picture. Get Brian on the phone. In time for next awards season—it wasn't a crazy goal, wasn't a totally unrealistic timeline. People wanted to help him. He had a million favors left to call in.

He shuffled to the guest room, still typing on his phone. "Now is the PERFECT TIME to do this MOVIE," he wrote. "we as a nation are hungry 4 meaning."

The curtains in the guest room were drawn, but the lights had been turned up to a blazing wash, a fat leather recliner pulled into the center of the room, a whole setup already plugged in and humming away—a bursting IV sack, a heart monitor, a silver tray of antiseptic swabs and packaged needles.

"NancY pls get Numbers pulled 2gether aSAP so I cn present 2 don delillo 2morrow eve, find out if thre is nice resto nearby, make a res, he can bring wife is f he has or gf?"

The doctor came in—tan, sexless, a chain around his neck, and hairless forearms. Plum-colored scrubs. Had he done that on purpose, removed all his body hair?

"Sir?" the doctor said.

Harvey didn't look up from his phone.

"Sir?"

"Jesus, what?"

"I just need your finger, sir. Let's just slip this on," the doctor said, clipping a pulse monitor on his ring finger. Harvey pretended not to notice the man's smirk. Fuck him. Fuck the hairless doctor.

"OK," the doctor said. "Remember the basics from the phone consultation?"

Harvey stared at him—Gabe had done the required phone call in Harvey's place. He nodded.

"We've been starting people at a hundred, for chronic pain like yours. How does that sound?"

Harvey shrugged. "Let's do more."

"It might be best to just see how you respond at a hundred."

"More," Harvey said, mildly, and watched the doctor start to respond. "More," Harvey said again, smiling a little, "more," and the doctor finally gave up, sensing, maybe, that Harvey could keep this up as long as it took.

"OK," the doctor said, brightly, "let's do one thirty-five," as if he had been the one to suggest it. He left, and a nurse came in.

The nurse was named Anastasia, a Russian with bleached hair and too-dark eyebrows. Shapeless scrubs, a pair of white Keds, tightly laced. She was brusque but not unkind.

"And how are you, Anastasia?" Harvey said.

"Good," she said, cheerful. She was maybe twenty-five.

"Having a good day?"

She made a face, then smiled. "Back at work, you know. It's fine."

"Right. You do anything fun lately?"

She didn't seem at all bothered by his questions, happy to chat. "I went on vacation with my husband."

"Oh, yeah?" he said. "Where did you go with this husband?"

"Have you been to Miami?"

"Have I been to Miami?" he said. "Yeah, sure. Sure I've been to Miami."

"We went. Me and my husband. I think he liked it more than me. He saw, he liked the—" She stopped, made a ballooning gesture in front of her flat chest. "All the swimsuits. His eyes were, like, pow," she said, a googly expression on her face. "I think he wanted to stay."

"Sounds like a real dick, Anastasia."

She giggled. Amazing, these Soviet girls, just happy to have a husband. Probably husbands who knocked them around a little, why not. The things he could do for Anastasia, if she gave even the slightest indication of receptivity. He reminded himself to ask Gabe to find out more about her. Who was this husband? Some pale Russian with sunken eyes, guzzling protein shakes from Costco, probably a pit bull in the backyard.

Harvey adjusted himself in the big leather chair.

"Comfy?" Anastasia said.

"Mmm."

They mixed in an antiemetic, and a little Xanax, too, so people didn't freak out, Anastasia explained. "So you won't even be worried."

The doctor came back in, smiley, fratty.

"And are we feeling ready?" He looked only at the air around Harvey, no longer making direct eye contact. Good. Let the doctor be afraid. He'd signed an NDA, they all did.

The machine was the size of a toaster. A thin tube hooked up to a port in the back of his hand. Anastasia prepared the area with a shot of lidocaine. Had him make a fist.

"Big strong veins!" she cooed.

He looked away when she inserted the IV. Didn't want to think of the veins right there, under the surface. Unsettling how it took mere seconds to gain access to his insides, open him up.

"OK," the doctor said. "OK. All set?"

Harvey felt his phone buzz in his pocket. "Hold on," he said.

"Don't jostle the IV."

It was not, as he guessed, an e-mail from the producers. Just an e-mail from his accountant: "Sending good thoughts for tomorrow." Yes, sure, Dave, thanks for your good thoughts. None of your thoughts are good thoughts, that's why you're an accountant.

Harvey said, "Is this going to be scary, Anastasia? Are you going to watch over me?"

She laughed. "Yes," she said. "Nothing to worry about." She put the eye mask over his face. Got even closer to adjust the strap. He wished he had used the trimmer—he had a corsage of wiry black hairs at each ear. He had the feeling, lately, when he looked in the mirror, that a pile of glue was staring back at him, like he was melting.

"OK," Anastasia's voice came, faint from the new darkness. "Now I put on the headphones. Yes?"

They were big, noise-canceling. "Blanket," he said. Then reminded himself to throw in a "please."

Yes. A heavy fur blanket pulled over his body, tucked by Anastasia right up under his chin. Maternally, gently. He couldn't remember if he had sent the e-mail to Nancy—he should do that, he thought, quickly, make sure that ball got rolling. But where was his phone? No matter. He no longer cared where his phone was. Because here it was, it had arrived:

The cool whoosh of the future in his veins.

Ah. Ahh.

Had he yelled the word "help"? Or just mouthed it? Whatever panic he felt had appeared and disappeared in the same instant.

Welcome, the void said. We've been waiting for you.

Then his body started to rise, like a balloon nearing the ceiling, bobbing lightly. Wow, he thought, mildly. A nice drift over the city. What city? I don't know. A city. Maybe the city from the Apple TV screen saver, a generic grid twinkling below. He was moving so slowly.

When he tried to squeeze his brain around any future plans, around making the movie, his thoughts just slipped away. All he could think of were the words "white noise." White noise, yes—how better to describe what this feeling was?

Why couldn't all of life be this way, this uninflected witnessing, the relief of being a vegetable? Keep him hooked up to the machine, doctor. Twenty-four hours a day, just let him rest.

Bye!

Bye, Harvey!

What was Harvey but a cardboard cutout, really, an idea of himself? How funny that he had ever cared so much.

After maybe an hour, the sensations started to fade. He felt a familiar sorrow, like when, as a kid, he could sense the end of a movie nearing, knowing soon it would all be over, knowing that soon he would be returned to the harsh reality of the world and its disappointments.

Harvey was legitimately bereft. He pushed the eye mask away from his eyes with a clumsy hand—it felt like he was wearing mittens. And then the feeling was replaced with the information—curious!—that he was now lying on the floor. It didn't feel any different from being in the chair. He remained on the floor, very still. Feeling his chest rise and fall.

Anastasia opened the door, made a noise of surprise, then left. She returned with the doctor. Together they worked to hoist Harvey back into the chair. His legs felt weak. But he was smiling, a big dopey smile.

"You fell," the doctor said.

"I didn't feel anything."

"That's normal."

He had to pee, badly, his bladder glowing.

Anastasia removed the IV, easing the medical tape from his arm, careful not to rip out the hair. She was so conscientious, he thought. Perfect blond angel.

"Have you. Ever tried it?" he said, with some effort.

"No," she said. "No, not yet."

"You should try it," he said to Anastasia. "You have to try it."

"I see all the people when they come out, some are crying. But mostly they are happy, they have a good experience. Did you have a good experience?"

"Oh, yes." Should he try to explain more? "Very good."

"So maybe I should try it."

"When's your birthday? Make him give you one for your birthday. The doctor."

"Next month, actually."

"OK," Harvey said. "It's settled. I'm getting you an infusion for your birthday."

She laughed, prettily. "Thank you."

She was not even a little bit afraid of him.

"We'll just set you right up in bed," she was saying. "Let's just lie down for a bit, OK?"

He hoped that she never stopped telling him what to do, never stopped explaining what was coming next.

"Right, up we go, right on the bed. Now your legs. Swing them up for me. Very good."

Harvey lay on the bed.

"Are you gonna stay here?" he mumbled. "Stay with me?"

No response. When he opened his eyes, she was gone—he was alone.

Lunch in the dining room. Gabe pouring ice water from a carafe. A square of black cod, the size and thickness of a pack of cards. Charred broccolini. A scoop of bland white rice, flecked with parsley. He still felt dazed, his thoughts dropping a little bit behind. He wasn't hungry—he forced down a few halfhearted forkfuls of rice. He felt different from the person he had been that morning, like he'd stepped off to the side of himself. His phone buzzed on the tabletop—Rory, the lawyers. He let it go to voice mail. After a few moments, the phone shivered: they had left a message. He read the transcription, auto-generated by the phone, with one squinted eye:

"Chow had Lee it's roar a couple be back"

He didn't click to see the rest of the gibberish, letting his eyes close fully, his head resting on his folded arms.

Kristin texted—five minutes away. Some sense of duty, visiting her father in his hour of need. There had been no way to indicate that he would prefer to be alone, in order to more effectively tranquilize himself: he'd rather spend the day with Anastasia or hunker down in the peaceful bowels of the screening room, knocking himself out with endless episodes. Life was in many ways worse these days, but you had to admit: God had given people the tools they needed to be happy.

Kristin was his oldest daughter, unmarried with an ADD kid, from designer sperm that had apparently not been so designer. Kristin ran a foundation aimed at improving graduation rates, and had signed a public pledge to give away at least half her wealth in her lifetime. Kristin, with her peculiar features, her downy cheeks. Kristin, who wrote an op-ed about choosing not to fly private anymore, for which she was roundly and deservedly mocked. She had never been able to see the wave coming, about to knock her down, though it was the clearest thing in the world.

Rory called again—Harvey answered. "Just wanting to touch base," Rory was saying. "I don't want to alarm you, but I know we're just concerned, about Jurors Three and Nine, especially. We fought tooth and nail to keep them off, and with good reason, and the consultant thinks they could be the vocal ones in a closed room—"

A vague image of the women jurors appeared to him, the one with a spider pin on her lapel, the other in a silky shirt buttoned to the neck, a tight cornrowed bun on her head, always staring his way. In any other situation, he would have been aware of the women's existence for half a second. If that. He resented having to think about them at all. Which one of them had laughed when they'd shown the photos of his naked body? His arms and legs starfished in that well-lit room?

"Just want to keep you up to date on our thinking," Rory finished.

"Well," Harvey said. Should he ask him to repeat himself? "I guess," he said slowly, "I'm glad to be up to date. On your thinking."

A nap upstairs, and now the elevator glided soundlessly down to the ground floor, depositing him, the vulnerable human, safely at his destination. He padded toward the front door, one hand trailing lightly along the wall, in case he needed the support. Kristin was milling around the entry hall, Gabe fluttering in the background. She was in a turtleneck and a quilted vest. Silver earrings and pulled-back ponytail. Awfully severe. She looked sober and anxious, her daughter clutching her hand tightly, though she was eleven or twelve.

"Grandpa!" the girl said, when she caught sight of him approaching, hobbling down the hall.

For a moment, Harvey was taken aback, his chest warming with legit joy. She sounded so guileless, Ruby, so cheerful and wholesome. When he smiled at her, already the girl seemed uninterested. Was this an ADD thing?

"Hello, you," Harvey said. He cleared his throat. He felt less groggy, less glitchy. "Hello, both of you."

"How are you, Dad?" Kristin said, hugging him with one arm.

"You know." He zipped and unzipped the half-zip of his sweater. "The bastards try to get you down." He blinked at the top of the girl's head. "Sorry. I mean the jerks."

Kristin patted his upper arm. "Well, we're here to get your spirits up. OK? We'll think positive."

He wished Gabe would just take over, like a cruise director, steer them toward the proper activities, keep them all energized and happy, maintain group morale, but Gabe had disappeared. "How was the drive?"

"Easy. Whatever."

"Boring," Ruby said. "How come there's an elevator in a house?"

"For people like me," he said, "people in pain. It's easier than the stairs."

Kristin's face rippled—who knows why?

"Are you hungry? Come in," he said. "Let's sit. Sit down at least—why are we just standing around?"

Gabe had put out silver bowls of potato chips, peanut M&M's. He appeared in the doorway to take their drink orders: Kristin wanted an espresso and a glass of seltzer, Ruby was already chewing the potato chips and shook her head.

"Water for me, too," Harvey said.

Ruby sat on the floor, leaned back against Kristin's legs. Kristin perched primly on the love seat, playing absently with Ruby's hair. It occurred to him that maybe she, too, was antsy, needed something to occupy herself.

"Having a good trip?" he said.

"We went to Ellis Island," Kristin said.

"You know, my grandparents are in the . . . book, register, whatever there. Did you see them? Find their names? Your great-grandparents. When they came from Warsaw."

"Uh, no. You didn't tell me that."

"You didn't tell me you were going."

A run of beeps from Ruby's phone, her head bowed in concentration. "And," Kristin said, "we saw a matinée of *Hamilton*."

"I've seen it twice already," Ruby said. "This one wasn't even the original cast."

"That's true," Kristin said. "Her friend at school is the kid of— what's the guy, the guy from *Cheers* who did that Broadway show a few years ago? They were living out here, for the run. Ruby visited for spring break."

Kristin looked at him expectantly, as if he would have follow-up questions. He folded his hands neatly on his stomach.

"How's your back?" she said.

"Better," he said. And it was true, since the infusion he had felt less pain. Had mostly just been less aware of pain, had not returned to the fact of the pain at the end of every thought. "I'm trying this new therapy. New thing, very cutting-edge. It was actually much better than the surgery. You should try it," Harvey said. "It's not just for, you know, pain."

How could he communicate what he had experienced earlier, how important it was that his daughter get an infusion as soon as possible? Maybe he could get Anastasia to come back this evening, get Kristin hooked up. Hell, even Ruby. All three of them zonked out in big easy chairs, drifting through space, attended to by a loyal blonde.

"And what about generally?" Kristin said. "Are you OK? Are you afraid?"

"Am I afraid?" He blinked, rapidly. "No, I'm not afraid." That's what he should try to make clear: how even though you felt, on the infusion, like you were floating through space and would never return to earth, it didn't scare you.

"I just," Kristin said. "I don't know. I'm here for you. I know Franny has not been the most supportive"—Frances, his other daughter, ensconced in Seattle with her bitchy tech husband; Frances, who sent him a lengthy e-mail, subject line "RAPE," and cc'd her shrink—"but you will always have me."

"Thanks. I don't think. I mean, I don't know but I don't think this is gonna go badly. You know? No one has given any indication that this is going to go sideways."

She didn't look entirely convinced. He suspected she thought that this scale of punishment made sense. It would have made him angry, usually—how could anyone believe he deserved this? Had he killed anyone? But that anger, so easily called forth, now seemed to exist on the other side of a pane of glass.

He pointed to where the roofline of the house next door was visible through the living room window, the jag of black gables. "You know who lives over there?" he said. "In that brick house?" He paused, to summon the appropriate level of drama. "Don DeLillo."

Kristin seemed distracted, not quite listening. "The writer?"

"Yes. Yes, exactly, the writer. Pretty wild, huh, right next door to your pops. We're actually doing a little project together, me and Don."

Hadn't Kristin majored in English? Shouldn't she look thrilled, instead of concerned?

"I'm gonna send you his books," Harvey announced. "Right now. For you, too, Ruby, a set for each of you." The gesture pleased him. He pulled up Amazon on his phone, squinting at the screen. "Now, let me just get this going," he said, pecking out letters in the search bar.

"Dad, I don't need all of Don DeLillo's books."

"Please, it's a pleasure. A gift."

"We're actually in the middle of decluttering right now," Kristin said.

"Nonsense," he said. "This is literature. Great literature. And maybe you'll want to help. I'm doing an adaptation of *White Noise*. It's going to be big, sweetie. Huge. Maybe Ruby can intern on the set, like what's-her-face Obama. Would you like that, Ruby? See how a movie gets made?"

Ruby shot him a thumbs-up without looking over, enchanted by her phone.

"You have something in development?" Kristin sounded skeptical. "But where's the financing coming from? I thought Bob was—"

"Listen, sweetie. Everyone wants to get in on my next project. You know how many calls I get a day, people sniffing around to see where I'm headed after all this wraps up? What moves I'll make?"

Saying the words made him even more certain—they sounded true.

"But what if. I don't know. You know, what if this doesn't go as you"—she seemed to be picking her words carefully, cognizant of Ruby at her feet—"as you planned?"

"Please. You think I'm going to jail? Look at me, I'm an old man."

An early dinner, a fire crackling pleasantly in the dining room. His appetite had returned, and he swabbed the steak juice from Vogel's embarrassing Wedgwood plate with a fat Parker House roll. Ruby ate plain spaghetti and an undressed salad. She drank ice water from a wine goblet. Kristin looked bored, ready to leave. Was it such a chore to spend time with him?

The clock in the kitchen was ticking so loudly he heard it from the dining room. Didn't Kristin notice? Didn't Ruby? Why were they all just sitting here eating as this steady tick marked every second?

"Gabe," Harvey said, clutching at the man's shirt as he refilled the Barolo. "Can we get that clock off, turn it off. Is it new? How come I hear every single tick?"

"Of course," Gabe said. "No problem. I'll take the batteries out right away."

Ruby watched this exchange with interest.

Harvey's phone kept buzzing on the table: texts of support. Last-minute exhortations from the lawyers, a request to RETURN MY CALL ASAP—he barely glanced at those. Some talk of bail, what to do if the judge denied their motion—"remanded," not a word he wanted to probe too hard. His eyes went soft, not exactly taking it in. Much better to focus on the other messages, the "Don't let this get you down" text, the "Soon this will all be in the rearview!" e-mail.

"Look at this," Harvey said, turning the phone toward Kristin so she could see the latest lengthy text, a fat bubble of blue filling the screen. "Paulie says he'll take me out the minute this is all over. Said to pencil in Capri in August." Nice to imagine August on the boat, the dinner at the cliffs, the low votives along the table. Maybe Don DeLillo could join. Make a note to have Nancy overnight Don DeLillo a DVD of *Contempt*.

"Great," Kristin said.

"What?" Harvey put his phone down. "Why do you say it like that, like it's bad?"

"It's just. I don't know if you should be, like, celebrating."

Ruby was eagle-eyed now, taking this in.

"Who's celebrating?" He gestured at the table, the staid windows segmenting the quickly darkening sky. "Is this a celebration, some wild party? I thought we were having a peaceful dinner. A quiet dinner with my daughter and granddaughter."

Kristin sighed, stared at her still full plate. "Sorry."

Another piece of steak, another Parker House roll. The green beans he grabbed with his fingers, everything speckled from the pepper mill wielded by Gabe. "Thank you," Harvey made a point of saying to Gabe. "Thank you," he repeated, to no one in particular.

Ruby gulped her ice water.

"You tired, sweetheart?" Kristin asked her. Ruby shrugged.

"She's getting tired," Kristin said. "We should think about going pretty soon."

"I'm not tired," Ruby said.

"It's a long drive back," Kristin said. "I don't love driving in the dark."

Harvey finished his wine. Tilting the empty glass back and forth. "What's the difference between the dark now and the dark in a few hours?" He had not meant it to sound accusatory—he really wondered.

"Dessert?" Gabe said, appearing in the doorway. "Angel food cake and berries, or crème brûlée? We have sorbet."

"I'm full," Kristin said. "Sounds so yummy, though."

"Cake," Ruby said, scooting up on her chair. "And, like, what kind of sorbet do you have?"

"Gabe, bring out all the sorbets," Harvey said, "and one of everything else. My family is visiting. It's a special occasion."

"Really?" Ruby looked at Kristin, who smiled tightly. On the table, Harvey's phone buzzed.

Joan, the reporter, had sent a series of question marks. *If you really want to talk with me honestly, I think we should set up a chat tonight.*

Harvey turned his phone over.

"You could spend the night," Harvey said. "We could watch something, downstairs." To Ruby, "There's candy in the screening room. You can pick whatever. King size."

"She's already had a lot of sugar today."

"Skittles have horse hooves in them," Ruby said. "Sick, right?"

"It is sick." He nodded at the gloomy horse painting over the mantelpiece, jittery in the light of the candle. "You notice all these horses everywhere? It's, like, every room has a horse painting. I saw on the, you know, hand towels, too. A horse caricature."

"You mean silhouette," Kristin said.

Harvey shrugged. "You're probably right."

Ruby patted his hand, once, twice. The gesture moved him. It would be fun, having Ruby intern on the movie. He had a swift and detailed daydream: Don DeLillo writing Ruby a letter of recommendation for college, Ruby waving from the dais of her graduation, beaming love at Harvey. But before he could respond, maybe even take Ruby's hand in his, Kristin had pushed her chair back, was gathering up her purse, folding her soiled napkin. "We should hit the road," she said.

"Are you sure you don't want to sleep over? There's so many rooms. You can ride the elevator."

Kristin smiled, sadly.

"Tea? Coffee? Anything? Let me call Gabe," he said. But their departure was already set in motion. Pretty soon he would be waving at their car as they pulled away and left him alone, and then that was exactly what he was doing. He lingered outside in the driveway, the barn jacket zipped up, his bare head cold, his nostrils sharpening with frigid air. The house next door, the house of Don DeLillo, was silent, all the windows black. No car in the driveway, no signs of life. Where had he gone, Don DeLillo?

Upstairs, Gabe had laid out his clothes for the morning: The suit hanging from the closet door. The red socks draped alongside the butterscotch split-toe bluchers. The walker probably folded and waiting by the door downstairs.

He sat on the closed lid of the toilet, waiting for the bath to fill. The ankle bracelet was waterproof, fine to wear in the shower, but he'd thought, at first, that he had to keep it dry, so he'd started taking baths. And now he preferred baths, liked feeling like a tea bag, steeping in the scalding water.

Around his body, the bathwater was cloudy with soap, tepid water he drained and refilled with more hot water. His phone and a heavy tumbler of Scotch on the porcelain ledge, the Scotch not exactly condoned by his doctors. But Gabe seemed to understand this was a special night, a night that deserved kindness. The pour had been especially generous. Harvey slipped the soap under each armpit, around the belly, the groin that he didn't quite acknowledge, a habit from childhood, hitting the area with soap but never looking at his body, his gaze focusing somewhere beyond. Then his legs, his knees poking out of the water like two bald monks. The soap shot out from his fist—he groped for it in the opaque water, then gave up.

A knock on the door—Gabe. "I'm just going to close up the house for the night," he said. "I left a sleeping pill on the nightstand with a fresh bottle of water. Can I get you anything else for now?"

"Thanks," Harvey called in the direction of the closed door. "Nothing. Thanks."

Another missed call from Rory. Forget Rory. He should get in touch with Joan. She had always helped him.

"Harvey," Joan said. She sounded weary. "I don't have time to do anything before tomorrow. You should get some sleep."

"Listen, listen. Just stay with me, OK? Joan? You know me. You've known me for years. I'm not a monster. You know I'm not a monster."

He'd worked hard, hadn't he? Bought his mother a house. Let Nancy's MS boyfriend piggyback on her health insurance. "You can tell the truth from the lies, can't you, Joan?"

"Harvey." Was she just going to keep repeating his name in that doomed register? Why was she acting like it was already over, like he'd already been convicted? His heart beat rapidly. He clutched the phone harder to his ear with wet hands. "Joan. I remember things, too, Joan. Remember that girl in Tokyo? Gold Bar," he said, triumphantly. "Gold Bar. You left her there. She was crying and you left her there. Remember that, Joan?"

"Jesus, Harvey."

"So you do remember?"

"What is this? Are you threatening me?" Her voice was a monotone, a professional monotone.

"No, no," he said, "not threatening, just—"

"Don't you dare threaten me, Harvey. Do not. Fucking. Dare."

He had never heard her sound like that. Her tone so careful, clipped. Like she was talking to someone doomed. A new and sudden panic was seizing him, a freezing bite at the nape of his neck, as if he'd been taken in the jaws of a terrible animal.

Perhaps a resolution would not be as clean as he'd assumed, not be as swift and total. All the things that had happened he could barely remember, so that at first he'd actually listened with some interest to the testimony, curious to hear what he'd supposedly done. But it had quickly become boring. He assumed everyone had felt the same way, assumed everyone was similarly bored. It had all seemed to occur at the wrong end of a telescope, far away and distorted—tales set in hotel rooms, hallways of restaurants that had closed almost a decade ago. Bar 89 no longer existed. The girl was saying he had called her once from his cell phone, told her he was standing out in front of Lady M and did she think it was totally naughty if he went inside and got a cake?

This made him look up—had he said that?

As the trial had gone on, Harvey had found himself fuzzing out, daydreaming, filling and refilling his water glass just to have something to do. The other girl said he had wanted to film her. Made her pose for him. "And did you pose for him?"

She nodded through tears. He glanced at the jury—no one seemed too distressed. Rory hadn't made eye contact with him, but Harvey could tell, by a slight upturn of his lips, that he, too, thought this was ridiculous.

"Did he invite you to parties?" the lawyer said. "And you attended, even after this incident?"

The girl looked at her hands. "I like parties," she said. "Everyone likes parties."

The trial could have ended right there. "Joan," Harvey said. "Wait."

But it was over. He had lost her.

"Goodbye, Harvey."

He called back. Once. Twice. Five times. The calls went straight to voice mail.

Gabe had turned down the bedcovers, dimmed the lights. Drawn all the curtains. Another slug of Scotch. Pajama pants drawstringed at his waist, a purple Lakers T-shirt he found in Vogel's top drawer. Fuzzy socks with snowflakes on them, white wool and ice blue, his pajama pants tucked into the top. Cozy, cozy. He could, at this moment, meet every one of his needs: always be warm, always be fed. What if that changed? Unbearable, unthink-able. Who knows how long he sat there in the dim room? How long until a sound outside broke the spell?

Harvey made his way to the window, and pulled back the curtain. The noise was coming from the house next door, Don DeLillo's house—it was his car, Don DeLillo's car, popping along the gravel, coming to a stop in front of the house. The car's inte-rior lights turned on, bright enough that Harvey saw the outline of Don DeLillo in the driver's seat. He seemed to be sitting very still, sitting very upright. Was he waiting for Harvey to join him? Waiting for their midnight meeting, there in the quiet country-side? An assignation amid its sleeping citizens, dreaming in their beds, unaware of Harvey and Don DeLillo vibrating on a higher frequency? Why else would Don DeLillo just be sitting there, the dome light like a beacon, summoning Harvey?

Harvey shrugged on the barn jacket, a beanie with earflaps that he grabbed from a basket of gloves and hats in the entry closet. A horse appliqué on the hat, hovering right over his brow.

One great yank and the front door was open—except the world was ending, an earsplitting, pants-shitting sound ripping through the silence. An alarm—he was in danger! Or, actually, he was the danger—he'd set off some security system, but no time to explain to Gabe. He strode out into the brisk night. A night, he noted, of no stars, a poetic observation, one he would share with Don DeLillo. The alarm continued its steady bleat, the volume seem-ing to increase. The covered patio furniture hulked in shadowy arrangement—he glided around it, heading toward the fence. He was moving fluidly, moving without any pain. The car came in and out of sight, the interior light still on, the beacon guiding his way.

Here was the fence, and there, on the other side, was Don DeLillo. He was still sitting in the car—talking on the phone,

Harvey could see now, a rectangle of light casting Don DeLillo's face in sickly blue. The radio was on, or music was playing, the chatter drifting through the night, in the intermittent silence of the alarm. Harvey started to wave. Don DeLillo would know what to do. How to fix the things that had gone wrong. The alarm behind him was louder, he wasn't imagining it. Don DeLillo had noticed, too, his head cocked, his face turning in Harvey's direction.

"It's me," Harvey called out, raising his hand, waving, hoping to be seen in the darkness. "I'm here."

Don DeLillo was unfolding himself from the car, standing with one hand cupped over his eyes—but why? There was no sun.

"Hello," Harvey said, and Don DeLillo paused, the driver's door ajar.

Harvey was pressed right up against the fence now, the slats coming to his chin, only his head poking over, like a gargoyle. "Good evening," Harvey yelled, in a rush. His hands were gripping the fence slats, which were, for some reason, damp. His loafers were soaked.

"Is everything OK?" Don DeLillo called.

"I just want to talk," Harvey said, "if you have a minute? Just a quick"—he rocked on his toes, his mind grasping for the word—"a quick chat."

"Hold on, I'll call you back," Don DeLillo said into the phone, then shut the car door, making his slow way on the gravel toward Harvey. He was coming closer. Every step was audible, an icy crunch.

"Are you all right?" Don DeLillo said, near enough now for Harvey to make out his face above his scarf, a face mooning out of the darkness—his eyes were wet berries.

"I'm fine," Harvey said. "And you?"

"The alarm?" Don DeLillo gestured behind Harvey.

"Oh, yes." He made as if to glance back at the house, then

actually did. The house was all lit up, a birthday cake hovering in the void. "I forgot the, uh. Security code."

"Right."

"I saw your light," Harvey said, trying to be crystal clear, to communicate, with every word he spoke, that he had received the message. "I saw you were awake, too. Both of us," Harvey said, with significance, "*couldn't sleep.*"

Didn't Don DeLillo see how alike they were, didn't he feel it? See how they were men, both of them, men up late on this dark winter night, pondering what the new day would bring?

Don DeLillo was studying Harvey, his face turned to the side. His brows bloomed on his old gray face.

"Maybe," Don DeLillo said, slowly, "maybe you just needed some fresh air. Sometimes that helps me. When I can't sleep."

"Yes," Harvey said, beaming. "That's exactly right. We both needed some air."

His fingers were freezing, almost numb. But his back didn't hurt, not at all. His nose was runny but he didn't make to wipe it. He tasted salt in his smile. "Don't worry," Harvey said, almost whispering. "I'm not gonna make a scene, or turn this into a big deal. I just," he said, "want you to know. It's an honor to meet you."

Don DeLillo looked bewildered.

"Do you want me to call someone?" Don DeLillo said.

Don DeLillo was close enough that Harvey could touch him, if he tried, if he made an effort. Did he reach out first, or did Don DeLillo back up, his arms flapping a little, his phone clutched to his chest? Why did he look confused? There was so much Harvey wanted to tell him—they had so much to decide. But there was time, he reminded himself. There was all the time in the world.

Asali Solomon
Delandria

THE STREETS OF THE TOWN could in no way be described as lively during the day, but at night they were even more deserted; the neat brick streets and ornate Victorians resembled the outcome of a pristine little purge. Rumor was that the students occasionally slipped into town after dark, calling at a certain ramshackle house to secure pills or powders too specialized to be found on campus. She almost never saw them.

Magna sped as she approached her apartment building, on Main Street, which was as desolate as it had been when she'd set out earlier that night. Suddenly a brown-and-white blur reared up in front of her. Meaning to hit the brake, she stamped on the accelerator. There was a violent, wet crunching sound and a scream caught in her throat.

With the helpless terror she'd felt at the top of roller coasters, she did not stop.

Before

It had become a habit for Magna—watching television, drinking wine, and then going for a drive. She and Jamal had ritually drunk wine while watching television every night, despite the fact that back then everyone in academia could be heard saying, "Oh, I never watch TV." Since no one in academia ever said, "Oh, I never drink wine," she wondered if they perhaps preferred to sip staring into the abyss. But eventually Jamal swore off TV, saying he wasn't getting enough done on his dissertation. Then he gave up drinking. Then he left her.

That was when Magna added the drives. It felt healthy to go out into the sharp air after the solo slide into the musty depths of the couch. Tonight she had given herself a quick assessment and decided she was okay to drive. She worried a bit about the fact that she had begun crying unexpectedly at the episode in season one when Wallace gets killed. She had not cried the first time she'd seen it. But poor Wallace! He had tried so hard to take care of the neighborhood kids, even though he was just a kid himself. Magna sobbed, remembering when the actor had been a hopeful teenager readying for the prom on *All My Children*. Nevertheless, grabbing her keys off the nail by the door, she concluded that she was not drunk, just sad. It was a sad time, on this show and in her life. The apartment building, a wide colonial, was quiet except for the blare of Mr. Oakley's TV set, which ran constantly, game shows during the day, weather and shopping channels at night. Mr. Oakley was a very nice, stooped old man, the type who looks like a baby, with an open smile. His loud TV and the large NRA bumper sticker on his car were the only problems with him as a neighbor. Magna never saw or heard anybody else in the building. She often wondered if she and Mr. Oakley were actually just roommates. The landlord was an upbeat, platinum-haired woman who lived elsewhere and suggested that Magna use "old-fashioned elbow grease" on the thick coatings of bird shit that had covered her back window and porch since before she'd moved in that summer.

Once outside, Magna inhaled the night. The stars looked crowded and close. "God's own country," she had always said to Jamal when they saw something pretty in this new town, which was often. She felt grateful to him for accompanying her to this hellhole, and was anxious to highlight its meager charms. And it was true that even the dump had a pastoral allure. "God's own country," she'd said among the soiled mattresses and splintered wood, where they'd come to bring a broken IKEA shelf that she shouldn't have packed in the first place. He'd laughed that time, holding his nose. After a couple of weeks she'd known it was becoming annoying, but she couldn't stop saying it.

"That's becoming a tic," he'd said.

"You say that about everything that gets on your nerves," she'd said.

"*Or* maybe you have a lot of tics."

Before he left, she and Jamal had sat on the second-floor back porch amid the bird shit and he had declared that the night sky was the only thing he would really miss. Oh, and her, of course; of course he'd miss her. Then he'd actually attempted a kiss. This was just after he'd announced that he was going back to California, where they'd been graduate students, because he felt like there was something special with Ananda, and he just had to figure everything out. He clarified that he wasn't breaking up with Magna at all, just putting things on pause. Instead of meeting his lips, Magna had put up an elbow, which he didn't see because his eyes were closed. She hurt his face and was not sorry.

Sometimes it was hard to remember why she had been with Jamal. Mostly he was the prototype of the bad boyfriend in a Tyler Perry movie. But then she would remember—he was handsome, smart, black, and well lotioned, the most undeniable man Magna had ever dated (like the bad boyfriend in a Tyler Perry movie). He had been several cuts above the other men in her graduate program. They were head cases: this one pretending to be gay to get closer to straight women; this one who'd written all of his coursework essays about feces; this one wearing an undershirt to class, approaching undergrads in Payne Hall, saying, "Can I holler at you for a minute?" Jamal, on the other hand, was beloved by everyone, and lived on secret fellowships that only the secretary and the department chair, and eventually Magna, knew about.

For the first few years in the program, he and Magna had been friends while he was on and off with a chalky black art history student who looked like a Goya painting. When that woman got a job in Texas off one dissertation chapter and Magna found herself in bed with Jamal, she couldn't believe it. She got high off the look on people's faces when they walked into a room together.

Before him, she'd never wanted children, but even with how unhappy they had begun to make each other, even after he left, she still ached to one day parade the streets with his baby in a stroller. It was a fantasy so familiar that it had become memory, painful to recall. As she drove down the dark street, past the quaint stores selling mugs and Lilly Pulitzer dresses, the Confederate junk shop and the one good restaurant, Magna knew she was trying to escape from what had happened that afternoon, her meeting with the university president. He was trim, silver haired, with burnished but not shiny shoes and the sharp facial planes of a film actor, but a Bill Clinton nose, a red medicine dropper there at the tip. She'd had to meet with him because she'd made the mistake of telling her most sympathetic colleague, the most liberal person in the English Department, about a slightly menacing incident, and the colleague had been upset enough to contact the president. "I hope it's okay," she'd said, only after she'd set up the meeting. Magna had said it was okay, feeling a sense of excited doom.

In the president's office Magna had found it hard to explain herself. She imagined that he'd postponed something more significant to take this meeting—a fund-raising call, a preliminary interview for an even fancier job, two fingers of whiskey. Was her story even a story? Two days earlier, she had been standing on the street near her apartment building when a car drove by and a male voice yelled, "Hey, girl!" in a voice like one of the Negro crows in *Dumbo*. She had heard laughter and seen a flash of white boy, clearly students at the school—they had a university bumper sticker. It was meant to be an imitation of her, Magna—how she would say "Hey, girl," because she was black.

"Hey, girl," she cawed to the thick burgundy carpet, the beautiful stone fireplace, and the portraits of landed gentry. She did not mention the crows in *Dumbo* to him, but the president nodded with some understanding. Magna had the absurd thought that she wished the boys in the car had instead called her a name, a historically certified epithet, which would have made for a better narrative. That had happened once back in her hometown, Philadelphia, a heavily black city that was also home to a lot of hateful white people. She'd been standing on a corner near her high school, headed to her therapist's office, and a girl's voice had screeched out of a passing car: "Nigger!"

"There is a need," the president said, after Magna's plotless yarn about the boys in the car, "for more dialogue about these issues." Here he paused as if someone were taking notes and needed to catch up. "I hope you always feel comfortable speaking about these things. And I hope that we can stay in touch." When his eyes drifted toward the door, she smoothed her skirt to stand.

As she saw herself out, Magna recalled the thin, quivering lip of her white colleague. She wasn't the only one who became distressed when Magna told her what it was like to be in the town and in the school; it was as if the well-meaning white people who'd been here for years, expatriates who had all gone just a tiny bit native, were meeting reality anew through her eyes.

"You can leave the door open," she heard the president say, but she had already gently closed it.

There were other things Magna would have told him if he had wanted to know about her life here at Lashington & Wiis. About how she was regularly mistaken for a student and told (with some stiffness) that this mistake was a compliment. About correcting the word *colored* in student essays. About the roiling sea of Bush-Cheney stickers on shiny SUVs in the parking lot (though who knew where the political sympathies of the university president lay?).

She could have told the president about how Benton Anders, a freshman from South Carolina in her Narratives class, had responded to Magna's "fun" assignment, a three-page imitation of June Jordan's memoir, *Soldier: A Poet's Childhood.* Benton Anders had attempted to imitate the deliberately childlike tone of Jordan's prose to rhapsodize about a woman named Delandria, his nanny from "baby all the way to eighteen." (He was currently eighteen.) Delandria was described by Anders as "cocoa brown" and "pillowy." He had apparently missed the venomous irony of Jordan's child-voice, which describes the violence, abuse, and insanity of her childhood; his piece culminated in a particularly cherished memory of riding a carousel at age sixteen while Delandria stood on the side, waving in the hot sunshine. "When I think of family, I think of my Deli," he had written. It didn't help matters any that Benton Anders called Magna "ma'am" instead of "professor," and that she had been too alarmed to correct him at the beginning and that then it had become too late.

"You must think it's cute," Jamal had said. Magna didn't think it was cute, not really, but Benton Anders was cute. That was undeniably true. He was over six feet tall with curly dark hair and light blue eyes. But he was less cute looming over her in her office in his pajamas, smelling beery and chemical, that time he'd overslept, missed class, and come running in five hours later to turn in his second paper. It said right there on the syllabus, "NO LATE PAPERS," and it seemed to Magna that, as a new black female professor barely out of her twenties, there were two ways to play this. She'd chosen the way in which they'd call her "professor" (even as her colleagues were "Lisa" and "Charley") and she'd point to the line that said "NO LATE PAPERS."

"So that's a zero?" he said. "But it's worth five percent of my grade!"

"There will be plenty of opportunities—"

There had been an exciting sequence of expressions and colors in the face of Benton Anders, as he had gone from slouching to erect and out of her office. He returned to her office fifteen minutes later, the flannel-shirted department chair in tow. With a hand on the shoulder of Benton Anders, Charley had backed Magna in a paternal I-wouldn't-do-it-like-this-they're-just-kids-but-I-get-it way, but she barely heard what he was saying for the shock: the child had run straight upstairs to the department chair to tattle on her. She tried to imagine herself, over a decade ago, a freshman back at the University of Pennsylvania, going to the department chair because of something a professor had done.

Even as the campus sat still and dark, she could feel it radiating malevolence toward her passing car. There in the grand Greek houses, the white students stayed up late to haze and rape each other; the black students crowded into dorms, testifying angrily and creating escapist personal dramas; the gay students hid under their beds, praying over transfer applications. Over it all, in the center of town, in front of the campus gates, there was the statue of General Lashington and his horse, Colonel Wiis, keeping faithful watch. Magna stifled the impulse to hold her breath while passing it.

As the town gave way to country, and the roads became more poorly lit, she could still see the rebel flags affixed to the houses. Her childhood was whatever the opposite of a rebel flag is; there was an invented Swahili grace, counterintuitive black supremacist narratives of world history, the spelling of *Afrika* with a *k*, and *Amerikkka* with three. But she'd had to take this job; she could no longer hide in graduate school. Her father had died of a heart attack that they had all seen coming but could not swerve to avoid, and her mother was comforting herself in an expensive apartment near the Philadelphia Museum of Art, hoping to die before her money ran out. Any day now, Magna's corporate attorney brother-in-law was going to be indicted on fraud charges, and Magna's sister would have to move back to the city with her two small children. The job Magna had been offered was in *this* place—not the place in Southern California whose English department had so many black professors that she'd gotten hairstyling ideas on the campus visit. They had given that job to someone with more interesting scholarship and better hair.

Magna arrived at the spot where you could really begin to see the mountain across a meadow. She had driven farther than she usually did at night; this was a spot she'd previously been to only during daylight hours. Shortly after Jamal had left, which was around the two-year anniversary of her father's death, she'd come here to look at the autumn leaves. It had not cheered her up, because even when no one died or left you, and even though she knew Jamal would eventually drop Ananda, too, fall was incontestably fucking sad.

She had picked up the phone three times tonight to call Jamal, to tell him about the university president. But it was not a reason to break their silence, just as the story she'd told the president was not quite a story, but an ugly little nothing.

Magna looked at the dark shapes of trees and the mountain looming ahead. She thought of the many horror movies she'd seen that included a version of this sequence, a clueless person alone in the woods. Not for the first time, she imagined running from slave catchers, and lamented that she had no notion of the direction of the North Star. After walking a few brisk paces in no particular direction, she decided to head back to what was home.

After

Had she maimed a person? Had she killed him? Fear squeezed her chest as she drove away from the accident, in the opposite direction she'd driven earlier—away from the woods and toward the towns that were worse than this one. Her heart thudded erratically and she cursed rhythmically to try to calm herself. Along this road there were no antiques shops or heralded berry pie and peanut soup (the slaves invented that!). These towns had no tourist offices bearing pamphlets about the general, his noble fight for family and the land worked by God-given slaves. In this direction were fly-specked diners, a massive Goodwill complex, hand lettered signs, and abandoned gas stations. But just as it is purportedly darkest before dawn, she mused that if she drove all night through the worst of towns, she might greet the sunrise in Washington, DC. Perhaps someone would hide her in a garret and help get her to New York. Maybe NYU had a job in her field this year? Soaked in sweat, she lowered the window, which brought on violent shivering. She rolled it back up.

In her mind she saw the prosecution reading off her privileges as the small-town Southern jury weighed her fate. (A subliminal flash of the yellow cover of *To Kill a Mockingbird*.)

"The defense will say that this woman was slowly driven crazy by so-called racism as if dying by one thousand cuts. But this woman was no slave! *Slavery ended over one hundred years ago!* And if attending good schools and being raised by a loving family and earning a PhD *unharassed* and a teaching position at one of the most elite schools in the country is slavery, then shackle me up, ladies and gentlemen, because slavery is the best deal in town!"

Magna felt herself swerving into the U-turn.

Back on Main Street, she parked the car with some deliberateness and walked over to the boy's long, twisted body, which he'd managed to drag out of the road and close to the curb. Though it was late November and near the mountains, he wore no jacket, just a pink, rumpled Oxford shirt and thin pants, no socks. "Help," he whispered. She knew that in his mind he was yelling; she knew because they were sharing a nightmare. He didn't seem to recognize her, though they saw each other twice weekly, every Tuesday and Thursday from 1:15 to 2:30 p.m., excepting his two absences (so far). "There's been an accident," she said, clamping her cell phone to her damp cheek with her shoulder as she used her hands to drape her sweatshirt over him. "Someone was hit."

She had called the police only once before, and it had been in this town. Not 911, but the other number, the one you call in a more leisurely manner, about nuisances. She and Jamal had been in bed listening to something she had not heard before or since—a party at a house nearby. Earlier that evening, while they had been watching television, arguing about their future during the commercials, the party had been background noise. But eventually they had lain awake, their argument unresolved, and the party had continued insistently. The town's usual silence had felt aggressive; Magna had been surprised to find this was worse.

At two thirty a.m. people yelled, "Whoooooooo!!!!!"

"I'm calling the police," she said.

"Don't," murmured Jamal. "That's bullshit. You're gonna call Boss Hogg?"

"It's not like those kids are black."

"Yeah, but you are. You can't get involved with the police here, Magna."

"Sometimes I really hate it when you use my name," she said.

Even with the pillow over her head, she heard the strains of a song she had loved lifetimes ago at college parties in West Philadelphia. Back then it had seemed that Ice Cube's defection from the West Coast to the Bomb Squad could unite all of black America—but now a white-girl voice started proudly yelling along:

Fuck you, Ice Cube!

Yeah, ha ha! It's the nigga ya love to hate!

Magna snapped on her bedside lamp and looked at Jamal. Even without sitting up, he nodded. *Release the hounds.*

"Do you want to leave your name?" the operator had asked.

"I'd rather not," Magna had said.

As she hung up, she wondered if not leaving her name meant that the complaint wouldn't be registered, but a few minutes later, she and Jamal heard the approach of the cruiser beneath the hoot-ing students, then the click of police shoes on gravel. Instinctively, Magna shut off the light again. Those kids sure had been sur-prised, listening again to "The Nigga Ya Love to Hate." She and Jamal had clung together, that night's argument now over, in her last, best memory of him. They used each other's bodies to stifle their laughter, though of course no one would have heard them. In the morning they awoke and laughed some more. It didn't sound like anyone was arrested that night, hauled off from the party to the small Southern police station. Magna imagined she would be going there now. This had been a long time coming, maybe her whole life.

"Do you want to leave your name?" the operator asked now.

"Oh, I'll be here."

Against the advice she'd always heard (advice she'd never imag-ined being useful to her, like "Stop, drop, and roll" or "Never let them take you to a second location"), Magna moved the accident victim, shifting him so that his head was now on her thigh. Using his name, she told him he would be okay. His eyes began to flut-ter, which alarmed her. Gently, she ordered him to stay awake. She could see him struggling with his eyelids; his gaze became glassy, then it focused on her with otherworldly calm. The calm of a sated baby, or, Magna supposed, someone giving in to death.

Back when Jamal was with her there in the town, Magna had made judicious use of the campus gym, climbing, pedaling furi-ously, and running nowhere. So the thigh was not quite a pillow, but was frankly headed there, full of human warmth between the boy's sweat-soaked, dark, curly head and the cold, hard street.

Ben Hinshaw

Antediluvian

THE YOUNGER MAN had been lingering for a while near the bar when a timid waitress asked Pointer if he might be willing to share his table. The two shook hands, Ned—that was the young man's name—apologizing as if he had just let a door swing shut in Pointer's face.

"Please," Pointer said, lifting his chin to indicate the other diners, European couples, holding hands across the tables, sharing bottles of chilled white wine they would finish off back in their rooms. "I'm just the old sod spoiling the mood."

Ned said he lived in Nairobi, where he taught English to business students. Before that, he'd been an estate agent in Clapham Junction—not a very good one. His hair was jaw-length, unwashed and uncombed, and he had a way of talking down and to the side as if unsure he had anything of value to offer.

"Mostly a girl," he said, when Pointer asked what, apart from the obvious, had inspired the big move. "Unless that's the obvious." Pointer kept his own hair neat, always had, even during long stints in the field. He detected a story Ned wasn't eager to share and he frankly wasn't desperate to hear.

Hotel Dahoma, sealed off by automated gates and high walls topped with barbed wire, was built into the heart of an old fishing village on the northeast coast of Unguja, the largest island in the archipelago. It had seen a spate of robberies the previous year, culminating in the murder-by-stabbing of a Dane who'd stumbled upon two thieves at work in his room, and off-season rates had halved.

"No way I could afford it otherwise," said Ned.

Pointer agreed, though in truth he was in the financial shape of his life. A recent flurry of interest had inspired new editions of two of his books and a retrospective at the Royal Geographical Society. At his sons' insistence he had booked this trip to Zanzibar— somewhere, for all his travels, he had never reached—as a sort of reward. Richie and James, both in London with wives and kids, had expressed concern about his moping around the Somerset cottage. He had always been an absent, active father, disappearing at a day's notice to cover a nascent coup against Amin or to dash in a Press vest down Ledra Street, reloading his Nikon F while, beside him, a Cypriot soldier plugged a hole in his own throat with two fingers. Though he was pushing seventy-four, it troubled his sons to see him languish in a routine of crosswords, gardening, and lengths of the local pool.

"Wasn't too keen at first," he told Ned. "Swanky hotels were never really me." He'd grown up in the Finsbury Park tenements, in a two-room flat with shared outhouse and neighbors upstairs smashing milk bottles in the sink so they didn't have to lug them down to the doorstep, and had always been more comfortable camping rough than lounging in five-star luxury. But getting something pricey at a bargain rate was irresistible. Like Ned, and probably everyone else, he wouldn't have picked the Dahoma were it not for that Dane's bad luck. But while the thought of what happened that night last year didn't trouble him, Pointer sensed, as they talked, that for Ned it cast a kind of shadow. More than one guest, turning in after dinner, would be knocking loudly before unlocking their door.

Electric light lapped at the top of the beach. Waiters in creased, ill-fitting white shirts hurried to relight lanterns blown out by the onshore wind. A new couple entered the restaurant. The woman looked to be in her late twenties, long dark hair, strong jaw, big alluring eyes, slovenly posture contrasting with a fine purple cocktail dress. The man, who had black hair styled like a little fin, seemed younger, though perhaps it was only that he hadn't dressed up.

"Hundred quid says they're Londoners," Pointer said.

As the two men ate their pineapple and ice cream, the woman mounted a bar stool, crossing her long, pale legs. Pointer succumbed to a vision in which she led him by the hand onto the dark beach, beyond the lights but still close enough to hear the murmur of voices; arranged him deftly on his back on the sand; stepped out of her knickers; lifted her dress. Afterward, leaving him sprawled, she returned to the bar for another cocktail.

"I suppose they want our table," Ned said. Pointer nodded and they finished their desserts.

The tide was out for much of the day, leaving a shallow lagoon protected by a reef. *Mashua* plied the deeper water beyond and cargo ships slunk across the horizon, heading north to the gulf or south to the cape.

On the second afternoon, while couples lay out around the pool, Pointer walked the beach. It was nice to watch the tiny white crabs dash back to their holes as he approached. Beyond the hotels lay the low shacks of the village. Fishermen, children, women wrapped loosely in yellow and orange cloth seemed surprised at first to see him out there. By the third day he had become unremarkable. On the fourth, Ned joined him on his long stroll, and a mile or two from the hotel they came upon a group of boys chasing a deflated plastic football. The two men were quickly absorbed into the game, Pointer accepting a position in goal, lumbering between his posts—clumps of dry wrack—as best he could. Diving was out of the question, but the boys cheered whether or not he made a save. They especially loved Ned, who had a mean Cruyff Turn in his repertoire, and argued fiercely about which team he would join.

"You've got a little fan club there," Pointer said as they made their way back, sore footed and sweaty. Ned only smiled, shook his head.

That evening the London woman came into the restaurant alone, carrying a paperback, barefoot this time in a navy tank top and denim shorts. The waiter cleared her husband's place. Without hesitation Pointer rose and went over, returning with her cutlery, napkin, and glass, the woman following behind.

Nicola lived in Battersea with her fiancé, or rather, husband— "Haven't quite got the hang of that yet"—who had gone down with food poisoning overnight. His name was Suve, which Pointer misheard at first as Sue. "He thinks it was the crab salad."

"We had that," said Pointer, "didn't we, Ned? We're both right as rain." He thumped himself twice in the gut.

"You must be made of sterner stuff." Nicola smiled.

"You've married the wrong man," Pointer said, winking at Ned.

Up close and dressed down she was less imposing, with narrow shoulders and small teeth, younger than she had seemed that first night. She was a barrister, she told them—long hours, but she loved it. As if under cross-examination, she confessed to a sheltered childhood, Home Counties suburban, the youngest of two girls. Her sister Melissa, eight months pregnant with a child conceived, as far as anyone could tell, during a holiday fling with an anonymous Frenchman, had apparently wept so loudly during the exchange of vows that the reverend had had to repeat himself several times, as if he were the one nervously pledging. Suve's family, meanwhile, had refused to attend, protesting his decision to marry a white girl in a church rather than wait for a match to be arranged.

"Good lad," Pointer said.

They wanted to talk about his work—people always did. But beyond specific anecdotes, it was hard to know what to say. He had traveled to places most Brits avoided, lived from one assignment to the next, been serially unfaithful to one wife and then another, missed most of the significant moments in his children's lives, spent too many nights in squalid little rooms, sniper fire streaking past the windows. People wanted him to be haunted, for his eyes to fill with tears at some memory or other—that Cambodian woman he'd photographed, say, cradling her sister's bloated corpse. They wanted guilt, trauma, desolateness, but he had never suffered like that. His work was an addiction he'd been glad to feed—what else was there to say?

Nicola and Ned seemed pleased to realize they knew the picture that had brought his name back into the lights. It had made the front pages the previous summer, including the international editions Ned picked up. Nicola asked how it came about.

When the trouble started, Pointer told them, he was staying with James and his wife in East Dulwich, mostly watching cricket on TV. The live footage of the riots had awakened something in him, and from the moment he emerged, camera in hand, out of the Tube at Bethnal Green into a chaos of burning cars and broken glass and shrieking sirens, he'd enjoyed himself immensely. He followed the skirmishes as they spilled from street to street, camera pressed to his face. More than one hooded looter howled at him, threatened to smash his camera. He was unfazed. That evening, on James's laptop, he studied the shots. One stood out immediately—a white man in his early thirties, apparently wearing plaid pajamas, no mask or scarf to shield his face, punching an Asian policeman in the mouth as another officer, a black woman, struggled to restrain him.

Send it in, James had said. There were fifty more filming on their phones, Pointer told him. But his reluctance sounded hollow even to him. Later that year the picture won a couple of awards and Pointer had to get his good suit dry-cleaned.

"We were in Brighton that weekend, thank God," Nicola said. She'd almost bought one of his books for her uncle last Christmas.

"Almost?" Pointer said.

Emptying the last of the wine into their glasses, she mentioned that she and Suve were booked to snorkel in the morning. No way would he be up to it, she said, and she didn't fancy going alone. Pointer saw at once that the younger man was keen. "I'm game if Ned is," he said.

That night he dreamed about the boys on the beach, kicking their ball around. The sunlight fell on them in waves, laughter on the breeze, the lagoon behind them smooth and blue. Then, one by one, they turned on him, glaring, each suddenly a replica of an Eritrean child he had photographed during the '85 famine—skeletal, bulbous-bellied, glint of accusation in the dying eyes—a memory that had surfaced now and then over the years but never so threateningly. Now the duplicates of that doomed boy dragged their wasted forms toward him, arms extended in supplication, until something shifted and the beach disappeared. As he lay on his bed, they tapped on the glass with crooked, bony fingers, unblinking, begging to come inside.

The dive center was half a mile to the north. The three of them walked along the beach, chewing warm bread rolls from the buffet, sun emerging out of the ocean, tinting the sand pink. Pointer detected a new ease between Ned and Nicola. "Late night for you youngsters, was it?"

"Someone decided sambucas were a good idea," Ned said.

"I'm honeymooning," Nicola said, "and my husband's got the shits. What's a girl supposed to do?"

Beyond the lagoon, the boat rolled with the swell. While the divers checked tanks and scrutinized gauges, Nicola threw up off the side. For twenty minutes they sailed over deep, dark water—a chalkboard back at the center had boasted four shark sightings in the last week—until the water paled and cleared over an offshore reef. They were close to uninhabited Mnemba, Unguja little more than a distant green layer. With a yelp, Nicola dropped into the water, adjusting her mask with the help of Alhaadi, their guide. Pointer followed and was greeted by a vision so startling he almost neglected to blow out his snorkel: hundreds of fish of every color and size swimming through the coral crags. The three of them swam behind Alhaadi, lost in their marveling, eyes caught by one fluorescent burst of movement after another. Sunlight filtered down through the clear water, casting their shadows on the reef.

Pointer began to detect some trace of nearby panic. He saw Nicola swimming scrappily away, kicking and flailing, notes of distress sounding through the chamber of her snorkel. Ned had stopped, too. Alhaadi dived again. Pointer signaled to him. Nicola was swimming for the boat, a hundred feet away, her mask discarded, floating behind.

"I've been stung!" she cried.

By the time they were all on deck, the other divers still off somewhere trolling the depths, welts had appeared on her calf. The imprint of trailing tentacles was clear, red and raw like a chemical burn. She winced and whimpered as Alhaadi doused it with hot water.

"Was it a jellyfish?" asked Ned.

She didn't know, she hadn't seen. Hunching over, she began to shiver. The pain was getting worse, she said, and spreading. "Spreading where?" With a shaking hand she indicated her kidneys, her spine. Soon she couldn't hold herself up, head lolling helplessly.

"She needs air!" Ned shouted, grabbing an oxygen tank from

the scuba gear and pushing the mouthpiece between her bluing lips.

Pointer pulled Alhaadi aside. "What does she need?"

The guide watched Nicola without urgency. Ned's arms were clasped around her, holding her up, his expression full of dread. "Maybe cortisone?" Alhaadi shrugged.

"Is it on the boat?"

"What's he saying?" Ned yelled. Pointer repeated Alhaadi's guess.

"He thinks? Does anybody know?" He looked frantically at Nicola and back at the guide. "For Christ's sake, she's—don't just stand there like a useless—get on the radio! Call a fucking doctor!"

Alhaadi whistled impassively across the glinting water to another man in a small RIB trailing the divers. Soon Pointer and Ned were lifting Nicola, by now grimly pale, barely conscious, shaking, down into the RIB. Alhaadi passed them the tank—he couldn't leave the boat.

Careening toward shore, outboard howling, Pointer felt more exhilarated than he had since that day in Bethnal Green. He watched Ned cradling Nicola, stroking her hair and talking in her ear. The younger man's face was ashen. Pointer thought of their conversation on the first night. There was, he saw, more than one woman in Ned's arms, more than one life at stake.

The tide was dropping fast as they neared the lagoon. Pointer and Ned carried her limp form up the beach into the dive center, laying her out on a bench, covering her with dry towels. The doctor, called by the girl on duty, was supposedly hurrying up the coast from Mambwe. Fifteen minutes, the girl said. Pointer lasted only five before he had to step outside. Nicola's condition was troubling, but it was Ned's anguish that finally became unbearable. The desperation in the young man's eyes, the devotion to this woman little more than a stranger and a newlywed at that, struck him as by far the more fatal affliction.

The doctor, a jovial, bearded Belgian with wire-rimmed glasses, helped her out of her wetsuit and administered the hydrocortisone. It was probably a man-o'-war, he explained, not strictly a jellyfish. As the pain eased, color returned to her face. Soon she was talking, thanking the doctor, shaking her head. Pointer watched Ned recovering too, straightening and moving away from the bench, seeming to gather himself.

"Ned, why don't you jog on down the beach and fetch Nicola's chappie."

"Oh, thanks, Ned," she said dreamily. She was sitting up in her black and red swimsuit, white smear of ointment on her wound. "Tell him not to worry though, would you? Tell him I'm not dying or anything."

Ned's head hung for a moment before he nodded.

Pointer dined alone that night, his last at the Dahoma. No sign of the others. The waiting staff broke into song, swaying in a line with their hands held up, smiling for the clapping guests.

The dream came again. He exploded into wakefulness, groping for the lamp. In his head, he listed men who had wound up caving. Some he had called friends. Hazlett, Constantini. Even Berman. For years, he'd pitied them, pansies the lot, not up to the job, doomed from the start by an in-built weakness, a fatal flaw like a crack through a plate; the work just widened the fissure. But now he sensed them gathering around him in the dark, arms linked in support.

Sunrise found him swimming in the lagoon. With open eyes he pushed down to the bottom, grabbing fistfuls of sand, watching it disperse. The light was dim but gilded. When he surfaced and saw the sky filling with color, he felt all the days behind him, strewn like spent canisters of film. Later, he walked south on the beach, hoping to find the football boys, but that stretch of sand was bare, just a collage of footprints and the clumps of dry seaweed that had been his posts. He walked on, into the wilder expanses beyond the village, monkeys moving and screeching in the branches, their long, tentacular tails never still. Up ahead, he saw a figure sitting on a hunk of driftwood. He raised an arm and Ned, in yellow shorts and a tatty short-sleeved shirt, hair blowing into his eyes, did the same.

"Beat me to it," Pointer said.

The younger man shifted, patting the bone-smooth wood, and the two of them sat side by side in silence, regarding the lagoon and the surf beyond. Gulls hung in the breeze and from their sandy catacombs the little crabs began to reemerge.

"What was her name?" Pointer said at last.

Ned shook his head. "I made a fool of myself."

Pointer waved that away. "If you hadn't, I would have."

Standing and stepping two paces forward, the younger man made marks in the sand with his toe. "Penny," he said eventually. "She was killed on the road between Nairobi and Garissa, riding on top of a bus that went into a ditch. It made all the papers back home, though I missed it at first. Someone said they saw her passing through the air. Isn't that perfect?"

"Where were you?"

"In London. She'd been away a few years by then, but I convinced myself she'd be back any day."

Pointer nodded, pushed his thin gray hair back off his forehead. "I was in Chad once, out in the desert. I've never been one for mysticism, but there's something about the desert when you're really out there in it. The guide showed us how to slide down the dunes on our bare feet—the sand was so smooth and tightly packed, it was like skidding down a wet pane of glass. Sang like a glass, too. You wet your finger and trace around the rim, you know? That beautiful note. It was just like that. Kept at it for hours, we did, till our feet were in ruins. Sang and sang, those dunes."

Ned turned to look back at him, his expression impossible to see with the sun so bright behind.

"Passing through the air," Pointer said.

He was packing when Nicola knocked on his door. She wore no makeup, hair tied back. Suve was at the dive center giving them hell; she was supposed to be resting. "But I didn't want to miss you before you left." He asked her how she was feeling. Much better, she said, though the sting still burned. Had she been to see Ned? "Not yet. But I will." She looked at his half-packed suitcase. "Bet you'll be glad to get home."

He shook his head. One night in Stone Town and then home, back to the empty Somerset cottage, back to the garden and Radio 4 and those endless unfinished crosswords. And that was just a prelude to the real shit—wasting away in some sterile dump, surrounded by other infirm old relics, the air rank with piss and soup, nurses lifting him onto the toilet, wiping him when he was done. Better to be dead. She leaned forward to say goodbye, arms clasped lightly around him. He pressed her body into his, feeling her breasts against his ribs, one hand just above her buttocks, one between her shoulder blades. Breathing in the brackish smell of her, he kissed her throat like a schoolboy trying to leave a mark.

"Bill," she said calmly. "Bill, come on now."

She let her arms drop but that was it. The lack of resistance was awful. He squeezed harder, stunned by the weakness of his arms—back in the day, he could've snapped such a skinny thing in two. She was waiting for him to let go, and finally he did, his head bowed.

"Forgive me," he said. "I—"

"No harm done," she said. "But I'm a married woman these days. Time to start behaving myself."

It was the most generous thing she could have said. He felt a flood of gratitude, so different from the hunger of a moment before. His throat was full and he had to swallow before he could speak. "He's a lucky man," he said.

She winked, and lowered her voice to a whisper. "You have no idea."

His driver, Philip, a serious man with prominent ears, declared himself an Arsenal fan, indicating the red-and-white paraphernalia scattered across the dashboard.

"Good lad," Pointer said. "If you ever make it to a home game, I'll show you my old stomping grounds." He shifted forward. "Tell me, the Danish chap killed last year, did you meet him?"

Philip shook his head solemnly. "No, sir. But his wife, yes. They are honeymoons, you know? I am driving her to Stone Town after, to the consulate."

"She must've been in rough shape."

"She did not speak, sir. Her eyes . . ." He shook his head again.

"And they caught the lads involved?"

"Oh yes, sir. Very easy, same day. It is over, this problem. No more trouble."

Pointer sat back in his seat, trying to imagine the young widow riding in this car. He could only picture her as Nicola. If it had happened to her—had Suve been the one killed—would she still have managed to speak with Philip as he drove? Yes. He was certain of it.

Suddenly, he was epically tired. Lush, ragged sugarcane fields blurred past. He watched them and, after a while, slept.

He was jarred awake by tapping on the tinted glass. They had stopped somewhere in the tattered interior amid low and half-built houses. A thunderous rain was coming down—it seemed another country. Drenched people surrounded the car, peering inside, knocking, men in torn T-shirts, women with infants strapped to their bodies, calling to him in a way he couldn't fathom. Was he dreaming again?

"They are wanting free taxi, sir." Philip pointed at the bus ahead of them, a pickup truck with a tarp stretched over the bed and passengers crammed onto narrow benches, spilling over the edge. "The bus is full and it rains very strong."

"They want a lift?"

"Yes, sir. Every day they are knocking, knocking-knocking-knocking." Philip shrugged. "Client is paying for nice ride, people are wanting ride for free."

Pointer looked around at the vacant seats. There were six, seven if he moved his bag, plus another two up front. With the babies they could squeeze in a dozen. The voices grew louder, the car lurching as the hands all pushed and pulled. Through the tinted glass, the wide white eyes stared, asking a question he'd been trying not to hear for as long as he could remember.

"Well," he said, "shall we let them in?"

Caroline Albertine Minor,
translated by Caroline Waight

Grief's Garden

ON A BENCH IN ENGHAVE PARK, we just gave up. As I sat and watched him limp off in his black half-length coat, I felt a deep urge to shoot him in the back. I wanted to see him collapse and lie unmoving in the gravel. A parody of a human being, though I was the inhuman one. I could barely make myself treat him with respect—just hit and bit and spat and kicked. In the year since the accident, I'd destroyed an antique magnifying glass, our door, a book of Milo Manara's drawings and several of his sweaters. Returning to the shop we'd left empty-handed, I bought a harmonica and a jigsaw puzzle for our son.

We were spending Christmas together, for all our sakes. He gave me two bottles of red wine and *The Hosier and Other Stories* by Steen Steensen Blicher. Me, five years ago: age twenty, doped up on love and sex, my head on his chest as he reads me "The Gypsy Woman" in our bedroom, which looks out onto the overgrown garden. His voice isn't cracked yet. It's composed, and rather lighter than you'd think to look at him—he's tall and dark and broad, my M, with a thick beard and a vaulting forehead. He read me "The Gypsy Woman" one evening when we first got together. But he doesn't remember that now. The memory exists in me alone, and he must have bought the book because he knows *he* likes Blicher. He asked me to open my presents before dinner, as though eager to see my reaction. Or maybe he wanted to spare his family? Maybe he was thinking that far ahead. I sat at the kitchen table and tore the paper off the first, then the second bottle, leaving the book till last in the hope that it would rescind the insult of the wine. It was disappointment that tightened my throat as I thanked him. My father-in-law put his arm around me and led me upstairs, into his office. There, love, he said, and I cried into his soft shoulder. There, there.

I go down to the water and follow it. Quarter past seven on December 24—there's nobody else on the street. Out above the sea it's blue and spitting. At the fort I see a family with five children, speaking a language I don't understand. As they climb the steps toward me, I sit on a bench and rock to and fro to the sound of my own breath. They don't slip on the wet steps, their faces bright against the darkness and their black hair. Did she give birth to all five? I'll never be able to kill myself, I realize. This is the closest I'll come, but I'm still a long way off. By the time I get back to the others, the roast duck is on the table and nobody asks where I've been. M is pleased with the gloves and the extravagant whiskey.

The neuropsychologist at Department 123 concluded one of our brief and useless meetings by quoting a Chinese proverb. *You leave grief's garden holding a gift*, he said, but he didn't answer when I asked what happens if you prefer to stay.

That day in Enghave Park marked five years, six months, and fifteen days since I took a job as a receptionist at the architecture firm, since the first time I saw and fell in love with M, nine years older, across a high-ceilinged model-making workshop; two years and seven days since I gave birth to our son; and one year and four days since his father hit his head—first against the taxi's windscreen, where it left a cobweb break in the glass, then against the asphalt, with such force that his brain ricocheted inside his skull. The worst part isn't the blow, they told me later. It's the recoil. I had a missed call from the man who found him. The sheer thought. The screen on my phone lighting up in my bedroom, his lying on the wet roadway as I continued to sleep. The sheer thought.

The officers used my name a lot. Maybe that is something you learn at police training college. My name like a hand reaching into the dread and holding me upright by the collar: *Put your clothes on, Caroline, and come downstairs, Caroline, we'll drive you to the hospital. Put your clothes on and come downstairs.* I was too shivery for socks. The feeling of my bare feet in trainers in December, my breasts, soft from nursing, sticking to my stomach beneath the woolen sweater. The two men were ordinary, clean, dressed alike in dark blue turtlenecks with gold buttons at the shoulder. One of them asked if I was going to vomit. The other sat in the backseat and took my hand. I'd been to the hairdresser's that day, and when M and I had sex afterward I'd briefly felt as though there were some third person, heavily perfumed, with us in the bed. In the waiting room at the trauma center I could smell the products in my hair again, feeling the prayer rise inside me like steam and sickness. To fill the time with something other than horror, I recited it ceaselessly. *Don't let him die / I'm not finished learning / I'm not finished loving,* I prayed, *Don't let it be him / Let it be someone else.* Could I transmute that body? Swap it at the last second for some random stranger's? He lay naked under a sheet on the hospital bed. That was his urine in the matte plastic bag, the smell of the party still on him. Kissing his forehead and cheekbone, which glittered with asphalt but hadn't yet swollen as it would do overnight, I scolded him softly. You promised me this. You promised me that.

The next few days, as I sat and watched M among the machines, I was afraid of more than simply losing him. Over the years I had fused myself with him, as surely and unobtrusively as a Siamese twin, and in his motionless body I saw my own decline. I didn't doubt the vital organs were his. I was the parasitic twin, the growth. If he left me, it wouldn't be long before I dried up like a child's umbilical stump.

As soon as the consultant removed the drip that kept him asleep, a quivering began beneath his eyelids, his legs stretched spastically and his mouth tasted itself. He coughed, frightened, his muscles trembling and twitching. I imagined his journey out of the coma as an increasingly painful ascent through dark water. Putting my face close to his, I whispered without conviction that he shouldn't be afraid.

His hands fumbled for the tube in his nose supplying his brain with extra oxygen, and the nurse had to bandage them. The hands I knew so well (even now I can see them before me, doing anything, and everything), compressed into two bound lumps. It upset me to see them waving in the air in front of his face, like cat's paws or tiny boxing gloves. The officers came to the ward and dropped off a plastic bag with the cut-up woolen coat. Inside, apart from his phone, I found an orange dummy, the nutmeg (an amulet) and a note I'd long ago secreted in the smallest of the inner pockets. The paper had rubbed thin and soft along the cross fold, and I envied the hands that had made those creases at a bar in Amsterdam four years earlier.

Someone had written his name and *welcome* on a board outside room 93. He slept a lot in those first weeks, and his waking gaze was blurred by sedatives. The therapists had built him an oversized playpen, a fence of blue mattresses held in place by two low cabinets. I lay down next to him and burrowed under his arm, trying to distinguish his sweat scent from all the rest of it. Chemicals leached through his pores, his skin flaked with eczema and his breath smelled metallic. He was a thousand worlds away, caught in vivid, swirling hallucinations. He was in Berlin. He was in Santiago. He was a guide at the science museum, nineteen years old again, then twenty-eight. There were animals everywhere. He caught fresh fish and ate them on the shores of a lake, offering me a piece of cod, and the birds had broken their wings. They had to be taken to the animal hospital. I was a dirty whore, I was his Japanese intern Natsuko. Recognition would shoot without warning across his face like leaking current, before it was gone again and I could be anybody.

For years his old apartment had been rented to a Czech family. Every so often they invited us to dinner. I remember dishes like chicken in orange sauce, yogurt with red berries and strudel filled in the middle with a sweet poppyseed paste. When Kristina became pregnant with their second child, they found somewhere bigger and M put the apartment up for sale. The contract had been signed a few days before the accident. The young woman who lives there now has a limp handshake and a silver lamp in the window where M's wiry basil plant used to stand. Her father kept messaging me while M was in the hospital. I'd told him that the previous owner of the apartment was in a coma, yet day after day he continued to send me lengthy messages about keys to the attic and a gate I didn't know existed. *We've got to sort this out*, he wrote, and I decided to let them see me. There were the same stairs where I'd slipped and fallen a few years earlier. Nothing had actually happened, but M had come home from work, and to be on the safe side I lay down on his bed. The problem was that I couldn't stop laughing. I laughed so hysterically and continuously that he phoned the emergency doctor, who asked to speak to me, and after that I fell silent and went to sleep. It was only shock. The whole family answered the door: the limp, blond-haired girl and her parents, their faces flecked with paint. I gave the father a handful of keys I'd found at home—I can't throw keys away, keeping them all without exception in a sugar bowl on my chest of drawers. The mother remarked that they looked like keys to a bike lock, and I had to admit she was right. They didn't ask about him. I said he could sit upright on the edge of the bed for nearly a minute. No need for the tube anymore. I said it wasn't anyone's fault. Thanks, said the girl's father, we'll try the keys. I craned my neck to see the empty room behind them. The floor was covered with plastic and where M's bed used to stand, a work light cast its garish beam across the walls and ceiling.

Once he became more aware of where he was, and they let him make short trips outside the ward, we took the lift down to the foyer and I pushed him into the hospital chapel by way of experiment. A high-ceilinged room that smelled of resin. *Get me out*, he shouted, *get me out of here*. I took it as a good sign. He—unlike me—had always been an avowed atheist, and whenever we visited a church on our holidays, he would stay smoking in the sunshine while I let myself be sucked in, wandering aimlessly through the spongy silence that accumulates in places like that. That's how I want to remember him: waiting in a strip of sunlight on the other side of the road, patient and proud and very, very beautiful.

I never stopped desiring him. Even after the baby came, love politely stayed nearby, and whenever we could we slipped away to be alone with it. His parents took care of our son while we went on long drives up the coast, where we'd turn off into a forest and do it among the trees or in the car. Our first night without the baby we stayed at a hotel in Granada. I remember the almond tart dusted with icing sugar, the fine rain that settled on my face as we wandered around the palace gardens.

On Christmas Eve I decided to let the child see him. Our son lit up and laughed at the sight of his father, but when M reached out for him and accidentally grabbed the boy's throat, I screamed so loudly that he began to cry. Taking the shrieking child to my parents outside, I told them I'd take the bus home, and that I'd be back in time for dinner. By the time I returned to the room, M had forgotten our visit. His short-term memory was in pieces, the minutes slipping through him like water. Nothing stuck. *Is that you?* he asked, and I said it was. When the tray of duck and sauce and potatoes arrived, I helped him lift the fork to his mouth, and I made sure he didn't drink so much apple juice that he threw up. The occupational therapist called his condition *non-critical*. His brain overlooked his body's satiety signals, but there was nothing to indicate that M was overeating. In the ten days since the accident, he'd lost so much muscle mass that his T-shirts were loose across his chest. When he was finished with the main, I peeled the lid off the plastic tub of rice pudding and put the spoon in his hand. *Can you manage?* I asked. He nodded. *Merry Christmas*, I said, kissing him goodbye. *I love you.* Say it again: *I love you.* M did his rehab without complaint, and if there was a group singing session or a games night on the ward, he always took part. After a month at the hospital, he was covering short stretches on a walking frame and could recall for increasingly longer periods of time where he was and what he was doing there. *An accident*, he said hesitantly. *Did I have a car accident? A fall?* He treated his carers with a distant politeness and took pains not to get them confused. Dorthe, Louise, Gitte, Yvonne, Vibeke. I felt deep gratitude for the strong and gentle women who looked after him, and although they occasionally talked down to him, I couldn't blame them. There's something unmistakably childlike about a person who's hit their head. An innocence, or just a lasting wonder.

Gradually, as I came to know the patients on the ward, I arranged them in a hierarchy of presence. At the bottom were those who still hadn't left, and would probably never leave, their vegetative states. Kevin's mother watched enviously as I came trundling down the corridor with M. She sat by her son's bed and waited for him to cough. *It helps me remember his voice*, she said without self-pity. On the door of the wardrobe hung a picture of a young man with a broad face smiling shyly into the room. The driver coming the wrong way down the motorway had died at the scene; his two friends got away with scratches. Kevin's mother envied me, while I envied the relatives visiting patients with broken legs and bad hearts and infections—even cancer. Somewhere between Kevin at the bottom and M, who seemed to be able to do something new every day, was a group of people who couldn't get out of their wheelchairs but could make gestures. People whose communicative abilities were reduced to signals of disgust and enthusiasm, or whose facial expressions were wiped clean, everything hanging slack or tightened into a knot around the nose. The variations were endless and brutal. A Turkish man made a particular impression on me. He was more than six foot six and because he was non-critical like M, but didn't have M's metabolism, all his sweaters crept too short, gradually revealing a soft, hairy belly. The man traveled the ward's rectangular corridors in short steps, his gaze fixed on a point in the air ahead. His arms hung straight and his fingers were curved, as though he were asleep. The only time I saw him even remotely animated was when a physiotherapist offered him a cup of hot chocolate from the machine in the lounge. Then he grinned, drank it in three gulps and immediately asked for more. I was told later he'd worked at the vegetable market—an accident at work, it was—and I couldn't stop seeing the truck bed hammer down on the roof of his skull, transforming Mehmet there and then into a man-child whom his wife regarded with such immense helplessness I had to look away each time the family brought their food into the shared kitchen. The children had each other. They could hide in their own world, fight and play in the halls. She was irrevocably alone.

We got onto the 1A bus at Lille Triangel. I stopped short and tugged the snowsuit down over the child's tummy, taking off his elephant hat. We were outside the world. It was a simple time. I had no expectations of the days. The bus glided past the Citadel and along Store Kongensgade, past the shiny and expensive things, and at Magasin the tourists arrived in groups, before we wove through the city toward the main railway station. As the bus turns off Tietgen Bridge and continues down Ingerslevsgade, you get a few seconds' glimpse of our courtyard gate. After the accident I'd been back to the flat just once. The plan was to fetch books and clothes, make sure the lights and hobs were switched off, empty the fridge and take out the bins. My mother waited in the car, and I pressed my face into a T-shirt he'd worn. Longing enters the body like no other emotion. It swoops and spreads so fast you think you're about to cleave from head to toe. I stood in our bedroom and breathed through the threadbare cotton until the smell of him was indiscernible from the smell of the room. I pushed the wire drawer back into place with my foot and shut the wardrobe, made the bed. In the kitchen I washed up glasses and wiped down the table. I filled three IKEA bags with clothes and books.

The Friday it happened, M had left work early. He walked into the salon while I was still sitting with the heavy collar around my neck and the gown hanging from my shoulders. The hairdresser asked him to take a seat on the sofa behind me. I caught his eye in the mirror, feeling awkward about my new hair, which she wouldn't stop fiddling with. It hung down over my face in smooth hanks. There's a picture of me taken at a café where we went afterward and which we left to go home and screw. I remember he took me from behind, but not if he came that way, or how I did. I took a picture of myself in the living room with Photo Booth. You only see me from the neck up, but I know I'm naked, that he's in the bathroom as I'm sending it to my sister, writing: *New haircut!* I saw him for the last time on the landing. The black beanie, the coat. He could really thunder down a set of stairs. I closed the door and went back into the bedroom to get dressed—black turtleneck, high boots. I picked up the handbag he had given me in Granada. Blue and soft, it bulged with the packets of rice pudding, the freezer bag of blanched almonds and the cherry sauce I'd bought that morning. The rain was fierce, and I tucked the bag under my jacket to protect the leather.

It was still raining when I called him shortly after midnight, on my way home in a taxi. I could hear the party behind him, and he sounded cheerful and sober. His blood alcohol level is written down in the medical notes somewhere in a folder in his new apartment, but it doesn't matter anymore. It makes no difference.

I don't know if we said we loved each other, but why shouldn't we have said it?

THE GOLDEN LADY. MAI'S MASSAGE. THE FLOWER CORNER. At one point on the motorway it would feel like we were driving somewhere far away, before the bus reached its final stop and swung into a holding bay outside Hvidovre Hospital. The passengers had mostly thinned out by then, just a few of them getting off. Sometimes I was the only one. In the three months, when I made that trip each day, I noticed a certain type of man using the hospital foyer as a shelter. Perhaps they were homeless, perhaps just lonely. Or they simply preferred the crowd to the silence of their apartments. One brought a bag of rolls to eat in front of a television screen. Another, older and clubfooted, bought an orange soda and drank it at a table in the cafeteria. A few looked more down-at-heel, their hair greasy and matted. The men were always there when I arrived, and I never saw them take the bus home again, although of course they did.

For a long time after the accident, M couldn't remember our son's birth. The past came to him in flashes, and I did what I could to seize his islands of clarity, connect and extend them, hoping a coastal string of memories would emerge that corresponded to my own. I described in detail extracts from our life together. Our last fight, what we used to have for dinner, the pattern on our bedclothes, the routines of caring for our child. The series we were watching. After a while the question took on the character of an entreaty: *Do you remember?*

It kept snowing well into spring. Gitte arranged for us to borrow a pram from Pediatrics, a moss-green Odder from the nineties with the number of the department written on the side in black pen. It made me uneasy to clip my son into the harness, as though the pram itself could make him sick. M and I took the lift down to the foyer and emerged from the swing doors. Cutting through the area where the buses turned around, we walked across the lawn between some residential blocks, crossed a single-lane road and went into the churchyard, where we wandered up and down the muddy paths. I felt a bottomless exhaustion. After a few laps I let him push the pram, but his gait was strange and stiff, and he dragged his feet. The sound woke the child, and I grabbed the pram in irritation and asked him to walk normally. *It's my shoes*, he said. *They're too big.* I told him the injuries had affected his balance. *It's because I'm not used to walking on anything except bamboo floors*, he muttered. *Smooth, shiny bamboo floors. No. That's not right. You hit your head, and you don't know what you're talking about. You're a patient at Hvidovre Hospital, right over there. See.* I pointed in the direction of the gray buildings, their flat roofs peeping from behind a row of black trees. He squinted, the hat concealing the fact that his hair had grown too long and stuck out boyishly around his ears. I had to be kinder to him, and more patient. One day he'd look at the world again as though it belonged to him—at me, as though I did. I smiled and slipped my arm into his. The hope was euphoric, and it lifted me up and made me strong, until it dropped me again with a suddenness that took my breath away. In that state it took everything I had to cling on and stay lifted.

At the end of March we were called in for a meeting to discuss discharging M. The sun was shining, and there was an expectant mood around the table. I sat at the head (we were the guests of honor) next to M, who had a calendar open in front of him. He wrote in capitals like before, but the letters were big and childishly tilted, as though pulled by a magnet in the bottom right-hand corner. The neuropsychologist spoke first, then the rest of the team took turns. By this point M had taken the bus into the city and visited the apartment twice. Last time, as part of the discharge process, he did the shopping and made an omelet with Manchego and asparagus. After watching him cook, the occupational thera-pist packed up her things and left us. We ate the omelet in the cold, because the radiators had been off all winter. Cutting it in half, he laid a piece on my plate. It was tasty, and we ate all of it. I longed desperately to be outside my body, like you do sometimes when you've got food poisoning or an upcoming exam. The illness that seemed almost natural at the hospital was impossible to ignore now that he was back at the apartment. We ate in silence, wearing our jackets. I smiled encouragingly at him. He had deeply and utterly changed for me.

Waking up is just starting the loss again from the beginning, only worse.

A few months after the accident, I found a CD-ROM with some grainy footage of him from before we had met. In the video M is the same age as I am now. Wearing a checked tweed hat, obviously high. He and a friend have built a makeshift catapult onto which, gingerly, he places a hand-rolled cigarette. Pausing for effect, he brings his fist down like a hammer onto one end of the ruler, and the cigarette flies up past his snapping jaws and lands on the floor. He mugs for the camera anyway, an agile look on his face, as though he actually managed to grab it. He keeps up the self-assured grimace for a few seconds before cracking into laughter, and the friend behind the camera does the same. Then it finishes. I don't have the courage to watch it again, because there you are, and I can't bear it, and I don't even want to try.

This unspeakable shame: to contain not a single sentence worthy of you.

I'm lying.

Your name. Say it.

Jianan Qian

To the Dogs

I GOT ON THE TRAIN ON A HORRID SUMMER DAY, wearing a white designer shirt soaked with sweat. My father gave this shirt to me the night before my departure as a farewell gift. As he handed it over, he told me that he wore it in his youth whenever he needed to feel strong—only twice, once for his wedding, the second time for his father's funeral.

On the station platform my father offered me last-minute advice. "Keep in mind, Zhao," he said. "Forgetfulness is essential to moving on." I nodded. We were both fighting back tears; we both knew this departure could be for life.

This was in 1972. I was fifteen, sent from my hometown of Shanghai to a remote rural town, X. According to central government policy, I needed to be reformed by the peasants because my class status wasn't right—both my parents were high school teachers.

For three days I changed onto smaller and smaller trains until I arrived at a wooden shed with a cardboard sign that read X Town Station, the handwriting big and wild. Though I held a slip of paper with the address of my new home, I still didn't know where to go. There was no road—east, west, south or north; all I could see was a vast barren land, yellow, dusty. I didn't dare ask the conductor. He seemed to be a violent man, his two wolf eyes glaring as he came to puncture my ticket. I was among the last five passengers; the other four men looked like locals—dark, sturdy and silent. I walked over to them to ask the way, but they showed their teeth and one of them pushed me. I stood quietly, trying to look as if I wasn't watching, while the four headed in the same direction across the dusty land. I sneaked after them until we passed a grove of poplars. Rows of low shanties, packed together, came into view.

In front of the shanties sat a dozen middle-aged women, naked to the waist. Their bulging breasts dangled like bags of rice. The toddlers climbed on their backs. When the babies whined for food, the women flapped their huge breasts over their shoulders so the kids could grab, hold and suck.

I had never seen a naked woman. I froze like a statue.

"Never seen a woman?" A stout man, much younger than the four locals I'd followed, approached me. I didn't answer, blushed. "You must be Savage Zhao from Shanghai?" he said, looking me up and down, and finally fixing his burning gaze on my shirt.

"Why am I a savage?" I asked.

Ignoring my question, he went over to one of the sitting women, pinched her right breast, and leapt away.

"Chen, you bastard, your thing itches, right?" shouted the woman. The baby on her back gaped indifferently at Chen.

"You bitch in heat. You must've had your husband *diao yangzi* yesterday!" Chen shouted to the woman from a stone's throw.

"What does *diao yangzi* mean?" I blurted.

All the women, and Chen, burst into laughter.

"*Diao yangzi*, the savage wants to know what *diao yangzi* is!"
"*Diao yangzi*. Dogs *diao yangzi*."

I had no idea what was so funny. I just echoed them, "*Diao yangzi*. Dogs *diao yangzi*."

．　．　．

Chen turned out to be the person selected to help me reform, even though he was only two years my senior. "I've been an orphan since I was twelve," he said. "You'll bring me a tiny allowance every month."

Chen reminded me of the brown bear I'd seen in the Shanghai zoo, with his long nose and his barrel chest. Sometimes when he didn't say anything at all, I could still hear heavy grunts from deep inside him. But all the locals said he was a very kind boy, except for his wicked ideas.

"Still, you'll find his wicked ideas useful," they told me, half smiling.

I stayed in the pigsty behind his one-room shack; all the pigs had been sold years ago to pay for Chen's father's medicine. The first night, I could barely sleep, straining to blink away the images of my old Simmons mattress and the chamomile tea my mother had made for me every evening. Now, the plank bed ironed my back. I heard what must have been the call of an owl.

"I knew you wouldn't be able to fall asleep," a voice said out of the darkness; it was Chen. "Lie on the floor, Savage Zhao. No one can sleep on a bed in summer."

I moved to the cement floor. Immediately I cooled down.

"Sleep tight. Tomorrow we've got to work." He went out, leaving the door open.

The next day I was assigned a job in the local factory, which produced magnets, working along with Chen. The factory was a two-story gray building, right beside X town's only septic tank. I couldn't help but cover my nose and mouth with both hands.

"Savage Zhao, you make me sick. Drop your hands. You can't work that way."

I put both my hands down, and began to cough heavily. A shoal of men soon gathered around me, smirking.

"What the hell's with this guy?" one of them asked.

"Oh, he's a savage. Just arrived yesterday."

They stared at my designer shirt, their eyes flaring. One

man—he had a scar across his left eyebrow and was markedly shorter than the others—took a step forward and raised his fist, ready for a fight. "Savage," he spat.

"Didn't I tell you yesterday? You should take off this disgusting shirt." Chen fumbled with the buttons, pulling off my shirt. Only then did I realize all the men in the factory were shirtless.

"Take this off, or they'll beat you," he whispered in my ear.

The men didn't walk away until Chen had rolled my shirt into a ball and thrown it into the cesspool nearby.

At least the job was easy enough. I was to pour chemical liquid into a metal mold. I strived to work hard, running to fetch another metal bucket right after I finished emptying the one at hand. Chen laughed at me.

"No need to work so hard. It's useless. The magnets, I mean. They just stack them in the warehouse."

I didn't reply. He continued babbling, saying we were here only for the sake of lunch. He told me I was lucky because it was July—so much to eat in summer.

At noon, a bell rang and he led the way to the canteen. "Whatever you see, remember—don't say a thing," Chen said in a muffled voice. I nodded.

Soon I realized what he'd been referring to. The stinky tank nearby had attracted swarms of flies to the factory, especially the canteen. They weaved a thick black carpet around the tables, sucking on the grease. I tried not to frown, or pucker my lips. Chen asked me to take his lunch pail for a second. He didn't sit down. Instead of fanning away the flies, he banged the table with both hands. A cluster of black bodies crushed under his broad palms; the survivors flew away, a black funnel reaching to the ceiling.

Chen took his seat and put down our lunch pails. He dunked the dead flies into his soup. Then he bit into the flies with a snapping sound.

Around us, I heard more bangs and snaps, and witnessed black funnels rising from other tables. Chen scooped the rest of the flies into my spoon and encouraged me to have a taste.

"You really think we can live on the food provided by the canteen?" He frowned at his lunch: a bowl of watery soup with two green leaves, and another bowl of rice.

"Take these. They're nutritious. You're lucky to have these summer supplements."

I was reluctant. Several young men banged and sat beside us. They stared at me, waiting to see if I would eat my spoonful of flies.

"Savages can't appreciate the wonderful side dish," one of them said.

"Then stay hungry." It was the short man with the scar. I knew now his name was Liu. He didn't bother to look up, but buried his head in his bowl—he'd dumped dozens of flies in the soup.

I poured the full spoon of flies into my mouth, and bit them with a snapping sound. "How do they taste, Savage Zhao?" Chen asked.

"Great!" I muttered, trying not to spit anything out.

Chen gave me a tour of X town on my first weekend. There was not much to see—only shacks and pens, except for two elaborate buildings: the local government office and the ancestral temple. The government building was the tallest in town, three stories. I saw a small red seal beside the left corner of its main gate, with two antique Chinese characters: Yu Household. Chen shook his head at me—he couldn't read; the only school was converted into the magnet factory when he was seven. "But I think you're right. My parents told me the richest family here used to be the Yus. They disappeared after 1949." The temple was the oldest building in X town, a high one-story wooden house not far from the station. Inside, floor-to-ceiling shelves lined three walls, and an altar stood at one end. There were no tables or chairs, only four giant pillars covered with knife marks. Chen told me this used to be the holiest place when he was a kid: the shelves held each family's ancestral tablets. Behind the scratches the teachings of Confucius were once inscribed.

"You're lucky," Chen exclaimed. "If the government didn't ban these superstitions, you wouldn't be in here. Women and outsiders weren't allowed to enter."

I looked around. The emptiness made me uneasy. But I smiled at Chen.

When in the countryside, do as the locals do. I walked around shirtless and swallowed flies as special treats at mealtime. When a woman worker bent to retrieve something from the floor, I joined the other men who stared at her nipples and laughed out loud. After work, I pinched the seated women's breasts before slipping inside my pigsty. There was no toilet in the village, so I learned to shit outside at night, whistling for a dog to come eat my stool, just like the locals did.

"Human shit is nutritious for dogs, just like flies are nutritious for us," Chen told me. "Why do the dogs here grow so strong? They're born to eat shit."

Most of the dogs were fierce and stayed away from humans, but a meek dog ate my shit almost every night—Little White, a male dog with a snow-white coat, rare to see in X town. Sometimes when he was enjoying the fresh food I provided, I talked to him in Shanghainese. I knew remembering Shanghai did me no good. Still, speaking my tongue with Little White was comforting. After having his late night snack, he'd lie beside me, listening quietly.

I sang Shanghainese nursery rhymes to him.

Yao A Yao / Yao Dao Wai-Po Qiao Wai-Po Jiao Wo Hao Bao-Bao
(Row a boat / Row a boat to Grandma's, where Grandma calls me
her dear babe)

Little White's fur blued in the moonlight. A hint of melancholy in his blinking eyes made me feel he understood the song. I tried not to think what my parents were doing, or whether they missed me. My father had told me at the station that I'd probably never get back to them, never get back home in this life. Tears would brim when I saw Little White run away—like Cinderella, he would start for home after the very first call of an owl.

I dared not talk in Shanghainese with any locals. They might mock me and complain that the reforming work wasn't being carefully done. They might even file a report to the local government, and have me sent to an even more horrible place. Chen might get in trouble too. I copied the way everyone spoke, though I didn't always understand their words. When we got up early and went to work, Chen greeted the first woman neighbor, "You had your husband *diao yangzi* yesterday?"

Then we'd hoot and run away.

I didn't ask again what *diao yangzi* meant. I guessed it had something to do with sex, and that was enough.

By the end of September, it was okay to lie on the plank bed. But to make my belly stop drumming, I had to imagine myself drinking a large bowl of my mother's rib soup as I fell asleep. Each day, it seemed, there were fewer flies in the canteen. Sometimes we were still lucky enough to collect a pile of black bodies when having meals. Other times we could only watch a black carpet drown in the cesspool, helpless. In late October, when we scraped the very last of the flies from the switch rope of an electric lamp, we were sad to see that they were already dead. They had gathered around the rope for warmth, but it wasn't warm enough to save them. They had remained there only because of the static electricity. Without the flies we were soon starving.

"Autumn's the cruelest season in X town," Chen said—even he was less stout. He sounded as if he felt sorry for me.

I felt sorry for Little White. He came to me every night, waited quietly as my face wrinkled and I groaned, but failed to produce anything solid for him. He showed no disappointment. He lay down beside me, let me tickle his belly and listened to my Shanghai song.

Yao A Yao / Yao Dao Wai-Po Qiao Wai-Po Jiao Wo Hao Bao-Bao

Little White was hungry too. I could see a harplike skeleton under his skin.

There was something strange about the autumn in X town. Despite the hunger, everyone seemed excited, cheeks reddening, eyes widening, as if they were expecting something unusual. At first I believed there'd be a large harvest awaiting us, but it turned out we had little to reap. Then on a Sunday in early November, I learned what we were waiting for.

The local boys and girls were chasing one another in the streets, calling out in excitement, "Dogs *diao yangzi*! Dogs *diao yangzi*!"

Chen saw the look on my face and said, "You want to know what *diao yangzi* is, go find out yourself."

I ran after the kids. They were happily chasing two dogs: a male dog who was pulling a female one along the street.

The kids skipped along and clapped their hands, shouting "*Diao yangzi, diao yangzi.*" They were five or six years old. I still couldn't figure out the exact meaning of this phrase. But I noticed something unusual with the dogs—the male dog wasn't dragging the female one with his mouth, but with his dick.

The kids darted across the street. The dogs were pulling and being pulled all the way around, groaning and grunting. Eventually the male dog was exhausted. He collapsed in a corner and drew out his long sausage-like dick, now soft.

. . .

November was the dogs' carnival. Every day I heard cries and shouts from the children and saw cheerful male dogs running and dragging female dogs—Old Wang's Little Brown, Old Li's Little Yellow, Young Sun's Young Black. Strangely, I didn't see my dear Little White. I realized I hadn't seen him for several weeks. He didn't even come at night when I whistled for him to take my shit.

I sang the rhyme all alone.

"Have you seen Little White recently?" I asked Chen.

"You mean the white dog raised by Old Zhang? Oh, that's a strange dog."

I waited for him to continue, but he only yawned and said he needed a nap.

In autumn, the workload broke our backs. We hoisted all the magnets on our shoulders from one warehouse to another—the authorities said they needed one more empty warehouse to stack ripe grain from the farm. We labored every day until the warehouse was cleared. Then they announced crops were short this year.

Furious, all the workers showed their fists and teeth, but we had no strength for a fight—our fists shook from hunger and fatigue.

"They're fucking with us," I said to Chen in a whisper. I had learned the word from him.

"Sure they are. But we have no choice. They're the leaders—*they move a finger and you'll die.* They play the same trick every year." Chen smiled a crooked smile. "Grin and bear it, Savage Zhao. Soon I'll show you something truly spectacular."

"What's so strange about Little White?" I asked Chen one Sunday afternoon when neither of us had the strength to take a walk. Two weeks had passed and I still hadn't seen the dog. I was careful not to let my voice show that I was sad.

"He hides himself in mating season. Strange, right?"

"But why?" I asked.

"He never goes after female dogs in the streets like other dogs. He's got a weird temper. Two years ago, Old Zhang took him to mate. Three weeks in, he finally grew intimate with his partner. Then they mated. Afterward, they were brought back to their owners. Little White behaved like a lovelorn boy—he refused to eat or go out. Maybe because that was his first time. You know what people say: the first time is unforgettable. But he's only a dog, right? Even men can fuck women they don't love. It's like having a meal." Chen drew a figure with a sharp rock in the dirt in front of our shack.

Luckily he didn't see me frowning.

"At last, after a month, he began to eat. For two years, he's refused to mate with any other bitch. He hides away in spring and autumn. An infatuated dog, isn't he? Hey, come see what I've done."

Now I could see he'd drawn a naked woman, chubby and full-breasted, no face. "That's great . . . But why don't they let the female dog stay with him?"

"You mean like a marriage? Don't be silly. Marriage isn't for dogs. And you know which female he was screwing? White Beauty. We need her. You don't know how important she is, do you?"

I shook my head.

Chen smirked. "You'll see. This time we'll use White Beauty strategically. She's one of a kind. We used Little Flower last year, but she didn't work well." He bent and put two stones on the breasts of the women he'd drawn on the ground—the nipples. "Wait and see, I'll show you something truly spectacular."

By late November it was freezing. Chen said winter in X town came earlier than in other parts of China. We were hungrier than ever. The trees were bald. Earlier in the month Chen had fried poplar leaves for us to eat. They were nasty, scraping our throats and stomachs. Now we'd even run out of leaves.

Strangely, the dogs were no longer emaciated. Male and female, they grew sturdier and sturdier. Every day, more dogs were seen having sex.

"They're catching the last bus," Chen said. "Their heat will be over as soon as December comes."

On the last day of November, Chen said it was time. I didn't know what he was talking about, but I'd learned it was better not to ask.

"Today, we'll make a beauty trap," Chen said. He told me they did the same trick every November. Before the long and bitter winter swept X town, they needed something to warm their bodies.

"Savage Zhao, you're lucky. This time we use White Beauty. You'll see with your own eyes how charming she is," Chen said.

There were four of us, Chen, Yang, Liu and I. Both Yang and Liu worked in our factory. They were the ones who'd threatened to rip off my shirt on my first day of work. Liu was the short, scarred man.

"Back then you were such a savage," Yang said with a smile.

"Still a savage," Liu said, looking serious and solemn. I'd never seen him smile, not even slightly.

Chen was in charge. "If you don't want to stay hungry and cold the whole winter," he told me, "then do what we tell you to do."

I promised I would.

"Watch out, Savage Zhao," Liu spat, eyes fierce.

We stole White Beauty from Old Wang's shack next to the ancestral temple. With the door closed, the windowless place was as dark as night—a perfect place for a trap. We gave White Beauty a bowl of fresh shit to keep her busy. When Liu chained her neck to the altar, she started to moan. Chen urged us to climb on the shelves. Holding clubs, we waited for the male dogs to come.

White Beauty grunted in the sexiest and most alluring way. Even though we were men, we got hard listening. Chen was happy with the noises she was making, said she was a real bitch.

He had told us already that even if White Beauty was locked in the temple, all the male dogs would smell her female odor from miles away. All we needed to do was wait and get the fattest dog. Chen was right. Soon we heard a fiery mix of steps, like heavy rain drumming on the roof. The male odor of the dogs, like rotten meat, hung in the air. I imagined their drool dripping, their tails wagging and their things itching. Scores of them, heads crowding the doorstep, peered in. We held our breath.

The dogs seemed to know what we men were up to. They waited, keeping a safe distance, and watched White Beauty swaying her hips. The air thickened with their smell and heavy breath, but no dog dared to sidle in. Chen gestured to us to have patience.

We waited and waited, listening to the male dogs moaning at White Beauty and her grunting back. We waited and waited, until our legs were numb and our private parts wet.

Eventually a dog was brave enough to step in. But he wasn't fat at all. My heart nearly pounded out of my chest.

"Damn it," Chen whispered. "Little White, you fool, you've screwed things up." Should we do it again? That dog is skinny, I wanted to say. But I didn't.

Zhao and Liu were disappointed too. They flared their nostrils and were about to jump down. "Hold on. We'll catch him, the foolish dog," Chen said. My heart was thumping with sadness. We remained where we were and held our breath.

Little White raised his head and looked up. I knew he'd seen us. He must've known what would happen to him. But he strode directly to White Beauty. His snout nudged heavily on her neck, then moved to her back, her belly and her hip. She too rubbed against him, licked him and even bit him. Eventually he smelled her pussy and took deep breaths, like I imagined a man would with a woman.

I almost shouted "run" to Little White. But I dared not. The other three men were entirely absorbed in the scene. Chen had told us that we needed to wait for the moment that the dog would *diao yangzi*.

We waited and waited. White Beauty seemed to hesitate. She dodged several times when Little White was about to mount. I knew she couldn't stand to see him die.

Still, Little White was strong enough to climb on her and enter her. Chen, Yang and Liu's faces glistened ecstatically. Liu and Yang wanted to jump down but Chen waved to us to wait, wait for the time when both sides of Little White's dick swelled like balloons. At that moment, he wouldn't be able to pull it out. Finally, I knew what *diao yangzi* meant.

Both the dogs moaned. And the scores of male dogs outside echoed their moans in a chorus. It was almost time. Chen fingered the door closed in a skilled maneuver. Hearing the door shut, we four jumped down simultaneously. Chen, Liu and Yang started to beat Little White with their clubs.

"Stupid dog, you bastard," Chen shouted. "You've messed things up."

"Now you've learned the bitterness of love," Liu raged. He kept striking Little White's head. His scar smiled when the skull cracked.

I watched for a long time with my club in my hand. Little White didn't look surprised; he didn't even attempt to bite us. He was ecstatic, enjoying making love with White Beauty until the very end of his life.

Chen carried a knife with him. After Little White was nothing but blood and pulp, Chen peeled off the dog's skin right away, in front of White Beauty.

"I'll go get something to cover her eyes," Yang said. "We want her to perform next year."

"No need to do that," Chen said, still cutting. "She'll be too old next year anyway. We'll find another White Beauty."

As we flayed Little White, removed his bowels, stomach, liver and heart, and chopped his flesh to pieces, White Beauty shuddered like an autumn leaf.

Yang took a wok and several logs of firewood from under the altar and began to make a fire. "You should taste this, Savage Zhao. Dog meat supreme," Chen said.

Liu went out to fetch some water from the well. I stood still, hoping no one noticed my trembling hands.

"First time you killed a dog, right?" Chen said. "You'll get used to this. We'll catch some old female dogs next month, after they give birth to pups. Not so delicious though. Their meat is tough and sour."

"Savage Zhao, sing a song for us. Chen likes listening to songs while cooking dogs," Yang suggested. "Liu used to sing Cantonese songs for us. He came from Guangzhou two years ago."

I shook my head, astonished.

Liu came back with the water. Yang laughed at him, "Savage Zhao can't see you're from Guangzhou. A-ha, Savage Liu. You've done a wonderful job of reforming yourself."

"Sing us a Cantonese song, Liu," Yang pleaded. "Beautiful songs you used to sing."

"I can't. I don't speak Cantonese anymore," Liu said, nonchalant. He poured the water into the wok.

"Savage Zhao, you sing. That song you sang in the night is a pleasant song. *Yu A Yu*, isn't it?" Chen said, mimicking my Shanghai dialect.

I should've been surprised and frightened to discover that even when I thought I was alone I'd been under surveillance. But I didn't feel a thing. I opened my mouth to sing for Chen, but no words came out.

The aroma of dog meat wafted from the wok.

"Sing, Savage Zhao. We'll let you eat an extra piece if you sing a pleasant song," Yang said. "Sing, please. It's a wonderful song." Chen stirred the stew.

Tantalizing aromas hung in the air. Drool trickled down from my mouth.

Yao A Yao / Yao Dao Wai-Po Qiao Wai-Po Jiao Wo Hao Bao-Bao

While I was singing, I felt the Shanghainese leap out of me, one word after another. I repeated the song again and again and, as I sang, the pictures of my old life faded away, my parents, my home, my town . . .

Yu A Yu / Yu Dao Wu-Pu Ju Wu-Pu Qu Wu Hu BeBe

"Come and eat, Zhao. Save this song for the next time." Chen offered me a chunk of Little White's steaming leg. It didn't make me sick. The image of the dog had already slipped my mind. The meat was chunky, thick and firm. I craved another bite, and another.

"Zhao, am I right? This is really spectacular, isn't it?" Chen said, nodding vigorously at me while I reached my chopsticks back into the wok.

I swallowed, and murmured in the local dialect, "Spectacular! *Diao yangzi.* Dogs *diao yangzi.*"

Sally Rooney
Color and Light

THE FIRST TIME HE SEES HER she's getting into his brother's car. He's sitting in the back seat and she gets into the front, closing the passenger door behind her. Then she notices him. She cranes around, eyebrows raised, and then turns back to Declan and says, Who's this?

That's Aidan, Declan says. My brother.

I didn't know you had a brother, she says mildly.

She turns around again, as if accepting the inevitability of having to speak to him. Older or younger? she asks.

Me? Aidan says. Younger.

The interior of the car is dark, and she narrows her eyes before concluding, You look it.

He's only a year younger, Declan says.

The woman has turned away now to roll down her window. She has to wind it down using the small lever on the door.

Your parents were busy, she remarks. How many others are there?

Only us, Declan says.

They got it all out of the way quickly then, she says. Sensible. Declan pulls out of the parking space and back onto the main road. Cool night air floods through the open window. The woman is lighting a cigarette. Aidan can see only the back of her head and her left arm, elbow angled.

I'll drop this lad home and then we'll go for a spin, Declan says.

Sounds divine, the woman says.

On their right is a row of houses and shops, which tapers off as they reach the end of town. Then the caravan park, the golf links. Does the woman already know where Aidan lives? She doesn't seem curious about how long it will take to get there. She exhales smoke out the window. The surface of the golf course glitters darkly.

What do you do, Aidan? she asks after a minute or two.

I work in the hotel.

Oh? How long have you been there?

Few years, he says.

Do you like it?

It's all right.

She flicks the stub of her cigarette out the window and rolls the window up. The car is much quieter then and things seem to hang unspoken. Declan says nothing. Aidan bites gently at the rough side of his left thumbnail. Should he ask her what she does for a living? But he doesn't even know her name. As if apprehending this very problem, Declan says, Pauline is a writer.

Oh, Aidan says. What kind of things do you write?

Films, she says.

For some reason Aidan does not wish to seem surprised by this knowledge, though he doesn't think he's ever been in a car with a screenwriter before. He just makes a noise like Huh. As if to say, Well, there you are. The woman, whose name is apparently Pauline, unexpectedly swivels around to look at him. Her hair, he notices, is pulled back from her forehead by a wide velveteen band. She has a strange smile on her face.

What? she says. You don't believe me.

He is alarmed, feeling that he has offended her and that Declan will be angry with him later. Of course I believe you, he says. Why wouldn't I?

For a few seconds she says nothing, but in the darkness and silence of the car she looks at him. In fact she stares at him, right into his eyes, for two or three seconds without speaking, maybe even four full seconds, a very long time. Why is she looking at him like this? Her face is expressionless. She has a pale forehead and her lips are pale, so her mouth appears as one delicate line. Is she looking at him just to show him her face, the face of a screenwriter?

When she speaks, her voice sounds totally different. She simply says, OK. And she stops looking at him and turns around again.

She doesn't speak to him again for the rest of the journey. She and Declan start talking instead, about people and events that have nothing to do with Aidan. He listens to them as if they are performing a play and he is the only audience member. Declan asks her when she's heading off to Paris and she tells him. She takes out her phone and starts looking for a photograph to show him. He says that someone called Michael never got back to him about something and Pauline says, Oh, Michael will be there, don't worry. Outside the windows, the darkness is punctuated only by passing headlights and, far up in the hills, the flickering lights of houses, hidden and revealed through the leaves of trees. Aidan has a feeling of some kind, but he doesn't know what the feeling is. Is he annoyed? Why should he be?

Declan indicates left for the estate. The streetlights grow brighter as they approach, and then the world is populated again, with semidetached houses and wheelie bins and parked cars. Declan pulls up outside Aidan's house.

Thanks for the lift, Aidan says. Have a good night. Pauline doesn't look up from her phone.

He sees her again a few weeks later, in the hotel. She comes in one night for dinner with a group of people Aidan has never seen before. She's not wearing a hairband this time—her hair is fixed quite high on her head with a clasp—but it's definitely the same woman. Aidan brings a carafe of water to the table. Pauline is talking and everyone else is listening to her, including the men, some of whom are older and wearing suits. They all seem fascinated by her—how unusual, Aidan thinks, to see grown men hanging on the words of a girl in that way. He wonders if she is famous, or somehow important. When he fills her glass she looks up and says thank you. Then she frowns.

Do I know you? she says.

Everyone at the table turns to stare at Aidan. He feels flustered. I think you know my brother, he says. Declan.

She laughs, as if he has said something very charming. Oh, you're Declan Kearney's brother, she says. Then, turning to her friends, she adds, I told you I knew all the locals.

They laugh appreciatively. She doesn't look at Aidan again. He finishes filling the glasses and goes back to the bar.

At the end of the night he helps Pauline's party to get their coats from the cloakroom. It's after midnight. They all seem a little drunk. Aidan still can't tell what they are to one another—friends or colleagues or family? The men are watching Pauline, and the other women are talking and laughing amongst themselves. Pauline asks him to call some taxis for them. He goes behind the desk and picks up the phone. She places a hand delicately on the counter, near the bell.

We're going to have a drink at my house, she says. Would you like to join us?

Oh, Aidan says. No, I can't.

She smiles pleasantly and turns back to her friends. Aidan dials the taxi number, gripping the phone hard against his skull so the ringtone shrieks in his ear. He should have said thanks, at least. Why didn't he? He was preoccupied, wondering where her house was. She can't live in town, or he would know her. Maybe she's just moved to town, or maybe she's working on a new film. If she even really writes films. He should have paused for a second to think about her question, and then he would have remembered to thank her. On the phone he orders two taxis and then hangs up.

They'll be here shortly, he says.

Pauline nods without looking back at him. He has made her dislike him.

I didn't know you lived around here, he says.

Again she just nods. He has the same view of her now as he did in the car the other week: the back of her head, and her neck and shoulders. When the taxis arrive outside, she says without turning to him, Give Declan my best. Then they all leave. Afterward the waiter who cleared their table tells Aidan they left a huge tip.

A few days later he's working the front desk in the afternoon, and a queue forms while he's on the phone. When he hangs up, he apologizes for the wait, checks the guests out of their rooms, wipes their keycards, and then sits down on the wheelie chair. Guests really don't have to do that—wait to be checked out. They can just leave their keycards on the desk and walk off, without the formal goodbye. But Aidan supposes they want to get the official go-ahead, to have their departure acknowledged in some way. Or maybe they just don't know that they're allowed, and assume they're not without being told so, because after all, at heart, human beings are so extremely submissive. He taps his fingers on the desk in a little rhythm, distracted.

Declan and Aidan are in the process of selling their mother's house. Declan has a house of his own already, a smaller one, closer to town, with a twenty-year mortgage. People thought Aidan might move back into the old house, seeing as he's renting outside town and has to share with housemates, but he doesn't want to. He just wants to get rid of the place. Their mother was sick for a long time, though she wasn't old, and he loved her very much, so it's painful to think of her now. And in fact he tries not to think of her. The thought creates a feeling—the thought might at first be only an abstract idea or a memory, but a feeling follows on from it helplessly. He would like to be able to think of her again, because she was the person on earth who loved him most, but it isn't yet possible to do so without pain—maybe it never will be. In any case, it's not as if the pain goes away when he doesn't think of her. A pain in your throat may get worse when you swallow, may be almost unbearably painful when you swallow, but that doesn't mean that the pain is gone when you're not swallowing. Yes, life is full of suffering and there's no way to be free of it. Anyway, they're selling the house, and Aidan will come into a little money, though not a lot.

That night Declan comes to pick him up from work very late, after two in the morning, and Pauline is lying in the back of the car, apparently drunk. Ignore her, Declan says.

Don't ignore me, Pauline says. How dare you?

How was work? Declan asks.

Aidan closes the door and puts his bag down at his feet. OK, he says. The car smells of alcohol. Aidan still feels that he doesn't really know who this woman is, this woman lying on the back seat. She's coming up fairly often in his life at this point, but who is she? At first he thought she was Declan's girlfriend, or at least a candidate for that role, but then in the hotel the other night she seemed different—glamorous in a way, with all those men looking at her—and of course Declan wasn't there, and she even invited Aidan for a drink afterward. He could ask his brother, How do you know this girl? I mean, are you riding her, or what? But Declan's sensibilities would be offended by that kind of thing.

How would you get home if you didn't have a lift? Pauline says.

Walk, Aidan says.

How long would it take?

About an hour.

Is it dangerous?

What? Aidan says. No, it's not dangerous. Dangerous in what way?

Ignore her, Declan repeats.

Aidan is my good friend, Pauline says. He won't ignore me. I left him a very generous tip in his restaurant, didn't I?

I heard about that, he says. That was nice of you.

And I invited him to my house, she continues. Only to be cruelly rebuffed.

What do you mean, you invited him to your house? Declan asks. When was this?

After dinner at the hotel, she says. He rebuffed me, cruelly.

Aidan's face is hot. Well, I'm sorry you felt that way, he says. I can't just walk out of work because someone invites me to their house.

I didn't get an invite, Declan says.

You were busy, Pauline says. And so was your brother, obviously. Can I ask you something about your job, Aidan?

What? he says.

Have you ever slept with any of the hotel guests?

For fuck's sake, Pauline, Declan says.

They are driving past the caravan park again now, where the smooth curved roofs of the caravans glow with reflected moonlight, white like fingernails. Beyond that, Aidan knows, is the ocean, but he can't see or smell or even hear it now, sealed up inside the car with Pauline laughing and the air smelling of alcohol and perfume. Doesn't she know that Declan doesn't enjoy that kind of banter? Or maybe she does know, and she's aggravating him on purpose for some reason Aidan doesn't understand.

Don't listen to her, Declan says.

A car flashes past and disappears. Aidan turns around to look at her. From this angle her face is sideways. It's actually quite long and oval, like the shape of a headache pill.

You can tell me, she says. You can whisper.

You're flirting with him, Declan says. You're flirting with my brother right in front of me. In my car! He reaches out and punches Aidan on the arm. Stop looking at her, he says. Turn around now. You're messing and I don't like it.

Who were all those people in the hotel the other night? Aidan says. Were they your friends?

Just people I know.

They seemed like big fans of yours.

People only act like that when they want something from you, she says.

She lets him continue staring at her. She lies there absorbing his look, even smiling vaguely, allowing it to go on. Declan punches him again. Aidan turns around. The windshield is blank like a powered-off computer screen.

We're not allowed to sleep with the guests, he says.

No, of course not. But I bet you've had offers.

Yeah, well. Mostly from men.

Declan appears startled. Really? he says. Aidan just shrugs.

Declan has never worked in a hotel, or a bar or a restaurant. He's an office manager with a business degree.

Are you ever tempted? Pauline says.

Not usually.

Aidan touches the window handle on the car door, not winding it up or down, just toying with it.

We did have a writer in the other night who invited me back to her house, he says.

Was she beautiful?

Pauline! Declan says. You're pissing me off now. Just drop it, OK? Jesus. This is the last time I do you a favor.

Aidan can't tell if Declan is still speaking to Pauline now, or to him. It sounded like he meant Pauline, but Aidan is the one receiving the favor of a lift home, not her, unless there's another favor running concurrently to this one. Everyone falls silent. Aidan thinks about the linen room at work, where all the clean sheets are stored, folded up tight in the wooden slats, bluish white, smelling of powder and soap.

When they pull up outside his house he thanks his brother for the lift. Declan makes a dismissive gesture in the air with his hand. Don't worry about it, he says. The shape of Pauline's face is visible through the back window, but is she looking at him or not, he can't tell.

Two weeks later, the arts festival is on in town and the hotel is busy. Aidan's manager has to call him in for an extra shift on Friday because one of the girls has laryngitis. He finishes work at ten on Saturday night and goes down to the seafront for the closing ceremony of the festival. It's the same every year, a fireworks display at the end of the pier. He's seen the display ten or twelve times now, or however many years the festival has been going. The first time he was a teenager, still in school. He thought that his life was just about to start happening then. He thought that he was poised tantalizingly on the brink, and that any day—or even any minute—the waiting would end and the real thing would begin.

Down on the beach he zips his jacket up to the chin. It's crowded already and the streetlights on the promenade cast a gray glow over the sand and the sea. Families pick their way down the beach with buggies, bickering or laughing, and boats clink in the marina, a noise like handbells ringing, but random and disconnected. Teenagers sit on the steps, drinking cans and laughing at videos. People from the festival hold walkie-talkies to their ears and stride around importantly. Aidan looks at his phone, wondering if Declan is around, or Richie, or any of the gang from work, but no one's said anything in the group chat. It's cold again this year. He puts his phone away and rubs his hands.

Pauline is already walking toward him by the time he sees her, meaning she has seen him first. She's wearing a big oversized fleece that drops down almost to her knees. Her hair is pushed back from her forehead by a hairband again.

So you do have days off, she says.

I actually just finished, he says. But I'm off tomorrow.

Can I watch the fireworks with you or are you with someone?

He immediately likes this question. Turning it over in his mind only seems to reveal additional angles from which it can be admired.

No, I'm on my own, he says. We can watch together, yeah. She stands beside him and rubs her arms in a pantomime of being cold. He looks at her, wondering if the pantomime demands some kind of response from him.

I'm sorry I was such a mess the other night, she says. When was that? Last week, or whenever. I think Declan was annoyed afterward.

Was he?

Did he say anything to you about it?

Me, no, Aidan says. We don't really talk about things. The lights overhead go down and the beach is in darkness.

Around them people are moving, huddling, saying things, taking out their phones and shining torches, and then at the end of the pier the fireworks begin. A line of golden sparks shoots upward into the sky and ends in a colored point: first pink, then blue, then pink again, casting its brief hypnotic light on the sand and the water. Then a whistling noise, as low as a breath, and above them in the sky, exploding outward, red blossoms, and yellow and then green, leaving soft fronds of gold behind. When the fireworks burst, it's silent color and light at first, and a second later the noise: a loud crack like something breaking, or a deep low booming that goes into the chest. Aidan can see the tiny missiles flying upward hissing into the sky from the pier, almost invisible, and then shattering outward into fragments of light, glittering like pixels, bright white fading to yellow and then gold to darker gold and then black. It's the darker gold, just before black, that he finds most beautiful: a low ember color, darker than a glow-ing coal. Finally, so high above they have to crane their necks to see the whole shape, three dazzling yellow fireworks, consuming the sky, eating the whole darkness. Then it's over. The streetlights come back up.

Beside him Pauline is rubbing her face and nose with her hands. Cold again. Aidan realizes, obscurely, that a lot depends now on Pauline's having enjoyed the fireworks—that if she didn't enjoy them, if she thought they were boring, not only will he no longer like her but he will no longer have enjoyed them either, in retrospect, and something good will be dead. He says nothing. Along with everyone else, they turn back and leave the beach. It's possible to walk at only one speed, the speed of the crowd, which seems like the slowest and least comfortable speed at which humans can move. At this pace Aidan keeps bumping into people, small children keep running out unexpectedly in front of him, and prams and people in wheelchairs need to move past. Pauline stays close by him, and at the top of the promenade she asks if he'll walk her home. He says sure.

She's staying in one of the houses on the seafront. He knows the street; it's where all the holiday homes are, with glass walls facing the ocean. As they walk, the rest of the crowd falls away behind them. When they reach her street it's just the two of them alone in silence.

There's so much he doesn't know about Pauline—so much, it strikes him with a different and slightly surprising emphasis, that he would like to know—that it's impossible to begin asking questions. He doesn't know her surname, or where she's from, what she does all day, who her family are. He doesn't know how old she is. Or how she came to know Declan, or how well she knows him.

You know, as to what you were saying the other night, Aidan says, I actually did sleep with a guest at the hotel once. I wouldn't go telling Declan about it, because he doesn't approve of that kind of thing.

Pauline's eyes flash up at him. Who was the guest? she asks.

I don't know, a woman staying on her own. She was a little bit older, maybe in her thirties.

And was it a good experience? Or bad?

It wasn't great, Aidan says. Not that the sex was bad but more that I felt bad about it, like it was the wrong thing to do.

But the sex was good.

It was OK. I mean, I'm sure it was fine, I don't even remember it now. Something at the time made me think maybe she was married. But I don't know for a fact—I just thought it at the time.

Why did you do it? Pauline says.

He goes quiet for a few seconds. I don't know, he says. I was hoping you wouldn't ask that.

What do you mean?

You just seem like someone who understands these things. But when you ask that it makes me feel like I did something weird.

She stops walking and puts her hand on a gatepost, which must be hers. He stops walking, too. Behind her is a large house with big windows, set back from the street by a garden, and all the lights are switched off.

I don't think it's weird, she says. I used to have a boyfriend who was married. And I knew his wife—not well or anything, but I did know her. I'm not asking why you did it because I think it's sick that you would sleep with someone who was married. I suppose I just wonder, why do we do things that we don't really want to do? And I thought you might have an answer, but it's OK if you don't. I don't either.

Right. Well, that makes me feel better. Not that I'm happy you were in a bad situation, but I feel better that I'm not the only one.

Are you in a bad situation now?

No, he says. Now I would say, I am in no situation at all. I feel like my life basically isn't happening. I think if I dropped dead the only people who would care are the people who would have to cover my shifts. And they wouldn't even be sad, they'd just be annoyed.

Pauline frowns. She rubs the gatepost under her hand like she's thinking.

Well, I don't have that problem, she says. I think in my case there's too much happening. At this point everyone I've ever met seems to want something from me. I feel like if I dropped dead they'd probably cut my body into pieces and sell it at an auction.

You mean like those people you were with, at the hotel.

She shrugs. She rubs her arms again. She asks him if he wants to come inside and he says yes.

The house is spacious and, though furnished, appears curiously empty. The ceilings are high up and far away. Pauline leaves the keys on the hall table and walks through the house switching lights on in a seemingly arbitrary fashion. They reach the living room and she sits down on a gigantic green corner sofa, with a flat surface so large it resembles a bed, but with cushions at the back. There is no television and the bookshelves are bare. He sits down on the couch but not right beside her.

Do you live here on your own? he says.

She looks around vaguely, as if she doesn't know what he means by "here." Oh, she says. Well, only for now.

How long is now?

Everyone always asks questions like that. Don't you start. Everyone wants to know what I'm doing and how long I'm doing it for. I'd like to be really alone for a while and for no one to know where I was or when I was coming back. And maybe I wouldn't come back at all.

She stands up from the sofa and asks if he would like a drink. Unnerved by her previous speech, about going somewhere alone and never returning, which seems in a way like a metaphor, he just shrugs.

I have a bottle of whiskey, she says. But I don't want you to think I have a drinking problem. Someone gave it to me as a present—I didn't buy it myself. Would you have even a small half glass and I'll have one? But if you don't want one I won't have one either.

I'll have a glass, yeah, he says.

She walks out of the room, not through a door but through an open archway. The house is confusingly laid out, so he can't tell where she's gone or how far away.

If you want to be alone, he says aloud, I can go.

She reappears in the archway almost instantly. What? she says.

If you want to be alone like you were saying, he repeats. I don't want to intrude on you.

Oh, I only meant that . . . philosophically, she says. Were you listening to me? That's your first mistake. Everything I say is nonsense. Your brother knows how to deal with me, he never listens. I'll be back in a second.

She goes away again. What does it mean that Declan "knows how to deal with" Pauline? Should Aidan ask? Maybe this is his opening to ask. She returns with two half-full tumblers, hands him one, and then settles down on the sofa beside him, slightly closer than where she was sitting previously, though still not touching. They sip the whiskey. It's not something Aidan would ever drink of his own volition, but it tastes fine.

I'm sorry about your mother, Pauline says. Declan told me she passed away.

Yeah. Thanks.

They pause. Aidan takes another, larger sip of whiskey. You're seeing a lot of Declan, are you? he says.

He's sort of my car friend. I mean he's my only friend who has a car. He's very nice, he's always driving me places. And he usually just ignores me when I say silly things. I think he thinks I'm a terrible woman. He wasn't impressed with me the other night when I asked you those vulgar questions. But you're his baby brother—he thinks you're very innocent.

Aidan pays special attention to the fact that she has used the word "friend" more than once in connection with Declan. He feels it can have only one meaning—a thought that makes him feel good. Does he? he replies. I don't know what he thinks of me.

He said he didn't know if you were gay or straight, Pauline says.

Ah, well. As I said, I don't talk about things with him.

You've never brought a girlfriend home.

You've got the advantage of me here, Aidan says. He's telling you all about me and I don't know anything about you.

She smiles. Her teeth are extremely white and perfect, unrealistic looking, almost blue. What do you want to know? she says.

Well, I'm curious what brings you to live here. I don't think you're from here.

That's what you're curious about? Good grief. I'm starting to think you really are innocent.

That's not very nice, Aidan says.

She looks wounded for a moment, stares into her glass, and says sadly, What made you think I was nice?

He doesn't think he can answer this question. In truth he doesn't think of her as particularly nice. He just thinks of niceness as a general standard to which everyone accepts they can be held.

She puts her empty glass down on the coffee table and sits back on the couch. Your life isn't as bad as you think it is, she says.

Well, neither is yours, he replies.

How should you know?

Everyone wants your attention all the time, so what? Aidan says. If you hated it so much you could fuck off on your own somewhere—what's to stop you?

She tilts her head to one side, places a hand gently under her chin. Move to a remote seaside town, you mean? she says. Live the quiet life—maybe settle down with a nice country boy who works hard for a living. Is that what you had in mind?

Oh, fuck off.

She gives a light, irritatingly musical laugh.

I don't want anything from you, he adds.

Then what are you doing here?

He puts his glass down. You asked me to come in, he says. You asked if we could watch the fireworks together, remember? And then you asked me to walk home with you, and then you asked me inside. And I'm the one who's inserting myself into your life, am I? I never wanted anything from you.

She seems to consider this, looking grave. Finally she says, I thought you liked me.

What does that mean? If I liked you that means something bad about me?

As if she has not heard him, she replies, I liked you.

He now feels utterly confused as to why they seem to be arguing, confused to the point of abrupt despair. Right, he says. Look, I'm going to go.

By all means.

He experiences this parting with her—this parting he himself announced spontaneously and called into existence—as an excruciating ordeal, almost a physical pain. He can't quite believe he's going through with it, actually standing upright from the sofa and turning away toward the door they entered through. Why is everything so strange now? At what point did his relations with Pauline begin to violate the ordinary rules of social contact? It started normally enough. Or did it? He still doesn't even know if she's his brother's girlfriend.

She doesn't rise from the couch to see him out. He has to make his way through the half-lit, cavernous house alone, fumbling through dark hallways and at one point a dazzlingly bright dining room toward the front door. Why did she say that, about settling down with a "nice country boy"? She was just trying to provoke him. But why? She knows nothing about his life. Why is he even thinking about her, then? At this moment, reaching the front door of Pauline's house, with its glazed glass reflecting back at him an unrecognizable image that he knows to be his own face, this strikes Aidan as the question without an answer.

. . .

Several weeks later he's in the back room trying to find a Continental power adapter for a guest upstairs when Lydia comes in saying that someone at reception wants him. Wants what? he says. Wants you, Lydia says. They're asking for you. Aidan closes the drawer containing the hotel's selection of adapters and, as if in a dream now or in a video game, his actions under the control of some higher intelligence, he stands up and follows Lydia out of the back room, toward the front desk. He already knows, before he sees or hears Pauline, that she will be there waiting for him. And she is. She's wearing a dress made from what looks like very soft, fine cloth. An older man is standing beside her with his arm around her waist. Aidan simply notices all this neutrally. His image of Pauline is already so confused and obscure that to see her in this situation cannot indicate anything really new about her.

All right, Aidan says. How can I help?

We're looking for a room, the man says.

Pauline touches her nose with her fingertips. The man swats her arm and says, You're making it worse. Look. It's going to start bleeding again.

It is bleeding, she says.

She sounds drunk. Aidan can see that her fingers are bloodied when she draws them away from her face. He bends over the computer at the desk but does not immediately open the room-reservations interface. He swallows and pretends to click on something, actually just clicking nothing. Is Lydia watching him? She's at the desk, just a little way to his right, but he can't tell if she's looking.

For how many nights? Aidan says.

One, the man says. Tonight.

They're not going to have anything at such short notice, Pauline says.

Well, let's see, the man says.

If you'd told me you were coming, I could have arranged something, she says.

Relax, the man says.

Aidan swallows again. He's conscious of a kind of throbbing sensation inside his head, like the flicking of a light, on and off. He moves the mouse around the screen in a show of efficiency and then, impulsively, pretends to type something although there is no keyboard input open onscreen. He's certain Lydia is watching him. Finally he straightens up from the computer and looks at the man.

No, I'm sorry, he says. We don't have any rooms available tonight.

The man stares at him. Lydia's looking over at him, too. You don't have any rooms? the man says. Every room in the hotel is taken? In the middle of April?

I told you, Pauline says.

Sorry, Aidan says. We can get you something next week, if you'd like.

The man moves his mouth like he's laughing, but no laugh comes out. He removes his hand from Pauline's waist, lifts it up in the air, and lets it drop against his own body. Aidan is careful not to look at Pauline or Lydia at all.

No rooms, the man repeats. All booked up. This hotel.

I'm sorry I can't help, Aidan says.

The man looks at Pauline.

Well, what do you want me to do? she says.

In response the man lifts his arm again to point at Aidan. Is this your boyfriend? the man says.

Oh, don't be absurd, Pauline says. Are you going to develop paranoia now on top of everything else?

You know him, the man says. You asked for him.

Pauline shakes her head, dabs delicately at her nose, and flashes a kind of apologetic smile at Aidan and Lydia across the desk. I'm sorry, she says. We'll get out of your way. Can I ask you to call a couple of taxis? I'd really appreciate it.

Oh, we can't share a taxi? the man says.

Coldly now, Pauline replies, We're going in opposite directions. Under his breath, with a kind of frozen grin on his face, the man says, I don't believe it. I don't believe it. Then he turns around and walks toward the large double doors of the hotel entrance. Lydia picks up the phone to call the taxi company. Pauline, without any change in her demeanor, lifts the hotel pen from the desk, takes the pad of paper, writes something down, and then tears the sheet from the pad. She takes out some money, encloses it in the note, and pushes it across the desk toward Aidan. Looking only at Lydia, she smiles and says, Thanks so much. Then she exits, following the man through the double doors.

When the doors swing shut, Lydia is still on the phone. Aidan sits down and stares into space. He hears Lydia saying goodbye, then he hears the faint click of the receiver replaced in its cradle. He just sits there. Lydia finds the note on the desk and nudges it in Aidan's direction with the end of a pen, like she doesn't want to touch it.

She left this for you, Lydia says.

I don't want it.

Lydia uses the pen to flick open the note.

There's a hundred euro in here, she says.

That's OK, he says. You take it.

For a few seconds Lydia says nothing. Aidan just sits staring blankly straight ahead. Presently, as if making up her mind, Lydia says, I'll put it with the tips. She wrote you a note as well, do you not want that? I think it just says thank you.

You can leave it, he says. Or, actually, give it to me.

Lydia gives it to him. Without looking at it, he places it in his pocket. Then he rises from the chair to return to the back room to find the power adapter for the guest upstairs. He won't see Pauline again before she leaves town in a few days' time.

The O. Henry Prize Winners 2021

The Writers on Their Work

Daphne Palasi Andreades, "Brown Girls"
Do you consider your story to be personal or political?

"Brown Girls" is both personal and political. Like the characters in this story, I grew up in Queens, New York, a place that's incredibly diverse and vibrant, possessing a tough beauty—much like these young women. While my experiences aren't identical to theirs, I did draw upon my observations and memories of this place and its people to create the scenes, conflicts, and atmosphere depicted in this fictional narrative. In terms of whether I consider my story "political," I am reminded of the author Toni Morrison, who said, "All good art is political." By "good art," I interpret this to mean work that's complex, thought-provoking, honest, and bold; by "political," Morrison isn't referring to work that pushes an agenda, but rather, art that engages deeply and unflinchingly with the world we inhabit.

To be specific, "Brown Girls" explores racism, class, colonialism, immigration, gender, and the way these forces shape the lives of young women of color. As an artist, I believe one's formal choices can be political statements, as well. For instance, by using the collective point of view—the "we"—I was interested in illustrating the shared experiences between second-generation immigrant girls of color belonging to various diasporas, now living in this particular location. I used vignettes to structure the story, a form I believe mirrors the fragmented way some people of color and immigrants experience life, as well as time and memory. Morrison said the best art should be "unquestionably political and irrevocably beautiful," which is how I aspire to approach my own work.

Daphne Palasi Andreades's debut novel will be published by Random House in January 2022. She holds an MFA from Columbia University, where she was awarded a Henfield Prize and a creative writing teaching fellowship. She is the recipient of a Bread Loaf Writers' Conference scholarship, among other honors. She resides in New York City.

Sindya Bhanoo, "Malliga Homes"
What inspired your story?

Almost always, I start my stories with an image in mind. In "Malliga Homes," it was an image of a husband putting his hand over his wife's when he wanted her to calm down. I knew, too, that the image was from the wife's memory. She was a widow and she was recalling the times her husband did this.

The story is set in a retirement community in southern India where many of the residents are upper-middle-class Indians whose children have moved away and settled abroad. I first heard about the growth of these retirement communities from my mother. I am a journalist and at one point thought I might write a newspaper article about these communities. They seemed like such lonely places, in spite of all the amenities they offered. I never wrote the article but the details I gathered stayed filed away in mind. It was fertile soil that I did not yet have use for. Later, when the image of this widow came to mind, I placed her in a retirement community. I did some more research to build the world and make it feel authentic, but the image of hand upon hand was the seed I knew I wanted to sow.

Sindya Bhanoo's debut short story collection, *Seeking Fortune Elsewhere,* will be published by Catapult in 2022. Her fiction has appeared in *Granta,* the *New England Review, Glimmer Train,* and elsewhere. She is the recipient of the DISQUIET Literary Prize and scholarships from the Bread Loaf and Sewanee writers' conferences. A longtime newspaper reporter, Sindya has worked for *The New York Times* and *The Washington Post.* She is a graduate of the Michener Center for Writers, UC Berkeley's Graduate School of Journalism, and Carnegie Mellon University. She lives in Austin, Texas.

Karina Sainz Borgo, "Scissors"
Do you consider your story to be personal or political?

The story fictionalizes an image that I witnessed on the border of a South American country where I was researching a novel. Everything I write is political, which does not mean that I'm an activist. I see the world as Doris Lessing, Natalia Ginzburg, or Susan Sontag might have looked at it. Everything from beginning to end in my story was very clear, because of the image itself, like seeing a barracks from the Europe of the Second World War in the twenty-first century. The misery and despair moved me and made me understand that migrants will always be a theme of my work. The force of unsettling facts leads me to write fiction, perhaps as an act of purging, or because I cannot keep them inside. Rather than cut my character Herminia, I tried to strengthen her tragic story with her silence. Her image burned me. I wanted to tell it with the precision, intensity, and neatness of the short story. I come from a Latin American tradition that gives enormous strength to the story as a literary genre.

Karina Sainz Borgo was born in Caracas in 1982 and has lived in Spain for over a decade. She began working as a journalist for the Venezuelan newspaper *El Nacional* and since then has dedicated her life to cultural reporting. She has collaborated with the Spanish and Latin American publications *El Mundo*, *Gatopardo*, and *Quimera*. She currently writes for the digital newspaper *Vozpópuli* and collaborates with the literary magazine *Zenda*. She is the author of two narrative nonfiction books, *Tráfico y Guaire* (2008) and *Caracas Hip-Hop* (2008), as well as a literary chronicle, *Crónicas barbitúricas* (2019). *La hija de la española* is her first work of fiction and an extraordinary debut, an instant international sensation. In 2019 she was chosen by *Forbes* magazine as one of the 100 Most Creative People.

Jamel Brinkley, "Witness"
What made you want to re-create this particular world/reality in fiction?

As I drafted and revised this story, I realized it wanted to be in conversation with work by writers like James Baldwin ("the line which separates a witness from an actor is a very thin line indeed; nevertheless, the line is real," from *I Am Not Your Negro*) and Gina Berriault ("Be an eyewitness to this too," from "Around the Dear Ruin"). The story deals with the atrocities of medical racism, and its effects on Black women in particular, but it also deals with a not-unrelated personal failure. The tone of the narrator, Silas, is soaked with regret, haunted, because he was only a partial witness to the suffering of his sister. He didn't see enough—he didn't do the very hard but necessary work of paying attention—and he certainly didn't say enough, or do enough. He didn't provide care. His telling of the story is an attempt to resurrect Bernice. It's also, at the same time, an attempt to fess up, but a confession has only so much efficacy when the emergency is over and done with, and when the loved one you've let down is already, and irretrievably, gone. By itself, regret has very serious limitations. At some point, it seems, you're again thinking only of yourself. Still, the problem he faced so inadequately isn't his alone—versions of it are quite common, I think—so perhaps his story can have value for us as we confront the emergencies that are ongoing.

Jamel Brinkley is the author of *A Lucky Man: Stories* (2018), a finalist for the National Book Award and winner of the Ernest J. Gaines Award for Literary Excellence. His writing has appeared in *A Public Space*, *The Paris Review*, *Ploughshares*, *Gulf Coast*, and *American Short Fiction*, and has been anthologized twice in *The Best American Short Stories*. He was a Carol Houck Smith fellow at the Wisconsin Institute for Creative Writing and a recent Wallace Stegner fellow at Stanford University. Raised in Brooklyn and the Bronx, he teaches at the Iowa Writers' Workshop.

Emma Cline, "White Noise"
What inspired your story?

I read an article about Harvey Weinstein, awaiting his trial in some borrowed house, and immediately I wanted to try to imagine what those days might be like. No monster can be a monster for twenty-four hours a day. This character, Harvey, is a predator, but he doesn't see himself that way. He's also irritable, hungry, bored, self-pitying, scared. I'm interested in exploring those moments of humanity, the banality and self-delusion, the recognizable foibles. Fictional Harvey is petty in the way we are all petty, he's lonely and afraid. If anything, this humanity makes his acts of predation more ominous, or underscores their deviance—it's not as though he's nothing more than an Evil Man. It's much more—frightening? disturbing?—to me that characters like the fictional Harvey might experience themselves as victims, pitiable and under attack, or that we can see elements of ourselves in this fictional Harvey.

Emma Cline is the author of the novel *The Girls* and the story collection *Daddy*. *The Girls* was an international bestseller, and was a finalist for a National Book Critics Circle Award, the First Novel Prize, and the Los Angeles Times Book Prize, and the winner of the Shirley Jackson Award. Cline was named one of *Granta's* Best Young American Novelists and was the winner of the Plimpton Prize.

Anthony Doerr, "The Master's Castle"
What inspired your story?

In 2015, a literary nonprofit in Boise called the Cabin asked Jess Walter and me if we might participate in a benefit in which we would each write and present an original short story. Jess, bless him, agreed. As a prompt, and as a way to demonstrate how art begets more art, we chose a sentence from three stories by three of the Cabin's summer writing students. Our only rule was this: the three sentences had to appear—in any order—somewhere in our stories.

They were:

1. "The drawbridge slowly came down, like the maw of a terrible beast," by Anna Price, grade 6.
2. "'Ow, what wa . . .' Basil stopped mid-sentence," by Avery Gendler, grade 6.

3. "April is the month to throw yourself off of things," by Ollie Siedl, grade 9.

It was the first time I'd written a story with the express intent of reading it aloud, so I desperately wanted to make it comic, but as usual it turned earnest and lonely. On the night of the benefit, the Cabin brought the three young writers onstage to share their work, and their three sentences glowed on a huge screen behind Jess and me as we read, and it was thrilling to see what Jess created with a drawbridge, the month of April, and a character named Basil. His story ("A Hard Day's Knight") was nine times funnier than mine, but what I most remember about that evening is feeling the anticipation build in the audience for the moment each of the sentences would appear in each story, and how, as Jess read, the theater filled with a palpable and golden goodwill.

For years afterward I didn't do anything else with "The Master's Castle" (the title came from Anna Price's story, too) until I learned that the literary magazine *Tin House* was going to publish its final issue after twenty amazing years. I'm deeply grateful to Cheston Knapp and Meg Storey at *Tin House* for so many years of collaboration, to Jess for devoting so much labor to another literary cause, to Chimamanda and Jenny for including my weird little story in this collection, and most of all to the three young writers who let us borrow from their imaginations.

Anthony Doerr lives in Boise, Idaho. He is the author of the story collections *The Shell Collector* and *Memory Wall*, and the novels *About Grace* and *All the Light We Cannot See*. His new novel, *Cloud Cuckoo Land*, will be published in the fall of 2021.

Adachioma Ezeano, "Becoming the Baby Girl"
What inspired your story?

I did not grow up in a living room with a television. My father called it an *unnecessary misuse of resources*. He called us to the living room at two p.m. every Sunday to tell us tales and Bible stories. The first time I heard of the speaking donkey, it was through him. My cousin who lived with us, Martina, also told stories. She told us about a goat that once spoke out in the village because it was stolen, and had heard its owner was searching for it, and she told us about a river that changed course because the villagers committed an abomination, and the gods needed to punish them. Martina was not really my cousin. But my mother insisted on explaining to our friends that she was. My mother wanted to avoid using the very degrading word "house-help." Martina is from my hometown, Okija, where she lived until my mother decided that house chores were too much for her, that she could no longer cope with taking care of her two daughters and her husband and cooking and still go to teach young children who jumped on each other.

Martina came to live with us. Her stories *became* a part of my life. In addition to the story of the goat and the absconded river, a story about possessed fair girls delighted me. According to Martina, fair girls were usually possessed by a Mammy Water spirit. And until their families made a certain kind of sacrifice to appease this Mammy Water spirit, they would keep milking men and discarding them, revolting against societal standards and gathering affluence as they went. I wanted to be a fair girl, to have that kind of power and freedom. Of course I was a child and silly and have gone ahead to forget all of that. But when I was an undergraduate, words like "runs-girls" and "baby girls" were as frequent as a rush of calmly gathered breeze. For these girls, money was the love language for sex. I was charmed by how they rose above the communal expectations for women and girls, their boldness, their wealth. And so that quiet afternoon, when *McSweeney's* e-mailed me asking for a story, I knew what to write about.

Adachioma Ezeano's work was recently included in *The Best Small Fictions 2020*. She is an MFA student at the University of Kentucky. In 2018, she made Chimamanda Ngozi Adichie's "Yes folder" for Purple Hibiscus Writing Workshop.

Tessa Hadley, "The Other One"
Did you know how your story would end at its inception?

That was one of the trickiest questions for this story. I had hoped for a while that I could make a story around a car accident like this one—where a man is killed when he's not where he's supposed to be, and with the wrong woman in the car. It's a story I'd heard about friends of friends a very long time ago, in fact in the seventies. But I'd only heard these very bare outlines; I have invented all the rest of the details and the personalities. I liked the power of the twisty, convoluted anecdote, which is intriguing and suggestive even while it's so sad for the protagonists. For a long time I couldn't quite see how to control the explosive, overviolent, melodramatic elements in the story.

I thought it would be too scorching to treat it all from very close quarters. It would be possible to write the events as they unfolded at the time—but it would take a lot of skill to stop that reading simply as excess, melodrama, blunt and unsubtle, tearing through subtlety and nuance. It was better—I thought—to experience all that melodrama at a considerable distance: thirty years later, as those buried ugly secrets get churned up in the later lives of those who've survived the accident. I knew, from the first moment I thought of the story, that the dead man's daughter would know a name—and that she'd then hear that name again, at a dinner party, and after a while recognize the woman who'd been in the car with her father when he died. That name, Delia, was one of the first things I had securely in my imagination. And then, following on the name, Delia's appearance and her whole aura. How attractive she is to Heloise, and how Delia's life seems so serene and composed to the younger woman.

But how to end the story? Something told me that by treating the whole melodrama of the accident at third hand, through Heloise's memories, I had cheated the reader somewhat. I should deliver on the accident itself, on what actually happened in that one past careless dreadful moment. I could only do this by switching my perspective from Heloise's unexpectedly to Delia's. Was this cheating—or too tricksy, too clever-clever? I didn't know whether I was going to swerve into Delia's perspective almost until I arrived at that moment of writing the end of the story. And then it was one of those endings that wrote itself; I launched into it, and it felt right. I was unwrapping the reality of the past, in a way that rewarded the reader for sticking with my story—rewarded myself, too, for holding out on its rich center and only skirting it. Here, now, this is how it was. This is how it happened, and what it felt like. In the last sentence, although we're still with Delia in her flat in London, waiting to set out on the fateful journey, I seem almost to set out how the accident happened, disaster striking from a clear sky in the very midst of happiness. A dazzle of light in the mirror—in a rearview mirror perhaps. Perhaps that's actually what happened. Light dazzling in a rearview mirror, a swerve into the path of an oncoming lorry. As I wrote, I felt I was satisfying—but with an obliqueness that pleased me—what? Curiosity. An appetite to know, to unravel the potent mystery of real things that happen. What might happen? What would it be like if it happened? And what could happen next?

Tessa Hadley has written seven novels—including *The London Train* and also *The Past*, which won the Hawthornden Prize—and three collections of short stories. *Late in the Day*, her latest novel, came out in 2019. She publishes short stories regularly in *The New Yorker*, and reviews for *The Guardian* and the *London Review of*

Books; she was awarded a Windham Campbell Prize for Fiction in 2016, and the Edge Hill Prize in 2018.

Ben Hinshaw, "Antediluvian"
What inspired your story?

The ordeal endured by Nicola in "Antediluvian" was inspired by my wife's encounter with an unidentified sea creature on our own East African honeymoon. The experience left a deep impression, and I knew it would eventually surface in my writing. Meanwhile, I had for a long time been interested in writing about an elderly photojournalist confronting the moral injury inflicted by his work. Don McCullin's incredible memoir *Unreasonable Behavior* opened up that world for me, providing the details and insights I needed to begin. After that, it was a case of letting those two elements cross-pollinate until the story found its shape.

Ben Hinshaw is a British-American writer, born on the island of Guernsey in 1981. His first book, *Exactly What You Mean*, will be published in the United Kingdom by Viking in 2022.

Jowhor Ile, "Fisherman's Stew"
What inspired your story?

As a child, I heard about dead people returning briefly to visit relatives in distant places, sitting down with friends only to vanish in a fleeting moment. I wanted to explore in fiction the wonder and unease I felt while listening to these stories. I was curious about the longing and love that can bind the living and the dead. I also wanted to write about food and sex, community, longing, and love. I believe we can traverse boundaries with love.

Jowhor Ile was born and raised in Nigeria. His first novel, *And After Many Days*, was awarded the Etisalat Prize for Literature in 2016. Ile's short fiction has appeared in *The Sewanee Review*, *McSweeney's Quarterly*, and *Litro Magazine*. He earned his MFA at Boston University and is currently an assistant professor at West Virginia University. Ile splits his time between Nigeria and the United States.

Alice Jolly, "From Far Around They Saw Us Burn"
Do you consider your story to be personal or political? What made you want to re-create this world/reality in fiction?

I always try to write stories that are both intimate and epic. I focus on a specific moment but I'm also tuning in to some echo of the eternal and the universal. "From All Around They Saw Us Burn" is written in an unusual way. There is a distant, omniscient voice in the story but also a first-person-plural voice that operates almost like a Greek chorus. A gentle argument is taking place between these two voices. I thought that it would be hard to make this work but the story fell into place quite easily. I only had to write down what I was hearing.

I am interested in fiction as a means of redressing historical injustices and interrogating the assumptions made by mainstream historians. If history is about understanding the present through the lens of the past, then the exact calibration of the lens matters. "Herstory" can't just be inserted into "history." We need to remake history itself. Does "a heroine" have to be a female version of a hero, dragging with her all the baggage of celebrity, romantic struggle, and success? Sometimes just the act of telling someone's story gives them their own version of heroism. I am not interested in laying ghosts to rest. I want to raise the dead and let them dance.

Alice Jolly's most recent novel, *Mary Ann Sate, Imbecile* (Unbound), was runner-up for the United Kingdom's £30,000 Rathbones Folio Prize and was on the long list for the Ondaatje Prize. Alice has also won the V. S. Pritchett Short Story Prize and the PEN Ackerley Prize for memoir. *Mary Ann Sate, Imbecile* and Jolly's memoir, *Dead Babies and Seaside Towns,* have just been published in the United States. Her stories have appeared in *Prospect, Ploughshares,* the *Manchester Review, Riptide, Litro,* and Fairlight Books. She teaches creative writing at Oxford University.

David Means, "Two Nurses, Smoking"
What inspired your story? Did you know how your story would end at its inception?

I live near a small, local hospital, and just about every day I walk by and see nurses and other workers, orderlies and ambulance drivers, outside the building smoking, huddling and hiding near the bushes—in all weather—looking somewhat clandestine, and a little guilty. One day, I saw a couple who inspired me to start imagining Marlon and Gracie. To paraphrase something Tom Waits said, to catch a story, you have to think like a story. Seeing them that day, I began to think like a story.

The urge to write this story goes back to seeing nurses outside the hospital down the street, watching the way they stood, moved, leaned toward each other—and then wanting to make a story about them. I was revising and really digging into the story as the COVID pandemic hit—and I live next door to an emergency room nurse who works in the city—so I was also, of course, thinking deeply about the reality of health care workers and the pain they face every day.

James Baldwin famously said that "morality is based on ideas and that all ideas are dangerous—dangerous because ideas can only lead to action and where the action leads no man [or person] can say." The feeling I get writing a story, watching and listening to my characters, seeing them move, trying to catch something that might get lost, is that story goes beyond ideas and into flesh and blood and touch. Again, this is just a feeling, and it might even be unreal, but no matter what, the story ends up going beyond my ideas, my political thoughts, my moral outrage—and settles into narrative. What you hope for is that the story will go beyond ideas into something that is essentially human.

No, I didn't [know how it would end]. I did feel—because when I was first writing it, I gave it a working title, "A Happy Story"—that it was heading toward what I hoped to be a tender, gentle resolution.

I had to do a lot of exploring—longer dialogues—and let the two characters speak with each other to learn more about their lives, and, above all, to understand their dynamic, to find the right way to see the intimacy between them unfold. And I wrote a few possible endings—mainly slightly different landscapes that ended up on the editing floor.

David Means's second collection of stories, *Assorted Fire Events*, earned the Los Angeles Times Book Prize for fiction, and his third, *The Secret Goldfish*, was shortlisted for the Frank O'Connor International Short Story Award. His fourth, *The Spot*, was selected as a 2010 Notable Book by *The New York Times* and won an O. Henry Prize. His first novel, *Hystopia*, was longlisted for the Man Booker Prize. His fifth collection—*Instructions for a Funeral*—was published in 2019. He lives in Nyack, New York, and teaches at Vassar College.

Caroline Albertine Minor, "Grief's Garden"
Why was the short story format the best vehicle for your ideas?

"Grief's Garden" is made up of series of short scenes, memory flashes really, oscillating between hope and dread, tied together by the narrator's longing for someone who is no longer there. It reads like a short story, but really it is my attempt to order (in time, with words) the chaos and nonsensicality of what then felt like death without dying.

Caroline Albertine Minor was born in Copenhagen, where she still lives with her partner and two children. She published her first book in 2013 and was nominated for the prestigious Nordic Council Literature Prize for her collection of short stories entitled "Blessings" (*Velsignelser*), published in 2017. She won several prestigious awards, including the P. O. Enquist Literary Prize 2018 as well as the Danish Fiction Writers' Association Prize. She was awarded a three-year working grant by the Danish Arts Council and is in the process of completing her master's degree in anthropology. Her new novel, *The Lobster's Shell*, will be published in seven languages, including English (Granta).

Jianan Qian, "To the Dogs"
Why was the short story format the best vehicle for your ideas?

Growing up, I always loved miniatures. I like building mansions with Popsicle sticks and stadiums with joker cards. If you do a great job, you get to see the whole thing all at once, and by controlling the details, you can freeze time and space.

To me, short stories are miniatures made of words. But my main intention here is not to build a time machine for readers to revisit a certain epoch, but to lay bare the dark side of humanity that is revealed in a crucial historical moment. Because the short story form requires the condensation of everything, there's a fascination with seeing so much—even though in a disturbing way—about humanity.

Jianan Qian writes in both Chinese and English. In her native language, Chinese, she has published four books. In English, her work has appeared in the *New York Times, Granta, Gulf Coast, Guernica, The Millions*, and elsewhere. Currently, she is a PhD student in English and creative writing at the University of Southern California.

David Rabe, "Things We Worried About When I Was Ten"
What inspired your story? Did you know how your story would end at its inception?

I was born in Dubuque, Iowa, where I went to grade school, high school, and college. Toward the end of high school, the work of the actor James Dean, along with his death, sparked in me a shocked awareness of the possibilities of what I'll call for the moment "creativity." It seemed the way out of a lot of confusion, and also a way to use that confusion. In college I tried my hand at acting, mainly at the neighboring women's college, where there was in fact a theater department. At the same time, I took creative writing classes taught by priest/poet Raymond Roseliep at the college I attended. After graduation, I moved east, and after two years in the army, I was no longer interested in acting. I focused on writing. Thanks to Joseph Papp at the New York Shakespeare Festival, I had my first play performed in New York in 1971. Since then I've written many plays; three published novels, *Recital of the Dog, Dinosaurs on the Roof*, and *Girl by the Road at Night*; a book of stories; and several films, *Casualties of War* among them, along with many other screenplays that were never made into films. Still, they paid the bills. "Things We Worried About When I Was Ten" arrived at the kitchen table one morning, interrupting whatever thoughts I was having. The first sentence and much of the first few paragraphs pressed for attention with a distinct quality I've learned over time to respect.

Such thoughts deserve focus in a way most don't. I typed them out, and then knew I had an approach to certain materials that had been hanging around in my head and notes. I think a story I read near that time by John L'Heureux might have opened me to the possibilities of the form, and the form, once it was clear to me, allowed flow that gave the disparate parts of the story continuity. Worry, and what to do about those worries, large and small, was the thread. It would be disingenuous not to allow that this story is personal. Certain elements, events, and figures in it have been with me for a long time. I can't say I knew the ending as I started, but I had a sense of it. After all, it involves the blackout game. What did we think we were doing?

Sally Rooney, "Color and Light"
What inspired your story?

After finishing work on my second novel, I wrote nothing for what seemed to me like a long time. For the first few months I convinced myself I was just taking a short break, but after about six months I started to get quite anxious and despairing. The simple fact was that I had no ideas. I have heard other writers, including some I admire very much, say that they get up and write every day regardless of whether they have ideas or not. But I am still mystified as to what that means. Without any ideas, what would I write about? So for six months, eight months, I wrote nothing. Then one afternoon that summer, I had an idea about a man getting into his brother's car and finding a woman sitting in the front seat. Immediately I opened up an A4 notepad—I can't remember why, since I usually don't write longhand—and started jotting down the opening scene. Rereading the story now, I can feel again how closely I identified with my protagonist—his sense of infuriating confusion at the events of his own life. Later and in an indirect way, these characters led me to the development of the novel I am working on now. For that I am very grateful to them, and I send them my best wishes. I hope they are doing okay.

Sally Rooney is the author of the novels *Conversations with Friends* and *Normal People*.

Joan Silber, "Freedom from Want"
Did you know how your story would end at its inception?

I had no idea how the story would end. I had the first sentence, "My brother's longtime boyfriend decided to leave him, once and for all," Rachel's agreeably acerbic voice, and the brother's cancer diagnosis. I do remember thinking, *Oh, I'm writing about illness again.* (Both of my parents died young, and it has clearly informed my sense of what happens in life.) As I worked with a cast of characters, including the brother's lover's lover, they clustered around the situation in ways unexpected to me. I see that I wrote in my notes, "Make the happier part in this story longer."

Who knows what I even meant by that? But when I wrote the last scene, I was glad to see the characters behaving a little better—ironies notwithstanding—than I'd thought they would. I hadn't known I was going there.

Joan Silber is the author of nine books of fiction; the most recent is *Secrets of Happiness.* Her novel *Improvement* won the National Book Critics Circle Award and the PEN/Faulkner Award, and she received the PEN/Malamud Award for Excellence in the Short Story. Her book *Fools* was longlisted for the National Book Award and a finalist for the PEN/Faulkner Award; *The Size of the World* was a finalist for the Los Angeles Times Book Prize, and *Ideas of Heaven* was a finalist for the National Book Award and the Story Prize. She lives in New York and teaches in the Warren Wilson MFA Program.

Asali Solomon, "Delandria"
What made you want to re-create this particular world/reality in fiction?

It has been true for decades (and is even more true after 2020) that you should not go into academia if you want to be employed while living where you want to live. If you're fortunate enough to get a tenure-track job (an employment condition becoming somewhat like a pension or a unicorn), you may well find yourself living in a place that was invented by your nightmares. It was in this fashion that a black person raised in West Philadelphia by politically engaged black cultural nationalists spent three years teaching at a college that was (and is) a loving monument to the Confederacy in a town that was (and is) a loving monument to the Confederacy. Early on I knew that I wouldn't stay there forever and figured I would write about the experience. I didn't know if it would be an opera, a sitcom, or a performance piece involving a bucket of pig's blood. I don't remember what exactly triggered the writing of this story in 2018, eleven years after I left and two years before the heated monument battles of 2020, but I can say that I was quickly overwhelmed by vivid memories. The invented violence in the story came to me instantly. Those three years featured some of the most consistent quiet violence I hope to ever experience.

My one regret about "Delandria" (which happens to have a title about which I'm particularly vain) is that I didn't get to work in a reference to *The Robert E. Lee Family Cooking and Housekeeping Book*. I once spotted this volume, published in 1997 (updated in 2002), on a gleaming end table in a campus mansion. It is described on Amazon as a "charming" "treasury of recipes, remedies and household history." When I saw it, I imagined that the book would have one page of household tips: "Have slaves." I've been laughing about that joke with myself ever since.

Asali Solomon is the author of *The Days of Afrekete*, a novel forthcoming from Farrar, Straus and Giroux. Her novel *Disgruntled* was cited as one of the best books of 2015 by the *San Francisco Chronicle* and *The Denver Post*; the short stories in her first book, *Get Down*, earned her a Rona Jaffe Foundation Writers' Award and the National Book Foundation's "5 Under 35" honor. Her writing has appeared in *McSweeney's*; *Kenyon Review*; *O, The Oprah Magazine*; *Vibe*; *Essence*; *The Paris Review*'s "The Daily"; and the anthology *How We Fight White Supremacy: A Field Guide to Black Resistance*. Solomon teaches fiction writing and African American and Caribbean literature at Haverford College, and has become increasingly chauvinistic about being a near-lifelong West Philadelphian.

Crystal Wilkinson, "Endangered Species: Case 47401"
What inspired your story?

I wrote a version of this story in 2006 when I was still living and teaching in the Midwest. I was away from my family in Kentucky. The landscape was different. I was homesick. The story was a secret way to work out my feelings of displacement. Every so often I would pull it out and add a paragraph, a line, a scene, a character. At some point a character who no longer exists in this version said, "The Midwest ain't nothing like being down South." I deleted that character and with it went what she said, but the through line of the Midwestern/Southern divide remained. Between writing my novel, working on a nonfiction project, caring for my family, and teaching, every so often I'd come to "Endangered Species" just to play, to luxuriate in this little secret world I'd created. I made a game of it. I made wild leaps, I added feral cats and mice. I added a crazy door-to-door sales consultant. At some point, I thought about adding a thread of magical realism or a UFO. All these efforts became my own little pleasure house when the other writing wouldn't come. I took great joy in pulling the file up every so often over the years and delving into the chaos when other things on my writing desk were not complying with my will. I always thought this story was too out of control to ever be published or completed. I was juggling too many themes, plot arcs, ideas.

Years later, I was at a writing retreat in Vermont and my novel was becoming really depressing. I opened my pleasure house and this final version of "Endangered Species" was born. I posted on Twitter on February 9, 2019: "Anybody interested in a short story about feral cats and mice and racism and the power of Black women and police brutality and the south and Appalachia written in Black English as defined by Toni Cade Bambara?" Thirteen years after that first attempt, I began to send the story out. It was time to abandon my pleasure house and return to the novel.

Crystal Wilkinson was born in Ohio and raised in Kentucky. She is the author of *Blackberries, Blackberries*; *Water Street*; and *The Birds of Opulence* (winner of the 2016 Ernest J. Gaines Award for Literary Excellence). She is a United States Artists fellow and was nominated for the John Dos Passos Prize, the Hurston/Wright Legacy Award, and the Orange Prize. Her stories, poems, and essays have recently appeared in *Story*, *AGNI*, *Oxford American*, *Kenyon Review*, and others. She teaches at the University of Kentucky.

Tiphanie Yanique, "The Living Sea"
What made you want to re-create this particular world/reality in fiction?

I wrote this material first in essay form for *The New York Times*. My grandmother had always told me, told all of us grandchildren, that her childhood in Vega Baja was charmed. I had been doing research about my grandmother's life for myself after her death—

the research was a way to feel connected to her. And because I am a writer, I was also doing this research for my first novel, which was based loosely on my grandmother's life. When I went to Vega Baja, I discovered something that I hadn't known before: that my grandmother had been raised in an orphanage. This was news not just to me, but to most everyone in my generation of our family. It felt vital to write this material as nonfiction as a gift to my family and to myself—here is another part of the truth, I wanted to tell them. And it wasn't a truth my grandmother wanted hidden forever, though she had hidden it from us her whole life. Before she died, she'd told me two things: 1) You should go to Vega Baja to research your novel. And 2) wait for certain people to die before publishing that novel. My grandmother was a librarian and a storyteller, so she understood the power of narrative. I tried to do as she told me: I waited for the certain people to die, but the material from my research in Vega Baja never really made it into my first novel. I couldn't come to terms with the facts, so I couldn't write them then into fiction. "The Living Sea," the fiction it is now, is a story in my upcoming book, *Monster in the Middle*. That book is about how the stories we are told about love inform how we enter into loving relationships. When I started to write that book, I remembered that my grandmother had had her first boyfriend in Vega Baja and that they often met at the beach. This gave me a new way to enter into the material. It also gave me another chance to be with my grandmother, who was the most important person in my life. I sometimes get asked if I will always write about the Caribbean in my fiction. I always say: yes, yes, the whole world is in the Caribbean. The Caribbean experience, like any experience, has all of humanity inside of it. But I have been thinking lately that I may always be writing about my grandmother. My grandmother unorphaned me by raising me when my mother could not and my father would not. She was my guide to humanity. As a fiction writer, this is how I understand my work—a thinking through of the very question of what it means to be human.

Tiphanie Yanique is the author of the poetry collection *Wife*, which won the 2016 Bocas Prize in Caribbean poetry and the United Kingdom's 2016 Forward/Felix Dennis Prize for Best First Collection. Tiphanie is also the author of the novel *Land of Love and Drowning*, which won the 2014 Flaherty-Dunnan First Novel Prize from the Center for Fiction, the Phillis Wheatley Book Award, and the American Academy of Arts and Letters Rosenthal Family Foundation Award, and was listed by NPR as one of the best books of 2014. *Land of Love and Drowning* was also a finalist for the Orion Book Award and the Hurston/Wright Legacy Award. She is the author of a collection of stories, *How to Escape from a Leper Colony*, which won her a listing as one of the National Book Foundation's 5 Under 35. She has won the Boston Review's annual short story contest, a Rona Jaffe Foundation Writers' Award, a Pushcart Prize, a Fulbright scholarship, and an Academy of American Poets Prize. She has been listed by *The Boston Globe* as one of the sixteen cultural figures to watch out for, and her writing has been published in *The New York Times*, *Best African American Fiction*, *The Wall Street Journal*, *American Short Fiction*, and other places. *A Living Sea* is included in *Monster in the Middle*, which will be published in October 2021. Tiphanie is from the Virgin Islands and is an associate professor at Emory University.

Publisher's Note

A Brief History of the O. Henry Prize

Many readers have come to love the short story through the simple characters, the humor and easy narrative voice, and the compelling plotting in the work of William Sydney Porter (1862–1910), best known as O. Henry. His surprise endings entertain readers, including those back for a second, third, or fourth look. Even now one can say "Gift of the Magi" in conversation about a friendship or marriage, and many people around the world will know they are referring to the generosity and selflessness of love.

O. Henry was a newspaperman, skilled at hiding from his editors at deadline. He spent his childhood in Greensboro, North Carolina, his adolescence in Texas, and his later years in New York City. In between Texas and New York, he was caught embezzling and hid from the law in Honduras, where he came up with the phrase "banana republic." On learning his wife was dying, he returned home to her and to their daughter, and subsequently served a three-year prison sentence for bank fraud in Columbus, Ohio. Accounts of the origin of his pen name vary: one story dates from his days in Austin, where he was said to call the wandering family cat "Oh! Henry!"; another states that the name was inspired by the captain of the guard at the Ohio State Penitentiary, Orrin Henry. In 1909, Porter told *The New York Times*, "[A friend] suggested that we get a newspaper and pick a name from the first list of notables that we found in it. In the society columns we found the account of a fashionable ball. . . . We looked down the list and my eye lighted on the name Henry, 'That'll do for a last name,' said I. 'Now for a first name. I want something short.' 'Why don't you use a plain initial letter, then?' asked my friend. 'Good,' said I, 'O is about the easiest letter written, and O it is.'"

Porter had devoted friends, and it's not hard to see why. He was charming and had an attractively gallant attitude. He drank too much and neglected his health, which caused his friends concern. He was often short of money; in a letter to a friend asking for a loan of $15 (his banker was out of town, he wrote), Porter added a postscript: "If it isn't convenient, I'll love you just the same." His banker was unavailable most of Porter's life. His sense of humor was always with him.

Reportedly, Porter's last words were from a popular song: "Turn up the light, for I don't want to go home in the dark."

After his death, O. Henry's stories continued to penetrate twentieth-century popular culture. Marilyn Monroe starred in a film adaptation of "The Cop and the Anthem." The popular western TV series *The Cisco Kid* grew out of "The Caballero's Way." Postage stamps were issued by the Soviets to commemorate O. Henry's one hundredth birthday in 1962 and by the United States in 2012 for his one hundred fiftieth. The most lasting legacy began just eight years after O. Henry's death, in April 1918, when the Twilight Club (founded in 1883 and later known as the Society of Arts and Sciences) held a dinner in his honor at the Hotel McAlpin in New York City. His friends remembered him so enthusiastically that a group of them met at the Biltmore Hotel in December of that year to establish some kind of memorial to him. They decided to award annual prizes in his name for short story writers, and they formed a committee to read the short stories published in a year and a smaller group to pick the winners.

In the words of the first series editor, Blanche Colton Williams (1879–1944), the memorial was intended to "strengthen the art of the short story and to stimulate younger authors."

Doubleday, Page & Company was chosen to publish the first volume, *O. Henry Memorial Award Prize Stories 1919*. In 1927, the society sold all rights to the annual collection to Doubleday, Doran & Company. Doubleday published *The O. Henry Prize Stories*, as it came to be known, in hardcover, and from 1984 to 1996 its subsidiary, Anchor Books, published it simultaneously in paperback. Since 1997, *The O. Henry Prize Stories* has been published as an original Anchor Books paperback, now with a brand-new title: *The Best Short Stories 2021: The O. Henry Prize Winners*. The year 2021 marks the exciting second-century start of the O. Henry Prize.

How the Stories Are Chosen

The guest editor chooses the twenty O. Henry Prize winners from a large pool of stories passed to her by the series editor. Short fiction originally published as short stories in magazines and online is eligible for inclusion in *The Best Short Stories: The O. Henry Prize Winners*. Stories may be written in English or translated into English. Sections of novels are not considered. Editors are asked to send all fiction they publish and not to nominate individual stories. Stories should not be submitted by agents or writers.

The goal of *The Best Short Stories: The O. Henry Prize Winners* remains to strengthen and add visibility to the art of the short story.

The stories selected were originally published between January 2019 and June 2020. There was a brief hiatus following the retirement of the previous series editor, so there was not a 2020 edition. We included as many stories for consideration in *The Best Short Stories 2021: The O. Henry Prize Winners* as we could read, including those from the very final issues of *Glimmer Train* and *Tin House*.

Acknowledgments

My warm gratitude to Jenny Minton Quigley, perceptive reader, and to LuAnn Walther.

—Chimamanda Ngozi Adichie

I am delighted by the amazing short story writers included here who affected us so deeply. Thanks to Joséphine de La Bruyère, a brilliant and spectacular editorial intern; Marion Minton, a passionately devoted bookworm; and insightful readers Ashley Gengras, Caroline Hall, and Sam Quigley. For their support on this project, I so appreciate Jen Marshall, Sarah Chalfant, Jackie Ko, Dan Quigley, Linda Johnson, Lisa Stevenson, Katie Aisner, Will Minton and Lane Minton, and at Anchor Books LuAnn Walther, Ellie Pritchett, James Meader, Angie Venezia, Linda Huang, Edward Allen, Aja Pollock, and especially Diana Secker Tesdell. I am most grateful to Chimamanda Ngozi Adichie; her brilliant vision and generous heart could launch a thousand story collections.

—Jenny Minton Quigley

Publications Submitted

Stories published in magazines distributed in North America are eligible for inclusion.

For fiction published online, the publication's contact information and the date of the story's publication should accompany the submissions.

Stories will be considered from July 1 to June 30 the following year. Publications received after July 1 will automatically be considered for the next volume of *The Best Short Stories: The O. Henry Prize Winners*.

Please submit PDF files of submissions to jenny@ohenryprize winners.com. Additionally, hard copies may be sent to Jenny Minton Quigley, c/o The O. Henry Prize Winners, 70 Mohawk Drive, West Hartford, CT 06117.

Able Muse
www.ablemuse.com
submission@ablemuse.com
Editor: Alexander Pepple
Two to three times a year

AGNI
www.agnionline.bu.edu
agni@bu.edu
Editors: Sven Birkerts and William
    Pierce
Biannual (print)

Alaska Quarterly Review
www.aqreview.org
uaa_aqr@uaa.alaska.edu
Editor: Ronald Spatz
Biannual

Amazon Original Stories
www.amazon.com/
    amazonoriginalstories
Submission by invitation only
Editor: Julia Sommerfeld
Twelve annually

American Short Fiction
www.americanshortfiction.org
editors@americanshortfiction.org
Editors: Rebecca Markovits and
    Adeena Reitberger
Triannual

Antipodes
www.wsupress.wayne.edu/journals/
    detail/antipodes-0
antipodesfiction@gmail.com
Editor: Annie Martin
Biannual

Apalachee Review
www.apalacheereview.org
christopherpaulhayes@gmail.com
Editor: Christopher Hayes
Biannual

Apogee Journal
www.apogeejournal.org
editors@apogeejournal.org
Executive Editor: Alexandra
    Watson
Biannual

The Arkansas International
www.arkint.org
info@arkint.org
Editor in Chief: Geoffrey Block
Biannual

Arkansas Review
www.arkreview.org
mtribbet@astate.edu
Editor: Marcus Tribbett
Triannual

ArLiJo
www.arlijo.com
givalpress@yahoo.com
Editor in Chief: Robert L. Giron
Ten issues a year

Ascent
www.readthebestwriting.com
ascent@cord.edu
Editor: Vincent Reusch

**The Asian American Literary
    Review**
www.aalrmag.org
editors@aalrmag.org
Editors in Chief: Lawrence-Minh
    Bùi Davis and Gerald Maa
Biannual

Aster(ix)
www.asterixjournal.com
info@asterixjournal.com
Editor in Chief: Angie Cruz
Triannual

The Atlantic
www.theatlantic.com
fiction@theatlantic.com
Editor in Chief: Jeffrey Goldberg;
    Magazine Editor: Don Peck
Monthly

Baltimore Review
www.baltimorereview.org
editor@baltimorereview.org
Senior Editor: Barbara Westwood
    Diehl
Quarterly

The Bare Life Review
www.barelifereview.org
barelifereview.submittable.com
Editor: Nyuol Lueth Tong

Bat City Review
www.batcityreview.org
fiction@batcityreview.org
Editor: Sarah Matthes
Annual

Bellevue Literary Review
www.blreview.org
info@BLReview.org
Editor in Chief: Danielle Ofri
Biannual

Bennington Review
www.benningtonreview.org
BenningtonReview@Bennington
    .edu
Editor: Michael Dumanis
Biannual

Black Warrior Review
www.bwr.ua.edu
blackwarriorreview@gmail.com
Editor: Jackson Saul
Biannual

BOMB
www.bombmagazine.org
betsy@bombsite.com
Editor in Chief: Betsy Sussler
Quarterly

Booth
www.booth.butler.edu
booth@butler.edu
Editor: Robert Stapleton
Biannual

Boulevard
www.boulevardmagazine.org
editors@boulevardmagazine.org
Editor: Jessica Rogen
Triannual

The Briar Cliff Review
www.bcreview.org
3303 Rebecca Street
Sioux City, IA 51104
Editor: Tricia Currans-Sheehan
Annual

CALYX
www.calyxpress.org
editor@calyxpress.org
Editors: C. Lill Ahrens, Rachel
    Barton, Marjorie Coffey, Judith
    Edelstein, Emily Elbom, Carole
    Kalk, Christine Rhea
Biannual

The Carolina Quarterly
www.thecarolinaquarterly.com
carolina.quarterly@gmail.com
Editor in Chief: Kylan Rice
Biannual

Carve
www.carvezine.com
azumbahlen@carvezine.com
Editor in Chief: Anna Zumbahlen
Quarterly

Catamaran
www.catamaranliteraryreader.com
editor@catamaranliteraryreader.
    com
Editor in Chief: Catherine
    Sergurson
Quarterly

Catapult
www.catapult.co
catapult.submitable.com/submit
Editor in Chief: Nicole Chung

Cherry Tree
www.washcoll.edu/learn-by-doing
    /lit-house/cherry-tree/
lit_house@washcoll.edu
Editor in Chief: James Allen Hall
Annual

Chicago Quarterly Review
www.chicagoquarterlyreview.com
cqr@icogitate.com
Senior Editors: S. Afzal Haider and
    Elizabeth McKenzie
Quarterly

Chicago Review
www.chicagoreview.org
editors@chicagoreview.org
Editor: Gerónimo Sarmiento Cruz
Triannual

Cimarron Review
www.cimarronreview.com
cimarronreview@okstate.edu
Editor: Lisa Lewis
Quarterly

The Cincinnati Review
www.cincinnatireview.com
editors@cincinnatireview.com
Managing Editor: Lisa Ampleman
Biannual

Colorado Review
www.coloradoreview.colostate.edu
    /colorado-review
creview@colostate.edu
Editor: Stephanie G'Schwind
Triannual

The Common
www.thecommononline.org
info@thecommononline.org
Editor in Chief: Jennifer Acker
Biannual

Confrontation
www.confrontationmagazine.org
confrontationmag@gmail.com
Editor in Chief: Jonna G. Semeiks
Biannual

Conjunctions
www.conjunctions.com
conjunctions@bard.edu
Editor: Bradford Morrow
Biannual

Copper Nickel
www.copper-nickel.org
wayne.miller@ucdenver.edu
Editor: Wayne Miller
Biannual

Crab Orchard Review
www.craborchardreview.siu.edu
jtribble@siu.edu
Editor: Allison Joseph
Biannual

Crazyhorse
www.crazyhorse.cofc.edu
crazyhorse@cofc.edu
Editor: Anthony Varallo
Biannual

Cream City Review
www.uwm.edu/creamcityreview
info@creamcityreview.org
Editor in Chief: Su Cho
Semiannual

CutBank
www.cutbankonline.org
editor.cutbank@gmail.com
Editor in Chief: Jake Bienvenue
Biannual

The Dalhousie Review
www.ojs.library.dal.ca
   /dalhousiereview
Dalhousie.Review@Dal.ca
Editor: Anthony Enns
Triannual

Dappled Things
www.dappledthings.org
dappledthings.ann@gmail.com
Editor in Chief: Katy Carl
Quarterly

december
www.decembermag.org
editor@decembermag.org
Editor: Gianna Jacobson
Biannual

Delmarva Review
www.delmarvareview.org
editor@delmarvareview.org
Editor: Wilson Wyatt, Jr.
Annual

Denver Quarterly
www.du.edu/denverquarterly
denverquarterly@gmail.com
Editor: W. Scott Howard
Quarterly

Descant
www.descant.tcu.edu
descant@tcu.edu
Editor in Chief: Matt Pitt
Annual

Driftwood Press
www.driftwoodpress.net
driftwoodlit@gmail.com
Editors: James McNulty and Jerrod
Schwarz
Quarterly

Ecotone
www.ecotonemagazine.org
info@ecotonejournal.com
Editor in Chief: David Gessner
Biannual

Electric Literature
www.electricliterature.com
editors@electricliterature.com
Executive Director: Halimah
Marcus; Editor in Chief: Jess
Zimmerman
Weekly

Emrys Journal
www.emrys.org
info@emrys.org
Editor: Katie Burgess
Annual

Epiphany
www.epiphanyzine.com
Editor in Chief: Rachel Lyon
Biannual

Epoch
www.epoch.cornell.edu/epoch
-magazine-0
mk64@cornell.edu
Editor: Michael Koch
Triannual

Event
www.eventmagazine.ca
event@douglascollege.ca
Editor: Sashi Bhat
Triannually

Exile Quarterly
www.exilequarterly.com
competitions@exilequarterly.com
Editor in Chief: Barry Callaghan
Quarterly

Fairy Tale Review
www.fairytalereview.com
ftreditorial@gmail.com
Editor: Kate Bernheimer
Annual

Fantasy & Science Fiction
www.sfsite.com/fsf/
fsfmag@fandsf.com
Editor: Gordon Van Gelder
Bimonthly

Fence
www.fenceportal.org
rebeccafence@gmail.com
Editor: Rebecca Wolff
Biannual

Fiction
www.fictioninc.com
fictionmageditors@gmail.com
Editor: Mark Jay Mirsky
Annual

Fiction River
www.fictionriver.com
wmgpublishingmail@mail.com
Editors: Kristine Kathryn Rusch
    and Dean Wesley Smith
Six times a year

The Fiddlehead
www.thefiddlehead.ca
fiddlehead@unb.ca
Editor: Sue Sinclaire
Quarterly

Five Points
www.fivepoints.gsu.edu
fivepoints.submittable.com/submit
Editor: Megan Sexton
Biannual

The Florida Review
www.floridareview.cah.ucf.edu
flreview@ucf.edu
Editor: Lisa Roney
Biannual

Foglifter
www.foglifterjournal.com
foglifter.journal@gmail.com
Editor: Chad Koch
Biannual

Fourteen Hills: The SFSU Review
www.14hills.net
hills@sfsu.edu
Editor in Chief: Rachel Huefner
Biannual

Freeman's
www.freemansbiannual.com
eburns@groveatlantic.com
Editor: John Freeman
Biannual

f(r)iction
www.tetheredbyletters.com
    /friction
leahscott@tetheredbyletters.com
Editor in Chief: Dani Hedlund
Triannual

Gemini Magazine
www.gemini-magazine.com
editor@gemini-magazine.com
Editor: David Bright
Four to six issues per year

The Georgia Review
www.thegeorgiareview.com
garev@uga.edu
Editor: Stephen Corey
Quarterly

The Gettysburg Review
www.gettysburgreview.com
mdrew@gettysburg.edu
Editor: Mark Drew
Quarterly

Gold Man Review
www.goldmanreview.org
heather.cuthbertson@
goldmanpublishing.com
Editor in Chief: Heather
Cuthbertson
Annual

Grain
www.grainmagazine.ca
grainmag@skwriter.com
Editor: Nicole Haldoupis
Quarterly

Granta
www.granta.com
editorial@granta.com
Editor: Sigrid Rausing
Quarterly (print)

The Greensboro Review
www.greensbororeview.org
greensbororeview.submittable.com/
submit
Editor: Terry L. Kennedy
Biannual

Guernica
www.guernicamag.com
editors@guernicamag.com
Editor in Chief: Ed Winstead

**Gulf Coast: A Journal of
Literature and Fine Arts**
www.gulfcoastmag.org
gulfcoastea@gmail.com
Editor: Nick Rattner
Biannual

Harper's Magazine
www.harpers.org
letters@harpers.org
Editor: Christopher Beha
Monthly

Harpur Palate
www.harpurpalate.binghamton
.edu
harpur.palate@gmail.com
Editor in Chief: Sarah Sassone

Harvard Review
www.harvardreview.org
info@harvardreview.org
Editor: Christina Thompson
Biannual

Hayden's Ferry Review
www.haydensferryreview.com
hfr@asu.edu
Editor: Erin Noehre
Semiannual

The Hopkins Review
www.hopkinsreview.jhu.edu
wmb@jhu.edu
Editor: David Yezzi
Quarterly

Hotel Amerika
www.hotelamerika.net
editors.hotelamerika@gmail.com
Editor: David Lazar
Annual

The Hudson Review
www.hudsonreview.com
info@hudsonreview.com
Editor: Paula Deitz
Quarterly

Hunger Mountain
www.hungermtn.org
hungermtn@vcfa.edu
Editor: Erin Stalcup
Annual (print)

The Idaho Review
www.idahoreview.org
mwieland@boisestate.edu
Editors: Mitch Wieland and Brady
    Udall
Annual

Image
www.imagejournal.org
image@imagejournal.org
Editor in Chief: James K. A. Smith
Quarterly

Indiana Review
www.indianareview.org
inreview@indiana.edu
Editor in Chief: Alberto Sveum
Biannual

Into the Void
www.intothevoidmagazine.com
info@intothevoidmagazine.com
Editor: Philip Elliot
Quarterly

The Iowa Review
www.iowareview.org
iowa-review@uiowa.edu
Acting Editor: Lynne Nugent
Triannual

Iron Horse Literary Review
www.ironhorsereview.com
ihlr.mail@gmail.com
Editor: Leslie Jill Patterson
Triannual

Jabberwock Review
www.jabberwock.org.msstate.edu
jabberwockreview@english
    .msstate.edu
Editor: Michael Kardos
Semiannual

The Journal
www.thejournalmag.org
managingeditor@thejournalmag
    .org
Managing Editor: Daniel Barnum
Biannual

Joyland
www.joylandmagazine.com
contact@joylandmagazine.com
Editor in Chief: Michelle Lyn
    King
Annual

Kenyon Review
www.kenyonreview.org
kenyonreview@kenyon.edu
Editor: Nicole Terez Dutton;
    Managing Editor: Abigail
    Wadsworth Serfass
Six times a year

**Lady Churchill's Rosebud
    Wristlet**
www.smallbeerpress.com/lcrw
info@smallbeerpress.com
Editors: Gavin J. Grant and Kelly
    Link
Biannual

Lake Effect
www.behrend.psu.edu/school-of
    -humanities-social-sciences
    /lake-effect
gol1@psu.edu
Editors: George Looney and Aimee
    Pogson
Annual

Lalitamba
www.lalitamba.com
lalitamba_magazine@yahoo.com
Editor: Shyam Mukanda
Annual

Literary Hub
www.lithub.com
info@lithub.com
Editor: Jonny Diamond

The Literary Review
www.theliteraryreview.org
info@theliteraryreview.org
Editor: Minna Zallman Proctor
Quarterly

LitMag
www.litmag.com
info@litmag.com
Editor: Marc Berley
Annual

Little Patuxent Review
www.littlepatuxentreview.org
editor@littlepatuxentreview.org
Editor: Chelsea Lemon Fetzer
Biannual

The Louisville Review
www.louisvillereview.org
managingeditor@louisvillereview
    .org
Managing Editor: Amy Foos
    Kapoor
Biannual

MAKE: Literary Magazine
www.makemag.com
info@makemag.com
Editor: Chamandeep Bains
Annual

The Malahat Review
www.malahatreview.ca
malahat@uvic.ca
Editor: Iain Higgins
Quarterly

Manoa
www.manoa.hawaii.edu
/manoajournal
mjournal-l@lists.hawaii.edu
Editor: Frank Stewart
Biannual

The Massachusetts Review
www.massreview.org
massrev@external.umass.edu
Editor: Jim Hicks
Quarterly

The Masters Review
www.mastersreview.com
contact@mastersreview.com
Editor in Chief: Cole Meyer
Annual

McSweeney's Quarterly Concern
www.mcsweeneys.net
letters@mcsweeneys.net
Founding Editor: Dave Eggers
Editor: Claire Boyle
Quarterly

Meridian
www.readmeridian.org
meridianuva@gmail.com
Editor: Suzie Eckl
Semiannual

Michigan Quarterly Review
www.michiganquarterlyreview
.com
mqr@umich.edu
Editor: Khaled Mattawa
Quarterly

Mid-American Review
www.casit.bgsu.edu
/midamericanreview
mar@bgsu.edu
Editor in Chief: Abigail Cloud
Semiannual

Midwestern Gothic
www.midwestgothic.com
info@midwesterngothic.com
Fiction Editors: Jeff Pfaller and
Robert James Russell
Biannual

Mississippi Review
www.sites.usm.edu/mississippi
-review/
msreview@usm.edu
Editor in Chief: Adam Clay
Biannual

The Missouri Review
www.missourireview.com
question@moreview.com
Editor: Speer Morgan
Quarterly

Mizna
www.mizna.org/articles/journal
mizna@mizna.org
Editor: Lana Barkawi
Biannual

Montana Quarterly
www.themontanaquarterly.com
editor@themontanaquarterly.com
Editor in Chief: Scott McMillion
Quarterly

Mount Hope
www.mounthopemagazine.com
mount.hope.magazine@gmail.com
Editor: Edward J. Delaney
Biannual

n+1
www.nplusonemag.com
editors@nplusonemag.com
Senior Editors: Chad Harbach and
    Charles Petersen
Triannual

Narrative
www.narrativemagazine.com
info@narrativemagazine.com
Editors: Carol Edgarian and Tom
    Jenks
Triannual

Natural Bridge
www.blogs.umsl.edu
    /naturalbridge
natural@umsl.edu
Editor: Shane Seely
Biannual

NELLE
www.uab.edu/cas
    /englishpublications/nelle
editors.nelle@gmail.com
Editor: Lauren Goodwin Slaughter
Annual

New England Review
www.nereview.com
nereview@middlebury.edu
Editor: Carolyn Kuebler
Quarterly

Newfound
www.newfound.org
info@newfound.org
Editor: Laura Eppinger
Annual

New Letters
www.newletters.org
newletters@umkc.edu
Editor in Chief: Christie Hodgen
Quarterly

New Madrid
www.newmadridjournal.org
msu.newmadrid@murraystate.edu
Editor: Ann Neelon
Biannual

New Ohio Review
www.ohio.edu/nor
noreditors@ohio.edu
Editor: David Wanczyk
Biannual

New Orleans Review
www.neworleansreview.org
noreview@loyno.edu
Editor: Lindsay Sproul
Annual

New South
www.newsouthjournal.com
newsoutheditors@gmail.com
Editor: A. Prevett
Biannual

The New Yorker
www.newyorker.com
themail@newyorker.com
Editor: David Remnick
Weekly

Nimrod International Journal
www.nimrod.utulsa.edu
nimrod@utulsa.edu
Editor: Eilis O'Neal
Biannual

Ninth Letter
www.ninthletter.com
fiction@ninthletter.com
Editor: Jodee Stanley
Biannual

Noon
www.noonannual.com
1324 Lexington Ave, PMB 298
New York, NY 10128
Editor: Diane Williams
Annual

The Normal School
www.thenormalschool.com
normalschooleditors@gmail.com
Editor in Chief: Stephen Church

North American Review
www.northamericanreview.org
nar@uni.edu
Fiction Editor: Grant Tracey

North Carolina Literary Review
www.nclr.ecu.edu
BauerM@ecu.edu
Editor: Margaret D. Bauer
Annual

North Dakota Quarterly
www.ndquarterly.org
ndq@und.edu
Editor: William Caraher
Quarterly

Northern New England Review
www.nnereview.com
douaihym@franklinpierce.edu
Editor: Margot Douaihy
Annual

No Tokens Journal
www.notokensjournal.com
NoTokensJournal@gmail.com
Editor: T Kira Mahealani Madden
Biannual

Notre Dame Review
www.ndreview.nd.edu
notredamereview@gmail.com
Fiction Editor: Steve Tomasula
Biannual

The Ocean State Review
www.oceanstatereview.org
oceanstatereview@gmail.com
Senior Editors: Elizabeth Foulke
    and Charles Kell
Annual

One Story
www.one-story.com
Executive Editor: Hannah Tinti;
    Editor: Patrick Ryan
Monthly

Orca
www.orcalit.com
Senior Editors: Joe Ponepinto and
    Zachary Kellian
Quarterly

Orion
www.orionmagazine.org
questions@orionmagazine.org
Editor: Sumanth Prabhaker
Quarterly

Outlook Springs
www.outlooksprings.com
outlookspringsnh@gmail.com
Editor: Andrew R. Mitchell
Triannual

Overtime
www.workerswritejournal.com
    /overtime.htm
info@workerswritejournal.com
Editor: David LaBounty
Quarterly

Oxford American
www.oxfordamerican.org
info@oxfordamerican.org
Editor: Eliza Borné
Quarterly

Pakn Treger
www.yiddishbookcenter.org
    /language-literature-culture
    /pakn-treger
pt@yiddishbookcenter.org
Editor: Aaron Lansky
Quarterly

The Paris Review
www.theparisreview.org
queries@theparisreview.org
Editor: Emily Nemens
Quarterly

Passages North
www.passagesnorth.com
passages@nmu.edu
Editor in Chief: Jennifer Howard
Annual

Pembroke Magazine
www.pembrokemagazine.com
pembrokemagazine@gmail.com
Editor: Jessica Pitchford
Annual

The Pinch
www.pinchjournal.com
editor@pinchjournal.com
Editor in Chief: Courtney Miller
    Santo
Biannual

Playboy
www.playboyenterprises.com
Executive Editor: Shane Singh
Monthly

Pleiades
www.pleiadesmag.com
pleiadescnf@gmail.com
Editors: Erin Adair-Hodges and
    Jenny Molberg
Biannual

Ploughshares
www.pshares.org
pshares@pshares.org
Editor in Chief: Ladette Randolph
Triannual

Post Road
www.postroadmag.com
info@postroadmag.com
Managing Editor: Chris Boucher
Biannual

Potomac Review
www.mcblogs.montgomerycollege
    .edu/potomacreview/
potomacrevieweditor@
    montgomerycollege.edu
Editor: John Wei Han Wang
Quarterly

Prairie Fire
www.prairiefire.ca
prfire@prairiefire.ca
Editor: Andris Taskans
Quarterly

Prairie Schooner
www.prairieschooner.unl.edu
prairieschooner@unl.edu
Editor in Chief: Kwame Dawes
Quarterly

PRISM international
www.prismmagazine.ca
prose@prismmagazine.ca
Prose Editor: Kyla Jamieson
Quarterly

A Public Space
www.apublicspace.org
general@apublicspace.org
Editor: Brigid Hughes
Quarterly

PULP Literature
www.pulpliterature.com
info@pulpliterature.com
Managing Editor: Jennifer Landels
Quarterly

Raritan
www.raritanquarterly.rutgers.edu
rqr@sas.rutgers.edu
Editor in Chief: Jackson Lears
Quarterly

Redivider
www.redividerjournal.org
editor@redividerjournal.org
Editor in Chief: Bradley Babendir
Biannual

River Styx
www.riverstyx.org
BigRiver@riverstyx.org
Managing Editor: Christina Chady
Biannual

Room
www.roommagazine.com
contactus@roommagazine.com
Managing Editor: Chelene Knight
Quarterly

Ruminate
www.ruminatemagazine.com
info@ruminatemagazine.org
Editor in Chief: Brianna Van Dyke
Quarterly

Salamander
www.salamandermag.org
editors@salamandermag.org
Editor in Chief: Jennifer Barber
Biannual

Salmagundi
www.salmagundi.skidmore.edu
salmagun@skidmore.edu
Editor in Chief: Robert Boyers
Quarterly

Saranac Review
www.saranacreview.com
info@saranacreview.com
Editor: Aimée Baker
Annual

The Saturday Evening Post
www.saturdayeveningpost.com
editors@saturdayeveningpost.com
Editor: Steven Slon
Six times a year

Slice
www.slicemagazine.org
editors@slicemagazine.org
Editor in Chief: Beth Blachman
Biannual

Smith's Monthly
www.smithsmonthly.com
dean@deanwesleysmith.com
Editor: Dean Wesley Smith
Monthly

The Southampton Review
www.thesouthamptonreview.com
editors@thesouthamptonreview
    .com
Editor: Emily Smith Gilbert
Biannual

The South Carolina Review
www.clemson.edu/caah/sites
    /south-carolina-review/index
    .html
screv@clemson.edu
Editor: Keith Lee Morris
Annual

South Dakota Review
www.southdakotareview.com
sdreview@usd.edu
Editor: Lee Ann Roripaugh
Quarterly

The Southeast Review
www.southeastreview.org
southeastreview@gmail.com
Editor: Zach Linge
Semiannual

Southern Humanities Review
www.southernhumanitiesreview
.com
shr@auburn.edu
Editors: Anton DiSclafani and
Rose McLarney
Quarterly

Southern Indiana Review
www.usi.edu/sir
sir@usi.edu
Editor: Ron Mitchell
Biannual

The Southern Review
www.thesouthernreview.org
southernreview@lsu.edu
Editors: Jessica Faust and Sacha
Idell
Quarterly

Southwest Review
www.southwestreview.com
swr@smu.edu
Editor in Chief: Greg
Brownderville
Quarterly

St. Anthony Messenger
www.info.franciscanmedia.org
/st-anthony-messenger
samadmin@franciscanmedia.org
Editor: Christopher Heffron
Monthly

Story
www.storymagazine.org
contact@storymagazine.org
Editor: Michael Nye
Triannual

StoryQuarterly
www.storyquarterly.camden
.rutgers.edu
storyquarterlyeditors@gmail.com
Editor: Paul Lisicky
Annual

subTerrain
www.subterrain.ca
subter@portal.ca
Editor: Brian Kaufman
Triannual

Subtropics
www.subtropics.english.ufl.edu
subtropics@english.ufl.edu
Editor: David Leavitt
Biannual

The Sun
www.thesunmagazine.org
Editor: Sy Safransky
Monthly

Sycamore Review
www.sycamorereview.com
sycamore@purdue.edu
Editor in Chief: Anthony Sutton
Biannual

Tahoma Literary Review
www.tahomaliteraryreview.com
fiction@tahomaliteraryreview.com
Fiction Editor: Leanne Dunic
Triannual

Third Coast
www.thirdcoastmagazine.com
editors@thirdcoastmagazine.com
Editor in Chief: Kai Harris
Biannual

The Threepenny Review
www.threepennyreview.com
wlesser@threepennyreview.com
Editor: Wendy Lesser
Quarterly

upstreet
www.upstreet-mag.org
editor@upstreet-mag.org
Fiction Editor: Joyce A. Griffin
Annual

Virginia Quarterly Review
www.vqronline.org
editors@vqronline.org
Editor: Paul Reyes
Quarterly

Washington Square Review
www.washingtonsquarereview.com
washingtonsquarereview@gmail
.com
Editor in Chief: Joanna Yas
Biannual

Water-Stone Review
www.waterstonereview.com
water-stone@hamline.edu
Editor: Meghan Maloney-Vinz
Annual

Weber
www.weber.edu/weberjournal
weberjournal@weber.edu
Editor: Michael Wutz
Biannual

West Branch
www.westbranch.blogs.bucknell
.edu
westbranch@bucknell.edu
Editor: G. C. Waldrep
Triannual

Western Humanities Review
www.westernhumanitiesreview
.com
ManagingEditor.WHR@gmail
.com
Editor: Michael Mejia
Triannual

Willow Springs
www.willowspringsmagazine.org
willowspringsewu@gmail.com
Editor: Polly Buckingham
Biannual

Witness
www.witness.blackmountain
  institute.org
witness@unlv.edu
Editor in Chief: Maile Chapman
Triannual

The Worcester Review
www.theworcesterreview.org
editor.worcreview@gmail.com
Managing Editor: Kate McIntyre
Annual

Workers Write!
www.workerswritejournal.com
info@workerswritejournal.com
Editor: David LaBounty
Annual

World Literature Today
www.worldliteraturetoday.org
dsimon@ou.edu
Editor in Chief: Daniel Simon
Bimonthly

X-R-A-Y
www.xraylitmag.com
xraylitmag@gmail.com
Editor: Jennifer Greidus

Yellow Medicine Review
www.yellowmedicinereview.com
editor@yellowmedicinereview.com
Guest Editor: Terese Mailhot
Semiannual

Yemasee
www.yemasseejournal.com
editor@yemasseejournal.com
Senior Editors: Laura Irei, Charlie
  Martin, and Joy Priest
Biannual

Zoetrope All-Story
www.all-story.com
info@all-story.com
Editor: Michael Ray
Quarterly

Zone 3
www.zone3press.com
zone3@apsu.edu
Fiction Editor: Barry Kitterman
Biannual

ZYZZYVA
www.zyzzyva.org
editor@zyzzyva.org
Editor: Laura Cogan
Triannual

Permissions